Confessions Of An Honest Man

A Novel by Arthur Rosch

Table of Contents

4

6

Chapter One

September, 1967. Detroit, Michigan

Aaron Kantro follows his colleagues through the labyrinth of the nightclub's kitchen and out the back door. A waft of cool air hits his face as he steps onto the concrete platform next to the loading dock. His sweat instantly begins to dry and he can see steam misting from the other musicians' tuxedos. It's the band's third break. They will play one more set of forty five minutes. Then their work for the night is done.

There are nine or ten people gathered around the rear entrance to the club. They are either jazz fans who want to hang out or they are so loaded they don't know how they got there.

A man with his shirtails dangling from his suit stumbles into Aaron. "I wan' shake your hand," he announces. He extends his unkempt digits and then pulls his hand away as if to recalibrate his arm's trajectory. Aaron, when he puts his hand out to respond, feels like an idiot. He puts his hands in his pockets and hopes the man will go away.

"I tell you somethin'", the man says. "You play some drums for a white boy. Some fuckin' drums. I close my eyes, can't tell the diff'rence. Sound jus' like a real drummer." He tries again to extend his hand and stumbles across his own feet.

"Excuse me", a young lady says as she passes between Aaron and the drunk. She wants an autograph from the legendary saxophonist, Zoot Prestige. Aaron's boss transfers a cheroot from his hand to his mouth. He leans down to inscribe his signature into the lady's little book, while trying to keep his eyes averted from the cleavage that is so conspicuously thrust into his face.

Aaron notes this little drama and loses his anger. Zoot Prestige is just too funny. Aaron quietly moves behind the imposing figure of his boss. The drunk rambles away, talking to himself.

Aaron is the only white person beneath the scalloped awning. There are perhaps ten white people in the club. It bothers him more than he likes to admit that he longs to see other white faces. It has been his decision to play jazz, and his brand of jazz carries him to black clubs in black neighborhoods. Sometimes, the moment he walks into a place, he feels the air freeze with racial tension. Sometimes he is scared. The only way through it is to play the music.

As the little throng disperses, Zoot butts his smoke in the sand of an ashtray. He steps off the concrete pad and walks across the lot towards his car.

After waiting about thirty seconds, the group's organist, Tyrone Terry, follows the lanky figure of his boss. Aaron waits another thirty seconds and follows his colleagues to the cream-colored Continental. This precaution seems a little silly but there are probably narcs in the club and Aaron has to admit that it is pretty obvious what's happening when three jazz musicians get into a car and don't go anywhere.

Soon the men are engrossed in the ritual of the pipe: lighting, inhaling, holding breath, exhaling. It's cozy in the Continental's plush interior. Air comes sighing through the upholstery's leather seams as the musicians' weight compresses the seat cushions. Zoot and his side-men are settling down, recharging their nerves for the next set, the last set. It is one o'clock in the morning.

"She wanted you to look at 'em," Tyrone says to his employer.

"I know," responds Zoot, "but it seems so...I don't know...un-chivalrous to put my nose right into a lady's cleavage. Besides, it's redundant. I seen titties before. Wan't nothin' special about hers...they's just...."

BANG! There is a huge sound, an explosion. The men's bodies react instinctively. They duck, and their arms rise to cover their heads.

The car lurches as a man dives across the hood, holding a pistol in his right hand. His legs swim wildly as he fights to stop his momentum. Whatever tactic he has in mind, it isn't working. The car's sheen and finish turn the hood into a sliding board.

"Jesus fucking Christ!" In the back seat Aaron curses loudly without thinking. He has never before heard a gun shot. In spite of this fact, he recognizes the sound. It is rounder, weightier, and more final than the sound of a firecracker.

The man on the car's hood waves the pistol frantically. Slithering to get his balance, he clutches at the windshield wipers and misses. Gravity and car wax slide him across the polished metal until he lands on the ground. The pistol fires as he hits the gravel. The bullet   penetrates   a   tire

with a loud hiss.

The man springs up and disappears among the ordered rows of vehicles in the parking lot.

Zoot Prestige holds a finger to his mouth, slides from under the steering wheel and drops quietly to the floor of the passenger seat. Zoot doesn't want to get shot. Zoot doesn't want to be a witness if somebody gets shot. Zoot doesn't want questions. Zoot doesn't want any dealings with the Poe-Leece!

Aaron scrunches onto the floor of the back seat until his arm rests on the hump of the drive shaft. Tyrone, on the other side, is hoping to disappear via the flawed logic of an ostrich. He is pulling his little pork-pie hat over his eyes.

A voice shouts, "I'LL KILL YOU MOTHERFUCKER!"

Two more shots are fired from the opposite corner of the lot. Two sparking ovals of muzzle flash light up the windshields of Cadillacs and Thunderbirds. A man's face appears, pressed to the window of Zoot's car. His cheek is distorted against the glass, with an eye like a panicked horse. His quick breath steams the window only inches from Zoot's face. With a slight turn to the right, Zoot becomes a virtual nose-to-nose mirror image of the man with the gun.

The enraged shooter doesn't see the human being an inch from his face. He raises his snubby revolver over the top of the vehicle, fires twice without aiming, and runs to cover behind a black Eldorado. The wind has changed. The shots are barely audible.

"Sheee-it!" Zoot grumbles, "I hope nobody messes up my short. I paid three hundred bucks for this custom paint job." The immaculately polished car is long and sleek as a submarine.

A voice shouts, "HEY LOOK HE'S OVER THERE!"

Bang bang bang! Flashes light up the musicians' faces. Guns are all over the place. Aaron looks at Tyrone. The keyboard player has twitched and spilled a pipe full of burning marijuana into his lap. He brushes and pats frantically to prevent embers from smoldering through the pants of his tux. Thrusting his hands into his pockets he makes a basket to prevent sparks from spreading onto the seat or the carpet. Aaron produces a handkerchief and helps contain the disaster. Tyrone is feeling little stings of fire burning their way into his palms. He is tossing the embers back and forth as he jumps and wriggles all over the tiny floor space behind the driver's seat. When   the

When the young musicians' eyes meet they realize that they have entered the realm of the completely absurd. They begin to giggle, as quietly as possible. Tyrone manages to empty his lungs without breaking into a hacking cough. The bodies of both men are convulsed with terrified hilarity.

Aaron's legs are crossed on the floor of the back seat. Zoot gestures with his fingers for the pipe. Tyrone hands it to Aaron as he muffles his cough and puts out the fire in his lap. Aaron gives the pipe to Zoot through the space between the seats.

The parking lot is a bedlam of running, screaming people.

Two men, fingers snarled in each other's sport coats, roll across the hood of Zoot's car. The metal on the Continental goes 'scroich! bunk!'. Zoot winces and hides his face behind his hands. The men vanish somewhere in the gravel of the lot, grunting and cursing. A grey fedora with a black band lays on the hood for a moment before a stiff breeze carries it away. Zoot elevates his head a few inches and tries to inspect his hood for damage. It's impossible. The windows are now opaque with steam.

Zoot relaxes. He sits with his face level with the knobs on the dashboard. His wrists are on his knees and his hands hang loose in the shadow beneath the glove box. He loads the pipe and hands it to Aaron through the crack.

"Don't strike no match!" he says. "Use that thing." He points to the black knob of the cigarette lighter. Each door has an ashtray and each ashtray has its own lighter.

Zoot sniffs the air inside the car. "I smell somethin' burning," he says. "You cats makin' barbecue back there?" His voice is good natured and mocking.

Observing Zoot's total poise, Aaron and Tyrone hiss through their lips with suppressed giggles. It is impossible to tell which part of the moment is funny and which part is terrifying. The giggles have

13

equal components of panic and the hysterical disbelief of pot heads in a bizarre situation.

Big cars roar to life and race from the lot in clouds of gravel and fumes. Sirens doppler past, right on their tails, red lights whizzing through the intersection. Crimson slashes of reflection light up the Continental's glass.

Then there is silence. People stealthily emerge from cover, crunch-crunching across the gravel. They run for shelter inside the club. The musicians straighten their bodies with the slowness of clock hands moving. Soon they are sitting normally on the seats. Zoot loads the pipe, lights and inhales. He holds his breath for a long time, then exhales an almost transparent cloud. He replaces the pipe in a leather pouch, conceals the stash under the seat, and twists his head from left to right and back again, loosening his neck muscles. He is sixty-two, and a tenor saxophone has hung from his shoulders for more than fifty years.

"Should we go back in and play?" There is a squeak in Aaron's voice. He makes a few mock rolls with invisible drumsticks.

Zoot looks at Aaron with a bare vapor of a smile, tolerant of his drummer's naïveté. "Why wouldl we NOT go back in and play?" The marquee lights of the street's clubs and bars glow on half of Zoot's face, shadowing the other half. This gives his eye a demonic glitter. He wets his thumb and forefinger with his tongue and smoothes the hairs of his moustache.

"Let me point out something to you, babe," says Zoot. "We're professional jazz musicians. We play music, and we get paid. Rather nicely, I might add, thanks to my modest fame and the fact that I placed at number eight in Downbeat's Tenor Saxophone category." He pauses for a moment and says with a trace of gloating, "AHEAD of Dexter Gordon, Stan Getz and Gene Ammons." He laughs a ripe and disdainful laugh. The magazine polls have such appalling power to determine a musician's pay level.

Opening the door, Zoot brushes a tiny flake of ash from his tuxedo pants with a dapper gesture, and corkscrews his six foot three inch frame upright. The saxophonist makes a quick but careful scrutiny of his vehicle. He circles it, running the flat of his hand along its sculpted façade. There are no bullet holes that he detects, no scratches. The hood has resumed its normal shape.

Tyrone and Aaron squeeze themselves out of the car. Aaron closes the door delicately, with the barest of clicks, as if he fears the automobile will fall to pieces if he so much as breathes wrong.

The world flickers. The young musicians' hearts race, their nerves tingle. They are playing a jazz gig with a famous saxophone player! Zoot Prestige has apprenticed with Duke Ellington, he's played with Charlie Parker. He is a legend.

Zoot straightens his lapels and moves his shoulders inside his jacket so the garment settles more squarely on his body.

"That's right," he adds. "We're hipsters, babe, we stay cool. We got a paying gig, we play until the club owner asks us to stop or it's two a.m." Zoot's voice is like velvet and sand, Scotch whisky and smoke. "Long as the drummer doesn't get shot. Gotta draw the line somewhere. Last drummer I lost was Bobby Beffords, in '65. And before that I had a good run, only lost two drummers in six years. Course, I never had a white drummer before. Everybody upset about that."

He aims a gentle look at Aaron, to check that he isn't being taken seriously. His smile is full of irony and play. He brushes a bit of ash from Aaron's tuxedo jacket. It is a tender paternal gesture.

Fourteen drummers had come to audition when Zoot was putting together the band for this tour. Thirteen of them were black. Aaron was the third drummer to play. As soon as he finished the tune, Zoot sent the other drummers home.

He knew he would take a lot of heat for hiring a white drummer. Fuck 'em. The kid was worth it.

"Ain't nothin' unusual happening here, babe", says Zoot. "It's just another gig, somebody's old lady got too friendly with somebody else's old man and things got ugly." The tall man shepherds his young friends toward the door of the nightclub. "It's human nature. Why don't we go inside and play some music to soothe the savage breast? We'll lay down some Recalcitrant Funk-itis."

Zoot has just coined another of his classic nonsense terms. Recalcitrant Funk-itis now joins the lexicon along with Groove-matic Ubiquity, Heliocentric Hot Sauce and other such crazy combinations from Zoot's fertile mind.

Tyrone pulls at his cummberbund to conceal the holes in the crotch of his pants. The young men follow the urbane figure of their mentor back into the humid noise of Mickey Tucker's Jazz Corner.

Chapter Two
1956: University City, Missouri
Aaron at Nine

There's always one of these kids at every school playground. On the blacktop at Daniel Boone School this kid is Aaron Kantro. He's the one with the "Kick Me" sign scotch -taped to his back. He knows people are laughing at him. His temper ratchets up like beans in a pressure cooker. He'd better get control of that rage, stuff it back inside himself. He gets into trouble when the rage comes out. He does crazy things that have big consequences. He knows what the word means. He's endured plenty of Consequences. They aren't funny, like on the TV show, "Truth Or Consequences". He's learning the trick: he's learning to put his feelings into a steel safe with ten combinations and gleaming chrome wheels that turn smoothly. He's learning to lock away his feelings. They're dangerous.

In baseball season, football season, soccer season, it's always the same: Aaron stands in line when the team captains chose their players. He waits slightly pigeon-toed, his shoulders held high and his hands fisted tightly at his sides. At school he can't compete with boys his own age, so he has been put back a year in gym class. It doesn't help. They might as well have put him back with the first graders. He is too little to hurt anyone. If he punches a bully in the nose the force is no more than a gnat landing on its six tiny legs. There's no power in Aaron's body. He barely weighs seventy pounds. He's uncoordinated. He isn't obnoxious or funny. Without these ingredients for childhood charisma, his place in the playground pecking order is at the bottom. Last. "Kick Me" dangles from the back of his shirt on an inch of Scotch Tape just below the collar.

Aaron isn't afraid of these jerks. The person he fears is his mother. He's terrified of his mother.

The dark shadows under Aaron's eyes give the impression that his soul is etched with some serious concern. His thoughtful demeanor earns him a nickname. He is called "The Professor". It's not a happy nickname. It isn't like "Slugger", "Speedy" or "A.J". One of Aaron's teachers started using it as a term of affection. The kids adopt it as their expression of contempt. When they drawl "Here comes the Professor" they use a throaty mocking tone that is the currency of sarcasm and insult. They draw things on sheets of paper. "Place Foot Here" with an arrow pointing towards his behind. They've drawn Aaron with a yarmulke and a tallis. He's on his knees crawling after a pig. Lock away that temper. Put it in the big black safe.

At school, he spends most of his time lost in fantasies about Vikings, looking out the window with unfocused eyes. He always delays going home. His mother's usually at home. He is completely terrified of his mother.

If he's lucky his mom has gone shopping or to a doctor's appointment. He grabs a snack and then slides like a ghost through his siblings' cries and demands and gets into the room he shares with his little brother. Avoiding his mother's attention is the highest priority. Little currents of fear race along his nerves when he thinks of Esther Kantro.

Aaron's mother frequently says, as if to excuse her rages, "I love you the only way I can." He doesn't understand what that means. He's sure his mother does not love him. She hates him! When she says she loves him "the only way-I can", that must mean there is something wrong with him.

Aaron is certain of his father's love. He wants to see his dad, wants dad to be at home all the time, wants dad to talk to him, ask him questions about what he's thinking. He wants his dad to understand that he isn't stupid, he's just…just too mad to think, maybe. He wants dad to tell him things are okay. He isn't afraid of his dad. Maybe love is just not being afraid. When his father's home, Esther is a different person. She doesn't shake him or scream at him, she doesn't squeeze his arms until fingernail marks show.

More than anything, Aaron wants his father to be at home.

Aaron can't have what he wants. Aaron is getting used to this state of being denied what he wants. It seems like it's always his mother who blocks him, taking away the things he wants.

It's a secret, this fighting that takes place when his father is away.

Esther makes threats. "I'll kill you if your father hears of this", she says one day. "I'm sick of it! I'm sick of you! You drive me crazy!" She is twisting a wet dish towel in her rough red hands. Aaron sees his neck between those hands. He is seeing the thoughts in Esther's mind.

While Aaron tries to banish this image, his mother enters her ongoing tirade. In some abstract way Aaron knows that his mother isn't really speaking to HIM, she is speaking to something or someone that made her angry a long time ago. "How did the toaster get knocked to the floor? It's broken into a million pieces! How did that happen? How? HOW? Your dad better not find out about this! I have to throw away the toaster and buy another one. I'm so mad I can kill you! I'm sick of you, I am, totally sick of you and your behavior. Dad has enough on his mind. He works all day and half the night, and he doesn't need stories about you, running around the house flying like an airplane, knocking things down right and left. You'll give your father a heart attack! You're going to kill him!" Her voice rises in pitch and volume until she's shrieking. "He'll drop dead and it'll be your fault! Is that what you want? Is it?"

The word "kill" is as common as pennies in the currency of the Kantro's domestic language. Killing, murder, suicide, death death death....the siblings scream at each other, "I'll kill you," and "no you won't, I'll kill you first!"

Sometimes Aaron slaps his hands to his ears. No no no no! His father can't die! He won't tell, won't utter a word about this strange ...strange...situation. That's a good word. It's a situation. For Aaron this is a new way of using a familiar word.. He likes to discover new words and new ways to use words. It is one of those pleasures that comes from inside his mind. This is a way of thinking that he enjoys. It's the USE of his mind that he enjoys. He loves finding new words and learning how to use them.

Aaron will protect his father at all costs from this...situation. It isn't dad's fault he has to work so much. Mother always says it: money's more important than anything, even love!

It isn't dad's fault that he goes to work so early and comes back so late. It isn't dad's fault that Aaron gets so mad he breaks dishes and never does his homework and throws baseballs through the living room window.

Sometimes Aaron's mom feels bad and sometimes she feels good but it's spooky good, there's something wrong with how she feels good. She dances by herself around the living room, singing corny old songs, and then she puts on her mink coat and drives to the stores in Clayton and Lake Forest. When she comes home she moves so fast she looks like two people at once while she hides the stuff she bought. She moves the heavy coats aside and gets into the deep shelves at the back of the closet. She pushes at bags and boxes until she makes room for the new shoes, earrings and bracelets.

She buys a lot of stuff and Aaron wonders if she is the reason why dad works all the time. Dad is scared of her, Aaron realizes. He lets her do whatever she wants rather than start one of those terrible fights where screams get so loud the neighbors call the police and mom hits dad so hard his eyes go black. Those fights are terrifying!.

Aaron has a vague knowledge that his mother hasn't always been this way. She was different when she and dad were first married. She looks different in the pictures. She looks happy and..and...nice! What has happened to change her from a nice person to such a mean person?

* * *

By late September school has already become boring. Aaron doesn't have the attention span to hold on to subjects that aren't related to his interests. Numbers, chemicals, categories, all these things whoosh past him without leaving an impression.

Then, on the last day of the month, a notice appears on the main board just outside the principal's office. It has symbols that Aaron recognizes as musical notes and a floaty cartoon of several men in top hats and tuxedos, tootling on various instruments.

MUSIC APPRECIATION. An elective course available to fourth graders begins in two weeks. Those who are interested should sign their names on the numbered sheet attached. A pencil dangles from a string. This IS interesting and promises to break the daily monotony of teachers' droning voices. Aaron picks up the bright orange nub and signs his name.

He waits eagerly. After the passage of two weeks, his home room teacher hands out a number of folded notices. One of them is for Aaron and he finds notification that today, yes, TODAY! At one thirty the kids who signed up for the class are to go to the cafeteria.

One thirty comes and Aaron is in the biology lab with Mr. Warren, the science teacher. He presents his note. The teacher scans it and nods Aaron towards the door. Aaron finds himself traversing the near-empty halls towards the cafeteria. A few kids converge on the double glass doors leading into the expanse of the lunch facility. They push the doors open and find an area where the long rectangular tables have been cleared away to make room for a chalk board, an upright piano and three rows of chairs.

The students find their seats with the usual clamor. After getting a glance at the teacher, kids are bumping one another to sit in the back row. They've done their lightning appraisal of the instructor and they don't like what they see: the music teacher looks mean.

It seems pretty stupid to Aaron to try and get away from this strange looking woman. He takes a seat in the front row at the right corner, next to the window. He counts the attendees: eleven students. Eleven out of a total of ninety seven fourth graders at Daniel Boone School. Of those eleven, Aaron guesses with accurate realism, there might be four who are actually interested in Music Appreciation.

The two minute bell rings before third period. Wooden floorboards in the halls amplify chatter and the sounds of hurrying feet. The staccato booming quickly dies as classroom doors close behind tardy students.

The teacher stands next to the blackboard with one hand on her hip, the other holding a long piece of chalk that she passes through her fingers with intricate dexterity. It twirls from thumb and index finger down to the middle finger, where it stops and whizzes around that long digit and somehow balances on its point in the teacher's palm. The chalk then continues and finds its way to the pinky and returns the way it has come. The teacher's fingers look like five perfectly trained snakes.

Aaron is transfixed by this skilful movement. Under his desk he attempts to work the pattern with his pencil, which he instantly drops and just as instantly picks up.

The kids are wary. A couple of girls whisper the word "ugly". Aaron looks at the new teacher and tries the word ugly, but it doesn't fit. He rummages his mind for a word to describe the woman. Not ugly. Not scary. Not mean. Not repulsive.

Then the word comes to him. It's a word he doesn't know he knew, but somehow he knows what it means. Maybe he read it in David Copperfield.

The word is Homely. The teacher is homely. Her hair is in a net. Its red brown coils are tucked in an orderly bun. She has large ears. She wears a green blouse and a pink sweater that covers a long bony torso. The sweater is too short at the waist and buttoned to the top over her large adam's apple. The long brown skirt looks as if it was made a hundred years ago. There are a pair of checked men's pajama pants visible beneath the hem of the skirt. The grey and green flannel pants swish over white tennis shoes as she walks.

"Take your seats, take your seats," the woman says in voice that's more like song than like speach. When the students sort themselves out, the teacher begins to write her name on the blackboard with brisk muscular strokes.

"I am," she says as she taps the chalk rapidly on the board. Tap tap. Tap tap tap. There is a pause as she finishes printing her name. "I am….Mrs. Leek."

There's an immediate titter throughout the class. Aaron agrees it's a funny name but feels that it will be rude to laugh at another person's name.

Mrs. Leek turns and puts her hands on her hips. The laughter diminishes but doesn't die out. Mrs. Leek looks at the students as if she can stab them with her eyes. Only one boy continues laughing. He's a big dumb kid named Bennie Shapiro. His eyes are closed and his head points towards the ceiling as he brays like a donkey.

"YOU!" The woman points to Benny Shapiro. She is holding the white chalk as if it can beam death-rays. "Do you think there's something funny about my name?"

Benny's face comes down and turns almost crimson. His long legs are splayed out beneath the chair in front of him, his shoes almost pointing in opposite directions. "Ummm," Benny murmurs, "I was just, uh…"

"And your name is?" The teacher demands. She takes a small pad of paper from her skirt pocket and holds a pen over it.

Benny is stunned into silence.

"Can someone tell me this young man's name?"

"Bennie Shapiro" emerges timidly from several children.

Mrs. Leek writes quickly on her pad, tears the leaf free and walks to Bennie Shapiro. She folds

the paper once and hands it to the boy. "You are dismissed from this class, Mister Shapiro. Permanently. I don't tolerate rudeness. Take this note to your teacher. I'm informing her of why you are no longer in this class. I'll want her signature, and a signature from one of your parents."

Bennie is confused and scared. He pulls his legs back under him and gets up. He looks around, appealing to his classmates. None meet his eyes.

Discipline problems are thus ended in Music Appreciation Class.

Aaron has never encountered a person so strange as Mrs. Leek. She sings rather than speaks. When kids are outside her danger radius, she is a ripe target for mockery. Everywhere in the school some piping voice imitates her trademark delivery.

"Students!", they sing, "Who can tell me the name of this music? Students! What instrument do you hear in this solo?" After two weeks the kids shave the imitation to a lilting utterance of the single word in two notes: Students! They become like bird calls, emitting from the playground, answered from the second floor, again from the gym. "Students!", they sing, and follow with fits of giggling.

Mrs. Leek doesn't care. She is terrifying. This capacity to instill fear is a combination of her stunning dour face and the expressions of contempt she can use to bore straight through a student's soul. Her lips are extremely full and marked with cracked vertical lines. Her skin has the texture of pitted leather. Sometimes her face looks like a tree knot, a place where a branch has failed to sprout.

Her teaching methods are strict and direct. She doesn't mind getting wrong answers. At least they are answers. One day she points a yardstick at a boy named Mark Rabinowitz.

"Can you tell me, Mister Rabinowitz, what German composer struggled with deafness throughout his life?"

The boy yawns, blinks, appears to think for a moment. "Umm, uh, Fats Domino?"

Mrs. Leek pops the yardstick across a desktop, making it snap so loud everyone jumps.

"All I want to know is whether or not you are alive!" the woman says. "I'm not asking so much. Make a guess, take a chance. You can't look more stupid than you do now. 'Duh, um, Fats Domino?,'"she mocks. "Beethoven's Balls, most of you kids are stupid as fire hydrants."

Mrs. Leek's curse has brought all the students to a state of fascinated alertness.

"I suppose I'll get fired now," she says calmly. "I'll only miss two or three of you."

Her eyes meet Aaron's and she gives him the slightest wink. Aaron's insides relax with unfamiliar gratitude as he realizes that he will be one of those few students.

The incident passes and the eccentric teacher does not get fired. She continues the arduous task of instilling music into the lives of her students.

She brings record albums from her collection. One day she brings 45's by Fabian and Elvis. She plays them side by side with old records by Mississippi blues men with funny names. Blind Willy this. Pegleg Joe that.

"You see how the rhythms and chords are really the same?" she asks. Two or three sets of eyes are alert. Aaron Kantro nods but is too paralyzed with shyness to speak.

When the teacher plays Benny Goodman or Duke Ellington, Aaron feels like he is on a rocket ship. He thinks a fuse has been lit under his chair. The music gives him goose bumps. He feels a strange warmth at the back of his neck.

One day Mrs. Leek brings an album in a sleeve painted in wild abstract colors.

"Students!" she says in her two-note fanfare. "Without further ado, I bring you 'The Prelude To The Rite of Spring', by Igor Stravinsky. For all of you eggheads, it's played by the New York Philarmonic and conducted by Leonard Bernstein."

She puts the 33 rpm record on the spindle of the school's little blue Zenith record player. She turns the knob and the record drops to the turntable. The tone arm automatically lifts and positions itself over the rim of the album. It drops onto the vinyl surface and there are a few seconds of crackling static before the music begins.

An instrument plays, solo. Maybe it's an oboe, or a bassoon. It seems to Aaron as if it's calling someone or something, maybe a bird in the forest. Soon its call is answered by another bird, and another. The music gathers power, momentum, and starts battering itself like a pair of huge mountain rams clashing horn to horn.

Nine kids put their hands over their ears, slump, jerk, make pig faces. Mrs. Leek tolerates this behavior. She knows she is asking a lot.

One child, Aaron, is transfixed. His eyes go soft and distant.

Mrs. Leek lets the music play for three or four minutes, then gently turns down the volume until it is silent. Taking care not to call Aaron "Professor", she asks him what he thinks of the music.

Aaron is aware of the other students watching. He thinks it best to shrug and say nothing. He fits in better when he pretends to be stupid.

From the first day of class, Aaron has felt Mrs. Leek's attention. He can tell that she knows something about him, and that she likes him. She does nothing to single him out, nothing to embarrass him. He will never admit it to other kids, but he likes her. Now he is overcome by his need to share his feelings with the teacher. She is homely, but Aaron sees a kindness in her face that makes the homeliness vanish.

"It sounds so weird!", Aaron says... "I can see, like, giant birds calling and dragons dancing, and planets moving through space. There are spooky vines and flowers growing really fast and then when it got loud and, um, rhythmic I, "...he pauses, looks around the room, and his voice tapers away in embarrassment.

Mrs. Leek's gaze penetrates him thoughtfully. Again, she restrains herself from calling him "Professor". It is such a perfect nickname for the precocious little boy.

"That's good, Aaron," is all she says. "That's very good."

Mrs. Leek enters Aaron's name as a candidate for the Comprehensive Musical Aptitude Test. This search for young talent emerges from The St. Louis Symphony Orchestra and its bundle of civic programs. The test to discover promising musicians between eight and ten years old is the obsession of Saul Lefkowitz, first violinist and Concert Master of the orchestra. The distinguished violinist has made careers blossom through the decades of his life. He is adept at finding grant money and has kept the Youth Orchestra thriving for more than twenty years.

Mrs. Leek is supposed to give Aaron a note to be signed by his parents, a simple consent form. She signs it herself, forging the signature of Aaron's father, and sends it on. There is something wrong in Aaron's family. She doesn't have to be a genius to know this. Her experience has taught her that talent often emerges from trouble. She isn't taking any chances. She knows that this child, this thin sad-looking child, has a real passion for music. He has been born with the soul of an artist.

A few days later Mrs. Leek hands Aaron a precious invitation with its date, time and address. The conspiracy is unspoken. Aaron knows he has been granted a favor. He doesn't want his mother to know about the test. She will tell him he can't go, and she will scream at his dad until he gives in. He knows that if something good comes of this test, he will have to fight for its possession. His mother ALWAYS says no. He has given up asking for things. He lives an alternate life, completely beyond the ken of his family. He has become a precocious virtuoso of bus, streetcar and other forms of transportation. He does everything in his power to avoid going home. He spends late afternoons watching the fifty cent double feature at the Varsity Theatre.

On a Saturday morning in early October, the chosen students are allowed into the presence of the maestro.

The big dark auditorium swallows the fifty children. They sit in the first rows, just below the stage. They can see into the mysterious empty orchestra pit. The stage and front rows are lit. The rest of the vast chamber is in darkness.

Saul Lefkowitz sits dangling his legs from the polished teak stage, holding a violin in his left hand, idly touching a string with his pinky finger.

The concertmaster is a short bald man with a plump torso and eyebrows that fly upward like flames from his bright blue eyes. He is a familiar type. Aaron dismisses him as completely unremarkable. He reminds him of his uncle Morris, the one who farts so much that it isn't funny any more.

When the children are seated and quiet, Saul Lefkowitz picks up a bow, puts the violin to his neck and begins playing with incredible agility and fire. He is completely transformed! His body rocks like that of an Orthodox Jew in prayer, his elbow slicing the air, the bow riding across the strings, bouncing into the air, then skipping like flat stones thrown across water. All of this motion unleashes a cascade of precise yet passionate musical sound. Aaron has never seen anyone who possesses this magic, this amazing skill!

Aaron Kantro promises himself that some day, he too will have this intangible thing, this Genius. He doesn't care how hard it will be, how much work it requires, how much time, how much sacrifice.

Having gotten the attention of the aspiring musicians, Saul Lefkowitz has a bundle of sheets passed around and begins to administer The Test.

An hour later, the violinist snaps his case shut, unplugs the tape recorders, the tone generators, and stuffs the envelope of tests into his briefcase.

"Thank you very much, children. It will take a couple weeks to process these scores. You will be notified if you qualify for a place in the Youth Orchestra. I'm sure you all did very well and I wish there was room for every one of you in the orchestra. Fech! It can't be. I will tell you now that perhaps five of you, at the most, will qualify. So I'm just asking you not to get your hopes up. And most of all, just because you don't get a place in the Youth Orchestra doesn't mean you should give up an interest in music. If you already play an instrument, keep practicing! And those of you who don't, find an instrument you enjoy, get a teacher and learn music! It's wonderful!"

Aaron finds the test stimulating but not difficult. Which chord is identical to the preceding chord? A, B, C, or D? It's effortless. Aaron knows the answers.

Aaron quickly marks his test sheet. He notices a boy in the row ahead of him who is his equal in speed. The boy is relaxed and marks his test sheet with nonchalance. As Aaron emerges from the auditorium into the light of an autumn afternoon, this boy approaches him, open and confident.

"Hi, my name is Lester Stiers. I'll bet you did pretty good. I was watching, I can tell. I already know about chords and intervals, my dad taught me. I'm lucky, my dad's a really good musician."

Aaron isn't used to friendliness. He blushes, and fights an impulse to turn away. He forces himself to respond.

"I'll bet you did pretty good yourself. What instrument do you want to play?"

"I'm already practicing woodwinds. I'm gonna be a tenor sax player, like my dad. He's a jazz musician. That's why I'm named Lester…after Lester Young? You know who that was?"

Aaron makes a sleepy-eyed face and pretends to hold a big saxophone sideways. "Doo ta dooo ta

doo", he tries to imitate one of The Prez' licks.

Lester's face goes slack with amazement. "Wow! We must be the youngest hipsters in the world! I get this all from my dad. He's so frustrated sometimes. To make a living he has to play a lot of schlock, you know, Mickey Mouse, bubblegum, ticky tick, but that's life for a jazz musician. Hey, what school do you go to?"

"Daniel Boone."

"You mean with Mrs. Leek?"

Aaron laughs. "Yeah, Mrs. Leek. Everybody hates her, but I think she's okay."

"My dad says she's nutty as a drunken camel but she's a bitchin' musician. Ha ha!" Lester mouths the curse word routinely, but his giggle betrays his nervousness. "I'm coming to your school in January. Dad's got a gig in Gaslight Square, and we just moved to U. City. I'll be in the fourth grade. What about you?"

"Me too," says Aaron. He hopes they will be in the same homeroom. Aaron is desperate for a friend, and he's never met anyone that he likes so much, so fast.

"So.... guess I'll see you at Daniel Boone School," Lester says breezily. A car, driven by a woman who must be Lester's mother, is pulling to the curb. Lester gets into the car. As he waves goodbye, Aaron can tell that Lester's mother is going to offer him a ride. He is overcome by shyness. He quickly disappears into the crowd and waits for the bus.

When a week has passed, Aaron takes to racing home from school so that he has a chance to be first to the mailbox. He has said nothing about the test, has betrayed none of his hope.

He is filled with dread.

When the result arrives eighteen days later, it is addressed to Mr. and Mrs. Max Kantro.

This is a complication Aaron has not anticipated. Why didn't he think of this? Oh, what a dummy he is! He can't open it. His mother will be the first to open it.

A hot poker of fear prods his heart. He can't remember when or how it began, this war with his mother, but he knows that if he likes something, if it's fun, if it gives him a sense of skill, then he will have to fight for it. He knows these feelings if not the words. He has no idea why he is locked in this contest with his mother, why it bothers her so much to see him happy. He accepts it as one of life's dark mysteries.

He places the mail on the end table in the den. Then he sets himself to wait. He is like a statue.

He has no attention for television, for books. He is preparing for battle.

Esther comes whistling into the house two hours later, arms full of packages. Aaron knows by the whistle and the packages that his mother is "up". This isn't good. He'd rather face her "down" than her "up". When she's "down" she is mindlessly brutal. When she is "up" she is unpredictable. She is capable of anything. She's devious. This is a word he has looked up in the dictionary. "Devious: departing from the proper or accepted way. Not straightforward. Deceptive or crooked."

Esther glances at her son, whose eyes are pointed at the television. Aaron recognizes an episode of Sky King, but it is nothing to him but moving figures and noise.

"Hello, Aaron."

"Hi," Aaron mumbles, seeing nothing.

Esther Kantro drops the packages on the couch and hangs her coat in the closet. She is dark-haired, dark eyed, stout, powerful. Her nose is like the blade of an ax.

"Did you have a good day?"

"Yes, fine." Aaron's voice sounds as if it has no breath behind it. When he was younger he was wild and angry. That had been shaken out of him. Now he is quiet. He has learned stealth, guile, even treachery. These are his weapons, his only means of waging war.

He has put the letter in the middle of the pile.

Esther gets organized and comes to the table and begins going through bills, advertisements and letters. She stands over the trash can, dropping envelopes from her hand to the grey bin.

Aaron watches her every movement from the corner of his eye. He sees his mother reach the distinctive grey and blue striped envelope containing the letter from Saul Lefkowitz. She opens it and reads it. She makes a little splutting noise with her lips, puts the paper back into the envelope, crushes the thing into a wad and throws it after the junk mail.

Aaron's heart begins to pound with terror. He knew this would happen! He knew it!

He will wait until she leaves the room, he'll get the letter and show it to his dad when he comes home. That's his plan.

"Look, the trash is full, Aaron. Why don't you take it out?"

Aaron lifts the plastic cylinder full of trash and heads for the back door. His mother follows him. "Get the other cans. It's collection day tomorrow. We'll put everything in the trunk and take it to Shepman's so his truck doesn't wake your dad in the morning."

Lev Shepman is the garbage man. He owns a dump on the other side of the highway. Taking the garbage to Shepman in his filthy grey jumpsuit is unthinkable, ridiculous.

Aaron hasn't reckoned with his mother's powerful psychic antennae. Is she some kind of witch? How can she know?

She knows. She has been deceived. Aaron has achieved something without her permission. He has lied and concealed things. That means Aaron wants something very badly. Esther is aggrieved; she radiates outrage, but says nothing. She will simply eradicate the letter before Max comes home. She can tear it to pieces but that's too simple. She wants Aaron to participate in its loss. She wants him to know that his desires are nothing to her but garbage.

Briefly, mother's and son's eyes meet. Aaron turns away, lest she see his hate and his desire.

Esther follows Aaron from room to room as he gathers the trash and puts it into a big plastic bag. His heart beats painfully against his rib cage, like mallet blows on some tympani of foreboding.

When everything is collected, Esther, dangling her keys, escorts Aaron towards the car.

He has to do it, now. Hefting the sack on his scrawny shoulder he lurches down the driveway, dodges a car, cuts through the neighbors' garden, squeezes through a hedge, and is gone. The sack is heavy with melon rinds, leftovers gone too ripe, newspapers and an old phone book. As he adjusts the clumsy weight of the sack, Aaron hears a muffled squawk of outrage from his mother. He knows she's too fat to run. He makes it down into The Dell, a tiny copse of wood and water that has yet to fall under the developers' tractors.

Terrified and exultant, he finds the letter near the top of the heap, straightens it and reads it by the fading light.

"Dear Mr. and Mrs. Kantro," it says. "It gives me great pleasure to inform you that your son, Aaron, achieved one of the highest scores for musical aptitude in the history of the Comprehensive Musical Aptitude Test. In the entire state, among thousands of children, Aaron ranks in the upper one tenth of a percentile. I strongly encourage you to enroll your son in the Youth Orchestra. We have openings at present for violin, flute, bassoon, trumpet and percussion. With his enrollment comes instruction in his chosen instrument, free of charge. In the future, should Aaron express a desire, he will be given training in Harmony, Theory and advanced musical forms. This is thanks to the Zellman Endowment, whose funds have been set aside to encourage those students with special promise. Please fill out and sign the enclosed form and return it to me in the provided envelope. I look forward to hearing from you. Sincerely, Saul Lefkowitz, Concertmaster, St. Louis Symphony Orchestra. "

The letter is crumpled, damp and stained with coffee grounds. Aaron looks at the form, a questionnaire with check boxes and signature lines. He studies it carefully, then sponges the sheets dry on his shirt and folds them. Aaron hugs the letter to his chest. He laughs hugely and silently and dances in a little hopping circle, throwing his arms to the sky, showing the letter to the gods in Heaven. Nothing like this has ever happened to him. He has never been praised, never succeeded, never been special.

Now he is someone! Upper one tenth of a percentile! That means he is better than ninety nine point nine percent of all the other fourth graders in the state. Oh God! An area in him is opening up, a place, a scent, a taste, a way of being that he has never known. Victory!

It is dark. There is an owl that lives in The Dell. It hoots, a familiar and beloved tone. To Aaron the sound means autumn. It means Halloween, burning leaves, Thanksgiving. It brings the spirit of the Indians to his imagination. They are laden with pumpkins and sheaves of corn. Something about this time of year shivers his very core with a thrill of olden days, of uncut forests and great running rivers.

Once, as he was playing Army with the other kids, the owl took a giant white crap right on his head. He didn't take it personally. He loves the owl, and wonders where it will go when the tractors come.

He still has to go home, to face his mother's wrath, his father's weakness. He isn't in the Youth Orchestra yet. He has pushed defiance to a new level. He knows, from bitter experience, that his mother will make him pay.

Through the trees he can see the lights coming on. He can hear the cars of fathers coming home from work, and knows that his father is still some hours away. He waits, trying to re-read the letter, but it's now too dark.

At last, seizing his courage as if it is a brick and he a workman, he starts home, with the letter and consent form folded neatly in his pocket. He emerges from the trees into the suburban night. Cicadas buzz and the ghostly glow of television light escapes from curtained windows. When he gets to the next-door neighbors' garden, he sees with great relief that his father's car is in the driveway.

His parents are in the den, watching television. Max has his supper on a portable tray. None of Aaron's siblings are present.

As the boy lets himself in the back door, Esther is silent.

"Where on earth have you been?" Max Kantro is concerned but not angry. Aaron is never frightened of his father. He advances, avoiding his mother's glare, and holds out the letter.

"Mom threw this in the trash. I had to get it back."

"What are you talking about?" Esther protests. "There is only junk mail. I threw nothing......"

Max sees his son cringe away from his wife, and it hurts, but he doesn't know what to do. He takes the letter. He wants to give the boy a big hug, but that isn't his way, has never been the way in his family. They don't touch, don't hug.

As he reads, the wrinkles in his face change direction. A proud blush flows from his neck to the top of his head. He had been exhausted. Now there's energy in him. His poor lost son may have found something to guide him through his difficult childhood.

"Look at this, Esther. How can this happen? He scored in the upper tenth percent. My god, this is fantastic. Aren't you looking, Esther? I've heard about these tests from everybody down at the deli. It's become the big status thing, to get your kid into the Youth Orchestra. It's a scholarship! Aaron, why didn't you say something? I didn't even know you took the test."

Esther sits with her shoulders rigid, her nose wrinkled. "Let me see." Max hands the letter to his wife. Aaron blanches, imagining that she is about to tear the missive to pieces.

Esther's expression remains fixed as she reads the letter. "That's very good, Aaron. We're very proud of you." She hands the letter daintily back to her husband, holding it with the tips of her fingers. "Music....hmm..uh huh." She says the word "music" as if it refers to a noxious gas.

Max smiles. He seems unaware of the tangled wires that grip his wife and son. "I can't wait to tell my sisters. One of my customer's kids took the test. He got a polite form letter. Nothing."

Esther brightens as she thinks of having something over her sisters-in-law. Aaron knows the signs; he knows that a battle has been won.

"Have you decided on an instrument?" Max refers to the letter. "Look, you can......"

"Drums." Aaron makes this announcement as boldly as he can. "See," he points at the application sheet, "It says 'percussion' but that means drums and everything about drums." Mrs. Leek showed the class a movie of the Count Basie orchestra, and when Aaron saw the drummer, Sonny Payne, dashing his way through "The One O'clock Jump," he found a new hero, a new kind of icon, a sweaty madman at the helm of a giant ship, a drummer-captain commanding the guns of the brass section, summoning the torpedoes of the woodwinds, driving it, steaming ahead, locking with the bass player in a majestic stomping wildness that thrilled every atom of his being.

"Drums," he says, hammering the word into the firmament like a mountain climber planting a flag.

"Well, okay," Max begins, but Esther interrupts.

"Anything but drums, Max. That will drive me crazy. My migraines...I can't stand it.....no way can it be drums."

Max sees a sudden bleakness ripping away the triumph in his son's face. Beside him, smoky thoughts waft from the crypt of Esther's mask-like countenance. The battle that has been proceeding between his wife and his firstborn son reveals itself in all its frost and frustration. The naked enmity that exists between the people he loves emerges like a buried archive from a melted avalanche. He understands suddenly that he is in a delicate situation.

"Aaron," he says, knowing that this will be a huge disappointment for his son. "Choose another instrument. Your mother's only being fair. She has it rough with her headaches. Maybe in a few years, maybe her headaches will get better...." his eyes plead back at his son's pleading.

Something ripes and gives way, and Aaron accepts his lot. He has anticipated as much. It can never happen, that he will get what he really wants. It will always be the consolation prize.

"Can I play trumpet?" he asks, timidly. "I want to play jazz, like Satchmo and Dizzy."

Where on earth is a nine year old getting this stuff? Max looks toward Esther, and sees an objection perched on the edge of her lips.

"Listen to that," Esther says, her spite gaining momentum. "He wants to play Schvahtze music. Not respectable music, not Lawrence Welk or Mantovani. He has to be a bum and go around with the coloreds. What kind of life will that be? Imagine me having to say to my friends, 'My son, the jazz musician'. He'll bring schvahtzes right here, into this house. He'll be nothing but a bum and a dope fiend. He'll end up like Mark Holtzman, playing bar mitzvahs and weddings with a bottle of gin in his pocket, nothing but a schlepper."

"Esther, for Christ's sake he's nine years old! He's not making a career choice."

"All right, then, but if I have migraines, he'll have to go out to the garage or down in the basement. And there will be no schvahtzes in this house except Etta and the lawn mower boy when he needs to use the spare bathroom."

"Let him play the trumpet, Esther, it'll be good for him. God knows he's no athlete and not much of a student."

Max knows all about Esther's racial views. She hates coloreds, she hates all Goyim, and she is a self-hating anti-semite. She has a special terror of schvahtzes, as they are called in the local Yiddish dialect. As a child she witnessed a robbery, she saw her father shoot a black man. It is one of many searing memories from her childhood. The things she doesn't remember, or half-remembers, are far more disturbing.

Aaron sags, limp with relief. The battle, for now, is over. He has gotten something, something big. He will be in the Youth Orchestra.

Chapter Three

1957: The Black Truck

Sarah Kantro is surrounded. Her nemesis, the hulking Stella Riseman, intercepts her as she walks up the steps to the school building. Stella's regular claque of friends act as reinforcements. They push Sarah from one girl to the other until Sarah is sitting on the steps looking up at four leering faces. With one great effort, Sarah lunges at Stella's knees, hugging them viciously so that Stella is thrown off balance.

Stella stumbles backwards harmlessly, falling into a sitting position on the next step. She takes the opportunity to howl, exaggerating her injury. She has one eye on Sarah and one eye on the teacher who is monitoring the schoolyard.

"Mr. Pelton!" Stella screams, "Sarah just knocked me down for no reason!"

"She did," the other girls confirm, as the teacher approaches to sort out the trouble.

Sarah doesn't wait for Mr. Pelton's intervention. She bursts through the ring of girls and runs into the cool dimly lit corridors of the school.

Now I'll get a note to be signed by mama, she thinks, telling her about my bad conduct. I'm stupid stupid stupid.

The bell signaling the end of lunch period rings through the building. Sarah takes refuge in a bathroom stall, and waits for the halls to empty of students. After a few minutes pass she goes to the door, checks in both directions, then leaves the school and runs to the park across the street. There she curls up inside one of the large concrete cylinders that are part of the playground equipment. If she huddles at the very center of the drum, no one can see her, but she can see out in both directions.

Sarah must have fallen asleep, because the sound of the school bell wakes her. Startled, she leaps from the cylinder before any of the kids can cross from the school into the playground. She has to get home. She hopes that she can get away with her bad behavior, that no one has called mama. She needs to reach the shelter of her room with her sketch pads and art books.

"Please, mama, don't be home" she prays, "don't be home don't be home don't be home."

Esther's car is parked solidly in the carport. Sarah enters through the back door and tries to make her way to her room without being seen. She is hungry but she still has part of her lunch. She listens but hears no sound, no television, no dishwasher, no voice on the phone. The door to her room is closed. Marilee isn't home. It's only ten past three. She presses one hand to the poster of Elvis on the outside of the door, turns the knob with the other.

Esther is sitting on Sarah's bed, fingers drumming, wearing a look that bodes no tenderness.

"Ma....mama," Sarah stammers, fear suddenly twisting inside her rib cage.

"You weren't in school this afternoon," Esther states with a frozen calm so menacing that Sarah winces.

"I was too," she protests without thinking, "who says I wasn't?"

Esther softens her tone. "You're sure you were there?"

Sarah jumps through the opening. "Yes, mama, I was there all day." As she speaks, she knows she has been trapped, that she has just added a dumb lie to her other crimes. The glint in her mother's eye tells her that someone has called from the school, that she knows about the fight, about the skipping out, everything.

It isn't a hard slap when it comes. Esther's blows are terror weapons. They are calibrated not to cause injury. When Esther needs to express her rage violently, she tends to shake, squeeze and throttle her victims. She is too smart to mark up her children. Still, the slap dazzles the girl, knocking her to a sitting position against the door.

Esther is standing over her, hands on hips. "Not only do you beat up Stella Riseman and play hookie, but you have the nerve to lie to me! What good are you? Why did I bother to have you? You're not like your sister, who's considerate and helpful and makes good grades."

Esther storms from the room, to return a moment later with a suitcase. She snaps it open, and begins taking Sarah's clothing from drawers and closet. "I'm sending you away." Esther's voice has deepened. It seems to have bubbles in it, hot bubbles. "I've arranged for an orphanage to take you."

"Oh god, mama! Please don't! I'll be good, I promise! I really really will.. I'll do everything you tell me. I'll be as good....even BETTER than Marilee. Please, mama, please!.."

She is hanging tightly to her mother's arm, hoping somehow to restrain the inexorable movement of clothing from drawer to suitcase. Clack! The next drawer opens. Swish, flop, swish, flop, dresses, blouses and undies go in random piles into the suitcase. Sarah, clinging desperately, slides this way and that, as Esther's arm moves, oblivious of the little-girl weight attached to it.

The suitcase snaps shut. With a powerful grip, Esther takes the child, running, stumbling, and thrusts her out the front door, tossing the case down next to her. "Just wait here," she orders.

"The Black Truck will come to get you pretty soon and take you to the orphanage."

The door closes. Sarah begins to scream with terror. The Black Truck! This image of impersonal menace is so horrible that it closes like a spider's legs around her heart. She will be taken away from everything she knows! Her brothers, her father! To go where? To an orphanage? Even Esther has to be better than an orphanage that sends out The Black Truck. Her screams echo up and down the street. They are too loud. Esther begins to worry that this is becoming a scene. It violates her fine-tuned sense of privacy. The door quickly opens and Sarah and her suitcase are pulled back inside.

"All right," says Esther. "I'll give you one more chance. But you'd better behave or so help me god, next time, you'll go."

"Yes, mama, anything, just please call the orphanage and tell the Black Truck not to come. I'll be so good you wont believe it's the same daughter. I promise, promise promise."

"Just go to your room and put your clothes back," Esther commands.

"I will, mama, I will, please call the orphanage right now."

Watching her daughter, Esther goes to the phone nook near the living room. She dials POPCORN, the number that gives the time . "Hello, this is Esther Kantro. I called you earlier about my daughter, Sarah. Well. I've changed my mind, you can cancel the Black Truck."

"The time is now three twenty two p.m.", the neutral female voice recites.

"What, they're already on their way? I'm so sorry for causing you the trouble. Please radio The Black Truck and have it return to the orphanage; we won't need it today. Thank you very much."

Sobbing with relief, Sarah meekly takes the case and returns to her room, where she puts her clothes back in their places.

When things have settled down, the tears dried, the fear subsided, Esther comes into the girls' room. Marilee has come and gone, indifferent to the tumult. Mark is in the basement, watching TV. No one knows where Aaron might be.

"You realize, of course," Esther says, very calm, very composed, as she moves across the room to where Sarah sits, quietly sketching in her notebook, "that since I didn't send you away, we'll have to think of some other punishment for what you did today."

Sarah can't summon enough emotion to be afraid of any lesser punishment. "Yes, mama. Of course."

"Well, I guess we'll just take away your art books for a few days, mm?" With a swish, Esther lifts the pad out of Sarah's hands. She tosses it through the open door. Then, as Sarah stands, silent and pale, her mother removes the other pads, pens and colored pencils from the desk's various drawers.

"Yes mama," she says again, meekly, as Esther gathers everything and takes the stuff from the room. When her mother's steps have faded down the hall, Sarah considers her options. Marilee's desk is off limits. Even if it wasn't locked, if Marilee finds out she's been rooting around in her very PERSONAL PRIVATE desk, it will be as bad as getting Esther angry all over again.

Sarah pulls her chair to the closet door. She slides open her side of the closet as soundlessly as possible. Standing on the chair, she reaches up to the shelf and feels around way in the back, where things tend to slide and get lost. After a moment, her fingers discern the shape of a fugitive pencil. Once retrieved, she runs it through the little hand sharpener and sweeps the shavings carefully into her trash can, then mixes the contents of the can thoroughly so no detectable traces can be found.

As for locating a surface upon which to draw, that is no problem. The family stores things all over the house. There are old ledgers inside boxes in the closet way at the back behind mom's hat boxes. Sarah finds one of these. They are all hand bound notebooks covered in faded blue cloth. They are filled with her father's notations. Quietly, oh so quietly, she tears an empty back page from a ledger dated "6 - 12 1959".

Listening for the clomp of her mother's angry stride, Sarah returns to sketching a delicate blue flower. It is an imaginary flower, though it looks somewhat like an orchid.

Chapter Four

1967: On the road with The Zoot Prestige Trio

Aaron at Twenty

Zoot Prestige twists his head as far as it will go. He wants to look into Aaron's eyes. He feels so sad. He has been gripped by Aaron's childhood trauma. It is a lot like his own trauma, but that is a thing of the past. These experiences are still alive in his young friend, they are still sizzling with the heat of a hot stove in Aaron's soul.

"That's like some concentration camp shit, man. You, your sisters and brother, you grew up in Hell," says Zoot. "Your mother's still alive, right?"

"Yes, she's a ghost, but she still lives."

"Man, your mother is an evil person. Evil. Evil!" Zoot's hands beat on the steering wheel. He is clearly upset. He is smoking one of his cheroots, biting it in his anger, and the white smoke comes from his mouth, hovers for a moment around the steering wheel and is sucked out the open driver's side window. The trio is on the way from Detroit to Cleveland. The landscape is mile upon mile of steel tubing running in mazes, rising to slender stacks from which flames shoot. Storage tanks with rusted ochre paint are filled with substances that can poison whole cities. It is industrial Hell and it drives the musicians into themselves.

Zoot Prestige is a prominent jazz musician. He isn't a titan like John Coltrane but he is an astute marketer of his own material and he stays within the top tenor sax players in the magazine jazz polls.

He lives a comfortable middle class lifestyle, supporting numerous children and ex-wives. Unless a gig is west of the Mississippi he choses to drive his plush Lincoln Continental, with its massive trunk and cargo space. If the gigs require the Hammond B3 organ and its speaker, he tows it in a black aluminum trailer.

Aaron talks about his childhood. It's difficult. The words emerge as if each is a toy wooden block stuck in his throat. Zoot listens intently to Aaron 's story. Tyrone Terry, a keyboard player near to Aaron's age, finds himself mesmerized. Aaron isn't sure he should be sharing these dark corners of his past. He looks at the face of Zoot, at his craggy mixed-race countenance. When he sees interest and sympathy, he keeps going.

Now, Zoot's comment jars him. "My mother isn't evil, she's sick. She can't help herself."

With this statement, Zoot puts on the brakes so suddenly that the car shimmies. He slows and finds a place to pull off the highway.

"Now wait a minute!" He points the skinny cigar at Aaron and sees that he has almost bitten the thing in two. He pushes it into the ash tray and squashes it to a nub. The car's engine rumbles in idle. Tyrone, in the back seat, plants his chin on the front seat's leather, to hear what is being said.

"My definition of an evil person," says Zoot, " is someone who avoids their own pain by passing it off to someone else. It's that simple. You don't need to get into ontological bullshit to define evil. It's real simple, least in the human realm. I don't know about evil as anything other than human. There may be some cosmic impersonal force of pure Evil, but I ain't qualified to know about that. The most evil shit I've seen in this world is from PEOPLE! Evil happens when people or even whole cultures decide to shift their pain!"

Zoot exhales and calms himself. He shuts his eyes for a moment, passes his hand over his eye lids, as if to dispel a wretched vision.

"Your mother is sick, for real," he continues, " she is hurting bad. But she chose to take it out on you and your family, and there ain't no excuse for that. It makes me angry that you make excuses for her."

Aaron wants to avoid Zoot's eyes, but he is aware of this, and makes himself look back. In this light Zoot's eyes have a subtle tint of blue-green, almost turquoise. They are full of suffering, humor and intelligence.

"If my mother's evil, what does that make me? The spawn of evil, the child of a devil?"

"Oh, now cut out that shit. You didn't ask to be treated that way. You were a little boy. No child should EVER be treated that way! But now you're a man; you've got to learn to deal with it. If you don't, you're gonna hurt yourself and other people too. I want you to listen to me, babe. Aaron Kantro, hear Zoot Prestige when he's testifying. I want you to remember this piece of advice. I don't give advice, hardly ever, it's a policy, a promise I made to myself so's I'd never become pompous. This...this ain't advice...this is more like a seed I'm planting. Let it go into your mind and just lay there and maybe some day you'll need it and then it'll be there, it'll be ready. Okay?"

Aaron nods. He looks toward the solemn face of Tyrone. The pianist nods, and gestures with his face toward the saxophonist.

"Okay, this is it," Zoot affirms. "Aaron Kantro, someday when you need help, when you hit bottom, don't wait to ask for it. You can't get up from the bottom all by yourself. Don't be too proud. Ask for help. Reach out for people. Don't be too proud. Ask for help when you need it. Okay? Do you hear me?"

"I will, I will," Aaron responds, at the surface of his mind. Farther down, he doesn't even register what Zoot is saying. He is ignoring it as useless information. "Why will I need help?" he wonders. "I'm gonna do fine, I'll be great, I'll be famous. I'm really going to BE somebody! What the fuck does he mean, 'hit bottom?"

Zoot watches Aaron with eyes narrowed to bare cracks, as if he knows what Aaron is thinking. He can only pray that his gifted young friend might remember this exchange before it's too late, before he slides down the endless chute that goes nowhere. That will be a terrible shame; a tragedy.

He gives a near-invisible shrug. This kid, this beautiful kid, this fine musician will some day find himself in a dark place, trapped in a cell of his own making. There is nothing that he, Zoot Prestige, can do except plant a seed that might help.

Zoot looks in the side view mirror, presses his foot to the gas pedal and roars back into the zooming traffic.

Chapter Five

Perception   **is**   **Reality**
1967: Indianapolis

Aaron leans forward to put his drumsticks and brushes into the trunk of Zoot's car. He is alone in the parking lot behind The Jazz Spot. Across the alley a dog is trying to open a trash can at the back of a restaurant. The thing topples with a crash, the lid pops open and a number of dogs converge on the scene, growling over scraps.

The gig is over. It is two twenty in the morning. Two brilliant mercury vapor lamps light up the almost empty lot, which is enclosed by buildings on three sides. On the fourth side a dark vacant lot full of weeds and rusty cans stretches emptily to the curb of the next street.

Aaron doesn't think about danger. He is in a parking lot, late at night, behind a jazz club in an urban black ghetto. He has seen gunfights, stabbings, throttlings, beatings, riots. What is there to think about? He and Tyrone have sneaked some Thai Stick on top of Zoot's carefully doled out Mexican weed, and the music is swirling through his head like the arabesques on the ceiling of the Great Mosque of Samarkand.

A force strikes him behind both knees, so that he is suddenly flat on his back at the rear of the Continental. A hand comes down upon his mouth, sealilng off his air, while another hand holds the blade of a knife to his throat. Aaron is looking up into the face of a man with a ragged Afro haircut. Another man is going through his pockets, while a third is inside the Continental, opening the glove compartment. The man on top of Aaron says "What the motherfucker got? He got anything?"

The man who has rifled his pockets holds Aaron 's wallet, takes out the money and tosses the wallet aside. "He got some twenties and some tens. Let's kill the ofay motherfucker and get out of here."

Aaron sees the hand holding the knife tense. He sees the bunching of muscle at the wrist, sees the clear intention to murder flowing down from his assailant's eyes, through his shoulders, through his ligaments and tendons.

I don't want to get stabbed, Aaron thinks. I'd rather get shot. I'd rather be blown up, I'd rather drown or be poisoned or get cancer, anything but stabbed. His mind is moving at convulsive light-speed.. I should pray, he thinks, or somehow address myself to God, Allah, Buddha, Krishna, I should be forgiving this fucking asshole on top of me, I shouldn't depart this life polluted by the murderous spirit of this pathetic killer who's about to cut my throat.

A voice comes from the rear door of the Jazz Spot. "Get off him, motherfucker, or I blow your head off."

It's Zoot. He holds his saxophone in the crook of his arm, pointing it like a shotgun. He moves forward, putting the toes of his feet down delicately. "Get up off him!" he commands. His voice has teeth, like a saw blade.

The pressure on Aaron's mouth eases, the hand comes away. Aaron takes a breath and turns his head to see Zoot, pointing the saxophone. There is plenty of light in the parking lot. No way, he thinks, these guys are going to believe that's a gun.

Zoot rattles the keys on the saxophone and it makes hollow clicking sounds.

"Get out of my car!" He pushes the sound of his voice with all of its metal, sharp, cutting.

"Take it easy, old man, don't shoot," one of the robbers says. It's the man who has taken Aaron's wallet. He holds Aaron's money between the fingers of one hand, then drops the bills onto the cracked asphalt.

Zoot takes another two steps forward, cradling the saxophone's mouthpiece in his left hand while he holds the bell down near his waist with his right hand. He is only three or four feet from the nearest of Aaron's attackers. The bright pale blue light glitters on the brass instrument, catching its curves and intricate engraving.

"If you get the fuck out of here right now, I won't kill you," Zoot concedes. "I mean RIGHT NOW!"

As he spits these last words like projectiles, the men bolt from the parking lot, feet slapping gravel and fine dust as they vanish down the alley.

Zoot kneels and helps Aaron sit up. He props the saxophone against the car's fender and brushes grime from his drummer's clothes.

Aaron can't breathe. He feels the impressions of large pebbles in his back.

"That was goddam close," Zoot says. "You okay? They didn't cut you?"

Aaron shakes his head, trying to form words. Zoot helps him to his feet and leads him to the open passenger door of the car, where he gently seats him on the soft leather. "I shouldn't have left you out here alone. I thought Tyrone was here. Guess he went up to the hotel, huh?"

Aaron nods. Air begins to flow into his lungs. "How the hell did you do that?" He flicks one shaking hand in the direction of the saxophone.

"What?" Zoot shrugs, looks at the horn. "Oh....that. Demonstration of a fundamental principle: belief determines reality. I hold it like a gun, i imagine the image of a gun, they think it's a gun, simple."

"But it's not a gun, and any moron can see it is not a gun," Aaron protests.

"Don't matter. If I had said 'bang', one of those fuckers would have fallen over dead. Least I think so; I never killed nobody with an idea, not yet. At that moment the saxophone was a gun." He looks at the beautiful instrument propped against the vehicle's tire. It is a most un-weapon-like device. "Well, fuck, it was worth a try and it worked!"

Aaron rubs his shoulder blade where it has met the ground. "This is Plato's postulation that idea precedes matter. Or Percival's thesis that thinking becomes destiny. Are you a neo-Platonist, Zoot?"

"Absolutely. The Zoot Prestige philosophy has its roots in Heraclitus and in such Renaissance mystics as Bruno and Ficino. Not to mention Gurdjieff, Ouspensky, Rudolph Steiner, Annie Besant...you been reading the same shit, man, only I been reading it thirty years longer."

Aaron picks little pieces of rock out of his forearms, and then gets up to retrieve his wallet and his money. "I almost got killed two seconds ago, and we're talking metaphysics in an Indianapolis parking lot. I like it."

Zoot sits on the seat Aaron has just vacated, extending his legs and sighing. "I'm tired. I need some sleep. Nothing like the nearness of death to beget metaphysical speculation."

"Either that or a raging hard-on," Aaron agrees, picking up the saxophone. He studies it carefully. He uses it to cover the sudden erection that pushes at his trousers. It seems as if the a primal life force has just been sucked into his body.

Zoot extends his hand and takes the instrument, cradling it in his lap. "Objects have souls, just like people. You never know when some rock or tree or piece of metal might turn into your friend."

"You're my friend, Zoot. How many times are you going to save my life?"

"Hundreds," Zoot announces. "Thousands. Don't worry about it. You've saved me in other lives. You've saved many lives. It's all for the best. You have a life worth saving."

Chapter
University City, Missouri
Aaron Is Eight Years Old

Aaron can't draw the way Sarah can. He has learned how to make one picture, a winter scene of a cabin on a hill, with a road leading up through pine trees. It looks, more or less, like that: smoke comes out of the cabin's chimney. It is a real picture, not a scribble, and he is proud of it.

It is Saturday afternoon, and Aaron isn't feeling well. He has learned that feeling sick provides him with a little margin of safety. He can hole up in his room, escape from whatever demands might be placed upon him to play baseball, badly, or go swimming and have to be naked in locker rooms with aggressive boys. Sometimes, if his mom isn't home, he can just practice his trumpet and watch TV all day. If she is home, he stays in his room and practices in the closet,with a mute stuck into the bell of the horn. He likes to sketch or read volumes of the encyclopedia from cover to cover. He started with W because he wanted to look up World War Two, and after that he read about World War One, and then just read the whole volume from cover to cover, then went back to A and kept reading. He is now at J.

He wishes he can draw as well as Sarah. He needs so badly to excel, and to have people tell him that he is the best in the world at something. He wants to draw pictures of exploding battleships and zooming fighter planes, but they aren't very satisfying. Oh well, Sarah can't play trumpet. When she tries to blow into his horn, it just sounds like a fart. Sarah likes stupid music, Fabian and Paul Anka, and can't understand a note of Count Basie or Jimmie Lunceford. Aaron knows that he is just a kid and that he isn't very good on the trumpet. He is the best trumpeter in his grade, but that isn't very much. He knows it will take maybe ten years to get pretty good, and the idea of it taxes his patience.

Aaron tried his first sketch when he was five years old, directly onto the wall of his room. Esther threw all his clothes into a suitcase and threatened to send him to an orphanage. It had been more terrifying than any experience of his life. When he told Sarah about it she turned ghostly white.

"You mean it's all a big fake?"

"She did it to you, too?" Aaron asks.

Sarah nods. Her face is slowly flushing red.

"For one thing,", he explains, "it's against the law. Parents can't send their kids away unless they burn the house down or chop somebody's head off with an axe...she just wants to scare you."

Aaron has taken all the charge out of the threat of being sent away. What a relief! The next time Esther pulls her orphanage trick, Sarah screams and cries, but she is doing it to give mother a show, the kind of show she wants. If she doesn't act scared, mother will know the punishment has lost its effect. She will invent something worse.

Aaron can hear kids playing outside. Next door, the Schimmels have a big plastic swimming pool, and all the girls are there, shrieking and splashing. Mark is at Grandma's and dad is at work. Aaron always knows where his mother is; his ears are like radar dishes turning and turning, keeping track of her presence. Bad things tend to happen when he is alone with his mother.

At the moment, he knows she is outside, gossiping with Emma Loewe and Florence Schimmel. They are sitting in chaise lounges, wearing floppy sunbonnets, watching children splash in the pool. At the moment, he knows she is outside, gossiping with Emma Loewe and Florence Schimmel. They are sitting in chaise lounges, wearing floppy sunbonnets, watching children splash in the pool.

Aaron runs out of paper. He goes through his desk and his closet. Then, timidly, he sneaks to the girls' room. They have just gotten new desks, with locking pull-down tops. He can't get into either desk.

He turns his head slightly, listening intently, to locate his mother. She is still outside. Aaron pads down the hall to the dining room, where his parents keep paper and business ledgers in a heavy dark cabinet that smells of cedar and mothballs.

The cabinet is also locked. Aaron is an impatient child; he hates being thwarted. As he begins to seethe with frustration, he sees on the dining room table a wirebound notebook. It is at the center of the large table, out of his reach. His eyes barely clear the surface of the table, and his arms are a few inches too short to grasp his objective.

Quietly, he moves one of the heavy chairs out from under the table. Checking to see that his socks are clean, he steps onto the chair.

The table is spread with a spotless white tablecloth. Fine crystal bowls are set out, containing nuts and foil-wrapped candies. Aaron reaches for the notebook. As he pulls it towards him, the wire loops that bind the book slide across the tablecloth. At one end of the wire binding there is an exposed arc, bent and sharply pointed. As Aaron hauls in his prize, this bit of wire catches and pulls at the tablecloth.

Aaron is so intent that he fails to notice the cloth moving and bunching until the crystal bowls topple over the edge of the table, crashing into each other and breaking, spilling nuts and chocolate all over the carpet.

This is a catastrophe of paralyzing dimensions. Aaron reaches for the dozens of glittering pieces, flirting with the idea of cutting himself to create a bloody injury, anything to distract from his crime. His hands go forward and back, not quite touching the glass, like parakeets fluttering around in a cage. He touches one big piece, lacks the courage to slash himself, drops it, gets up and runs across the room, then runs back, making sounds of alarm.

"Uh...uh..uh..." little bubbles of panic and terror come from his mouth. Then it is too late. Esther is there, bull-like, shocked and wrathful.

She has gained a lot of weight over the last few years. She is five foot four and weighs over two hundred pounds. Her breasts and belly sag; her face is gray from drugs. Her eyes normally have a glazed quality, but now they are dilated with eager alertness, and they fix upon the little boy with stunning malevolence.

"I'm cleaning it up right now, mom. See?" Aaron is on his knees, attempting to shovel the fragments of glass onto the notebook. He holds two large pieces together, placatingly, as if to demonstrate that it can all be repaired.

"Stop it!" Esther bellows. Aaron snaps upright and backward in one grasshopper motion. He wants to be out of her reach.

"My mother gave me those bowls for my wedding. They are family heirlooms, handed down from generation to generation." Esther bends down and picks up the larger pieces, and puts them into the bunched tablecloth, where it has drooped to the floor.

"I'm sorry," Aaron whines, "I didn't mean to..."

"You never 'mean to', you worthless little bastard." Esther's voice has the texture of broken glass, and Aaron twitches with every movement of her hands. Her body is jerking with the suppressed urge to kill her son, to wring his ugly little neck. Something stops her. Perhaps she recognizes that she is so angry that if she begins to beat her son, there will be no end to it until he is dead.

"Go to your room and stay there," she commands. She is thinking about her mother, and how the old bitch forced her to work through the Depression, keeping her out of school. How the old bitch turned a blind eye to the games that her brothers played with her and her sisters, lewd brutal games that made her burn with shame and hate. At the topmost level of her mind, she is enraged because the bowls are very expensive, and now they are broken and gone. Underneath that greedy evaluation, she is dimly aware that she hates the bowls. She is glad they are gone, glad that she doesn't have to look at a reminder of the family she loathes. But Aaron has done wrong, and Aaron has to suffer the consequences. Her rage isn't so much at the loss of the expensive bowls. Her rage is at Aaron's very existence, at the way Aaron resembles her brother Sonny, the lousy bastard who made her play sick games in the basement.

Stunned and unbelieving, Aaron runs, clutching the notepad to his chest. He knows there is more to come. He waits in his room like a small animal trapped by a predator, cut off from any further retreat.

He waits. And waits. Nothing happens. When an hour has passed, he begins to relax. Finally, he resumes sketching.

The day passes. His brother and sisters come home. Sarah pokes her head in the room and gives him a spooky look but says nothing.

The family routine resumes its normal rhythm. Dinner is served. Everyone watches TV. The kids go to bed at nine o'clock, leaving Esther free to watch Milton Berle without being disturbed. At about eleven, Max comes in, tired, drooping, and eats the lukewarm dinner leftovers. Esther tells him about the loss of the bowls, outraged all over again, but Max stares at an undefined spot on the floor, barely hearing.

The next day, Sunday, Max has arranged to be with the family while someone else manages the deli. The Kantros go to a movie matinee and then eat at a Chinese restaurant. Nothing is said about the broken bowls. Aaron begins to think the calamity is receding into the past.

It isn't until Monday afternoon that he receives the first installment of his punishment.

He has been reading volume K of the encyclopedia. The Kachin people of northern Burma supplied guerilla forces to the allies during World War Two. The area is invaded by China in 1945, but it is a lawless area of mountain wilderness, and is still controlled by local warlords. Aaron's imagination loves to soar to remote geographies. Summer is almost over. Insects buzz against the window screen. Lawn sprinklers hiss all over the neighborhood as their arcs of water move backwards and forwards across close-trimmed yards.

Aaron is getting thirsty. He doesn't want to leave the safety of his room and the historic adventures of the encyclopedia, but an image forms in his mind, the image of a cherry popsicle, and soon this image becomes so compelling that he is forced to bow to its demands.

The problem with such a demand is that he will have to ask Esther for this cherry popsicle. The freezer is not a help-yourself place in the Kantro household. It is the repository of special treats, ice cream, frozen Snickers bars, dreamsicles and cherry popsicles.

Aaron's thirst and this image of a popsicle rule him. It becomes him, until he disappears so far into it that it outweighs his caution.

Gingerly, he taps at the door to his parents' bedroom.

"Mom?" His voice ends on a high note, as if he is a squeeze-doll.

"What do you want?" Esther does not glance at the little face craning around the door-frame. A wet towel is wrapped around her forehead. The room is dark except for the glow of the portable TV that is perched high on a shelf opposite the double bed. Canned laughter spills from the little blue and white box. Esther's hair is in curlers, a white cream is daubed on her face.

Aaron knows that she has a headache. The image of the popsicle pushes that fact aside.

"Can I have a cherry popsicle, mom? I haven't has one since Friday, and I haven't has any candy either, except for one at the movies. Sarah had a dreamsicle yesterday and Marilee had two fudge-sicles. And Mark, Mark got a sno-cone and a licorice bar and...."

"Oh shut up, Aaron. I'll get you a popsicle." Esther heaves herself upright, grunting, holding the cloth to her head. Aaron follows her into the kitchen, the image of the popsicle now making way for the promise of the popsicle, soon to be the deliciously melting reality of the popsicle. It seems as though he has never looked forward to anything so much in his entire life.

Esther opens the freezer, at the top of the refrigerator. From within its dark humming interior, she withdraws a large manila envelope. From this she takes a shard of one of the broken crystal bowls.

"Here's your cherry popsicle, Aaron." She hands the boy a large piece of broken glass, as if it is an actual popsicle, as if nothing is amiss, askew, strange, twisted, unreal, as if the sharp glass is sweet and frosty, with white wisps of steam emitting from a cold paper wrapping.

Aaron's hand is already out. He takes the piece and holds it, looking from his mother to the glass shard, and back. He tries to read in his mother's face a clue, an explanation as to the nature of this game. The face is closed, so closed and distant. For a moment the world does a flip and shudder, and black is white, hot is cold, love is hate and glass is sweet water ice. Then everything rights itself, and Aaron comprehends his punishment.

This is but the first piece of glass. He receives another each time he asks for something good: a treat, a sweet, permission to go out and play. Piece by piece, Aaron obtains every bit of both crystal bowls, down to the tiniest sliver. It takes a long time, because he simply stops asking for things after a while. Then he realizes that he'd better start asking for things or this punishment will go on forever. He begins asking for things that he doesn't need or doesn't want.

There are times when his father is present, and as one of the envelopes comes out from its place in the house or the car, Aaron looks hopefully and futilely at Max, his eyes begging, "Please stop this craziness, please help me." But Max needs his wife more than he needs to protect his children. Max has made his own bargain with the devil.

Chapter Seven

Bebop Nazi

1961: Suburban St. Louis, Missouri

Aaron is Fourteen

Aaron Kantro goes up the wide semi-circle of steps that funnel students through the brass doors of Normandy Junior High School. The light dims and he is sun- blinded as he passes into the vast atrium. He stands still while students flow past him. The sound of rushing people strikes Aaron like a cold ocean breaker. When his vision adjusts he moves towards the stairwell, staying close to the wall. He looks at the sheet of paper taped to his notebook. Room 210, it says. Mr.Goodwin. Home Room. That's his destination.

Aaron wears a knit sweater and a pair of cream-colored slacks with cuffs and a belt. He notices with the lightning perception of terror that some of the boys are wearing pants without cuffs or belts. They wear richly colored plaid shirts, which Aaron recognizes as Bleeding Madras, the magical shirts from India with their rectangles of color that change with each washing. The fashionable shoes are Florsheim Penny Loafers. These boys stride like roosters with gorgeous plumage. They look as if they own the school.

Aaron knows this feeling of terror like an old companion. As his spirits plummet he senses that junior high school is bigger and scarier than he imagined.

Status is as necessary as oxygen in this world. Status is fragile. Who is he? The best musician in the school? What a joke. A musician is like a sewing pin in an armory of broadswords. No matter that he can scream double high C in the Jazz Orchestra. He doesn't share the nifty hand-shakes, he's not invited to participate in the latest nonsense slogan. This autumn, the jocks have devised a new goofy phrase: 'Bwadda bwadda hamm-ba!" This incantation is an integral part of the ongoing ritual of popularity. "Bwadda bwadda hamm-ba!" is the official greeting as they puff out their chests and wiggle their fingers in suggestive signals. Last year for the entire year the jocks were howling "Ja Deek Wow! Ja Deek Wow!" Aaron has enough sense not to attempt a "Bwadda". He'd be humiliated. Swimming against the stream of social ritual is dangerous. He is not "Bwadda-qualified", just as he had never enjoyed the privilege of saying "Ja Deek Wow!"

It is the dress code that sits atop the pyramid of status cues. Clothes make the man, it's so often said.. Failure to dress correctly, to wear cool rags, carries the stench of dire stigma. Aaron learns by watching the athletes, the jocks, the guys who get the girls.

It's late September. School has been in session for two weeks. That night Aaron finds his father in his favorite spot, prone on the living room couch, engrossed in a spy novel.

"Dad," Aaron's voice is tentative. He loves his father. He doesn't like bothering him. Aaron is remotely aware that here is a man who carries a load that would crush him were their places reversed. Still, he wants something and this is one route to getting better clothes. "I need some money for pants and things..."

Max looks at him as if he's crazy. He's in his boxer shorts and a t-shirt, with a light blanket thrown over his body. Max yawns and vocalizes a languid "heeee..yah!" He beholds his son with great patience. "You have clothes. What happened to all those nice things we bought?"

Aaron's embarrassed, but he says it anyway. "We bought that stuff at Sears, dad. At Sears! People are laughing at me." How can he explain to his father? He HAS to buy tight-fitting slacks from the most fashionable men's store. He must also wear Bleeding Madras Shirts, Florsheim Penny Loafers, a silver ID bracelet and black Marnier socks. Dad doesn't get it, he doesn't understand the IMPORTANCE of such items of fashion .

Max slips a bookmark piece of napkin into his spy novel. His eyelids are blinking with advancing sleep. "I'm not made of money," he says. "Those clothes seem perfectly acceptable to me. Wear what you've got. Maybe you need different friends, not different clothes." Max turns off the lamp. He's exhausted from sixteen hours of work. He begins to snore with his book riding up and down on his chest..

Aaron is forced to wear the pieces of his paltry wardrobe over and over again. The slacks don't fit the way they are supposed to fit. He isn't built right. Instead of hugging his frame from hip to ankle, the pants are too tight around his butt, then hang shapelessly from the thighs down. They have to be the PERFECT length. If they are half an inch too short, half an inch too long, the whole effect is lost. On Saturday he goes to H.I.S. Men's Apparel and uses all of his savings to buy a pair of continental slacks. No cuffs, no belt. The pants, despite their high price, fit him the same way his Sears-bought pants fit.

The tailor at H.I.S.Men's Apparel wails mockingly when he sees Aaron return for yet another fitting. "Again? Again?!"

"Mr. Rabinowitz", says Aaron, "If you could take in an inch here, and here..?" He uses his thumb and forefinger to grip the tiny area of trouser leg to demonstrate where he wants a change to be made.

"You're meshuggenuh,," the old man wheezes, "crazy. An inch this, an inch that. It doesn't work that way. It'll throw the whole line off." A blue tattoo shows on his liver-spotted wrist. His accent is thick with refugee anguish. ""Ehhh..." he raises his shoulders in an epic Hebrew shrug. "The customer is always right.That's what they say. Whoever 'they' are." He takes the trousers and tosses them onto his pile or pending alterations. "Come back Thursday evening. I'll see what I can do."

No intervention will ever make these pants right. Aaron must live with his continental slacks, fitting as they do, too short, too long, a bit of sock showing above the loafer, a bit of drag over the heel. It's humiliating.

And the shirts! Bleeding Madras shirts are just, just.....mystical. Each one is unique, each one a masterpiece of rectangles, lines and colors. He has a green one with purple vertical lines and pink horizontal stripes, and he loves it! The smell of it after ironing is like cotton candy. The shirts are disastrously expensive. If he doesn't wear a different one every day, he won't be popular. After determined pestering and many odd jobs to generate cash, Aaron has acquired three Bleeding Madres shirts and is desperately hoarding couch change to get a fourth. Once or twice a week he wears one of his crappy imitation Arrow shirts from Sears. Dreadful!

Of course, the shirts don't fit right.. Aaron can almost weep when he sees Tom Schweikert, the varsity quarterback, wearing a madras shirt. Tom's biceps fill the sleeves, they meet and move with the cloth. Aaron's shirts balloon around his pathetic skinny arms, as if he can fit both biceps into a single sleeve.

Thus his life proceeds as a junior high school student. Boring classes eat up thirty hours each week. Twice a week his trumpet teacher, Mr.Hanspiegel, comes to the house from six thirty to seven thirty. Four days a week, from four thirty to six o'clock, Aaron attends Hebrew School, loathing every moment of it, preparing for his Bar Mitzvah. Then he goes to Lester Stiers and listens to jazz and looks through the family's books at pictures of Coleman Hawkins and Duke Ellington. Having put off going home as long as possible, he finally sneaks through the back door, avoiding his mother. He goes to the room he shares with his brother Mark. A plaster-board partition has been constructed by Max to split the room into discreet areas. Aaron retreats to his desk in the corner beneath the window and reads about World War Two and The Holocaust. He turns to a series of images of mountains of Jewish corpses. He struggles with the implications. He doesn't like feeling numb, but he is numb. The tragedy is too huge, the evil too vast to be understood by one twelve year old boy. He can't make room for it. He closes the book with a shudder.

He is full of shame about being Jewish. He hates it, being a Jew. His mother has always despised her origins. Esther's constant litany of clichés seeps from her mouth and contaminates the entire family. "Once a Jew always a Jew" she repeats. She takes luxurious pleasure in her anti-semitism. "It can't be helped, we're stuck with it, making money's the only thing a Jew's good for, and your father's not even good for that. Your father's a complete failure." This statement drops like excrement from her mouth. She gloats when a Jew is caught in a crime or a scandal: "Hitler should have finished us off when he had the chance. What a shame, what a shonda, we still walk the earth, cheating people right and left."

In his highly developed fantasy life, Aaron is not a Jew. "I was adopted," he thinks, "after the war. I'm a pure Nordic child who got lost in the post war chaos and has somehow wound up in this Jewish family."

It's hard to swallow this tale when he looks in the mirror. Staring back at him is a boy who looks as if born to wear a yarmulke. His eyes are hazel, his hair is brown. His nose is medium sized but slightly convex. He does not consider himself handsome. His forehead is high and thoughtful, his gaze questioning, confused and sad. It is hard living with this visage but he has no choice. This is his own face. His own Jewish face.

A class field trip to the symphony leads him to an electrifying discovery: the music of Richard Wagner. The grandeur and color of the opera sends him into transports of ecstasy. It's better than TV, better than movies, it's better than what he thinks drugs are like. He is fascinated with the Nordic myth, with the Germanic Ideal. Inevitably, his thirst for Wagner's Ring Cycle leads him down the crazed labyrinth of Nazi ideology. He collects Nazi-era stamps, reads everything available on the period and the personalities. He has a copy of Mein Kampf. He finds it boring, stultifying. Forty or fifty pages and he's had enough. What horrible horrible stuff!

He keeps this preoccupation to himself. It's a hobby, nothing more. He's interested in history..

Aaron feels that he is the opposite of Tom Schweikert, the mystic quarterback god of Normandy J.H.S. Whenever they pass in the halls, Aaron fixes upon Tom a gaze of wistful jealousy, resentful yearning. Tom has no idea Aaron exists. Tom is Aaron's obsession, the person he wants to be, the embodiment of his longing for power.

It's the middle of October. The leaves have changed colors. The wind carries the bite of winter. Aaron loves this season, its mystery and its gloom. He is in the school library studying a map of General Rommel's desert campaigns. He feels a tap on his shoulder. Looking back and up, he sees Tom Schweikert bending forward, his face a few inches above Aaron's face. Tom is looking intently at the book on the table.

"You interested in the Wehrmacht and stuff like that?"

Aaron feels a chill of terror and excitement. "Yeah, " he manages to squeak. "I think Rommel and Guderian were great generals. Maybe the best in the German Army."

"He was a good soldier, that Rommel," Tom says smugly. "Too bad he got involved in the July Twentieth Plot."

Aaron is aware that he is being tested. "There wasn't conclusive proof about Rommel being a conspirator. A lot of talented officers were destroyed in Hitler's reaction."

"Hmm!" The handsome boy tries to conceal his surprise when Aaron provides the correct responses. He scratches his chin and sucks his lips over his teeth. The left side of his mouth slides downward. It transforms his face into a mask of cruelty that vanishes before Aaron can be sure of what he has seen. The big athlete looks down at Aaron speculatively.

"By the way," he says after a moment, "I'm Tom Schweikert. I think your name's Aaron something."

"Kantro," Aaron says, hoping it doesn't sound too Jewish. "I'm Aaron Kantro." Then he decides that it's no good to pretend to be something he isn't. "I admire the skill and dedication of The Wehrmacht," he says in a small brave voice. "But if they'd won the war, I might not be here. I might never have been born. I'm Jewish, you know." It takes a great effort to get the words out. He feels better for having said them.

"I wouldn''t be so sure". Tom speaks with an air of conspiratorial portent. "There were some special Jews who were indispensable to the Third Reich."

"I suppose that's possible," Aaron responds cautiously. "How do you know? You talk as if you were there with Hitler's inner circle."

"I've done a lot of research. I have a collection of rare documents and photos. You ought to see my stuff sometime."

"This is destiny" Aaron thinks. "This meeting is mystically pre-ordained." His mind fills with visions power, of a change in his status as he becomes the friend of an athlete who is already being scouted by the NFL. He can barely speak. "I'd..I'd like to see your collection," he finally stammers. "I'll bet I can learn a lot."

Tom picks up Aaron's pencil and writes his phone number on a piece of paper. He tears it out of his tablet and gives it to Aaron. "Call me Saturday. I'm busy with football workouts all week, but you can come over maybe Sunday and have dinner with us."

Unbelievable! To be singled out by the school's hottest jock is an electric ego boost. Aaron leaves school that day in a trance. Everyone in the library has seen Tom talking to him. As he walks down the long school corridors, he feels less fear, he feels as if people are saying, "Hey, he's Schweikert's friend. Leave him alone. He's cool."

God, he might even get some girls. He might get Michelle Dalton. Keep dreaming, Aaron, he tells himself. Keep dreaming.

On Sunday Aaron rides his bicycle to the Schweikert house. It is only eight blocks away, in the part of town where older houses sit comfortably in the shade of huge oak trees.

Tom's mother is raising him alone. She does some mysterious science work for the government. Her voice is hoarse and thick with a German accent. She wears her graying brown hair in a braid that circles her head. To Aaron it resembles some kind of pastry.

The woman regards Aaron with suspicion. She won't speak to him directly but as she speaks to her son she refers to Aaron as "Your little Jewish friend."

They eat roast pork, applesauce and sweet potatoes. Tom and his mother speak German at the table, discussing Aaron. The word "yooden" is repeated several times and at one point the conversation grows heated. Aaron understands parts of what he hears. Tom seems to have command over his mother. He speaks sharply and she subsides.

Aaron soon forgets his discomfort. After the meal, the boys go to Tom's room, located like an aerie, high up in the gables of the old house. At the door is a gothic-lettered sign: Berchtesgaden.

The room is a museum of Nazi memorabilia. Intricate models of ships, tanks, submarines and airplanes hang from the ceiling and adorn every shelf. One wall is covered with a scarlet flag with a black swastika inside a white circle. Tom has hundreds of photos of Hitler and all the Nazi chieftains. Aaron feels their occult presences in his blood with warlike fervor. Valkyries sing in his cells. He knows that he is the reincarnation of a great Nordic warrior, being tested by his exile in a puny Jewish body.

Tom brings out a full S.S. uniform, black with silver death's heads and piping. He dresses himself in it, and gives Aaron an ill-fitting Wehrmacht helmet and tunic. Then the boys goose step around the room, saluting and shouting Heil Hitler! Hours pass, as they pore over Tom's incredible collection of photos, detailing all the intricacies of Hitler's reign. Tom explains each picture to his eager new disciple. Here is Hitler and Eva Braun, dining on the veranda at the Eagle's Nest. Here is Goering addressing the Luftwaffe on the eve of the Battle of Britain. Here is Hitler in a moment of relaxation, charming a circle of beautiful women. They hold their schnapps glasses delicately and stare at him as if at a god, their eyes glazed over with erotic frenzy. There is a woman in a cup-shaped hat with a short veil that rests on her forehead. A fox stole drapes her shoulders. She looks like a blind person seeing an interior vision of heaven. Her eyes seem not to register a single object of the external world. Her pretty young face glows with a quiet yet overwhelming ecstasy as she sits with the Fuehrer.

Aaron basks in this weirdly charged history, nurturing himself with vicarious glory. When he thinks, as well he must, about the camps and the slaughter of millions, he makes an elaborate effort to rationalize. Stalin was a butcher. The British and Americans bombed Hamburg, Dresden, Hirishoma and Nagasaki.

Tom, reverently placing the photographs in their leather case, speaks in a hushed voice. "You know, I'm not supposed to tell this to anyone who isn't cleared. Are you a true believer? Can I trust you?"

"Of..of course," says Aaron. Tom's square-jawed face burns with fanatic fervor. In his S.S. uniform he looks like an adolescent version of Reinhardt Heydrich.

"Hitler's not dead," he intones, formulaic. "There was a special Einsatzpruppe that got him out before the Russians came. The Reich is only dormant. It has not fallen; the war is not over. Soon there will be a Fourth Reich."

Aaron mutters meaningless awed syllables and tries to look appropriately stern A squiggle of fear works like a worm in his stomach. This is some really weird stuff, he thinks. I don't want it to be true. The important thing, however, is not to put off Tom Schweikert. Okay, he may be a bit strange in the head. I can deal with it.

Aaron now has a new friend. He has two places to go after Hebrew School. Esther doesn't seem to care where he is, and his father is so busy he just assumes that Esther keeps track of her son. He is wrong. Aaron has long since become expert at deceiving his parents. He does not want them to know about Tom. He is queasy about the relationship. He can't quite identify this feeling as shame.

Lester, his music buddy, is more socially appropriate. His parents may be suspiciously liberal and possible beatniks or anarchists but they live in a nice house in a decent neighborhood. Esther is prepared to disapprove of Lester on principle, because that's what Esther does: she disapproves.

Aaron has dinner at Lester's house several times each month. Lester's parents are like friends. They are on speaking terms with negro jazz musicians, many of whom turn up at the Stiers house for weekend parties. Lester's pretty mom wears a beret and his dad can play every woodwind instrument in the orchestra. Max urges Aaron to reciprocate with a dinner invitation. The idea is terrifying. Aaron is afraid of his mother. He never knows what she'll do. After many long delays and excuses, Aaron is obliged to bring Lester Stiers home for dinner.

It is Monday night, the slow day at the deli, the one night Max can be home to eat with the family. They are all there, sitting in their places at the ovoid table with its yellow formica top. Esther has made a tuna casserole with a side dish of string beans. Butter and Wonder Bread are laid on a platter at the center of the table. Cans of Coca Cola stand at attention beside tall glasses filled with ice.

"Thank you for inviting me to dinner, Mr. and Mrs. Kantro." Lester is on his best behavior. He has heard things from Aaron that make him cautious. He doesn't know what to expect. Mrs. Kantro looks bad, really bad. She is fat. She wears a green house dress beneath a terry cloth pink bathrobe. Her skin sags under her eyes and beneath her chin and she looks twenty years older than his own mom. Her gait is a shuffle that goes "shhhs shhhhs" as her bloated feet slide around inside loose slippers.

"You're very welcome, Lester," says Mr. Kantro.

"My son says that you're a nice boy,". Esther Kantro's voice is dry and nasal, as if it is missing some essential lubricant to create a functional voice.

"Go ahead, help yourself." Max Kantro passes the serving dish of casserole. Lester dutifully lifts a portion with the serving spoon and puts it on his plate. The other dishes are passed in silence. Aaron's siblings are unnaturally quiet. The eating proceeds in a silence that makes Lester uncomfortable. He is accustomed to banter and joking around his family table. The tautness among the Kantros pushes words from Lester's mouth that he isn't thinking about.

"As long as my homework is done," he says, "my dad told me I can stay as long as I'm welcome."

Aaron gives his friend a push with his foot, under the table. He's warning Lester: be cool!

The silence stretches. "Aaron, what about your homework? Did you get your assignment finished?" Esther Kantro's words seem loaded with a kind of pleasurable anticipation. She knows he hasn't finished his homework. The details don't matter.. Aaron is supposed to write an essay for his Social Studies class. It is due the next day. The subject is boring to Aaron. He hasn't read the material. He will leave it to the last moment before going to bed, glance through it and absorb enough to write a paper worth a C plus. This is Aaron's normal method of skating through school.

Esther begins pestering him. "Have you even started it? You don't study at all. What kind of future do you think you'll have?. If you study more and apply yourself, your grades will go up and you might get into...."

"Don't worry, I'll get it done!" Aaron responds sharply. Then he adds, "I'm a fast worker." He nudges Lester. It isn't much of a joke, just a smug little quip. Lester, acting from a sense of loyalty, joins his friend in a barely audible snicker.

Esther takes her cup of hot coffee and flings it into Aaron's face. Max catches her hands in a powerful grip, but it is too late. The coffee cup flies across the room and smashes into the stove. The humiliation sears through Aaron like flame from a welder's torch.

Lester looks away with embarrassment and confusion. He has never seen anything like this. He is totally unprepared for family violence.

Aaron resists all impulse to cry, flinch or scream. He sits there with sweet brown liquid dribbling down his face, onto his favorite Madras shirt, eyes fixed upon the bloated face of his mother.

Esther is locked into a quivering combat with Max. Slowly, pitting his strength against that of his wife, he impels her toward the kitchen door. He is arresting her, removing her. Their arms knot and bulge with effort. Grunts of wrath come from deep in their throats. Max pushes his wife through the door, down the hallway, and then they are gone, with a violent slam of the bedroom door.

Lester and the Kantro kids are left in the kitchen, pale and silent. The fact that Max is now attempting to protect his children is new and comforting, but it is too little, and way too late.

....

"Heil Hitler," Aaron makes his body rigid as he raises his right arm in the Nazi salute. He pauses, feeling intensely ridiculous. He glances at the wall clock, sees that it is almost four o'clock. His right arm quavers, his fingers tremble and he drops his limb back to his side. The next words out of his mouth come with great reluctance.

"Uh...Tom... I've got to go now."

He looks at his..what?..friend? What is Tom to him, anyway? He is no longer sure. Four days a week, Monday through Thursday, Aaron endures the crushing boredom of Hebrew School. It lasts from four thirty to six o'clock. How can he go from this...

to THAT?

Tom has opened a card table and unfurled a poster that is about four feet long. It is a genuine propaganda print from the late thirties. It shows a Brown Shirt, a trooper from the SA, the Sturmabteilung. This symbol of Aryan brutality is standing in the doorway of what is plainly a Jewish shop. He holds a truncheon, the shaft of which rests in his left hand. A cringing family of Jews make their way under his pitiless gaze, out of their own shop. The poster's message is terse: JUDEN RAUS!

Tom plans on hanging this poster during the night at the front entrance of Shaar Zedek, the largest synagogue in town. This activism makes Aaron profoundly uneasy. The game has escalated from harmless fantasizing at Tom's home to tossing leaflets and delivering threatening letters to various targets. The implicit conflict in Aaron's situation is building. Tom is beginning to hint that soon Aaron must make a choice. His Bar Mitzvah is only a few months away. He is under siege. He is getting scared. Tom is talking about burning synagogues, planting flaming wooden swastikas in people's yards. This thing is getting crazy, it is far beyond harmless research into history. Aaron is being swept into the whirlpool of Tom's obsession.

Tom looks at the clock. "Four o'clock. Where are you going, Aaron?" His tone is nasty, mocking.

Aaron doesn't answer.

"Where are you going!" This time Tom's voice is a demand.

"You know where I'm going," Aaron responds queasily. "Do I have to say it?

I'm going to Hebrew School. Like I do four days a week, every week, until the damn thing is over."

Aaron is struggling. He wants to end this farce, but being Tom's friend brings many benefits. Girls talk to him, football players call him by his first name. He is on the verge of being able to date Michele Dalton. She says hello to him in the halls at school. She smiles flirtatiously. Why will she notice Aaron Kantro? Short, thin Aaron Kantro with the ill-proportioned body, the butt too large, the legs too skinny, the arms without muscle. A thousand rumors swirl around Michele. She screws college guys. She gave Tom a blowjob under the seats in the gym.

As a trophy, Michele will elevate Aaron to a new social status. The people who count will respect him. The sharp dressers with their skin-tight pants and madras shirts. The girls on the cheerleader squad and the guys whose fathers will buy them Thunderbirds and MG's on their sixteenth birthdays.

It is ironic that since he has begun to flirt with being a Nazi, there are aspects of being Jewish that have begun to haunt Aaron with their strange power. He despises Hebrew School but he is aware of the tremendous passion that has sustained Judaism throughout a long terrible history. The melodies of the prayers sprinkle his soul with an eerie antiquity. The stories of the Old Testament, the warlike heroism of the armies of Israel rival anything to be found in the Nordic sagas. When he stares at the synagogue's turquoise tiled dome, he feels that he is looking out upon the universe. The sounds of prayer that echo off the gilded vault affect him with their cries of discovery, despair and adoration.

No Jewish boy goes without a Bar Mitzvah. The entire social world of his age group revolves around the weekly Bar Mitzvah. It is an opportunity to reap numerous presents of goods and cash. Aaron wants a good stereo system. He is insane for a stereo system, he needs something better than his ridiculous old automatic Harmon Kardon with its cranky tone arm and its scratchy sound. There is no question of his refusing to be thrust into Jewish manhood.

It is time to get away from Tom, to break off the relationship.

Aaron watches Tom carefully for his reaction. He watches Tom the way he will watch a snake about to strike. Tom has recently acquired two guns: a Luger pistol and a bolt action Mauser rifle. Ammunition for these weapons is archaic, difficult to purchase. Tom's mother tells her son firmly that if she catches him with ammunition, she will take the guns and break them into a thousand pieces.

Tom is wearing his S.S. uniform. He picks up the Luger from his desk and lifts the hinged cocking mechanism. He snaps the trigger a few times, casually pointing the pistol in Aaron's direction. His face assumes that gruesome mask Aaron saw the first time they met. The lips draw back over the teeth, the left side of the face slides downward. This time Aaron has no difficulty identifying the meaning of the expression. It terrifies him.

"Aaron, we're going to have to make a decision, soon."

Aaron sighs and acts stupid. He gives Tom a blank look.

"You know what I mean," Tom says. "Your racial impurity. If you go through that disgusting ceremony, you'll be a Jew forever, and you won't be able to remain with us."

Tom always refers to a mysterious "Us". So far as Aaron knows, there are only the two of them. Tom will occasionally show off strange envelopes from South America, addressed to "Herr Thomas Schweikert". These, Tom explains, are from the "High Command" of the hidden Fourth Reich.

"I have to get my Bar Mitzvah," Aaron protests. "My parents will never let me back out of it."

"Your parents are Jews," Tom spat. "Do you want to be a Jew, too?"

"I...I don't know, Tom. I don't have any choice. There will be a party, and I'll get a lot of money and everyone's expecting me to.

"You'll sell your little greedy Jewish soul for five hundred dollars. Oh, you are a Jew, a contemptible little Jew. I should have known better than to try to lift your spirit into Aryan glory. Give up this abomination before you actually seal your Jewishness." Tom lays the pistol back on the desk. He stands so quickly that Aaron flinches backwards a step. Tom paces with his hands clasped behind his back. Aaron notes the imitation of Hitler's mannerism. "There is a path to the Higher Initiations. One such as you, with Jewish blood, can still reach a certain level. The disgusting ceremony of Bar Mitzvah will close that path forever. Your use as a Nazi will be finished." He walks to the large rear window that looks out upon his back yard and then turns to stare at Aaron with hard eyes. A leafless oak tree stretches its branches towards the house. As it shakes in the wind, Aaron sees the branches as fingers, reaching, trying to get through the glass and invade this chamber full of horrific souvenirs.

"Tom, I've got to go...you know at this point it's better not to draw attention to ourselves." He moves towards the door of the room.

Aaron finally admits to himself that not only is he a Jew, irrevocably, but that Tom Schweikert is totally mad. These things are okay for a game. That's all it is, a kid's game. Tom doesn't see this. He can't separate fantasy from reality.

Aaron suddenly feels as if he is being pushed by a wind, a gust of fear. This blonde muscular hulk with the flaming eyes is capable of anything. He wants to get away, to never see Tom again, to be rid forever of this silly puttering around in German outfits, saluting an evil dead tyrant. He flushes from head to toe as he faces the obscenity of what stands before him: a very big teenager in a complete S.S. uniform.

He feels unbelievably foolish. He is embarrassed for himself. He is deeply ashamed.

Taking off the steel helmet, the Wehrmacht overcoat, Aaron begins to edge out from under the menacing shadow of this deluded adolescent. He tries to get to the door, but the bigger boy grips his arm with fingers like a tourniquet.

"Answer now," Tom breathes. "What will it be?" His eyes become adamantine, a blue stone garden in which buds of murder bloom.

Aaron forces saliva past the lump in his throat, and the grainy vapor of terror in the pit of his stomach rises to meet it. His breath comes in quick short gasps. He turns over the temptation to use a cowardly lie to buy his way out. He is tired of being puny, tired of compensating. If he can't be a big strong boy, physically imposing, he realizes in this moment of choice that there are other kinds of largeness. This is what he wants, and it seems to him that if he can't be a hero in his own eyes, he doesn't care to live.

"I'm a Jew, Tom. Let me go. It's what I am, what I'll always be. I'm not a Nazi anymore."

Tom retains his fierce grip. "You leave me no choice, then. Too much has been revealed to you about the New Reich. I have to eliminate you."

Aaron sees Tom reach with his other hand towards his neck. It is almost large enough to completely encircle his scrawny throat. Tom begins to shake him, to strangle him, and it is a strange echo of similar punishments inflicted by his mother. For a moment, he isn't sure who is choking him. Then he realizes that where his mother will stop short of killing him, this lunatic has no such boundary.

Aaron kicks at Tom's crotch, but he is being held at arm's length with the full strength of an athletic grip. There isn't enough air in his lungs to cry for help. He is going to die. He catches hold of the metal struts of the shelves that support Tom's collection of model ships and planes. He pulls on the bracket, and its wooden planking comes tumbling down with a crash. Plastic model instruments of war come hurtling down to break into shards. Helmets, books, framed pictures shatter on the floor around Aaron's kicking feet. The air is nearly gone from his lungs when Mrs. Schweikert enters the room and screams something in German that translates itself to Aaron's desperate mind as "You'll ruin your life for this Jewish trash!". Tom's grip slackens, and Aaron takes the chance to run, to flee for his very existence back to a world where people are crazy. They just aren't THIS crazy.

Chapter Eight

Apprentice
1967: Cincinatti

"Gimme some more sauce, man." Tyrone has a big napkin slung under his chin, and his beard is slathered with sticky orange grease. The Continental is parked on a corner outside a place called Sal's Barbecue, a legendary pork'n'grits house in the black ghetto of

Cincinnati. Several towels and a white sheet have been arranged on the dash and covering the car seats, to protect Zoot's precious "short" from vagrant barbecue drippings. It is a huge concession, eating in Zoot's car. It is made necessary by the racial realities of their milieu.

Zoot passes a tube from the big red and white cardboard box full of ribs. He makes an underhanded gesture at a man who is giving the occupants of the car the evil eye.

"Think he never saw a white boy in a Continental before, shee-it. Can't even sit inside a rib joint without starting a riot. What do I gotta do to calm down all these racist motherfuckers?"

He points at Aaron with a greasy finger.

"Help us out. Become a black man!" He orders his young drummer. "Immediately!"

Aaron holds his breath and closes his eyes as if he is attempting to conjure this transformation. "Yes sir!" he complies. "I am now black!"

Tyrone leans forward from the back seat. "Amazing!" he says. Then he hesitates. "Ooops! Damn! You was black for a second, but you slipped back."

"Aw shit," Aaron mourns, splitting one meaty rib from its tenderloin tip. "I thought I had it there. Let me gather some strength and I'll try again."

Another car pulls up beside the Continental, waiting for the traffic light to change. The occupants point at Aaron and seem to be discussing his presence. Zoot presses the button on the automatic window and it rolls down smoothly.

"What are you lookin' at, motherfuckers? He just high yellow." Zoot uses a term for a light-skinned Negro.

The car pulls away.

"Sorry, Zoot, " Aaron says, "I didn't mean to become a crusade."

"Don't flatter me, young brother, I ain't no Martin Luther King. My reasons for bringing you on are purely selfish. You ain't a crusade, you the most funky goddam drummer I've ever heard and no racist bullshit is gonna deter me from keeping you in my band. I enjoy playin' with you like I ain't never enjoyed playin with NO drummer....well....Jimmy Cobb, Roy Haynes. You got to appreciate the gods of drums, but you...you something special, you pull shit outta your self I ain't never heard before. You restore all the pleasure to these endless gigs, that's the simple heart of the matter. After forty years of playin' Embraceable You, a little fresh input is a valuable thing. Truth is, I can't live without you. I NEED you...like dope or somethin'."

An unaccustomed warmth starts in Aaron's throat and descends like a cup of his granma's chicken soup, all the way to his guts. This is what love feels like, he realizes. His father is the only other person that can give him such a feeling. Aaron swallows and awkwardly wraps his stripped rib bones neatly together in white paper.

"Don't neither of you animals drip no rib juice on my upholstery," Zoot says. He gathers the containers of eaten ribs together, gets out of the car and deposits the whole mess into Sal's trashcan. He goes into an exaggerated version of "the walk," his lanky version of a strutting black man on the street, hands swinging, hips grooving, head bopping. Zoot has a way of carrying his hands as if they are not attached to his body, as if they are independent sentient

beings that have given themselves into his care.

Aaron taps Tyrone on the shoulder. "Check it out, Zoot's doin the dance."

Zoot Prestige cocks his finger, winks and makes a pop sound inside his cheek. When he returns to the car, he removes a clean white handkerchief from the glove compartment and wipes down the steering wheel and dashboard, then hands the cloth to Tyrone, who wipes up the backseat and the window perch. The musicians gather all the sheets and towels and put them into a paper grocery bag. Tyrone dashes out of the car while Zoot pops the trunk lever, and puts the bag into a plastic milk crate. The trunk is immense, and contains instrument cases, clothing, sheet music and other paraphenalia. As Tyrone takes his place in the back seat, Zoot turns the key in the ignition and the engine gurgles to life, the car vibrates elegantly.

"Let's see if we can play this gig tonight without getting nobody killed. No psychopathic mumflummery."

"Mumflummery." Tyrone considers the implications of the invented word.

"Mumflummery," Aaron repeats and pretends to write it down in an invisible notebook. "The Zoot Prestige Dictionary of Hip Terminology," he intones. "Mumflummery. Psychopathic variety. That's next to Monsterific Groove-natiousness."

Zoot guns the car into traffic. A Pontiac on their fender honks its horn.

"He high yellow, man," Zoot reiterates. He swings the wheel easily, assisted by power steering, and makes a U-turn. With a touch of the gas pedal, the Continental cruises down Grand Street, carrying the musicians to the next gig.

Chapter Nine

TheSubtleGroove
1967: Des Moines,Iowa

Zoot and his musicians are comfortably installed in two Holiday Inn motel rooms in a suburb of Des Moines, Iowa.

"This is high living, Zoot," Aaron says, pounding a fist into the bed on which he lay. "Not like the usual funky urban hotel rooms you get for us."

Tyrone is on the floor, with his home-made flat keyboard, an eighty eight note piece of cardboard that he uses to practice Bach and Rachmaninoff. He can barely read the English language but his facility with music is that of a virtuoso. His education is strangely lopsided. He has attended school sporadically up to the fourth grade. By that time he could already play piano by ear. At twelve he found he could make more money than his father did, by playing house parties and dives. When that begins to bore him, he seeks out a local legend named Willie Fredricks. Willie teaches him to read music so that his future might have some opportunity. It was a prescient decision.

Tyrone doesn't hear the conversation going on over his head. He is lost, his fingers whizzing up and down the cardboard, each digit seeming to have eight joints. The articulation of his hands is a challenge to nature, an apparent mutation.

Zoot is wearing his glasses. Seated in the easy chair near the door of the room, he is reading a copy of Jung's "Modern Man in Search of a Soul".

"Have you read this?" he asks Aaron.

Rooting through his suitcase at the foot of the bed, Aaron tosses four or five books over his head so they land near his pillow. He always reads. Every night, before sleep; while traveling. While on the toilet. He produces a copy of Freud's "Civilization and its Discontents."

"When you're done, I'll trade you."

Zoot grunts, then scratches himself, raking his chest with his free hand. "This motel shit makes me hinky. I can't smell any chitlins."

"You're an incorrigible Negro, Zoot." Aaron regards his employer sardonically. "Your blackness is legendary."

The saxophonist peers over the top of his glasses. With thumb and forefinger he pulls at the little goatee that sprouts beneath his lower lip. His eyes are dark green, his skin the color of unharvested wheat. It doesn't matter that he is a mix of black, white, Choctaw and Seminole. To society he is a black man and he has grown up in American black culture.

"The negro has a great history," he riposts. "The negro has a profound creative impact on society. "

The three musicians look at one another. The exchange has caught Tyrone's interest. "The negro," he says, "has strength and dignity."

There is a silence while they hold their collective breath. Then they burst into sloppy spitting laughter. They lean toward one another and manage a three way "high five".

"And the Jew," Aaron adds, "because of three thousand years of suffering and persecution, experiences solidarity with all oppressed peoples."

"Right on, motherfucker. Right on." Zoot leans back into his chair, raises his eyes to the paperback with the yellow and white cover, and continues to read.

Chapter Ten

The Pit and Plastic Money

Esther has that wonderful feeling of unstoppable energy. Her heart is pounding a little too fast, but that's okay, she can always take something to calm her down. The important thing is that life seems brand new today; she is sure her problems will soon be solved. The sessions with Doctor Weiner are making everything turn out all right. She doesn't understand how talking about herself for an hour each week can accomplish this result, but she is excited. She is in therapy, isn't she? She has a sickness. Nowadays people know how to treat these illnesses of the brain, the same as they can set a broken arm or cure a fever.

In a couple of weeks she will start feeling better, she will be less hyper and not fall victim to the black depressions that follow on her hyper states. There are new miracle medications. If she takes them as instructed, she won't need so many Valium that she gets from Doctor Pell, so many amphetamines from Doctor Grantham, she can cut back on the codeine from Doctor Maltz, the percodan from Doctor Rabinowicz. She has acquired a lot of medications from different doctors and Max doesn't pay attention. Some of Esther's doctors are paid by insurance, and others are paid in cash.

She goes to so many doctors because she isn't satisfied with any of them. She needs second opinions. What is causing her migraines? She has a pain at the right side of her neck that is just crippling, crippling, and she wants the opinions of at least two orthopedists.

Her teeth are rotten. She has two dentists who are good for prescriptions of Darvon and Codeine.

Seeing doctors has simply become a way of life. She has two main avenues of activity. One is seeing doctors, the other is shopping.

Now she has adds a psychiatrist to this team, as she calls it, her team of physicians.

And why not? Sarah Feldman is seeing a psychiatrist. Rose Podolski is, too. There is no shame in it. Quite the opposite. If you aren't seeing a psychiatrist, people think there must be something wrong with you.

Psychiatry isn't like regular medicine, but it shouldn't be like regular medicine. Should it? After all, it is about fixing her thoughts and feelings so she isn't so unhappy and taking it out on everyone else. She wishes she wasn't so angry but she can't help herself. She seems to be controlled by rage so often that she has turned to medicating herself as an ongoing project that can prevent some of her worst behavior and in turn that will protect the family. Her motives are completely unselfish.

She doesn't feel good about her behavior, the screaming and the scratching, the hitting and tantrums. She feels a guilt so deep that it almost paralyzes her and when it gets really bad she choses a cocktail of medications that will help her get through her crisis.

Doctor Weiner has pointed out to her that she is treating the children the same way she was treated by her mother. She has only told the doctor half truths, she has omitted darker, more unspeakable memories from her childhood, things she only dimly remembers, things she choses not to remember. She can not, WILL not, talk to a stranger about the way her brothers used her. She isn't sure about a lot of things. Her mother knew what was going on, she is sure about that. Her mother had caught Sonny in the basement with Esther several times, and with her sister Annie, making them do things with him that she doesn't want to remember.

Her mother knew. Her father was always at the business, struggling to keep the depression era darkness from overwhelming Zimmerman Wholesale Tobacco and Candy.

He had to pay a lot of people to keep the business afloat. He had been forced to take a "partner", an Italian, a Catholic Goy son of a bitch who did nothing but sit in the back room and count money.

This is secret family business and no one will ever know, not her husband, not her psychiatrist, no one.

Every time she sees Aaron, she sees her brother Sonny. The resemblance is very powerful. She feels hatred, raw hatred. Everything about Aaron sets her nerves on edge, makes her sick. He is an embarrassment, he is never going to amount to anything, never going to reflect anything but failure onto the family. This thing about music....how useless! If he pursues it much further, there will be no time for him to get into a profession. He will never be a doctor. But a dentist, maybe? A lawyer? Something respectable....something that won't take him around schvatzes all the time.

Maybe it is enough, just talking about her mother and father, and the beatings she got, the work she was forced to do instead of going to school, the depression- era slavery she endured while the sons went to school, leaving the daughters to work in the family business.

If she does this talking to the doctor, and takes her medications, things will change, things will get better.

Now that she is in treatment, she is bound to turn over a new leaf. Why not go shopping today, to get some things for the house? Nothing selfish. She cares only for the family. A woman is a hollow shell without a family. That's why she has to go to the store. Fix up the kitchen and the den. The house needs better things.

She has credit cards to get everything she needs. This isn't for her. It is for the family.

* * *

Max receives a call that afternoon, around three o'clock. It is Marilee.

"Dad, did you tell mom she can buy a bunch of stuff?"

"No Marilee...wait. What...., what is she doing?"

"You better get home fast. I just got here from school, and mom's really done it this time."

When he pulls into the driveway, Max sees huge crates and cardboard boxes lined up from the garage to the front door. As he runs to the door, Max sees the names of washing machine manufacturers, boxes of fine China dinnerware, a refrigerator crate that has not yet been opened.

Inside, he finds Esther singing at the top of her lungs. Mark is playing inside one of the big boxes. Marilee and Sarah are standing around looking frightened. Aaron is in the basement, where Max has built an extra room as his son's sanctuary. At the moment he is in the midst of his music lesson with Mr. Hanspiegler. The boy is playing exercises of fiendish complexity. Each one is faster than the previous one. The notes float up like a sound track to bedlam. Their very orderliness gives ironic counterpoint to the chaos unfolding in the large family room.

There are chairs, sofas, carpets, a cornucopia of consumer items, all with tags still on them, gleaming new, bits of packing material and excelsior clinging to them. Esther is in the process of wrestling a washing machine into the laundry room off the kitchen. The old machine is halfway out the back door. The bulk and weight seem to have no meaning to Esther. She pushes, rocks and lifts the new machine towards the empty slot with its hanging black hoses.

"Esther, what are you doing?"

Esther beams and points toward a roll of carpeting. "Doesn't this color look nice? We needed some new carpeting."

"Esther, Esther, stop it!"

She sings, dancing around the room with an invisible partner. "I could have danced all night, could have danced all night, and still have begged for moooore...." her voice is a pathetic monotone, but she evidently regards herself as the princess of the ballroom. She pauses to snip more packing twine with a scissors. Max gapes helplesssly for a moment. Then he goes to the extension phone in the bedroom.

Within the hour, an ambulance has taken Esther to the psychiatric ward at Jewish Veteran's Hospital. Dr. Weiner is waiting for his patient. He has canceled an appointment (for which Max is charged) and driven from his office to the hospital.

"She's having a severe manic episode," the psychiatrist explains to Max.

Tell me something I don't know, thinks Max bitterly.

"So far, sedation hasn 't touched her. At the moment we've got her in an isolation room, where she can 't hurt herself. If we can't bring her out of it with Thorazine, we may have to go to Electro-Shock therapy." He hands Max a set of papers. "I'll need your release to go ahead. I'm reluctant to use shock, but in extreme cases it can be very effective. Otherwise the patient goes on and on, and there's a danger of cardiac damage , stroke, or self inflicted injuries."

At that moment Esther is hurling herself against the padded wall. She is still singing the refrain from the musical"My Fair Lady". Her toneless rendition is almost inaudible outside the cell. She sings, spreading her arms to embrace an invisible partner. The hurling against the wall is just part of the dance step. She doesn't see the wall. Doctor Weiner has his back to the observaton window, but Max can see his wife, panting between lines of the song, then rushing into the wall as if she is trying desperately to tackle someone just beyond her reach.

Max signs the forms glumly. He sees the bill, the insurance forms, the co-pay, a Niagara of falling paper, dollar signs being sucked up into a giant funnel, a vacuum cleaner called Health Insurance. He has to extend his coverage to pay for Esther's treatment. He reads endless forms filled with fine print, he signs papers with a queasy feeling, knowing that he needs a lawyer to guide him through all this obscure verbiage.

Dapper in his double breasted suit, Dr. Weiner, a small blonde man with a fixed smile, takes the form and leads Max diplomatically away from the observation port. He makes an inconspicuous signal to an orderly, indicating that Esther is to be prepped for Electro-Convulsive Therapy.

With their mother gone, the children's feelings burst forth in a geyser of impish exuberance. Max understands that his home has become as oppressive as a prison camp.

He blames himself.

What kind of father am I, to have let this happen? That my children should rejoice because their mother's in the hospital? What kind of husband am I, to have let her become so unhappy that she must resort to such extremes of behavior?

Guilty as he feels, he knows that he will atone. There will be payment. It will go on for years, affecting the children, and perhaps the grandchildren. How long do family curses last? His intuitive grasp of the human psyche shows him a continuum, an interior ecology of family. He bitterly examines the dark undersides of both families, his own and Esther's. Crimes have been committed and passed from relative to relative, from generation to generation. These things don't just pop out of nowhere! Perhaps such behavior is genetic, perhaps it is some early childhood imprinting, or perhaps a combination of both. He feels frustrated at the limits of his knowledge. He needs to learn about psychology but he doesn't have the intellectual equipment to comprehend Freud.

Perhaps there are other books, easier books to help him through this labyrinth.

Max cleans up the mess of crates and packing. He returns the merchandise. It seems for a while as if there is an endless parade of trucks pulling into the driveway. Black men in overalls wrestle the appliances up the ramp and accept Max's tips without a word. Then he brings in his nephew Richard to manage the deli in the evenings. Richard is working his way through law school. He is grateful for the extra work. Max needs more time at home, to be with the children.

Things are going to change.

Without Esther's presence in the house, the kids are roaring around, being brats without inhibition, feeling free. Let them, Max thinks. They need to shout, to be obnoxious. Rock and roll blares from the radio, Marilee and three friends are shrieking with laughter. Mark is probably drawing a mural on the wall of his room. Aaron is in the basement with his friend Lester. It is the first time the kids have brought friends over since the terrible coffee-throwing incident. The boys are practicing One O'Clock Jump. They sound impressively good.

Making a tour of the house, Max shouts until everyone hears him. "Kids, I need you to be quiet for a few minutes. I'm calling the hospital."

With uncanny expectancy, the din subsides.

Max speaks briefly on the phone. "The head nurse says it's okay to visit for an hour. We'll go in about fifteen minutes."

There are groans from various corners of the house. "But dad," Sarah protests, "I've got homework to do."

"Homework. You weren't doing homework five minutes ago. You're going to see your mother, all of you, and I won't hear any excuses. How would you like to be sick and have no one come to visit you?"

"I wanna see mom," Mark chimes in. "I wanna see what the shock machine did to her."

"Get dressed in clean clothes," Max instructs softly. His belly feels as if he has stepped into an elevator that has snapped its cable and is falling, falling, with deadly velocity.

The head nurse lets them into the ward, through a series of locked gates. Inside, there is an office with double dutch doors, through which medications are dispensed. There is a lounge, then a long hallway, off which are rooms, then another lounge, which lets out onto a sun deck sealed in by a high, ornamental brick wall. One can view the park across the street only through decorative chinks in the brick. In the lounges are ping pong tables, a tv set, games like Clue and Monopoly. Everything is painted light green. Staff uniforms are of the same color, with dashes of blue lettering in name-badges and insignia.

Esther is in room eighteen. It is on the south side and has a window overlooking the city from five stories up. Max feels his heart pounding in his hands, his arms, at the backs of his knees. He knocks. Without waiting for an answer, he opens the door, holding it for his children.

The room is dark. "Esther? Esther?"

The only sound is of blocked breathing, like someone with a bad cold. Max can make out his wife's shape on the bed. He can smell her smell: perfume, perspiration and terror. Groping, he finds the light switch next to the door.

"Esther? You awake? The kids are here to see you."

"Max". Her voice is weak and cracked, as though her throat is full of the dust of many condemned buildings.

When he flips the switch, he is filled with regret. It is a switch he will never be able to unswitch. The children inhale and are silent, until Mark assesses the situation with typical juvenile bluntness.

"Wow, mom," he says with awe. "That shock machine really fucked you up, didn't it?"

Esther moves her lips, moistens them with a swollen tongue. Her voice is like that of a very old woman.

"How are you...k...kids? I can't talk so good....it's ...." She can't finish the sentence. Her hair is like black straw. Her eyes recede behind a huge grey expanse of puffed cheeks, and two large bruises show at either side of her forehead.

Max's fists are clenched around the small bouquet of flowers he's purchased in the hospital gift shop. He has squashed the stems into a green pulp. He wants to reprimand Mark for his language but gives it up. This has become Mark's routine method of address. Max won't be able to stop it.

What have they done to Esther? She looks like the victim of medieval torture.

The children gape, horrified and embarassed, and Sarah rushes into the bathroom. They may hate their mother, but no one can hate this brittle cocoon, housing only the shadow of a person, awaiting a spring that will never return.

Esther is released after two weeks. Max has visited her every day, but he doesn't force the children. None of them volunteers.

Re-established in her own bedroom, Esther spends most of her time sleeping. She often forgets the names of her children, or will address them with the names of her sister's children. She keeps calling Max by his brother's name, Sammy.

Max increases the hours of their cleaning woman, Vernice, and shaves some hours from his store manager's time, juggling desperately to be everywhere at once.

The children, who fix upon Vernice as a mother surrogate, are delighted.

Throughout these terrible experiences, Max mourns silently.

Chapter Eleven

Menace of the Death's Head

One day, dialing the combination of his locker at school, Aaron finds a folded slip of white paper in the door's ventilation slots. He reads the bold wide letters, done in blood-red crayon. His body turns ice cold, as if someone has just opened a freezer door in a butcher's warehouse.

DONT THINK YOU'VE GOTTEN AWAY. THE SOLDIERS OF THE NEW REICH WILL REACH OUT AND EXTERMINATE YOU AND ALL JEWISH VERMIN

It is signed with a swastika. Tom's friends aren't Nazis, but they will follow his lead if he wants to persecute a freshman. Aaron mentally lists all the ways that Tom can make his life miserable. From the moment of reading the note, Aaron begins to look in every corner for a potential ambush.

So begins his torment at the hands of a mad adolescent.

That afternoon, on the baseball field, he is waiting to be chosen for one of the teams. He is accustomed to being chosen last. On this day, however, he isn't chosen at all. After the squads have been picked, he stands there, alone, between two lines of boys, his face scarlet as he feels his mortifying conspicuousness. Someone snickers.

Coach Lyle shouts at his usual level. "All right, boys! One man left! Rothman, your team's got twelve, so you take him."

Off they go, to their positions. Aaron sits on the bench with the three other replacement players, who are rotated in and out of the game. Everyone but Aaron gets an equal amount of play. Coach Lyle finally notices, and instructs the team captain to send him in.

He is usually consigned to the oblivion of right field. This time Philip Rothman perversely gives him second base. He discovers the reason for this when the first runner to get on base bulldozes into him, sending him sprawling on his back into the mud. Aaron finds himself in the way of a series of accidents, savage slides and high-speed over-runs. No matter how he places himself, the base runner will make an elaborate detour to knock Aaron down into the soggy field. "Oh excuse me," each boy sneeres, "I didn't see you there."

When the ball is in play, and it falls his lot to catch it, he is thrown stinging pegs, or batters suddenly find the uncanny ability to drive burning liners right at his face.

Aaron grits his teeth and concentrates on catching each ball perfectly. The harder he tries, the more poorly he plays. Each error

114

elicits gales of laughter, cat-calls and derisive names. "Hey bloop-stoop, can't ya catch the ball?" Screaming with exaggerated laughter, cries come from every corner of the field. "Wimp-wrist!" "No pud, no pud, can't catch a soap sud!" The contempt is delivered with the acrid nastiness so highly developed in boys of young puberty. At one point, the center fielder sneaks in to crouch behind him, and when the pitcher comes up for a conference, Aaron is pushed over into the stickiest mud puddle.

His face is rigid as he fights the tears. He can not give anyone the satisfaction of seeing him cry. His nostrils quiver, he is continually wiping moisture from his eyes.

This is hell. He is headed for the showers, where he knows it will be worse. As he tries to wash away his coating of mud, the boys continue to deride the size of his penis.

"

Where did it go, where did it go?" They cackle, getting down on their hands and knees as if to search Aaron's crotch for the existence of his genitals. As he backs away he is stung by the swipe of wet towels. The boys howl, "A girl's in the locker room, girl's in the locker room! Girl alert! Girl alert!"

Aaron's chest works up and down with the agony of suppressing his tears. Shaking, he dresses and runs, just as his control gives way and wet streams began to slide down his face. The screams of adolescent boys follow him down the halls of the school building.

At the end of the day, Aaron sees Michele Dalton at her locker. Whenever he sees her he feels an emotion that is equal parts awe and fear. The awe is at her dreamlike features, the honey-blonde hair, blue eyes, glowing pink skin. Her breasts are like canteloupe halves, perfectly round, taut beneath white cashmere.

His fear is that she will find him ridiculous and humiliate him. She is the most sought-after girl in school. The other girls hate her and call her a tramp. The boys flock to her like pigeons around a peanut thrower.

Michele has been warm to Aaron during the period of his friendship with Tom. She has promised him a date at some vague time in the future.

Now, trying to keep the heartbeat out of his voice, Aaron approaches the girl.

"Hi, Michele. You need some help with those books? If you want, I can walk you home."

Getting the sentence out is an accomplishment that, a few months ago, he could never have achieved. Michele continues to pile books, one atop another. Her nipples show clearly through the thin sweater. Aaron's palms are moist as he watches her press the books into the crook of her arm, thrusting her glorious breasts forward. She closes her locker, spins the combination lock, and walks away, melting into the crowd of students hurrying toward the exits. She has not even glanced at him. He does not exist.

Looking around, Aaron sees several boys from his class, snickering pointedly behind their palms. He is hoping to escape the school without further trauma. As he nears the exit, he sees Lester Stiers.

"Hi, Lester," he says, gesturing ruefully, shoulders up, arms extended dismissively, as if to explain to his friend that a lot of crazy unfair things are happening, but they are inconsequential.

Lester grins without sincerity. "Hi, Aaron. I gotta hurry now. Talk to you tomorrow, okay?"

"Hey, Lester, wait a minute. What about our rehearsal tonight?"

Lester is walking at a rapid pace, looking around uneasily. "I don't think so, Aaron, call me next week or something."

"Dammit, Lester, not you too!"

"See ya man, take it easy." And Lester is gone, with a final look about him to see if anyone has spotted him talking to the class pariah.

Aaron begins to think of ways to kill himself. He casts about for ideas, yet each of them is too gruesome. Hanging? He can not bear the thought of being unable to breathe. His mother has pills! But that…that is his mother's way. And then, as he thinks about dying, and about the victory it will give to his mother, he casts away suicidal thoughts. Somehow he will bear this weight until it passes.

He skips school the next day, and the day after that. With Esther little better than a shade confined to her room, he is able to extend his fake illness throughout the week.

With the beginning of the new week, he knows that he must return to school or risk flunking out and having to do the year over again. He has to maintain a C average. That is part of the deal of getting a new stereo. He cann't afford to miss any more classes.

The torture continues. In gym class, in every class. Notes are passed from student to student, in which Aaron is sketched in ridiculous positions, in which he is portrayed as having a vagina and breasts. There are sketches in which he is shown dressed in Hassidic garb, wearing big black hats and absurdly long sidelocks. He is often shown eating the feces of a pig directly from its anus, or approaching a donkey with a giant and conspicuously circumcised erection. When he walks down the halls he passes through a blizzard of paper wads. In classes he is pelted by rubber bands and spitballs. The giggles and shrill taunts of his classmates flay his humiliated personality into a thousand shreds. It is as if his mother has been exploded into hundreds of fragments, each one with a mouth reiterating all the words that have been killing his soul throughout his childhood. He is useless, impotent, ugly, weak, a failure, stupid. All that stands between him and utter breakdown is his skill with his trumpet.

Walking home from school that Monday, the reassuring weight of the instrument case in his right hand reminds him that there is something he does well, something at which no one else can compete. Now his trumpet is his only friend.

"Damn you all!" he thinks fiercely. "Screw everybody! Screw Lester Stiers! I'm going to be the best musician in the world! That's what I want; to play my own music, something new and beautiful. I'll be rich and famous while all you jerks will be selling clothes at Sears or peddling insurance!"

Tom and several of his friends catch him halfway home.

Aaron swings the trumpet case in a wild arc as they close in. He runs but they are faster. They wrestle the case away from him and force him to the ground, kicking at him until someone drives by in a car and shouts that the police are coming.

The boys run, leaving Aaron in shock, bleeding. Through a buzzing haze, he sees the face of Coach Lyle.

"My trumpet, where's my trumpet?"

The coach helps him into a car.

"My trumpet!"

"I've got your trumpet, don't worry. Everything's okay. Let's get you to the hospital for some X-Rays."

Max leaves work early and drives with barely controlled frenzy to the hospital. He feels as if he is standing still and the canvas of life whirls around him, the same canvas repeating and repeating but giving the illusion of change.

Aaron is sedated when Max arrives. There is a mild concussion, a broken rib and two fingers broken on his left hand.

That evening, when Aaron awakes in his hospital bed, he immediately asks about his trumpet. Max hands him a brand new, shiny Selmer. Aaron's old horn has been stomped and twisted into a tangled, brassy piece of junk.

Chapter Twelve

Minus Mother

Esther's behavior takes on a metronomic quality. She begins to bounce in and out of certain states. Deprived of credit cards, she goes to stores thinking she is entitled to whatever she wants.

One afternoon in February she goes to Sears to have a second set of keys made for the Chrysler. As her behavior becomes more erratic she is losing free use of the car. She feels it might be more convenient if she has another set made behind Max's back. While she wanders through the aisles packed with merchandise she begins to think about the need for a new television set. The family should have its first color TV.

She wears her mink coat and carries herself imperiously. She has forgotten to change into shoes. Her house slippers make hissing sounds as she walks the aisles, observing the quality of pictures in the new color television sets.

If she waits too long, Max's sister Iris will be first to have a color television. The youngest Kantro girl is on her third marriage. This time she has bagged a real estate developer who spends half the year in Florida. In late spring when Iris returns from Florida towing husband number three she invites the less exalted families for a get-together at her new house, way out in the western fringe of St.Louis. The fringe keeps creeping farther west as affluent St. Louisans flee the expanding tide of black middle class homebuyers. The house that Iris and her husband purchased is in Frontenac, past Lindbergh, past I-70 where the treeless suburban housing developments give way to gated mansions at the tops of forested hills.

The acquisition of a color television set acquires some urgency because Esther knows that Iris has just begun to buy furnishings.

"Can I help you, Ma'am?" The salesman smiles mechanically. He is evaluating Esther's buying potential. She is wearing a very expensive coat. She looks unhinged but that doesn't mean she lacks money. Sometimes rich people got so unhinged they don't care what they look like.

Esther can tell the salesman isn't Jewish. Her world is clearly bifurcated into Jews and Goyim. She considers Goyim to be some primitive life form built for the purpose of making Jews suffer. The salesman is tall and thin, the sort of bloodless gentile that makes Esther recoil. He is in his forties, wearing a white shirt, a red bow tie and dark slacks. Esther doesn't like the sneering way the man looks at her. She is unconscious of the fact that she walks in slippers. She is counting on the mink coat to overawe sales personnel.

"How much is the RCA?" Esther points at the largest set in the TV department. Its remote control is mounted on a special stand above the screen with its surrounding woodwork.

The salesman stands a bit away from Esther, as if he can smell the tang of dementia on her. "That, ma'am, is the RCA XL 20, really our best set, the most advanced color features available today." He takes the remote device from its stand, points its business end at the TV set and clicks a button. The channel changes from NBC to CBS. The salesman does it again, until he has cycled through each of the five channels available in the St. Louis Metro Area.

Esther is impressed. In fact, she is thrilled, but she doesn't intend to show her pleasure. "All right, I'll take it, if you'll deliver it today." Esther haughtily extends a hand so that her index finger slopes a bit forward of her other digits. It is a dismissive pointing, as if the television set is no more important than a carton of milk.

"A very good choice, ma'am. You and your family will be very pleased. How will you pay for that, ma'am? Store account, cash or charge?"

"You can put it on my account," Esther says vaguely. She does not ask the price.

The salesman, whose name tag identifies him as Harlan, decides that he has a sale. He places himself behind a waist high counter. After dexterously jiggling a few keys on an adding machine he says, "That'll be one hundred eighty eight dollars and seventy nine cents with the sales tax and delivery fee."

Esther has followed the man, slippers shushing as she drags her swollen feet across the tile floor with its deposits of fine dust.

"What's the name for the account, ma'am?" Harlan takes a moment to pick up a silver microphone from the counter and presses the rectangular button on its top "Phil," he speaks. His voice rebounds throughout the store's second floor. "Wanna get me an XL20 and bring it to the loading dock?"

Harlan squares himself behind his counter, feeling pretty good about the commission he's just earned selling a TV to this middle aged broad who looks like she's been shot out of a cannon and landed face first in a bed of gravel.

There ensues a strange standoff. Esther does not answer his last question.

"Ma'am," Harlan reminds her, "the name on the account, please?"

"Just have your person bring it to the house and put it in the living room," Esther wheezes. She is starting to feel tired. She needs another couple of pills and shakes her purse to listen to the sounds of medications rattling in plastic and glass bottles.

"Is there a ladies room?" she asks. "I need to wash up just a little."

Harlan points past the hardware section. "You go through Power Tools all the way past the escalator and you'll see it in the far left corner. How 'bout your name, ma'am, so I can start this receipt." If the customer walks away from the counter without closing, the sale is a goner. He needs this sale. His oldest daughter is getting married in May and it's killing him.

"Kantro," Esther says over her shoulder, quickly spelling the name. She lurches towards the ladies' room, her purse sounding like a piñata full of hard candy.

She has to have a color TV before anyone else in the family. She has to. She is the first to get a new Chrysler. It isn't a Cadillac, she knows where to stop and Cadillac is where she stops when Max gets a look on his face that clearly says, "no more, you can pester me like one of our children until I give in but something will never happen and this is one of them. A Cadillac will never happen. A swimming pool will never happen. A twenty six foot cabin cruiser will never happen."

She tries. But she knows which things will never happen.

Harlan pulls a rolodex full of little cards out from beneath the surface of the counter. He marches his fingers towards the letter "K" and deftly separates its bunch of names and addresses from between "J" and "L".

Esther loses her way in Hardware and forgets where she is going but the pounding in her head merges with feelings of increasing fatigue. The signal is quite clear. It is time for another cocktail of Black Beauty and Blue Heaven.

As she finds the restroom her arms relax and her mink coat falls open to reveal the shapeless light blue housedress she wears beneath. A mother and daughter are just emerging from the facility and the mother pulls her child close.

Esther jangles her purse open on the counter top where a row of sinks stands before a long mirror. Fifteen or twenty bottles of medication roll loose within the confines of the large bag. Esther sees the fat plastic bottle and unscrews the top. Her hands shake and she has trouble lining her finger up so that she can press one capsule against the side of the bottle and slide it upward and outward into her hand. It isn't working. She tries an alternate technique, holding her hand out and carefully up-ending the bottle so that a pill falls into her palm. This results in two capsules landing in her hand and another three dropping to the floor. Before she can get into any more difficulty, she pops the two Black Beauties into her mouth and works them down her throat without water. She puts the open pill bottle and its cap on the counter and kneels down to retrieve the three spilled capsules. Her voluminous coat makes this difficult; it keeps swooshing the capsules around so that Esther is turning this way and that.

There is a hiss and a woman comes into the restroom and stops briefly in a moment of shock. Then she reverses course and leaves the room. Esther finally has to take off the coat and lay it gently across one of the stall doors.

She sees two of the capsules. She'll be damned if she'll let herself lose a Black Beauty. She knows there is a third one somewhere. She gets the two errant caps back into the bottle and returns to her search, pulling a stall door open with her fingers and crawling towards the toilet. Aha! There it is, the little son of a bitch. Right up against the rim of the toilet where it meets the floor. Disgusting! But...A Black Beauty is a Black Beauty. Maybe she can clean it later, with a dry towel. But she has to put it in her pocket to keep it separate from the others. All right. She gets the capsule between her fingers. She is in a bit of a situation. The stall door has swung inward behind her. It rests against her rump and as she crawls backward, carefully clutching the capsule in her right hand, two more women come into the restroom. They give little screeches and leave quickly. Esther finally manages to use the closed toilet seat to prop herself up. The capsule is so hard to hold onto that she gives up on her plans to clean the cap and just tosses it into her mouth. Three Black Beauties. No big deal. She will take three valium to smooth it out and she'll be fine.

The restroom is a bit of a chaos. She has hung her coat on the door of the stall next to the stall in which she is searching. It has slid to the floor. The fat bottle of Black Beauties has tipped and dropped perhaps a dozen capsules onto the counter. Some of them have rolled into the adjacent sink and are resting perilously at the lip of the metal plug, which is partially open. She gets the bottle and uses her palm to sweep the accessible capsules into a pile near the bottle's throat. She returns them to the bottle two at a time. Then she gets a comb from her purse and breaks off the handle. It makes a good spike with which she can pop the capsules out and away from the drain. The first two come away and she is able to get them onto the counter surface. She retrieves them and gets them into the bottle. Two more are still in the narrow gap between the drain's steel pipe entrance and the plug that can be opened or closed by way of the handle between the hot and cold water faucets. It occurs to her that she should close the drain and recover her capsules without going through all this nonsense. She turns the lever to the right. It opens and swallows the capsules. This sends her into a fury.

"You goddam son of a bitch bastard momser poison pipik. A geshvir dir in der

shpitznoz!" The Black Beauties are beginning to hit her without the mediation of the Valium and she knows she has to get some Blue Heaven in her gizzard. Her mixture of English and Yiddish curse words lend virulence to her expression that can't be equaled in mere English. She feels now as if the entire megilla is aimed by God at her personally and God can fargelt unt fargrint zoltsu vern!

She has a powerful instinct that she should get out of the bathroom, out of the store quickly, or she will be spending another week in the hospital with those faygeleh schvattzes!

She is all hands and knees and elbows and aching feet. She puts the purse down, opens it and roots around through her various bottles until she finds the clear glass container of valium. Her hands shake so badly that when she gets the bottle cap off the top, she drops it on the floor.

"Yemakh shmoy ve zikroy!" It is the worst curse she can think of: It means "May your name be blotted from the Book of Life". It is an invocation to annihilation. In this case she is cursing God and wants Him to die!

She isn't going to fool around any more! She takes the bottle and puts her lips around the opening and tips a random number of pills into her mouth. She can count with her tongue. There are no more than five or six. That will be okay. She has to get away!

She seals the capless bottle with a plug of toilet paper. She gets her coat back on and her purse zipped up. Her blood is pulsing with rage. She hits the door with all her weight and pushes. It opens outward. It stops when it meets resistance and almost bounces back into her face. She raises her arms protectively and prevents the door from crushing her nose.

There follows an interval of confusion as two of the store's security guards attempt to restrain Esther. The momentum of her exit from the bathroom is so great that one guard goes down to his knees. The other guard, who is bringing up the rear, lunges for Esther instinctively. All he sees is a furry beast with wrathful eyes that is attempting to escape. He thinks, quite relevantly, of getting a net but realizes that this is a large woman and not a rabid bear and that use of a net might be cause for a lawsuit.

"Fardreyen zolstu mit de fis!" Esther has abandoned English completely. "Krikken zolstu affen boykh!"

The security guard on his knees manages to rise and puts his hand around Esther's wrist. She

swings her arm with a strength fueled by advanced chemistry and ancient terror. The Cossacks are here! The pogrom is beginning! Next thing, the sabers will come out!

The salesman, Harlan, observes this scene from a safe distance. He has found the Kantro account closed and a special notation added: Do Not Sell To Mrs. Kantro. He already knows he has lost the sale as soon as the woman rushed off to the restroom. Then he hears the commotion and has a powerful sense that the demented woman is involved. He goes at a walk-run towards the restrooms. When he sees the wrestling match, he rushes to the nearest sales counter and picks up the microphone. He depresses the button and calls, "security backup quick ladies' restroom second floor!"

It takes some time to subdue Esther. It results in bloody noses, a broken femur and two cracked ribs.

It also results in putting Esther back in the locked ward at Jewish Veteran's Fifth Floor South. Her metronome has begun to swing. Every four or five weeks Esther behaves in such a way as to be arrested and confined to the ward.

Without Esther at the dining room table, the family has no difficulty expanding to fill the gap in its newfound cheer. For a few days Sarah continues to set a plate and silverware, out of habit. Then, as if erasing her mother's presence, she takes to setting five places, and moves the chairs a little farther apart. Only Max seems disturbed by the change.

Vernice, so handsome and maternal, is serving them a superbly cooked Italian meal. She vibrates such dignity and womanhood that Max is forced to acknowledge that he envies her husband. Then, inevitably, he questions himself: what is it in me that wanted to marry a woman who is so dreadfully unhappy? He knows that Esther has always been unhappy. He remembers the early years of their marriage. With brutal hindsight he recalls a thousand little discomforts that over time merged into several large agonies. There are arguments over trivialities. There are the sexual fears and failures. There is rejection followed by dependence, followed again by rejection. It has never been a good marriage.

Mark's birthday is coming up. He is getting that self-important air that seeps into a child's demeanor a week or so before the event. Max has already selected a birthday gift, but thinks to sound out his son 's ideas on the subject.

"Mark's got a birthday coming up," he points out to his other children, as if they don't know.

"He's getting so big, he's going to catch up with me, soon," Aaron says.

Mark puffs up.

"What will you like for a present?" Max asks playfully.

Without hesitating, Mark says, "I want a gun."

Ah well, Max thinks, boys will be boys. He has purchased a fine telescope in kit form, and looks forward to assembling it with his son. It is a gift the whole family can enjoy. He is confident that it will appeal to Mark's natural curiosity.

"What do you want a gun for?" Marilee frowns, looking so much like Esther, the way her bottom lip tightens and pushes forward over the upper lip.

"To kill mom."

The kitchen is silent, everyone stops chewing, forks and knives are interrupted in their dips and twists.

There is no more playfulness in Max's voice. "Mark, you shouldn't say things like that."

"Why not, she wants to kill me."

"That's nonsense. She's your mother. Even though she's sick, she still loves you very much."

"She does not. I don't believe you. She hates me and I hate her back."

Tomorrow, Max thinks, I'd better get a referral to a good child psychologist. I have to see if there's room for more mental health coverage. My premium will go up again. Mark's not just mouthing off baby talk. He means it.

"Eat your dinner," Max grumbles.

* * *

Aaron can no longer put off his return to school. He wants to sleep, that Monday morning, sleep all day and not face what he knows awaits him. When the alarm clock goes off, it brings him out of nightmares where he runs from rotting skulls in Nazi helmets, runs without going anywhere, fighting his way through air as thick as molasses.

Laboriously, he begins to dress, wondering whether or not to tell his father about what is happening in school. He feels so foolish about playing Nazi, sees it now for the stupidity that it is, and he can not bring himself to confide in Max. At some dim level of consciousness he feels that he is being punished for denying his roots. He has to atone, to face it and take it, and just brace himself for the misery that lays ahead.

Then the telephone rings. It is an unusual hour for phone calls.

He picks up the phone. It is Lester, and there is morbid excitement in his voice.

"Hey Aaron , did you hear?"

"Hear what? You know I've been home with a bashed head and numerous broken bones," he says bitterly. There have been no visits or calls from Lester.

"It's Tom. Tom Schweikert. He's dead."

The hair on the back of Aaron's neck rises with a ghostly thrill. He has been praying with every breath, wishing through the very pores of his body that Tom will disappear, will die, will have never existed in the first place. Can God provide such an unlikely escape? Aaron has long since learned that prayers usually take the long way around the universe before being returned to their senders in the form of an answer. The answer is usually some perverse lesson more baffling than the situation from which the prayer has emerged.

"It's true,"says Lester. "Somehow he shot himself with a gun. Nobody knows if it's an accident, on purpose, or what. They say he got the bullets from somebody on the varsity football team, so the whole team's been down at the police station, and man are they in trouble. That's all I've heard so far."

The tension flows out of Aaron in an almost heavenly release. He does not feel the least bit guilty. Tom and his guns. He knows it is no suicide. That bullet was meant for Aaron Kantro, the little Jew, and god has intervened. Justice has been administered with subtle efficiency, the bullet started its journey prematurely, finding a different target. Ever after, no matter how sorely tried, Aaron will believe in miracles.

His hate for Tom evaporates as he considers the crazy boy and his ilk. They seem so powerful on the surface, yet riddled with decay and horror inside. It reminds him of his mother, as she was before her decline: strong as a beast, vital with wrath, yet doomed to a lifetime of misery and insanity.

Am I doomed, as well? Aaron considers the riddle of his future. No, he thinks, I'm going to make it, I'm going to be a great musician. That's my destiny.

Chapter Thirteen

1967: The Zoot Prestige Trio At The Esquire Lounge

The Esquire Lounge is an archetypal venue: a pure urban jazz club, on the 'circuit', right down on Euclid Avenue between the steel mills to the west and Western Reserve University to the east. The club's sign has martini glasses jiggling in neon pink and green. Every time Aaron sees it, he senses that some day it will be a priceless artifact in a museum, "Esquire Lounge" and its dancing long-stemmed martini glasses being studied by serious observers of semiotics and folk art.

Zoot and the boys have f inished a week's engagement at the Jazzland Grill in Columbus. The drive to Cleveland is a little over two hours. It is a perfect example of Zoot's genius for scheduling gigs in different cities yet avoiding the road fatigue that can turn a musician's life into a nightmare.

Before checking into the hotel, before doing anything, Zoot wants to see old friends and examine the new soundboard at the Esquire. The gig is going to be recorded for Blue Note Records. Rumors are flying in the jazz world that the new band is something special, that Zoot has found a pair of "monsters", as they are called, to back him up as he plays his distinctive bop'n'blues style. For Aaron and Tyrone, it is their debut. Downbeat Magazine is going to review the record, it will be written up by critics like Leonard Feather and Nat Hentoff.

It's big. It's important. The album is going to be called "Hot Sax".

Zoot enters the club majestically, placing his feet on the carpet as if he is dancing, doing his lanky walk, all his joints subtly undulating.

"What's up, buttercup?," he inqures of the man sitting on a stool behind the bar. There are five or six people in the club, nursing drinks and chatting quietly. Two women spread white cotton tablecloths below the bandstand.

"Zoot motherfucking Prestige!" says the club's proprietor, "What is happenin'?" He puts out his cigarette and comes sailing from behind the bar, a tall fat man with a medium afro. He does a series of finger snaps and arcane handshakes with Zoot, then embraces him with a huge laugh.

Aaron knows these sounds and gestures; they are the greeting rituals of adult black males. They are tunes of loose laughter, arms and hands swinging wide and making noisy contact. The words mean little. The tones of understanding and recognition are everything. He tried, for a while, to imitate this hip black language. He felt ridiculous. What kind of spectacle must he be? A "white Negro". What's that nasty term? A "Wigger"? Does he want to be a slang term? Wait, let's not forget the Jew. What is he? A Nigyid?

A Yidgro? Oh God, he's a Yigger! No, he will speak the way he speaks, act the way he acts, just as he is.

Zoot does quick introductions. The club's owner is Hilton Stubbs. When Aaron is introduced, Stubbs looks at him coldly. Then, as if Aaron doesn't exist, Stubbs points to him and inquires of Zoot, "What is this?"

Zoot bristles. "What do you mean, 'what is this?', motherfucker. This is my drummer."

"This is a white kid from Shaker Heights, man, this won't go down."

"Hilton, you don't know shit." Zoot extends a protective arm around Aaron's shoulders. "You wanna cancel the gig?" Zoot picks up his saxophone case. "I can tell Blue Note we ain't playin' here. I'll go talk to Alvin at Loose End and I'll have my ass another gig."

"Naw, shit man, I won't do that; but I don't believe no white kid can play drums with Zoot Prestige and sound like the real deal."

"Why don't you talk to him like he's here in front of you, fool?"

Stubbs looks at Aaron. "Hmmmph." He lights a cigarette languidly, sizing Aaron up. "Zoot is legendary for being able to find monstrous drummers but I'm havin' a hard time taking you seriously. You can't be more than fucking twenty years old, kid. What do you know about soul?"

Aaron shrugs. "Gig starts at nine. You'll find out."

At that moment, several other people come from the back of the club, see Zoot and the greeting rituals are repeated. Aaron is ignored or treated to a cold stare, a lingering gaze of contempt and then a dismissive de-focusing of the eyes, as if he has simply vanished. Traveling with Zoot on the circuit, he has gotten a lot of racist attitude. He lets it bounce off him. He knows that later things will be different.

The equipment has to be unloaded and set up. There is already a Hammond organ and a Leslie speaker on the stage. Tyrone helps Aaron with the drums. At half past five, the recording crew arrives, hauling in a big Ampex eight track recorder in a wheeled case. Aaron is miked just above his head and in front of his bass drum. Zoot gets a single mike, Tyrone gets two, and two mikes are placed at strategic points on the stage. By six thirty the instruments are assembled and a sound check completed. The band and the recording crew order a few slabs of the Esquire's legendary barbecue and drink a few beers.

Zoot leads his band to the Hotel Onyx, next door, where they check in. Zoot has a room. Tyrone and Aaron share a room. They shower, shave, lay on their respective beds and relax.

Aaron falls asleep. At eight o clock, Tyrone shakes him awake. He has a familiar, crazed look on his face, as if he's about to do something naughty.

"Hey man, check this out." Tyrone holds two sugar cubes in his palm. They resemble pistils at the center of the long mocha petals of his fingers. Tyrone's digits are like the tentacles of a carnivorous plant.

Aaron sits up. Outside the window of the room, a neon sign is going bing! bop! bing! bop! Rooms! Hotel Onyx! Rooms! Hotel Onyx!

"Aw shit, what is that?" Aaron rubs his face, yawns.

"Hee hee. Owsley acid. The purest." Tyrone is full of mad mischief. His eyes seem to melt and harden like molten glass. Aaron loves him, loves his playing, loves his daring. He is virtually illiterate, dropped out of school in the fourth grade, but he is a thinker, a philosopher, a musical intellect.

"Owsley acid. It's always Owsley acid. How do you know it isn't bathtub PCP? With all the shit I just went through being white, you want me to take a psychedelic and play a gig?"

"I am Tyrone Terry, man, THE Tyrone Terry. Nobody twacks bullshit dope on me. I will kill them with my lethal B flat. What the fuck, man, it's not like you aint done it before. Here." He hands a cube to Aaron, then sucks the remaining cube into his mouth. His cheeks dent inward so that the goatee on his chin goes down like a sword blade. Behind his glasses his eyes are like the fires of a kiln. Aaron eats the cube with a tiny twist of fear. He knows taking a psychedelic is like going for a ride on a tiger's back. It can connect him to the primal power; or it can turn on him and eat him alive. He will risk it.

Having made this commitment, Aaron now has other preparations to make. He wishes he hadn't eaten the barbecue. It sits in his guts like a greasy snake. No matter, he will sweat it off. He sits in a quiet corner of the room, putting himself into lotus position. There is a terror of annihilation in him, residue from other psychedelic experiences. He has learned to let go of himself, has even learned to function, to play music, to walk around in the 'ordinary' world of people. It is the initial phases of the drug rush that are the most difficult. Suddenly, one finds oneself....utterly....without significance, lost in a vastness beyond vastness, so that the personality of Aaron Kantro is some kind of silly joke. It is this silly joke that Aaron has learned to dismiss with a figurative wave of his hand. What does it matter if I matter? Move forward into the risk, take the grotesque with the beautiful, take it all. Inhale and exhale universes with each breath.

Aaron hears Tyrone settle down beside him. Yoga is something Aaron has imparted to his friend, only to discover that Tyrone has a natural ability to settle into a deep silence. He is, perhaps, less intellectually encumbered. Whatever the reason, Tyrone is a natural yogi, he meditates and conjures mind exercises of stunning imagination.

Zoot will come to fetch them at quarter to nine. The young men must don their tuxedoes. The drug is working, beginning as they meditate, stretching their imagery into an immense hall in which they can hear one another's thoughts like echoes from walls of a cave.

"We got a gig," Aaron reminds Tyrone as he uncurls his legs. Tyrone opens his eyes slowly, and they are like search lights being uncovered, a mighty glow emits from their orbs. Pulling themselves into the mundane world, the musical brothers dress and look at their reflections in the mirror, giggling. "Be cool, be cool, " Tyrone admonishes, sinking his head between his shoulders as if to mimic stealth. "The Zoot will be wise to this, and he won't be happy if we're melting."

"Promise I won't melt," Aaron confirms. He is serious, he knows he has a responsibility to his mentor to behave and play like a professional jazz musician.

Zoot enters the room, sits in the one easy chair and lets both legs splay over the chair's arm rest.. He brings out his little pouch and crumples some weed into the corncob pipe. He examines his compatriots with an air of suspicion, but he has seen this before and has a measure of faith in his sidemen.

"Dudes look good," he sayes. "Feelin alright? Tight? Outtasight?"

"Just fine, Zoot. Lookin' forward to it, " Tyrone replies. Aaron nods agreement.

Zoot eyes his sidemen speculatively. "Gonna get cosmological on me? Gonna do Coltrane riffs?" This is one of Zoot's cautionary admonitions. He loves John Coltrane but knows his bread and butter, knows what the patrons of the Esquire Club have come to hear: stompin' blues shoutin bop-till-you-drop tenor saxophone organ trio music.

"Don't you trust us, Zoot? We know the gig." Aaron's hands are rattling complex drum patterns on his kneecap. Warming up.

"There's something about you two, tonight. You're glittering a little bit." It is impossible to tell whether or not he winks, because when he wants to, Zoot can wink but not wink. Aaron suspects he has winked. The saxophonist lights the pipe and inhales. Then he loads it again and passes it to Aaron. "I will righteously appreciate some discipline from you young monsters. Don't think I don't know what's going on here. This ain't speculative fiction. This is the Kingdom of Funktonics. Aaron, you gotta stay inside the groove and let these Black Nationalist motherfuckers know you can play some shit."

"We will play some shit," Tyrone affirms, making it sound like a solemn oath. Aaron repeats it.

"We will play some shit."

Each of them has the requisite two hits of weed, enacting the pre-set ritual that is as much a part of their working life as their instruments and their PA system. They head down the long stairs with its purple carpeting, into the foyer with its thousands of tiny hexagonal tiles and green trim. Euclid avenue is a parade of horsepower vanity. Caddies, Continentals and Grand Prix convertibles gurgle toward the traffic lights. A bit of rain has fallen and the smell of wet pavement and gasoline fumes mingle in the air. Reflections from neon lights bounce up from the sidewalks. Aaron inhales and marvels at the wild beauty of the world.

They walk around to the kitchen entrance of the club. Zoot gives a signal to Hilton Stubbs. The proprietor nods and goes to the bandstand. It is a good house. The tables are taken. The bar is already two rows deep. The recording engineers are perched at their boards like alchemists over tables of potions and unguents

"Ladies and gentlemen," Stubbs says into the microphone. "The Club Esquire is honored to present the reigning Master of Funk, the Prestigious One, The Zoot with the roots and his smokin' recruits, the one and only...... Zoot..... Pres.....tige!"

They come through the swinging door and make their procession to the bandstand. When the applause and whistles die down, Zoot looks at Tyrone and Aaron, snaps his fingers and counts off a blistering tempo for "All the Things You Are". They are off! Tyrone's organ vamps behind Zoot's solo like butter rolling down a split yam. Aaron is crisp as a new hundred dollar bill. The stick in his right hand comes down on the ride cymbal almost lazily; just enough behind the beat to give it tension, to make that indefinable suspense that is the elusive quality of swing. He pop pops with his left hand on the snare, talking to Zoot's cadences. It is a glory. It is jazz.

They play Monk's tune, "Well You Needn"t. Then, to slow things down, Zoot calls for "Angel Eyes". That's when the LSD begins working at its full intensity. Tyrone plays the dark moody chords of the song. Its story is that of an urban bar-room drama, of souls sliding toward damnation but gripping their humanity with ferocious desperation. When Tyrone's solo comes, he lands on one of those blue tones that the organ can sustain forever, while his right hand trills and trills pure funkiness. It is musical laughter. Aaron's smile grows larger than his face, a Cheshire Cat grin where the rest of him disappears into the curling lips and glowing teeth. Zoot rocks his horn and arches his back. The audience is screaming approval. The walls start to melt. Hilton Stubbs looks like a goat or a devil, behind the bar, smiling so that his gold tooth flashes across the room. Tyrone glances at Aaron, wicked sly wit oozing from his eyes.

Stay inside, Aaron mentally signals. Don't get crazy. Tyrone nods. Don't worry; I can get crazy and still stay inside. They are IT. They are tradition. They are milking all the conventions, all the known things of jazz. Tyrone arpeggioes to get to the head of the tune. It is like ocean waves, surf rolling in perfect cylinders toward the shore. Zoot hears the cue and they restate the brooding melodrama of Angel Eyes. The tune ends in a splash of cymbals, organ and saxophone. Perfect.

Zoot knows what's happening but says nothing. As long as they play well he will let it slide. He can't sit on these two young horses. He can go with them, out to the boundary. If he feels them slipping off, he will give them the infamous Zoot Stare. If he can keep them right there, right at the boundary but still within the vocabulary, the vocabulary itself will become the realm of exploration.

It works. It works all night. During the final song Aaron takes a drum solo and feels his arms multiply, feels as if four right hands and four left hands are striking and bouncing off the drums with incredible speed. He is a Hindu God, he is eight-armed Ganesh, the elephant god, the lord of Jupiter. He rolls and crackles and flames but keeps it together, never gets abstract, hits the One, the downbeat, right where he is supposed to. He pops his rim-shots and starts a snare roll, one that builds and builds as if the construction of a Great Pyramid is under way. Then, suddenly, he pulls the sticks away from the drums. There is silence. Perfect, beautiful silence. How long can he hold it? Well....exactly...THIS long, and he takes the roll from where he left and mellows down, slows and softens. Then vanishes, for just the count of one...two...three...four. Zoot and Tyrone land together on the song's ending: B-daaaaah! Climax! And the night of music is over.

There isn't anyone in the room who is wondering if Aaron can play drums. There isn't anyone in the room who is thinking about black or white, soul or without soul, paid dues, ain't paid dues, hipness or squareness.

There is only the miracle of music.

Chapter Fourteen

1961: Lions, Tigers and Crutches

One week before Passover that year, Esther makes her first suicide attempt. It is a near-miss, a classic underdose, an inchoate plea for attention.

Max changes psychiatrists. The new one, Dr. Potts, has theories about chemical imbalances. He prescribes. He uses no shock treatments, very little analysis. He does a lot of fancy brain scans with elaborate hospital machinery. Then he makes his oracular diagnosis, scribbles on a pad. Voila, the New Hope. MOA Inhibitors. Anti-depressants. Regulation of Lithium levels. Serotonin serenity.

Max has grown skeptical of shrinks and their glib reassurances. He can't stop trying to save his family. He can't abandon Esther to an institution, or watch Mark grow more and more violent, or witness Aaron descending into isolation and fantasy. If they can only hold on long enough, maybe science will find an answer. Researchers are discovering the biochemical nature of mental illness, the hormonal imbalances of depression. Maybe Esther is incapable of helping herself. Maybe her thoughts and responses are robotically tied to some vagrant juices squirting through the wrong synapses. We're all so helpless, Max thinks. Victims of substances microscopic in size but tyrannical in their effects on our lives.

The echoes of the Tom Schweikert nightmare are fading away. Aaron can walk the halls at school without fearing for his life. His adolescent misery remains. He still tries valiantly to look the right way, to say the right things with the right amount of macho swagger. Only the energies of youth can keep up with such ridiculous demands. Only the ignorance of youth will put up with them.

The only tool Aaron has to improve his social standing is his music. He is aware that the school's music teacher, Mr. Blackstone, is unusually sympathetic. The long-suffering young teacher has an allocation of a few hundred dollars with which to purchase sheet music of big band jazz.

There are auditions. Aaron and Lester quickly pass and are put in charge of the brass and reed sections. A clumsy but enthusiastic drummer named Jerry Koyne materializes from out of the ranks of the robotic snare drummers in the school marching band.

Mister Blackstone assembles a sixteen piece big band and starts rehearsals. The teacher is fresh out of college. He is a short, powerful looking man of about thirty with buzz cut black hair that forms a widow's peak. He has spent four years in the Marines before going to college. He exudes authority without being intimidating. He is now tasked with organizing a classical symphony orchestra and a school marching band.

The kids like him. His fellow teachers like him.

The jazz band is a labor of love. It is his own time and sometimes his own money that propels this collection of mostly awful musicians. It will cause him more grief than any experience he has endured as a Marine.

He persists because of the possibility that perhaps one or two of these children will have real gifts. The band rehearses, two hours Friday afternoon and two hours Saturday from seven to nine. The early rehearsals are nightmares. When he is frustrated, Daniel Blackstone has a habit of clutching his eyebrows. He will trap them between his thumb and fingers and pull them so that his forehead stretches tight. His hair is too short to tear out.

Dale Blackstone is a man of almost infinite patience. It will take a couple of months just to get these young people to play in tune, on cue. They might never "swing".

So far, the band sounds like a lumbering old elephant with a broken leg.

Jerry Koyne has been diligent with his drum practice. He has acquired a modicum of technique. He is the perfect demonstration of that maxim, "a little knowledge is a dangerous thing."

Jerry's parents have bought a full trap drum set for their son, and he leaves it in one of the sound-proofed practice rooms until rehearsal day. Then the drums are assembled,

the musicians take their seats, the music scores are passed out and rehearsal begins.

Jerry plays with such volume and intensity that it is impossible to achieve any work. He is mad with power. He has been listening to Buddy Rich and thinks he can play in that flashy style.

Mr.Blackstone admonishes the young man to tone it down, to listen to his fellow musicians, to blend in, to be part of the group and not a soloist.

Will do, says Jerry Koyne. Sorry Mr. Blackwell, I'll turn it down.

Two charts later, and the volume has returned to its former level.

The solution is to forbid Jerry the use of drum sticks. Instead he is to play every chart with brushes, those bundles of wire shaped like bird's tails. Brushes are for ballad playing, for accompanying vocalists. Jerry grits his teeth and begins to acquire more finesse.

After some months the band is honking its way through Basie, Duke, Woody Herman, Stan Kenton.

Aaron is capitvated by one song. It is Dizzy Gillespie's "Night in Tunisia." This song has everything: it is exotic, mysterious, its rhythms build and change, its dynamics go from quiet to screaming, and back to quiet. Best of all, it has a trumpet solo at the moment of the song's most dramatic break.

This is Aaron's showcase. He listens to the record over and over, memorizing the solo that Gillespie played. It is beyond his skill. The sheet music has provided a simpler version of the solo and Aaron masters it after a week of dedicated study.

Aaron hasn't forgotten his first love, the drums. He works out a schedule with Jerry to use the drum set for his own practice.

It is incredibly boring. Tapping patterns with his sticks, paradiddle paradiddle paradiddle, he persists with his will focused and his mind on cruise control. Double paradidddle double paradiddle double paradiddle. Fifty times. A hundred times. Faster, faster, slower, slower. Ratamacue ratamacue, over and over he taps out these stultifying but oh so important fundamentals. After a while they start falling naturally under his hands. After a while, he begins to PLAY and not merely practice. He gets a double paradiddle going. It is amazing! His hands control the sticks but the sticks seem to have a mind of their own, flying, flying, diggi diggi bam bam a diggibubba. Aaron watches the sticks blur, he floats out of his body and simply allows the sticks to do what they want. He can lean to the left and change hands so that the accents fall differently, then lean right, change again, lead with his right stick, back and forth, bam a bam. He moves around the drum kit, repeating the pattern from drum to drum and for the first time as a drummer, he feels control and wildness, together.

No one has a clue how good he is getting. He keeps it to himself. He is getting good, but he isn't good enough, not yet.

The jazz band begins to appear for school assemblies and other special occasions. Aaron always feels a cathartic thrill each time he stands up to play the transcribed trumpet solo cadenza in "Night in Tunisia". He loves to perform. It brings attention, status.

It brings girls

Mr. Blackstone, the young hip jazzman, is waiting for his moment. A slight push might open Aaron, might give him the courage to leap into the unknown, to close his eyes to the written music and begin playing from his dreams. After listening to Aaron embellish a number of written solos, he decides his student is ready to taste the exhilirating waters of pure improvisation.

There is a school assembly before the spring break. It is tailored to show off the burgeoning talents of the school. The drama club plays a scene. The glee club sings two songs. The Normandy Jazz Orchesra has six minutes at the assembly's end, before Principal Longley speaks about the importance of discipline in building character.

The band is going to play "Night In Tunisia". The lights are down in the auditorium. Aaron knows that everyone will be watching him as he stands. He is keyed for the dramatic trumpet break. On the record album it is a moment when Dizzy's high screeching exhortations leap out of total silence like a charge of saber-wielding Berber cavalry.

The measures tick away. Aaron is keeping his mouthpiece warm and his horn free of spit, marshalling his big breath for the surging break. The brass section is building to a crescendo. Aaron's eyes are leaping ahead of the score to the notes of his solo. He does not see Mr. Blackstone leave the podium and stealthily walk behind the bleachers toward the trumpet section.

Now, before five hundred of his peers, Aaron's cue is played. He stands, four measures in advance, and the spotlight falls upon him. Then it is time. The break chops off the previous measure, which echoes briefly and dies to an anticipatory pause. Aaron looks down at the music stand in time to see Mr. Blackstone's hand snatch the sheet away. There is no time for suprise or vacillation. He is at the mercy of his musical wits.

He plays. Feeling the modulations intuitively, he makes a new solo, nothing at all like the original. Mr. Blackstone beams, feeling the highest kind of success to which any teacher might aspire: to create a creator.

After the concert, glowing with his success, Aaron has more than his usual share of confidence. The band is patting him on the back, strangers are shaking his hand and professing their admiration. After he packs his horn and is ready to depart, he finds Michele Dalton, demure but attentive, waiting for him.

"Aaron, I had no idea you play trumpet so beautifully....ooooh, it just gave me goose bumps." The coquettish modulations in her voice raise sympathetic bumps on Aaron's skin.

"Did you make all that up? My father likes jazz. He plays records all the time, but I've never heard anything so modern sounding."

With these revelations, Aaron is willing to rationalize Michele into a sophisticate with an unjustly smirched reputation. "I've only learned to improvise," he confesses.

"Will there be another concert soon? I'd love to hear you play some more."

"Well, nothing's scheduled," Aaron says, struggling to control the tingle in his face that he knows is a vivid blush. Though he is puffed up with victory, his habitual shyness nearly obstructs what he knows is an opening. Now's your chance, idiot! he lashes himself. What can you lose?

"Some of the guys in the band get together on weekends to rehearse a small combo. You can listen to us play, even though its just rehearsal, it isn't all that good or anything. Will you like for me to call you next time we play?"

"I'd love it if you will," Michele oozes. Aaron is enchanted, enslaved, befogged with the implicit promise in the way she holds herself, in the drippings of her voice.

Telephone numbers are exchanged. Observed by Aaron's bandmates, his stock rises considerably. Mel Tillman, the bass player, leers as he struggles to fit his huge instrument into his mother's car. "Hey Aaron," he whispers, "You just got a come-on from Miss Put-Out. If you're still a virgin, here's your chance."

"You talk like you're not a virgin," Aaron whispers back.

"Well....." Mel evades suggestively.

"Don't hand me that shit. We're all virgins, except for maybe Johnny Trasker. And if you tell me different, you're full of it. We're probably going to be virgins for some time to come." Johnny Trasker has made a notorious visit to a local hotel that specializes in half hour rentals. None of the other boys have sufficient nerve to brave the neighborhood in which it is located.

"Well, maybe not us peasants, but your chances just went up about a hundred percent. Michele goes out with college guys," Mel smirks enviously. "And I'm sure they don't just shake hands when the date's over. It's not every day she bestows her amorous glance on one of us tenth graders. Of course, if you don't want her......"

"Just shut up, Mel, shut up. She's probably not like that at all."

"Suuuure," Mel groans, rolling his eyes. Finally, but not gently, he pushes his big fiddle into the back seat.

The following Saturday brings the combo rehearsal, at Jerry Koyne's house. Aaron has invited Michelle. He finds it impossible to concentrate. His stomach feels like a hailstorm, his lips are too dry to emit more than perfunctory notes. Michele promised to arrive at two oclock. It is now ten after.

"What's wrong, Kantro? Thinking about your girlfriend?" Jerry is ribbing him. The drummer, with his big ears and goofy face, is obsessed with Michele. Every one of the boys is obsessed with Michele, but Jerry is almost beyond obsession; his desire verges on the psychopathic.

"Not Kool Kantro," quips Simon Liebergott, a trombone player. "He can care less. After all, nobody wants to get laid, not at the tender age of fifteen."

Aaron is taking a lot of this. He resents it, but he also basks in it. The pressure to prove his manhood is so intense that he regrets inviting Michele to the rehearsal. He has done it for many reasons, and one of them is to impress his friends. Now he is stuck with it.

They play another arrangement. In the middle of it, Michele appears, letting herself in through the screen door. Suddenly there is new fire in the band's playing. Jerry twirls his sticks and grins. Simon and Larry Steinberg rock back and forth. Everyone tries to solo at once. The music suddenly sounds like an incompetent fusion of Dixieland and New Wave.

Michele sits demurely through the song. She is aware of her effect upon the boys. She blows Aaron a kiss, which results in a giant clinker. The band nearly drops the beat and wanders far out of tune. Eyebrows go up, there are grunts, coughs, elbows in ribs.

Michele nourishes herself on this attention. She can not believe in her beauty. Gazing in the mirror she sees only a plain and ragged girl, but if men think she is beautiful, that is power. Consumed by the need to be adored, she is well equipped for a lifetime of receiving the wrong kind of love.

The band plays one more tune with obvious relish. Then the boys discreetly vanish, one or two at a time. They wink, they tiptoe like Wily Coyote, they collide and tumble on the stairs, but finally leave Aaron alone with Michele.

"You guys are fabulous." She sits on a white wicker chair with her fingers intertwined beneath her chin. Her eyes go 'blink blink' so that her lashes seem to create a breeze. "How long have you been playing together?"

Aaron is grateful that she asks a good question, an ice breaker. It is easy for him to talk about the band, about jazz. Beneath his facile talk he feels queasy with nerves. He knows that the other boys are huddled at the top of the stairs, listening.

The house is built on a slope, so that the basement rehearsal room is below ground at one end, yet opens onto a patio at the other. The room is wood paneled, and several other rooms are adjacent, a laundry room, a store room and a guest bedroom.

Aaron has no idea how to seduce Michele. She has a reputation as a tramp. What does that mean? Is it true? And even if it is true, how does that help him in this situation? Is he required to take her out first? She might expect him to date her, give her a few presents. Should he try to kiss her now? Or should he play the gentleman, and pretend not to want her?

He keeps hearing his friends' jibes: This is your big chance, Aaron, don't blow it. She loves to put out. All the seniors have been in her pants. If you can't score now, you're never going to score.

He feels that if he fails to live up to their expectations, he will never hear the end of it, never be able to face his friends. Pressure, pressure. Everyone wants a vicarious thrill, and you, through sheer luck, happen to be the vehicle. By some fluke Michele's taken a fancy to you, she's looking at you doe-eyed, this very moment. Better use your big chance, before she decides to like some other guy. They're waiting, listening upstairs. Do something, quickly, before she loses interest and leaves.

He is utterly frightened. Feeling unreal, suspended in a dream, every movement is sluggish as he swims through his fear and moves his lips toward her lips, meeting them in an awkward, close-mouthed kiss.

It is a test. He has committed himself to undergoing it. Failure or success now depends on Michele.

"You certainly are bold," she says, flapping her eyelashes, head slightly lowered, looking up at him with timeless coquettishness. Obviously she doesn't mind. Aaron lets out his breath. He kisses her again. He feels as if he has just broken free of congested traffic, and is now zooming full speed ahead.

This time Michele opens her mouth, using her tongue to push past Aaron's lips, meeting and darting around his tongue.

Aaron is astonished. They are both breathing heavily. Forging ahead, he says, "Um..Michele, there's a guest room down here. You want to go in there? For more... privacy?"

Michele's eyes are misted, lips parted, breasts rising and falling. This is not Michele but a sex-exuding animal. Aaron has never seen such a look before, or such a change come over a female. It is shocking, exhilirating, frightening.

"Yes,"she breathes.

As she rises, guiding him with her hot moist fingers, Aaron's fear intensifies, his exultation vanishes. It is actually happening! Something sexual is going to occur with this fantastically gorgeous girl. Yet somehow he has become detached from his body. He looks down on himself from far above, and his remoteness is terrifying.

"I should be feeling something" he tells himself. "I should be excited, but I'm not. Instead I'm just cold, my heart is numb."

They go into the room and close the door. A little nightlight provides wan illumination. Awkwardly, Aaron removes Michele's sweater and brassiere as she sits upon the bed. Feeling nothing, he kisses her nipples. He keeps telling himself he should be excited. He is cold and afraid. Feeling nothing, he removes her skirt and slip, her shoes, socks, underpants. Michele slides back, to lie supine on the bed, her knees slightly bent, her figure softly visible in the dim yellowish light.

His clothing is half on, half off. Michele seems oblivious, her lungs heaving. God, she is beautiful, Aaron thinks, gazing at her nude body. Why don't I feel anything?

With a dreadful start, he realizes that he does not have an erection. He is outside himself, passion is utterly alien to this detachment. Frantically, he strokes himself, trying to get hard. His pants are around his ankles and he remembers the rubber in his wallet. With one hand he caresses Michele's vagina, puts his finger inside her moist opening. Michele is blind to everything, lost in another realm miles away. She receives his gestures passively, doing nothing in return. Her eyes are three quarters closed, staring into nothingness.

With his free hand, Aaron fumbles at his wallet, sliding the rubber out. With fingers and teeth he tears the package open. He is afraid to take his other hand away from Michele's body, afraid if he stops touching her breasts and vagina that her "hot"state will disappear and she will change her mind.

He continues to simulate passion while feeling cold emptiness. Struggling, he manages to get the rubber over his limp penis. Vaguely, at the periphery of his perception, he is aware that his friends are back in the basement, that their ears are pressed to the door of the guest room.

Michele moans, but does nothing to help. Aaron flails at his penis, willing it to become hard. If I can just get it into her, he thinks, it'll get hard, I'll be at home base. I'll have nothing to worry about. The fact that I am fucking her will, in itself, be so exciting that I'll get hard, automatically.

But getting it in is a problem. He moves over her, tries to thrust up, but feels it slosh around limply without going anywhere. Lying atop her, he reaches down to stimulate himself, panicking, thinking too many thoughts at once, about his friends, about what Michele will say to people if he doesn't get it up.

He isn't even sure whether the rubber is on or not. It seems to have slipped off his shrunken penis when he caressed himself. He raises himself off of her for a moment, looks down. Her breasts are so perfect and beautiful that he can not imagine anything more enticing. His penis partially responds. By this time Michele is moist enough that a thrust of her hips enables him to slip halfway inside. Involuntarily, with a spasm of terror and heat, he pushes all the way into her and his juices spurt. He gives a short cry, tries to stop himself, but it is too late. He has failed miserably.

With the technical fact of ejaculation, he gives up in hopelessness and rolls off of Michele. After a few moments of panting, she opens her baby blue eyes and inquires innocently, "Aren't you going to screw me?"

Chapter Fifteen

1964: Princess Wasp

Max can't afford a bigger house but he feels he has no choice. If he doesn't get a mortgage on a newer, larger home, Esther will become a bed of nails upon which he will spend every moment of his life.

Credit is easy. Over the years the deli has become a flourishing business. Goaded by Esther, Max has attempted to branch out into several quick-buck ventures, all of which are disastrous. Following the hula hoop fad, it seems that the way to get rich is to anticipate the next fad. Max doesn't learn his lesson until he has lost money on a trampoline center, a miniature golf course and a drive-in movie theatre.

One day, the house on the corner of his street goes up for sale. A week later it is sold, and a week after that, a family is seen moving into a house on the street where the Kantro family has lived for eight years. When Max comes home from work that night, Esther is sitting in bed, watching the television. Her hair is in curlers, her face is covered by cream. She wears a blue house dress with a white lacy collar. She looks like a barrel dressed up to be a scarecrow. Her eyes are like bludgeons, and Max sighs as he hangs up his jacket, because he can tell just by the way she is breathing that something is coming, a complaint, a major kvetch, a repetition of the kvetch she has been making for the past two years.

In his tank t-shirt, the skin of Max's shoulders is sallow and spotted. He hesitates, not wanting to sit on the bed, thereby sealing his fate for the next hour. He decides to turn around, go back to the kitchen to make himself a corned beef sandwich. Esther's voice beats him to the door of the bedroom.

"Shvahtzes," she says, using the pejorative yiddish term for negroes. The word is simply a corruption of the German word, blacks, or schwartzes. Her pronunciation is idiomatic of the shtetl, the ancestral village from which her family emigrated a hundred years ago. There is no "r" sound with this accent. It caused the word to sound even more dismissive, more vile and laden with contempt. "Shvahtzes" she says. "Right on this street. Do you know they bought the Melman's house?"

"So? I have no problem with colored people," Max answers patiently, but he knows his wife's mind. He knows the direction of her thinking.

"You have no problem," she mocks. "But when you're the last Jew on this street, the last white person in a sea of Shvahtzes, who will be laughing at you from a better neighborhood, out in Ladue? My sister, Rose, your brother Sammy, all your customers. 'Max Kantro can't afford to get away from the Schvahtzes', they'll say. And who will come to you with their business? Shvahtzes? You need to move the business and buy a new house, it's that simple, Max, or you'll end up a schlepper in your old age, working for some nice deli in Ladue as a meat cutter. I can see it now, you in your funny little paper hat, the eternal Jew, tired, oh so tired, and your feet hurt like hell. Is that what you want to happen?"

Max has been mulling this problem for some time. The house in which they live is a box made of concrete, brick and drywall. The kids are outgrowing it, they need their own rooms. If he looks through Esther's sneering prejudice, he has to admit that she is right. It is time to give in.

"All right, Esther. Tomorrow I'll talk to Leonard at the mortgage company. And we'll start the move. Are you happy? We'll move everything, the business, a new house, we'll run from the blacks and stay in our golden ghetto as it moves ever westward, to further suburbs. How long will we run? Will our kids run even further westward? The coloreds are making money now, they deserve better homes than the tenements on Delmar...."

Esther is snoring. Her nighttime barbiturates have kicked in. Max spends the rest of the night awake. His jaws are tight, the muscles of his temples bunch as the rows of his teeth meet and tighten. He wishes, just once, that he can beat Esther to a pulp before plunging into ever-greater debt.

The new house offers a bedroom for each of the children. It has spacious lawns, front and back. It is located in a school district that accommodates children from upper middle class families. The district also encloses a wide swathe of homes belonging to the absurdly wealthy. The Kantro offspring will attend classes with kids whose parents are listed in the social register.

Marilee has graduated high school and is now attending St. Louis University. For the remaining three children, the change of school district is momentous. Gone are the scrapings of the white social barrel. Gone are the greasers and the scions of carburetor kingdoms, the girls with the stiffened hair, the entire pinball mentality.

The new high school still has its natural share of football tribalism, but it is a school catering to an economic class that is several rungs up the ladder from the high school in the old neighborhood. The intellectual quotient is higher, the small talk revolves around Sartre, Camus, T.S Eliot, e.e. cummings and Ayn Rand. The beat poets are coming into vogue. It is a genteel, tweedy environment where the boys wear sport jackets to school and have roman numerals after their names. The girls who are looking to marry a rich boy after college tell one another a joke: find a boy whose first name sounds like a last name. Shelby. Tremaine. Thurston. The girls are already lining up for Bryn Mawr and Vassar. Every one of them, to the delight of their parents, is saving it for marriage.

To be a musician or a painter is no bad thing. A touch of talent makes being bad a good thing.

In this new-found social warmth, Aaron falls in love.

The party is held in the back yard of a long, elegant house, on a warm September night. The stereo is playing Peter, Paul and Mary, Pete Seger, and the occasional Beatles tune. Colored lanterns hang around the perimeter of the lawn, happy noises and splashes emanate from the swimming pool. Adults have discretely vanished.

Aaron wanders around, shyly but happily. He has a few acquaintances to whom he attaches himself. He avoids contact with strangers but his reticence is compensated for by the fashionable open-ness of his peers. People approach without hesitation, tell him their names, ask him about himself and seem genuinely delighted to meet him.

He wanders until he encounters a group seated around the fireplace, listening to a youth declaiming from Ginsburg's "Howl". There is a girl, nodding with her cronies in ecstatic understanding of the beat poet's profundities. She has long straight blond hair, blue eyes, finely cast Anglo-Saxon features. Aaron is stricken instantly. She is the archetype of his romantic fantasies. He has always dreamed of girls who are opposite to The Jewish Princess. He dreams of girls that will enrage his mother. Now, she is here, in the flesh.

He hangs at the periphery of the group, trying not to stare, averting his eyes whenever she looks at him. After a few minutes he knows that she is looking at him, and he raises his nerve to prolong an eye contact. The girl saves him his typical agonies of indecision. Unabashed, she approaches him.

"Hi. You're the new star musician, aren't you? I've heard about you from the guys in the band. They think you're the greatest thing since Miles Davis."

"You know who Miles Davis is?" This is something new. No one knows anything about jazz. Hipness is as rare as a precious jewel.

"Of course," she answers tartly. "Do you think I live in a closet? I love classical music, but lately I've been listening to some old Charlie Parker records."

Aaron almost faints. Fantasies like this occur only when he is asleep.

"I don't pretend to be an expert," she confesses modestly. "It's my older brother who collects the records. He's at Yale, now, so he sends me down to Moe's Jazz Nook for the records he can 't find. I listen to them before I mail them." She abruptly looks down at her shoes with unfeigned shyness. "Actually, I'm just name-dropping. I'm trying to impress you."

"I'm totally impressed," Aaron acknowledges with utmost sincerity. He is afraid he will wake up. "But why me?"

"I don't know. Something about you. If I knew you better, and you improved with the knowing, I think I might like you very much."

Her name is Katherine, and, as Aaron soon learns, she is not easily pleased. She makes it clear that in order to win her love, Aaron will have to prove his excellence in many ways. Grades are not important, but creativity, originality, poetic sensitivity, honesty, these are the qualities Katherine seeks in a man. By needing these things, she is exactly what Aaron needs.

That year Aaron surpasses himself. He is well-liked, learns to dress with chic indifference, begins writing poetry and gets a lot better at the drums. Though the pressure to conform still existes, it is conformity to a higher standard.

Coincident with these changes, he experiences a sudden and powerful burst of hormonal adjustment. In ten months he grows two inches in height and gains thirty pounds of muscle. His scrawny legs and narrow shoulders suddenly burst forth with taut flesh, spreading up and down across his body. He can run fast, play baseball and football, lift weights and wrestle. He has suddenly become one of the guys.

Max is pleased as he sees how the new situation suits his children. Esther is becoming more impossible. Her obsession with money becomes more pronounced. She doesn't really care if she has money. She cares that she looks as if she has money.

One night in January the kids are in bed and the house is quiet. Max is trying to get to sleep before Esther begins her set-piece speech. He has heard it a hundred times and now, as he begins to reach for the bedside light, Esther's voice forestalls him. He is too late.

"Now that we've got a respectable house, Max, why don't we get a pool?"

"Esther, a pool is six, seven thousand dollars. Just getting this house will keep me in debt for the

rest of my life. What do you want from me?"

"If we have a pool we'll look like we're doing well. People will think you're doing well and they'll trust you with their business. It's an investment, Max. Money attracts money. You have to look rich to get rich."

"Yes, and if I go to an early grave getting all this stuff, what will you do? Who will take care of you? You can't take care of yourself."

Esther's face goes scarlet. Max is already retreating, his body slightly hunched, turning sideways to present a smaller target. Esther reaches for the nearest object at hand, a glass of water on the bedstand table. She hurls it at Max. The glass strikes his abdomen a glancing blow and falls to the carpet. Water is spread in a trail of droplets from the bed to where the glass has fallen and now lays in a puddle. Max gets out of the bedroom and goes to the closet in the hallway next to the front door. There are blankets, and he takes one and retires to the living room couch. He has books there, and a reading lamp. Switching it on, he finds his place in Gore Vidal's historical novel, "Burr". He loves American History, can't get enough of it. Vidal is one of his favorite writers. Pushing everything else from his mind, he settles under his blanket, reads for five or ten minutes, and then begings to drowse away. He is asleep, perfectly, blissfully in that one moment where sleep overtakes awake, and he is suddenly aware that he has forgotten to turn off the reading light. It isn't really this awareness that brings him back to wakefulness. He often falls asleep with the light on. It is Esther. She is standing beside the couch like a basilisk, moving her fingers strangely. Her elbows are bent and her hands are at shoulder height, and she is wriggling her fingers as if they are covered with something sticky. Her eyes are unfocused, and she begins shaking her fingers as if to dislodge whatever substance has gotten there.

"Do you know," she says, " that Aaron is going with a schicksa? I happen to know that her parents are rabid anti-semites. You think they'll allow it to continue? I forbid it, Max. I absolutely forbid it. He should not see that girl again, for his own good. The goyim will never accept him. "

"Esther, for god's sake, will you leave it alone? She's made a man of him. He's happy, he looks so good and his grades have improved. I don't care if she's colored, polka dot or Moslem."

He turns his body, putting his face against the couch. He is practiced at letting his wife's nagging roll off his back. But Esther is in some kind of new agitation. At this point, usually, she loses steam and goes back to bed, locking the door behind her.

"Don't you tune me out!" she rasps, her voice loud enough to wake the whole house. She grasps Max by the shoulder and forcibly turns him back to face her. What he sees in her eyes is something he has never seen before: a vision of hell, dizzying in its violence.

Esther falls to her knees next to the couch and puts her hands on Max's face, rubbing forcefully, painfully. Max grabs her wrists, but her strength is incredible. "A schikisa,"she repeats, "Our son is going out with a goyische whore, a no good bitch!"

Max sits upright, trying to defend himself. He struggles to keep Esther's hands from his face. She tears at his eyes, and he stands to get away from her. She pursues like some monster-movie creature, shaking her hands, shaking, trembling. "Are you going to do something about it, Max? You're the father, it's your responsibility to see that our children don't end up marrying poison, goyim, niggers, anything they feel like marrying…."

Max retreats across the living room, knocking over the big lamp as he does so. The crash brings Aaron to the corner where the hallway leads into the living room. He stands there transfixed. Esther closes on Max and slashes with her fingernails, a powerful slap across his face. Three lines of blood ooze from his skin.

There, standing in his tank top shirt and his boxer shorts, looking like a pitiful middle aged Jewish man, Max makes a fist of his right hand and punches his wife right in the face. She staggers back, falls onto her behind, house dress disarranged, showing fat legs marked with varicose veins all up and down their length. Then she rises again and charges her husband like a maddened water buffalo. The two of them go down together, toppling the couch.

Aaron runs to the phone and calls the police. Quickly he gives their address. The police know the problems of the Kantro family. Someone will be dispatched. Then Aaron helps his father overpower his mother until she lays exhausted, sweat dripping from her forehead. Max has his knees on Esther's arms, and Aaron holds her legs. He feels revolted by her flesh, sees the blotched, bruised skin, the veins and swellings. He feels nauseous.

Esther's eyes fix on him. "YOU!" She hisses. "It's your fault! You've made me this way! Since the day you were born I've been suffering and sacrificing for you, working myself to the bone, trying to get you to make something of yourself. You have made me this way! YOU! Do you think I don't want to be a normal mother and housewife? I can't! Not with a son like you, never! You block me at every turn! You have to have this, have to have that, music, instruments, lessons, you want everything except what makes sense, to become something respectable, a doctor, a lawyer. YOU made me this way, you worthless little bastard!" Then the strength goes out of her and she begins to weep. Aaron feels a deep sadness welling up; the sound of his mother's tears seem to be those of a heartbroken child. For a moment it is possible not to hate her.

When he glances at his father, he sees something there that he has never seen before: pure rage. It is a rage that has been kept locked in a deep cellar of Max's psyche, a rage that he fears to let loose, for in letting it loose it might wreak havoc, it might maim and destroy, it might kill, it is capable of absolutely anything. Max is breathing hard, gulping for air and shaking all over. He swallows, with difficulty. He swallows again. Then he visibly takes conscious charge of his breathing. He holds the next intake of breath. He lets it out slowly. Again, he inhales, more slowly still, exhales. And a third time.

He is back in control of himself. He has taught himself this breathing trick decades ago, and he has never needed it so much as he needs it now.

Aaron understands that in himself just such a rage exists. It must also be kept locked carefully in a dark region of his psyche. In this he is like his father. He has absorbed some of his father's tricks. He hides his rage under a mask of mildness.

* * *

It seems, for a while, as if Sarah has also discovered a new life. Soon her old habits follow her to the new location. Before long she is picking up rides from the school parking lot, running with a fast crowd, an elite of super-rich boys with gaudy cars and the girls willing to pay the price of being in their company. In but a few months Sarah is infamous as the girl who will give a hand job in the back seats of cars. She has discovered that masturbating her male companions is infinitely safer and more hygienic than any alternative. It has the added benefit of neutralizing them quickly. After their orgasms they are like sleepy house cats.

It is the Year of Masturbation. Aaron's relationship with Katherine has proceeded to the petting stage. His arousal in her company is so painful and explosive that some release is necessary. Katherine is saving herself for marriage. If begged sufficiently, she will masturbate Aaron, with a mixture of greed and reluctance. She makes him feel guilty about it, about asking for it, relishing the power it gives her.

Aaron never gets farther than stroking the hairs of Katherine's pubic region. When he tries to find that moist inner sanctum with his finger, she squirms away.

"If you marry me, you can do all you want, but not until."

They are on the school bus, sitting in the very last seat. Aaron groans with passion. His balls ache so badly he can barely move. If he gets up to walk he will look as if he is straddling a horse. He givesKatherine a look that attempts to convey his helpless pain.

"All right," she says primly, "put your coat over us." Aaron offers her a wad of kleenex from his pocket and Katherine balls it into her palm. Under the coat, she unzips Aaron and takes his throbbing penis out. With a few deft strokes she brings him to orgasm as he muffles his cries of pleasure, his fluid squirting into the tissue paper.

"There, that's done with," she says. She has a plastic bag ready, into which to throw the kleenex. Katherine looks out the window to see how near they are to her stop. "Almost home," she observes with relief. "I need to wash my hands."

Chapter Sixteen

Fugue

Mark is sharpening his pencil in school one day when he has his first "episode". The pencil sharpener is located on the long tan-colored heater vent that runs the length of the room, just below the windowsills. Outside, fall is settling over the world, its wind carrying the last petals off the flowers, ripping apart white dandelions as the approaching winter's breath sweeps the vacant lot next to the school.

It is mid-afternoon, and the sun sends a rich but enfeebled orange light through the clouds. Everyone can feel a thunderstorm coming. Perhaps a tornado warning will be posted. The big thunderheads always generate a sense of danger and excitement. School has been in session several weeks. Halloween decorations are going up in the rooms and corridors, and Mark is getting that eerie mystic chill that preceedes his favorite holiday.

His hand continues to crank the pencil sharpener, but his mind is lost and gone wherever the wind has taken it. The next thing he knows, he is waking up in a hospital bed with stiff white sheets. He has not heard his teacher say, in her acrid voice, "Mark, will you stop dreaming at the pencil sharpener and let Sally use it?" He is not aware of the fact that he has wheeled on poor Sally Klein and attacked her with the pencil's finely sharpened point, poking her above the breastbone, frightening her so much that she and a dozen other girl students remain hysterical for hours afterward. He is not aware of any of these things. His mind is in the mystic October fugue until his awakening to the crinkle of sheets and the strong hospital smell.

His eyes clear and he discovers his father next to the bed, and there, in the corner, in the shadow she always carries with her, is his mother.

Max can not help but ask the question, though he knows it will only generate more questions. "Mark, why did you do that to the Klein girl?"

"Do what? I didn't do anything. How did I get here?" He is frightened. His eyes have a hunted look.

"You don't remember?"

"N..no, I don't remember anything except...let's see...I was sharpening my pencil at school, and then....." his voice trails off. "Did I fall asleep or something?" He wails desperately. "Did I faint?"

Then the shadow with his mother in it speaks. "He's a monster, Max. He has no guilt. Listen to him lie through his teeth."

This is too much for Max. "Shut up, Esther, or just leave the room. You, of all people, should know better."

Mark finally wakes up. The previous sentences have still been part of his dreams. He has never heard his father speak this way to his mother.

"You were sharpening a pencil," Max says patiently, "and you turned around and stabbed Sally Klein with the point, so that blood came, and she had to go to the hospital and get a shot. Now you tell me you don't remember any of that?"

Tears spring to Mark's eyes. "I didn't do it on purpose. I'm sorry. I don't remember." But, in fact, he does remember. He remembers being aware of Sally Klein standing behind him, and of having an overwhelming urge to scare her so badly she will wet her pants. He really wants to scare someone, and Sally has called him a 'putz', which is a word he has never heard before but knows it is not something nice. After that, it all goes blank. Or…not quite blank. He remembers a savage glee. It was fun scaring Sally Klein!

Max's own anger melts with his son's tears. That is all he needs to know: whether his son acted through malice or through sickness. He has always tried to distinguish between the two, though the effort leads him into subtle ethical and emotional minefields. Without that distinction he can never have endured his wife, or accepted situations in his life that would otherwise have been unconscionable. Knowing that human beings are often driven to do things beyond their control keeps the wellsprings of his heart open.

He takes Mark's hand. "It's all right, Mark. You did something terrible but you had a blackout. Let's just see if we can prevent it from happening again."

Esther and her shadow rise from their chair in the corner. "He's a monster, a beast. Just trying to see what he can get away with." Her voice drips the word 'monster', serpentine and elongated.

"I think I told you to be quiet," Max says through his teeth.

* * *

The new psychiatrist, Dr. Potts, is speaking from behind his imposing antique desk. He is tall, thin, sandy-haired, in his mid-forties, with the thoughtful enigmatic air seemingly endemic to psychiatrists. The freckles around his nose and slight sunburn indicate a recent ski vacation in Switzerland. He steeples his fingers and taps their tips together as he speaks.

"Mark can be very dangerous, both to himself and to those around him."

Max is thinking, God, I'm sick of psychiatrists, but I don't know what else to do.

"I think it's mandatory," the doctor says, " that we keep Mark hospitalized for a while, for observation and to administer a full battery of tests. We need to know if there's a neurological cause for this behaviour before we can proceed to other treatment modalities."

Max rubs the little ridge of flesh above his nose between thumb and forefinger, squeezing until his eyes feel a useful pressure. He has been picking up Esther's migraines recently. "I have to go along with you, doctor, I don't see any alternative. Mark's a good boy at heart, he doesn't mean to do what he did. He just blacked out. What do you call that? How do you treat it?"

"It's too early to diagnose, but my best guess, knowing your family history, is that he's a very angry and hostile boy. He represses the material of his violent thoughts and actions, things that he's ashamed of, then fugues, that is, blacks out, so as not to have to confront them. That way he evades responsibility, and it becomes morally permissible to take out his rage on someone."

"I know what a fugue is, doctor. So what you're saying is that this disorder might be of a moral nature, might simply indicate a weakness of character."

"That's an interesting way of putting it. We don't really know, do we, where character ends and illness begins." Dr. Potts is used to speaking over people's heads. As long as he sounds complex and authoritative, he can do anything.

Meanwhile, he needs to address this surprisingly astute man seated in front of his desk. "Mr. Kantro, every psychiatrist has to develop his own techniques. The field is still so new, there's so little data. We're not the same people we are in Freud's time. We don't have the same problems. Procedures change every week. What's correct at this moment can be criminal in a month's time."

"That's what I'm afraid of," Max says. "So how do I know that your treatment of my son and my wife may not include some of these so-called future criminal practices?"

Dr. Potts goes frosty. "You're welcome to go to any psychiatrist you chose. You've tried a few others, I know. Since you're here, I will appreciate a modicum of trust on your part. I'm not a butcher, I don't like the use of electro-shock or powerful antipsychotic medication. Right now, our priority is to keep your son calm and await developments. He's fortunate not to be in serious legal trouble. I know what your family's been through. Your oldest daughter seems well enough adjusted. The middle children at least have artistic pursuits through which they can channel their energies and frustrations. Does Mark have any such channel?"

"Not yet. He's very curious, but he hasn't developed any great interest, other than a fascination for weapons. And this, we can do without."

"Perhaps his intellectual curiosity will lead him to something more healthy. So far, from the tests I've administered, I regard him as a potential sociopath."

"A sociopath? A person without empathy or conscience?"

"That's close enough, " the doctor agrees.

"Never Mark, doctor. Sick, troubled, enraged with his mother, angry at the world, yes. Without a conscience? Never." As he speaks, Max isn't sure he believes himself. He desperately wants Mark to be a good but misguided kid. He ransacks his memory for signs and indications, for a moral nature that lives at Mark's center. If he is painstakingly honest with himself, he finds a cold, distant child who has a passion for lethal devices. He has begun taking Karate lessons, and Max encourages this as a potential discipline, as an interest that can become something to lead Mark out of his isolation.

It can also make him more dangerous.

Chapter Seventeen
June 1965: Journey to New York

Interstate Forty is less than two miles from Aaron's house. He takes a bus to the off ramp and then stands there, like an innocent lamb, his thumb sticking out. At his feet are his trumpet and a duffel bag full of clothes. In his back pocket is a wallet containing two hundred dollars.

Three days ago he was a high school student. Now he is an aspiring jazz musician on his way to New York City. It does not occur to him that there are flaws in his strategy, that he is unprepared, that his mastery of music is insufficient, his experience almost non-existent. He believes in his talent. He has spent nine years practicing and studying, listening to great jazz musicians like Charles Mingus and Miles Davis. He knows he can play. All he has to do is get to New York and present himself to his hero.

For the past two years, Aaron has been absorbed in the controversial jazz of Avian Coulter. Aaron's classmates are now worshipping The Beatles and The Rolling Stones. Aaron's idol is this man who is obscure to all but the most sophisticated jazz fans.

Coulter has overthrown the entire structure of jazz simply by dispensing with the pianist and the obligatory chord changes. The saxophonist writes touching and witty songs, then improvises according to the nature of the song itself rather than the chords. It is a step of great audacity. Musicians with less imagination will be lost without the architecture of chords. Coulter's wit and boundless inventiveness have earned him a worldwide reputation as a genius. It has also polarized the world of contemporary music between critics who regard him as a charlatan and critics who regard him as a messiah.

The music is pure revelation to Aaron from the very first note. It opens a pathway towards his individuality. He wants desperately to find Avian Coulter and present himself as a student, a friend, perhaps even a potential colleague.

Big cars full of families heading for vacation whizz by indifferently. The midwestern sun beats down, causing the sweat to form at Aaron's hairline. Road grit sticks in his hair and mixes with the sweat, so that it runs down his face, brown and dusty.

For almost half an hour, Aaron stands there futilely waving his thumb. He tries to make eye contact with drivers, but that doesn't work. He tries looking away from the drivers, and that doesn't work. He never thinks about giving up. He will stand there all day and all night, until someone gives him a ride.

Finally, an old beat-up Ford woody station wagon wheezes to a halt twenty feet down the ramp, then backs up. The driver leans toward the passenger side window and gestures.

"Get in, man! I saw the instrument case, that's why I stopped. What you got in there, trumpet? Alto sax?"

Aaron grips the handle of the door, which comes away in his hand. The driver laughs and pops the door from the inside.

"I just bought this thing yesterday for twenty five bucks. I don't know everything that's wrong with it yet."

Aaron sits on an exposed spring. The driver reaches into the back seat and tosses Aaron a cushion. He places it under his rump and finds a comfortable way to arrange himself.

Puttering on a bad muffler, the station wagon grudgingly accelerates to insert itself into traffic. The driver turns to Aaron. His eyes are blue and maniacally bright. He has short wavy red hair that tops a long aesthete's face. "I'm Greg Barnes," he says. Then he points to instrument cases in the back of the wagon. "Double Bass and electric bass. Got a rock and roll gig in New England, and, tell the truth, I don't give a fuck if I get there or not. I just want to drive, man, drive. I just read 'On the Road', you know, Kerouac's book? You read it yet? Great fucking book. I scored some weed down in the projects this morning and I got some black beauties and some benzos so I figure I'm set for just about everything except somebody to drive for me when I'm too fucked up."

Miracle miracle miracle, thinks Aaron, wiping his face with his shirt tail.

It takes the boys two weeks to reach the vicinity of New York City. This agonizing pace is due to marijuana and youthful fecklessness. The car breaks down almost daily. It runs out of gas frequently. There is a crack, a leak, a faulty pump, something prevents the old woody from functioning on a full tank. Fill up the fifteen-gallon tank and half hour later the gauge reads one quarter. It is a mystery. It is also a miracle that the boys haven't been incinerated in a ball of flame.

Greg is arrested twice on traffic violations and Aaron's money quickly disappears into the maw of bail and roadside bribes.

It is raining when they hit the Jersey Turnpike. Aaron is at the wheel and tosses a quarter into the receptacle and passes through. Then a series of tollbooths loom up at them as if each is a gate to Oz. There is no money! The boys dig frantically in seat crevices for change but there isn't enough. Aaron barrels through the tollbooths without stopping. The sound of bells follows them. There are four more booths before they reach the Lincoln Tunnel. Aaron drives through each of them, waiting for red lights to blink, waiting for the cops.

They get into the Lincoln Tunnel without attracting a trail of police cars. It is eight fifteen in the morning. The traffic is more sluggish than a snake digesting a rat. The Woody belches about halfway through the tunnel. There are hundreds of cars ahead of them, hundreds behind. The Woody is out of gas.

There is pandemonium. Motorists behave as if Aaron and Greg are personally responsible for destroying the business and social fabric of Manhattan. In a few minutes a tow truck from the Tunnel Authority comes along a special access lane. The boys are unceremoniously hooked up and towed to the pay booth, where, of course, they have no money. A contemptuous city employee questions them as to their destination, makes them fill out a promissory note to pay the City of New York a dollar fifty, and puts two gallons of gas into the car.

They have arrived. They drive about, lost in the immensity of the great city. Greg has a cousin who owns a seedy hotel on West Eighty Fourth Street. Heading in the general direction of uptown, they make it to Sixty Eighth and Amsterdam.

The Woody erupts with a dense cloud of smoke and coughs to its last halt. They abandon the car with little sentiment but less regret. Laden with instruments and duffel bags, they stand like idiots on the sidewalk.

Their destination is a run down flop called The Hotel Majestic. It belongs to one of Greg's distant cousins. A month's rent has been paid in advance at a substantial discount. The two young musicians, sitting on their pile of instruments and belongings, manage to panhandle enough change to pay a cab to take them the final half mile to their "suite" at The Hotel Majestic.

Chapter Eighteen

The Truth Is False

Aaron swallows his pride, phones home and gets his dad to wire another two hundred dollars. Nothing in his fantasies has prepared Aaron for the immense and charged reality of New York City. The hotel room looks out onto brick walls. It funnels sounds up to him, and he spends the nights listening. In the dark, echoes bound and rebound through the glass and brick canyons, sirens and taxi horns. Fragments of music and television shows escape like odors from briefly opened windows and doors. Hearing it, he feels closer to the secrets of jazz, the skewed voicings of Mingus, the elegance of Ellington. He can close his eyes and see richly dressed people emerging from beautiful cars, going into clubs. He can be closer to the wildness of Coltrane, imagine the saxophonist sitting atop a Pandora's box, keeping the lid from opening by a lofty effort of will. All jazz has this in common: an element of massed human striving, a crying for release, collectively incarnating above the skyline like a spirit materialzing out of the energy below. It is personified yearning, arching high through the night. Here, in the scudding bebop foam, the city is like a single acoustic horn focussing its random sounds until they become music. All these sounds and ideas populate Aaron's night, drawn up into the flue created by the three wings of the hotel, whose courtyard Aaron can see, eleven stories down, filled with bits of trash and broken glass.

Lester Young? Bird? Fats? Eric Dolphy? Dead musicians walk the streets, breathing their legacy into the living, praying to be heard above the cacophony of the millions scrambling to survive.

These uncommon people turn the city into beautiful sculptures of sound. They are often doomed, destroyed by the effort required to fit their visions into the world that spawned them.

The next day Aaron begins his search for the greatest of all his jazz heroes, Avian Coulter. The phone book has several A. Coulters. None will admit to being the jazz musician. Aaron goes downtown, into the Lower East Side, to a well-known jazz club called Slug's Saloon. He gets off the subway at Washington Square, to walk though the Village. Sitting on the fountain are several dilapidated old drunks. One of them sees Aaron and jumps up. He stinks of booze and his beard looks like something has crawled out of the subway tunnel and attached itself to his face..

"I'm talking to you, boy!" The man falls into step with Aaron, matching him stride for stride.

"I'm talkin' to you!" He puts his hand on Aaron's arm, so that Aaron stops. The man gestures to his pals, who sit at the lip of the fountain, indifferent. "Look at this white boy!" he demands. "Look at his eyes. God put some blessin' in this boy's eyes!"

Then, whatever battery pack has been animating the old wino, it seems to lose power, and he shuffles back towards his drinking buddies.

Slug's Saloon is closed. Outside, there is a black man wearing a woven Moroccan skullcap. Aaron conquers his shyness. "You don't know where Avian Coulter is playing, do you? Or where I might find him?"

The man scratches the bottom of his lip with his index finger. "Who the fuck are you?"

For a moment Aaron doesn't know what to say. He has come this far, he has exposed himself to every kind of weird adventure to get to this place.

"My name's Aaron Kantro. I'm a musician. I came a long way to hear Avian Coulter."

This is apparently acceptable. "Well shit," the man says, "he ain't playing nowhere. He's taking a sabbatical. That's what everybody's calling it. A sabbatical. He around here somewhere." The man sees someone farther down the street. His eyes move off, then his body follows.

Aaron has been growing a beard, to look older. He needs to get into clubs. He needs to be something other than a suburban white kid. He buys a Moroccan cap at a crafts store on Bleeker Street. He walks the city, stopping at Fifty-second Street on his way back to the hotel. Nothing is left of the glory days of jazz. The ghosts of bebop now compete with flashy disco clubs and jewelry stores.

That evening he goes to the Village Vanguard to see Sonny Rollins. Greg is already hooked up for his gig with Bob Wisdom and the Sages, rehearsing and getting ready for the tour. Aaron launches himself, alone, into the gaping maw of the city.

He is ridiculously early. Hardly anyone is in the club. Aaron takes the opportunity to talk to the bartender, whose name is Philip.

"Avian moves around a lot," the man says cryptically, "but you can try this address."He writes down a number on West Fifth Street. Aaron is elated.

He hears Sonny Rollins. He is mesmerized by the drummer, Billy Higgins, who plays with his tongue hanging out, smiling mightily, inventing endless rhythm on a minimal drum kit, no more than bass drum, high hat, snare and cymbal. It is an act of defiance. "See," he is telling the world, " I don't need all the fancy bullshit. I'm not some rock drummer sitting behind ten cymbals, eight tom toms, four high hats and two bass drums. I'm a drummer. I'm a musician. I can play on the top of a bucket and be great."

Aaron feels like his skin is a cloak, and someone has just taken two hands to the seam of it, and opened it wide.

When he leaves the club, an unexpected feeling suddenly overwhelms him. He feels alone, and terribly vulnerable. It is two thirty in the morning. He knows himself to be an innocent lamb, walking among wolves. The sheer magnitude of the city, his insignificance in it, sits with unaccustomed weight on his mind. He has always pumped himself up with ideas of his special destiny, of his imagined importance. Here, as the sophisticated jazz aficionados stream from the club behind him, he feels flattened, tiny. All these people have homes and friends. They disappear into cabs, laughing, talking jazz talk and holding hands, kissing. There is no one, other than Greg, in this entire city who cares about Aaron Kantro, who knows of his existence. His only link to this megalopolis is an abstraction, Avian Coulter. Ridiculous! A slip of paper in his pocket with what is probably a useless address. The street life is active around him. Huddled tormented looking people wait in doorways. Junkies pray for their powdered savior. A pair of tall, gaudily dressed homosexuals eye him with an acquisitive air, and as they begin to approach him, Aaron quickly moves off.

* * *

Afraid to face the dangers of the subway at this hour, Aaron flags a cab. Back at the hotel, he is tempted to wake Greg. He needs to talk. He thinks of Katherine. He aches for her. She is in Wisconsin, at a religious summer camp. A thousand miles and another world away. The passion is fading. It is time to admit to himself that he has moved out of Katherine's sphere and is now moving into a new, and as yet undefined, sphere of creative endeavor.

Greg is leaving in the morning. The band is going to Boston, then Providence, and on throughout New England. He will return to New York in a month, and then do the recording sessions. After that, things are up in the air. It depends on whether Bob Wisdom can keep getting gigs. And whether Greg can tolerate the music.

Alone on the foldout bed in the living room of the three room "suite," Aaron is aware of more than the glorious jazz whispers, the romance of his heroic visions. He hears now in the roar of the city the threat of imminent violence. He knows there are ten thousand aspirants like himself who come to the city every day, looking for success, only to drown in the sea of faces.

In the morning he looks at the slip of paper with the address that he'd been given by the bartender Philip. He is no longer sure of himself and his right to impose upon this man, Avian Coulter, who feels so close to his spirit, yet now seems so unattainable. He sits for an hour with Greg and says his goodbyes. They eat scrambled eggs and look out at the brick facades and the wired windows.

"What am I doing, man? I've got two hundred bucks, no job, nothing, and I'm looking for a musician who is considered a madman by most of the world, and a god by a few weird people. He isn't gigging. He's got ten record albums that everybody hates and calls useless noise."

Greg snaps his suitcase shut. "Don't sweat it. You're sixteen years old. Whatever happens, you've already done something amazing. You took this huge risk, made this big adventure. You'll find him; I know you will. And he'll love the way you play. Here, you wanna help me with this?" He opens the case for the bass fiddle. Aaron holds it upright while his friend places it into the velvet lining and fixes the bow into its discreet box. "Hey, I wanna leave this with you." He holds out a matchbox. "I just got it last night. Michoacan. It's grown by a tribe called the Tamuto. They've spent the last thousand years perfecting their farming techniques. They live in the inaccessible mountains and pack this stuff down on mules. They fertilize it with fossilized seashells that are all over the place from when the mountains were at the bottom of the sea, a million years ago."

Aaron takes the box. "You're full of shit, Greg, but you're never boring." The door buzzer honks.

"That's Wisdom. Egotistical motherfucker. By the time this gig is over I know I'm going to hate him. Maybe you'll get me a gig in the Avian Coulter Quintet. That will be refreshing after a month of Mustang Sally. Shit."

Their eyes can not meet. They are embarassed to feel love for each other and be unable to acknowledge it. "See you, man," Aaron says.

"You too. Hope you're still here when I get back."

"

Well, thanks for the hotel room." Greg has paid his cousin for a month. Aaron has the remainder in which to make something happen.

Aaron eats lunch in a coffee shop and takes the subway back to the Village, then walks east. He feels exposed and uncertain. The area is so run down, papers are blowing in the street, filthy three and four story brick buildings line the neighborhood. They look like empty facades with boarded up windows and peeling painted woodwork. There is a mix of people from many classes and social strata. There are young, white, hip looking longhairs, walking purposefully, books in hand, probably students at NYU or Columbia. There are also shivering, drooling derelicts, scheming junkies, old men and women sitting on chairs in front of their tenements, speaking Russian and Yiddish.

The address he has been given is in a building much like the others. A flight of concrete steps leads up to a locked glass door. There are rows of buzzers beneath mailboxes, with names written on white paper across individual slots. There is no Avian Coulter, but Aaron buzzes the apartment anyway. The occupant is irritated, and is not the jazz musician. Aaron's disappointment is palpable.

He walks the length of Manhattan, back to the hotel room. He thinks with bitter longing of Katherine. Their plans have diverged, their futures no longer intertwined in his carefully wrought fantasy. She will be in college come fall. And he..he doesn't know where he will be. Maybe he should go to college after all. The security of another four years in the womb looks very tempting at this moment.

No....he is committed to this solitary quest. He has to see it through.

A week passes and Aaron makes no headway in finding Avian Coulter. He knows a few more people by name, and has been invited to a jam session. To his embarrassed chagrin, he finds himself out of his depth. It is easy to feel superior to his school chums back home, but when he finds himself in the company of seasoned jazz veterans, he flounders in the speed and complexity of the music. On trumpet, he can play nothing of emotional consequence. On drums he feels awkward and tight. The musicians are friendly and encouraging, no one ridicules him. Upon returning to the hotel, he spends the next three days practicing furiously. He buys a practice drum pad and goes over his rudiments with stubborn intensity. He runs exotic scales on the trumpet until he is flying around the key signatures.

The city is wearing thin. He has seen all the museums, visited every tourist site, gone to all the jazz clubs, coffee houses and bookstores. He is too young to be at ease with the Village beatniks and folkie hipsters, too white to penetrate to the core of the black music scene.

Maybe I should go visit Katherine at her camp in Wisconsin. Oh shit, that will be a hit, won't it? Jewish ex-sort-of-boyfriend crashes Baptist summer camp. Maybe I should go home, and work in the deli until the next semester of community college starts. Oh man, have I made a mess of things. I can go home and play in bands for fraternity parties. That sounds great, doesn't it? Shit. What am I going to do?

He forces himself to leave the hotel, thinking to see a matinee in one of the midtown theatres. There are Samurai flicks on Forty Second Street. That will pass the afternoon.

Aaron pays for tokens and gets on the subway. Shortly, he emerges at Forty Second, in a heavy crowd. He scans the faces around him, searching for the knit hats, the black faces of musicians. Ahead of him, thirty or forty feet, is the retreating back of a man burdened with too many instrument cases. They are slipping from under his armpits, sliding down his side, flute cases, oboe cases, a saxophone case in each hand. Aaron runs forward, to offer his help.

"Excuse me," he says, "it looks like you've got more axes than you can deal with. Do you need a hand?"

The man stops and turns around to take a look at Aaron. Seeing a young man with what looks like an innocent and trustworthy face, he smiles. "Sure. You're just in time. My arms are about to fall off."

The man has a face that is familiar to Aaron.

"Hey, you're Avian Coulter!" he stammers, his heart suddenly beating wildly.

"That's right. You know my music?"

They are like an island in a flowing crowd that parts to pass around them.

"Oh yes, I've been listening to every one of your albums since they started coming out."

Coulter hands Aaron two cases. He is short, lean, with a full beard and eyes that are startlingly intense in a face the color of slightly creamed coffee. His voice is soft, and a pronounced lisp gives it an effeminate sound. Aaron has expected something completely different. It takes him a few moments to absorb the man behind the album cover photographs.

"I have to be in the studio in ten minutes. It's a couple of blocks from here. Do you mind?"

"No, of course not." Aaron walks at Avian Coulter's side and they resume their journey. Despite

Aaron's bashfulness, words come of their own accord from his mouth.

"I came here to thank you. I don't want to intrude on your privacy, but it's important for me to express what your music has done for me, to tell you how much it's freed me to find my own music."

Coulter grins wryly. "That's the best thing I've heard this year. At least I've done somebody some good. Thanks. Thanks a lot. Sometimes it seems like I'm just playing for nobody. What's your name, anyway?"

"Aaron Kantro. I play trumpet, drums, a little piano. Do you think it will be all right if I come to one of your rehearsals sometime? I won't get in the way."

"I don't see why not. Ain't playing much with groups these days. Just composing and taping. Give me a call sometime soon and I'll see what I can arrange. Got a pen? This is the studio, right here. It's my last album with Atlantic. I'm doing some overdubbing, finishing touches, polishing it up, you know?"

Aaron fishes a pen from his shirt pocket and copies Coulter's number.

"Thanks, Mister Coulter. You don't know how much I appreciate it."

"Call me Avian, please. Only cops and prosecutors call me Mister Coulter."

They shake hands and the musician takes his instruments and disappears into the building.

Aaron sees nothing for the rest of the day but Avian Coulter's face, as he has turned to Aaron on Forty Second Street. Of all the crazy coincidences!

He calls the musician the following day but there is no answer. He tries again the next day with the same result. He isn't worried. Avian Coulter has been open, friendly and accessible.

Suddenly his outlook on New York has changed. If fate can pull such a strange trick, there must be a reason to stay. He is filled with visions of some special angelic task force, whose job it is to oversee his destiny, to nudge him subtly through a sequence of events that will lead to the ultimate flowering of his genius.

He reaches Coulter on the third day after their meeting. After six rings the saxophonist ansswers, his voice slightly cobwebby, as if he has been sleeping.

"Hi, this is Aaron Kantro. Remember from Forty Second Street? I hope I didn't wake you."

"Oh sure, man. How you doing? I have to get up anyway..what time is it? One O'clock? Time to get moving. What can I do for you?"

"I was wondering if I can pay you a visit in the next day or two, maybe bring my horn...." Aaron's shyness and awe make the words difficult to force through. He is trying to step into this stranger's life so baldly.

"Let me think for a minute, what my schedule is," Coulter says. He sneezes four times. "Scuze me. I'm allergic to New York....hell, why don't you make it today. I'm doing some stuff with the tapes I made yesterday, here in the apartment. How about four oclock?"

"Fantastic. I really don't know why you're bothering with me. You must have hundreds of people breathing down your neck all the time."

Coulter laughs. "I got people breathing down my neck, but they aint' fans. Forget it, man. If I don't help younger players, pretty soon there won't be any more jazz. It's part of the job. I got a responsibility to cats like you. Let me tell you something. A jazz musician's life ain't like no movie star's. Nobody knows Avian Coulter from Black Adam."

Shaking with eagerness, Aaron packs his horn and boards the subway at three thirty. Coulter lives on Sixth Street on the Lower East Side. It is difficult for Aaron to imagine such a famous jazz musician living in such dilapidated circumstances. His naivete has been a wonderful defense against the realities of being a creative person. It is now, slowly but painfully, being peeled away.

Running the gauntlet of panhandlers and addicts, he finds the address without difficulty. It is a narrow grey building with a broken window on the first floor and a graffito saying "SPIDER" that shows a large zebra-striped tarantula just above the boarded up basement window. There is no lock on the entrance. The stairs are treacherous and ill smelling.

Aaron climbs three flights and finds Apartment 3C and knocks. There is no answer. He knocks again. He knocks for five minutes. There is no sound from inside, no response. Finally, a man in the apartment across the hall opens his door just a crack and says, "He's gone. He left an hour ago."

Feeling an agony of disappointment, Aaron leaves a note on Coulter's door.

"I was here at four o'clock. If you have the time or the desire to bother with a young stranger, please call me at this number....."

Descending the stairs, Aaron doubts he will ever hear from the man. He is hurt. He would be angry if he knew how, but it is difficult for Aaron to be angry.

A gloomy day passes. Aaron waits in the hotel room, wanting the phone to ring.

He is still asleep at eleven oclock the following morning when the telephone's bells come like chariots through his dreams. He does not want to wake up. The bells ring again, springing up like a forest of giant mushrooms. Towering over Aaron's head, they are bastions of fantasy and pleasure. His eyes open. He is lying on his side, staring without recognition at the knit pattern on his sweater, draped over the chair across the room. The phone rings once more. Aaron reaches out to pull the plastic eighth note to his ear. "Hello" he croaks.

"Hello," Avian's distinctive voice echoes. "Aaron?"

"Yes." Aaron is fully awake now.

"I'm sorry about the other day. Something really important came up and it grabbed my mind so much that I forgot about you. That's the truth. I'm very embarrassed."

Gratified, Aaron instantly forgives his hero. "That's okay, things like that happen. At least you're honest about it."

"Let's try again today," Coulter suggests. "I have to split for an appointment around four thirty, so maybe you can get here at one. Okay?"

"Fine, I'll be there," Aaron affirms.

* * *

It seems imperative, in adapting to New York City, to grow a set of psychic callouses. Aaron reflects upon the changes that have overtaken him in so short a time. He is developing the ability to shut things out: sights, sounds, the constant intrusion of machines and of other human beings. On the most routine journey onto the streets of Manhattan, Aaron feels as if he is crossing the circles of Hell. Poverty, decay, despair, every perversion, every misery of the human spirit parades before his senses. There is unbelievable opulence and comfort, surrounded by badlands of ghetto. Never before has Aaron seen the city as a prison. But now, after so short a time, he is becoming jaded to the cries of the other inmates.

Up the three flights of stairs again, carrying his horn, through the crying babies and squawking radios, multiple stations adding their ingredients to the sonic stew.

There is a note on Coulter's door. It says, "Aaron, I had to leave for fifteen minutes to run an important errand. Wait for me. There's a good coffee shop on first av. Good place to kill a few minutes. Avian."

This is progress. A note on the door. Maybe he ran out of tape or needed a new pad for his horn. Aaron finds the coffee shop and drinks capuccino for half an hour. When he returns to Coulter's the note is still on the door. He knocks anyway. No answer. Aaron decides to wait a little longer. He walks over to the West Side and looks into the windows of Village clubs. When next he checks the time, forty five minutes have passed.

The note is still on the door. How can his hero, the messiah to his creative mind, be so irresponsible? Unwilling to let his mentor be human, he makes excuses for the man. He walks the streets for another half hour, then returns. This time the note has been taken from the door. Aaron knocks. He hears sounds from within, but there is no answer. Footsteps are clearly audible when he presses his ear to the door, he hears what sounds like drawers being opened and shut. Once more, he knocks, this time vehemently. Steps come toward the door. Aaron steps back, just as a peephole opens, to be filled with an eye.

"Oh. Aaron." Coulter begins to unlock the door. The act consumes time, sucks the marrow from the bones of two minutes. The door is apparently secured with multiple devices. Aaron hears clicks, chains rattling, swiveling of tumblers, the sliding of bolts and a whoosh as the long floor bolt of the police lock slides across the wood of the foyer.

"I'm sorry, Aaron. I didn't think you'd wait around this long. You must think I'm incredibly rude. It's just that my life is sort of chaotic right now. It's hard sometimes for me to keep commitments. What else can I say? I didn't hang you up on purpose. Life's' a struggle, and sometimes you do things you don't want to do, and that you don't like yourself very much for doing."

Aaron has already forgiven him. He shifts his trumpet case into his left hand. "My arm is getting sore from carrying this thing. Do you still have some time?"

"Sure," Coulter gestures him into the apartment. "Why don't I get you something to drink. You want pop? Coffee? A beer?"

"Pop will do fine. We call it soda in St. Louis."

Coulter goes into the cubbyhole of a kitchen. Aaron looks around, slightly confused. Coulter is no pop celebrity but he is a world famous musician. His face appears on magazine covers in Holland, his records sell well in Japan. He is admittedly "far out" but critics write essays about his innovations, and a huge controversy has swirled around his methods during the first years of his career. How can such a famous man be living so marginally? It is a shabby studio, one room with bathroom and kitchenette. Coulter has only folding chairs, to save space, one of which he offers to Aaron. Other chairs are folded flat against the wall. Next to a window looking out onto East Sixth Street, a pallet is raised from the floor by cinderblocks. On the ledge of the window rests a panoply of tape equipment: decks, tapes, piles of patch cords, sheet music. A single chest of drawers is against the inner wall at the foot of the makeshift bed. The entire remainder of the room is filled with a mass of instruments. There is an electric piano, with amp and speaker, numerous reed instruments, a trumpet, a violin, a small set of drums, a bass. Coulter has an entire orchestra at his fingertips.

"Do you play all of these?"

"Just enough to lay tracks on tape." Coulter hands Aaron a Seven Up, then opens a beer for himself. He sits opposite Aaron at a small coffee table, wedged into the foyer, which serves also as a closet.

This is Aaron's first opportunity to study the man whose music means so much to him. His feelings are ill defined as he realizes that Coulter looks a great deal older than his thirty nine years. He looks haggard, there are dark circles under his eyes, as if he has not slept in days. Unwillingly, Aaron senses that the musician's smile comes from politeness, but that something is going on below the surface. He seems distant, his movements are reluctant. His attempts to accommodate Aaron make him even more uncomfortable.

"Listen, Avian....you're being very kind to me, and I'm grateful. But I get the feeling some other time might be better. You say you have an appointment at four thirty and it's almost four, now. I should go."

Coulter's smile fades, and his eyes meet Aaron's. There is a moment of unspoken but penetrating

candor between them. It is a jolt for Aaron, he is abruptly frightened by the suffering that lodges so deeply in the man's eyes, a pain that seems to reach out, quietly but desperately.

"I'm sorry, man. Shit, I must have said 'I'm sorry' a dozen times already. I'm having some problems. I haven't really worked in a year and a half. I can't keep the band together, and things are very tough. You know a musician like myself can be famous all over the world and still starve. If you want to give your life to music, don't expect much in return. It's not a very glorious life. But you're here now, you've gone through a lot to spend some time with me. I can wait about forty five minutes before I have to leave. Let's talk for a bit, and maybe you can play something for me."

Aaron has been praying for just such an informal audition. He is ready to play; he has been practicing like a maniac.

"Tell me about yourself, " Coulter prompts. "You're from the midwest. I'm from Little Rock, which is sort of the Midwest. Sort of. How does a kid as young as you from the suburbs know about music like this? It's really uncommon, you know, you're a very rare young person."

Aaron speaks about himself, his lifelong love of music, his creative evolution. "I guess I thought it was glorious, heroic, even holy, to be a jazz man. I'm afraid I'm getting slapped in the face by reality. Things aren't the way I thought they would be."

Something in the lines of Coulter's face resonates. Aaron can see the music embodied in the features of the flesh. The man's experiences have etched crevices upon his brow, creases running down his cheeks. Briefly, their eyes meet, and Aaron touches upon a revelation, catalyzed by the strange but familiar face of Avian Coulter. The face floats in space before his tunneled vision. The musician's expression conveys a spectrum of emotions, of detailed and persistent suffering and many failures. There is also a note of confidence, a stubborn kind of belief in himself that has enabled him to turn those failures into compelling art. With his tough but sad demeanor, Avian Coulter's look gently but thoroughly demolishes Aaron's fantasies of the jazz life.

Oddly enough, Aaron is no longer frightened or paralyzed with awe.

"You're trying to move pretty fast, you know." Coulter looks bemused as he uses his index finger to wipe a rivulet of sweat from his eyes. "How old are you? Sixteen, seventeen?"

The man's voice has mocking warmth. "You're pushing yourself pretty hard. Slow down a little, take it easy. Prodigies burn out. You don't have to be great yet. You just have to keep practicing. So.....you ready to play something for me?"

Aaron feels a twinge of stage fright, his mouth dries up and his legs feel weak. A vivid terrible memory flashes through his mind. It is the moment of his first trumpet solo before a school assembly, in the fourth grade. His mother has come up to him before his performance and says,

"If you make a mistake I'll kill you."

Of course, he made a lot of mistakes. The solo was a disaster.

He pushes the memory away. He has time to be great. Avian Coulter gave him permission to be himself, to be sixteen.

"Anything special you want to hear?"

"No, just pick it up and go. Warm up a little first. Don't try to prove anything."

Aaron's hand shakes slightly as he fits the mouthpiece into the horn and wriggles the valves. He takes the time to warm up, playing low long tones, trying to get the quaver out of his breath. Still, he can hear his heartbeat in each held note.

Gradually he moves to scales and they get faster as Aaron moves through the chromatic spectrum. Then he passes into more complex combinations, but it is all technical, all just ways of easing himself into something deeper.

He closes his eyes and begins pure improvisation in the leaping polytonal style that owes much to his mentor. He reaches inside himself for emotion. He slows the music and becomes song rather than note. Music is song, music is passion. Aaron knows he has passion; his life is a passion, his survival and creativity is a passion. He wants to echo the wails of the city outside the apartment, the tragic awareness of human life. He needs to relax. His heart will not stop pounding, his lungs will not allow him a full breath of air. But the fear too can be used. Like adding a log to a burning fire, he tosses his fear into the emotional cauldron and lets it flare with the rest of his longings.

At length he feels that he has said enough. He knows he has played well.

He looks with embarrassment and trepidation at Coulter's enigmatic smile.

"Before I say anything, I want to hear you play some drums. You say you're a drummer, right? I want you to play me some brush work. Adjust the kit any way you'd like. Warm yourself up."

Aaron smiles shyly and goes to the little drum set and takes a few moments to move the snare and cymbals into comfortable positions. For some reason, it is easier to drum for Coulter than play the trumpet. He remembers the awesome performance of Billy Higgins playing with Sonny Rollins just a few nights ago. He knows he isn't Billy Higgins or Elvin Jones or Max Roach. But he can play. He sets one brush on the snare and moves it in a circle. Smooth, with the left hand, circling. Then he taps with his right hand, at different places along the circle. Ch..fizzz, the drum says. Ch..fizzz. Aaron listens to the voice of the drum. Ch..fizzz...bop. Ch..fizz..bop. Bat. Then he tries a bass drum bomb. Just boom. And he adds Ch.fizzz to bop and then hit boom. Ch...fizz.Bop Boom. Boom boom. Ch....fizz bop.

Now for the high hat cymbals. Chick chick. ch...fizzz chick. Ch...fizzz chick. . Boom. Bop. Bat Bat. Chick Boom.

Little by little he ties each piece of the drum set into an everchanging but subtle movement of rhythmic circles, that always return to the beat, to one –two- three -four, but stretches the beat like taffy, makes suspense of where and when it will return.

In a couple minutes he has developed a lovely, loose commentary on the history of jazz drumming. He plays a while longer, then stops.

Coulter applauds. His smile is huge, and he breaks into pleased laughter.

Aaron's heart drops with relief.

"That's all right, man." The saxophonist reaches out and slaps his hand, gives him a high five.

"You want me to tell you what I hear?" Coulter asks.

"Of course. Please...."

"Okay. First thing is, you're a drummer. You're a good trumpeter, you got a lot of original shit going on, but you love the drums more. I can feel it, I can hear it. You aint' been playing as long on the drums, but you're a drummer. You need to practice on your speed and do some technique work, but you the real deal and I like the way you play. You got more originality than ninety nine percent of the musicians playing in this town. Don't ever give up on your vision. Music's hard, man. But it's so rare to have originality. Now, I got to say something that might be more difficult for you to hear. And that is that you're too young to know that you're too young. You think you can conquer the world. You're just beginning to find out it ain't that easy. That's okay. You need to live, Aaron. Sixteen is sixteen, and I know Mozart and Tony Williams are both motherfuckers but that's the exception and you don't want to be that great that young. It's important to ripen yourself at a good pace. Experience is what you need. Difficulty deepens your art, experience that might be humiliating or terrifying or exhilirating. It all has to go into your art. There is no way to live but to live. If I get a band together again and you're around in about a year, I will want to hear you. Can you accept that?"

Aaron feels both disappointed and gratified. There is a pain in his heart that nearly brings tears to his eyes. He has been both accepted and rejected. There is no Avian Coulter Quintet. His fantasy has to be reorganized. He has done that before.

"You're right" he says. "I'm a kid from the suburbs, up against the real world for the first time. What I think will be simple is complex, everything is more painful and sordid and frightening. But I'm staying with it. Music is my life. I'll make the best music I can."

A knock sounds at the door. Coulter, who had been relaxed a moment before, jerks visibly and rises to check the peephole. His manner is changed, anxiety is written in the set of his shoulders as he checks out his caller.

Then he relaxes, and begins the unlocking ritual. The visitor is a white man of Coulter's age, sporting a moustache, goatee, turtleneck and sport jacket.

"It is gettin' kind of late," the man says, "Just wanted to see if everything is okay."

"Phil, this is Aaron Kantro. Aaron, Phil Overton."

The name is familiar from jazz records and magazines. Overton is a respected bassist and composer.

"Aaron's been playing for me, Master Phillip," Coulter explains. "Sixteen and the kid's a monster. Trumpet and drums and who knows what else. Eddie Poncet should hear his action. He'd turn purple."

Aaron and Phil shake hands. "When I was sixteen I couldn't read a chart and didn't know A minor from G major. Coming up fast, aren't you?"

Aaron is hugely gratified. Eddie Poncet is winner of DownBeat's Best New Drummer of the Year award.

"Okay, I'll let you guys finish your business here. You'll be over soon?"

Overton casts a sharp glance at Coulter.

"Couple minutes. We'll go over those charts."

The bassist lets himself out.

Aaron replaces his trumpet in his case. "I better get going, I've made you late. Will it be okay if I call you sometime soon, and come back? You've been so kind to bother with me."

"No problem," Coulter says. "I might even set you up with somebody who's looking for a drummer. You got your own kit?"

"Not yet, " Aaron replies, "but that can be remedied."

"Okay, I'll be in touch. See you."

Coulter lets him out. Aaron has set down his trumpet to shake the man's hand. He is so flushed with pleasure and excitement that he forgets to take it with him. He is at the bottom of the stairs when the absence of its familiar weight impinges upon his mind. He turns and climbs the stairs. How his life has changed since he first climbed them, earlier in the day!

His knock on the door brings a shuffling sound from within. "It's me, Aaron. I forgot my horn."

The unlocking operation is again played out. As Coulter admits Aaron he looks ill at ease.

"Sorry, man," Aaron says, "just let me get this thing and I'll be out of your hair." He takes the trumpet and turns to leave. He has to wedge up against the coffee table in the cramped space of the foyer. There is a newspaper spread across its entire surface. As he squeezes past, Aaron's trumpet case is pressed to his abdomen. It slides along the table's edge, pulling at the newspaper until it comes off the table and falls with a rustle to the floor. Aaron mumbles an apology and bends to pick up the printed sheets. Then he freezes. Several items are concealed under the paper. Aaron recognizes them instantly, and in that moment a vast gestalt of assumptions and secure moral ideas come toppling down in his mind like a tower of dominos pushed by a child's mischievous finger.

On the table is a dinner plate containing a hypodermic syringe, a leather strap, a lighter, a spoon and a glassine envelope containing white powder.

Confusion, fear, disappointment surge like breakers against the crags of Aaron's heart.

"I....I didn't mean to...." he begins. What should he do? Back out the door? Run? Never come back?

Coulter quickly shuts and locks the door. He seems to have recovered his wits and gently offers Aaron a chair.

"Sit down," he says in that soft voice of his. "I wish this didn't have to happen. I owe you an explanation, an apology. I don't intend to be the instrument of the destruction of your innocence. Maybe instead I can help you, steer you clear of this shit."

Aaron sits. Coulter sighs and looks at Aaron for a moment, with the drugs and paraphernalia displayed between them. He seems to be deliberating his first words. The situation is like two people being pushed out of an airplane, with only one in possession of a parachute. Avian has the chute. Aaron is falling fast into a world where he doesn't know right, wrong, talent, mediocrity, morality, the permissible, the appropriate. He has come here with what now seems an idiotic assumption: that a famous genius will also be responsible, organized, comfortable....that he will have his shit together.

He knows about junk and jazz. He grew up listening to Bird. He knows the stories about Miles, Philly Joe and Bill Evans. The stories have not been real to him, until this moment.

"Aaron, " Coulter finally intones, tapping his fingertips together, having gone from deliberation to decision. "I'm a heroin addict. You don't have to be afraid of me. I won't ask you to do drugs. If I catch you doing drugs I will personally whup your ass and ruin your reputation as a musician. The fact that I'm an addict does not make me a stereotype, a lurching zombie thief, boosting TV sets from apartments. Smack is a disease that you give to yourself, and, once you've got it, the only medicine to cure the disease is the disease itself. You're constantly reinfecting yourself. It's a ridiculous trap, it's terrible, it's a waste of so much energy. I've tried to stop and I can't. So I find ways to live with myself and this mess I'm in. Are you with me, Aaron? Do you want to leave?"

"I'm okay. It's just such a shock. I've seen the junkies out here, and I don't think much of them, I have to admit. They're pretty disgusting."

"Well, it's too late to spare you shocks, man. You put yourself in the way of them. I'm going to give you another one, right now." With this, Coulter reaches onto the table and begins to set up his injection kit. He rises to get a little water. He dissolves the heroin into the spoon with the water and heats it with the cigarette lighter. He drops a tiny spot of cotton into the spoon. He uses that as a filter and draws the liquid up into the syringe.

He pulls the belt around his arm tight, using his teeth. He hits his upper arm several times with his right hand while making a fist of his left. Aaron notices scar tissue around the skin inside the elbow and a few livid spots. It isn't bad, it isn't a horrible set of tracks. Most of the marks vanish into the creamy brown skin. Still, it takes Coulter a few tries before he finds a place in the muscle of his forearm that will allow the needle to contact a vein. Coulter grunts when a tiny snake of blood floats up into the clear liquid inside the syringe. He draws back on the plunger so that the inside of the cylinder turns all red.

Calmly, deliberately, the musician injects heroin into the vein. The belt loosens as he releases the grip of his teeth. His arms come down onto the table, now relaxed.

A thing occurs to Aaron.

"You've had this dope all the time I've been here. That's where you were, earlier today. I just got right into the middle of your scoring and fixing."

"That's right." Coulter's voice grows even softer. In a few seconds, his face and bearing undergo a complete transformation. The age lines seem to disappear. His eyes take on sparkle and wit, audacity and kindness. He looks ten years younger. He looks, literally, as if he has been Fixed, Healed. It is more shocking than anything else Aaron has seen.

Aaron realizes that all the time he has spent playing, all the last hour and a half, Coulter has been sick and getting sicker.

"You let me come here, interrupt your fix, listen to me play, do all that, even though you're sick, you're in withdrawal, and you must have had the craving so intensely."

"This is true, "Coulter replies, exhaling with relief.

"I don't know how to take that in....it's like you're an addict, but you didn't rush me out of here, you gave me your full attention. There is sacrifice, something noble in that, but up to this point in my life, 'noble' and 'heroin addict' don't go together. Not at all."

Coulter purses his lips, inhales for a long time, then exhales. One hand goes to scratch his armpit, the fingers kneading at the cloth of his t-shirt. A fan in the corner says clop clop as it turns on its relentless axis, fighting the summer heat.

"When I was young, when I was your age," Avian says, "I knew exactly who I was going to be. I was cocky! I knew I could do anything. When you're young you're grandiose. You think you're gonna set the world on fire. But I grew older and the world resisted me. It took about ten years for me to realize that people aren't flocking to me in droves. I have always thought of myself as a genius, but Genius is a stupid word, prone to overuse and hyperbole. I always figured the world will reward me for making beautiful new music. I played the way I wanted to play, and no one gave me a gig, other musicians laughed at me. Can you dig it? Laughed at me!

Okay, so this is gonna be harder than I think, I tell myself. It's gonna take some effort. Problem is, I lack patience. I started to turn into someone I didn't like. I did things that I knew were wrong but I did them anyway. I got married. And I cheated, and that made me feel ashamed of myself.

I started fooling around with drugs and I thought, 'You shouldn't do that, Avian, it's self destructive', and then I'd do it anyway, get loaded, drunk, smoke something. Why can't I do the right thing? That's what I kept screaming at myself. What's wrong with me that I have the judgment of right and wrong yet I can't follow the right? I was getting acquainted with the basic problem of human nature. We aren't just one person, not in our psyches. We're many people and there are two basic people, Mr. Right and Mr. Wrong and you know what? It seems like Mr. Wrong is the stronger. He has the power of the irrational. " Coulter blows on his hands. He has the classic saxophonist's hands. The bottoms of his fingers are flattened where they press the keys.

Aaron struggles to understand. It seems as if Coulter is just warming up, as if he is preaching a sermon.

"The power of the irrational", Coulter says, almost angrily, "always wins in a pitched battle with the rational. We're still primitive animals, my friend. We're not apes straight out of the trees, but we're way too complex and I'm still basically confused about myself. I have a situation where demons are rampaging all through my psyche, leading me astray from my youthful heroic self image. My mother raised me in the church. She taught me right from wrong. I am doing things I know are wrong. I am crushed, I have betrayed myself beyond measure."

Coulter's elbows are on the table. His hands rest on his face so that his eyes above them seem to peer over a fence.

"So I cleaned myself up, I got pure, so to speak. I held down all my appetites, all my desires, all my craziness. I forced myself to behave rationally, even though my impulses were pulling me in the other direction. Oh man, I was torn! The result was that I became paralyzed. My very best was just to stand still and not-sin, to treadmill, avoiding the evil in myself instead of confronting it. In that period I became very smug. I thought I had conquered the beast. What a fool I was! Now I know that the beast is always there, it always rises again, and it laughs when you think you have destroyed it. The beast just goes down the subway tunnel, and you can hold down the manhole cover with all your will power, but it will be traveling down other sewer pipes in your mind, it will gather stronger monsters, more frightening enigmas, more blinded alligators of paradox to join its army. It's like holding back a huge lake of water with a dam made of a few sticks. It finally breaks and all the power of my unconscious comes roaring through me! Oh, hell! The stronger I think my will power is, the more ravenous are the snapping hungers when they burst forth, carried in the waters of my own being."

Coulter makes an inarticulate sound, "Aaach!" His fingers arch and he scratches his temples with his well-kept nails. He catchees Aaron's gaze and observes the way the young man is responding to this flood of words. Then he continues.

"I fought, again and again, until I learned that the beast can't be conquered by willpower. I admitted to myself that I still craved dope. Still have that wild need to assuage my pain the only way I know how. So I had to call a truce between my idea of myself and the reality of myself, the reality I am stuck with. I have to accept everything in myself, without condemnation.

I went nuts! I just let the darkness off its leash, I wanted to see how much dope I could do, how many women I could fuck, how many lies I could tell. And all this time, I'm still trying to get my music across, and I'm still being laughed at. I got so angry, I got mean. I beat on some people, got arrested and did time. Don't ever go to jail, son, don't ever!

By this time I was old enough to be aware of my limitations. I got an appetite for dope. It's a terrible obstacle to a successful life. It's a terrible symptom of a deep pathology in my soul. I was lucky, I found a good teacher, a psychologist who helped me understand that pathologies can be the doorways to deeper understanding of yourself. Your sickness, your darkness, is a vital component to your creativity. What will you understand about people if you've never been in their shoes? How much compassion can you have if you've never been at the same level as the most pathetic vile creature walking the streets of this city? I KNOW I am one of them! I can't ever forget that".

Coulter pauses and rubs his hands around his face in a gentle patting motion. It seems as though he wants to ascertain that he is still all there, that he is alive. He scratches the end of his nose elaborately and sighs.

"I've hurt a lot of people and I deeply regret that. Meanwhile I'm doing the best I can. I have a therapist. I'm preparing to go into serious treatment. I have a date set to enter a rehab place, a gift from a doctor who's a great jazz fan. The idea scares the hell out of me. And I'm really really sorry you got involved with my problems."

Coulter pauses, and the pause grows into a conclusion.

Aaron understands only fragments of what he has heard. He is aware that something unusual has just taken place, that Avian Coulter has delivered a verbal improvisation on a theme that he can't quite comprehend. Not yet.

Aaron works his jaw as if words want to come out of his mouth but they are too large to fit through the opening of his lips. He doesn't know what to say, how to respond. He has been able to play music for the great jazz musician but this is another matter, this is a more intimate opening to his soul. He stalls for a few moments and finally gives in to his own incompetence and just lets himself talk, lets himself say what he is feeling.

"I understand parts of what you say. I've been naive, arrogant, stupid. You're twice my age, you've done things that I can only dream of, you've made great music, you've taken the world by the throat and said 'Listen to me!' and some people have listened."

"At times, that's all I have," Coulter says. "Without music, I would have been in an insane asylum long ago. Dammit, Aaron, it's hard to reach across the years between us, to show you what I mean. You were worried sick an hour ago that I wouldn't accept you. Now it's the other way around. I want you to accept me, Avian Coulter, with the dope habit. I've learned to live with it, to get around it. Nothing will stop me from creating."

Aaron wipes his face with the sleeve of his shirt. It is hot, the air in the small apartment is stifling. "I love your songs," he says. His lips twitch in a shy smile. "I think my favorite is 'Woman Alone'. It has an almost Hebraic quality to it. It sounds like a Jewish Cantor singing one of the psalms. That's a great song, and your solo on the theme, it just makes me want to cry. I can see this woman, sitting at a window, with the breeze blowing a white lace curtain into her face, into her tears. I've never heard such pure emotion in music."

Once again, Aaron forgives his hero for being human. Nothing can change the fact that Avian Coulter has given great music to the world. Nothing else is important. Aaron extends his hand across the table. The older black man takes it in his. They shake on it, sealing an agreement between the generations of jazz.

Chapter Nineteen

1965: Aaron's Footsteps

Avian Coulter has not performed in public in more than two years. When Coulter tells Aaron that he has booked Carnegie Hall for a concert in a few weeks he is surprised. Avian offers him a modest payment for becoming the roadie, go-fer and all purpose utility man for the group.

It gives him a front seat in the making of jazz history. When Avian's first recording was released in 1958, the controversy was overwhelming. The jazz world was split down the middle as if by an axe blow. Avian's style is dismissed as pure hoax. He is accused of having the technique of a five year old, or of a monkey pressing down keys at random. A minority of jazz critics leap to his defense. There are bitter arguments in magazines, shouting matches on radio shows, a fiery brouhaha that leads to the legendary fist fight outside the Five Spot between Leonard Shapiro and Amir Mubarak, two of the world's most influential jazz critics.

None of this hurts Avian's record sales or attendance at his gigs, but the craziness surrounding his music breaks his heart. It is a simple matter to him: he has arrived at this style through years of arduous practice, through mastery of old forms, through thought, intuition and inspiration.

His fourth album is an exposition of so-called "conventional" playing. He plays bop standards. He makes it clear to everyone that he has total mastery of the jazz saxophone, its history and its multiple languages. Critics of all persuasions hail the record as a masterpiece. The world of jazz gradually begins to accept Avian's methods, and musicians begin to show what a pervasive influence he has become.

Aaron clutches the package of sheet music and descends through the circles of Hell as he heads east. Crossing the bowery, he leaves behind the tourists with their cameras, the pizza-slice hawkers and pretzel wagons. The texture of the city changes. Here, he thinks, is the real world. Here is my world. In the fading light he watches people come and go on their desperate missions. To rob and score. To steal, turn tricks, cop dope, and start all over again. On the sides of buildings, peeling posters for old boxing matches are glued on plywood window coverings. There are faded ads for long-defunct restaurants. They make odd juxtapositions: Kid Valencia versus BBQ TAKE OUT.

He reaches Avian's building and climbs the stairs. Up a flight, turn at the landing, up another flight in the opposite direction. From the top of the stairs comes the sound of saxophone, live. Then, along with the sound comes a subtle throbbing. Drums? Yes! Avian has been talking about gathering the Quartet. If that is Eddie Poncet!

Aaron knocks. Avian has only a few locks fastened. He is waiting for Aaron to return.

How does one react when meeting a musical giant, a man whose drumming has penetrated to one's very soul?

Poncet makes it easy. He has a goofy, charming grin, and he rises halfway from the drum chair, extending a hand. He is small, lithe, with a curving moustache framing large horsy teeth. "Hey man," he says. "It's a genuine pleasure. Avian says you're a true friend and an honest man. And you're gonna help us put together this gig."

Aaron is thrilled and embarrassed. "This doesn't seem real. I've got maybe thirty records with you on them. You've recorded with Sonny Rollins, Jackie Mclean, Roland Kirk. It's an honor to meet you."

Poncet's presence is direct, crisp, like his playing. Though he is Avian's age, maybe forty, he has none of the haunted melancholy that makes Avian seem so much older.

Again there is a knock on the door. "That's Donald and Charlie," Avian observes. "They're early. They're only an hour late."

* * *

Three days after the concert the quartet plus Aaron gathers at Avian's apartment to listen to tapes of the event. It is almost impossible to move in the tiny flat. If anyone needs to use the bathroom, or to reach the fridge, the others have to squeeze against banks of equipment, careful not to dislodge anything.

They are quite pleased with themselves. The concert has been a triumph, an event, written up in newspapers and magazines around the world. From the first notes, the audience was enthralled. Aaron, who was helping the recording technician, feels himself to be an intimate part of the proceedings. This is why he has come to New York, this is his jazz nirvana. He knows his own musical abilities need ripening. All he needs to do is practice, pratice, practice. And associate with the finest jazz musicians in the world.

It is eleven o'clock at night. At ten, Avian considerately turns down the volume. The room is fragrant with marijuana smoke. The trumpeter, Donald Plum, drinks steadily from a bottle of tequila. Eddie Poncet produces joints the size of cigars.

Avian is rewinding one of the tapes when a knock sounds at the door. It isn't a code-knock, it isn't "salt peanuts, salt peanuts". Everyone freezes.

Avian begins to rise from his chair when the door explodes inward, locks and all. It hangs briefly from hinges and assorted chains. Then the head of a sledge hammer appears, coming through the wood in the center of the frame. Another blow and the thing falls into the room, knocking over cymbals with a tremendous crash.

T

hree men wade into the room. Two of them are enormous black men, the third is a small fat white man holding a gun. With a brisk wave of his hand, he gestures everyone in the room to move to the bathroom. Paralyzed with fear and confusion, Aaron is rooted to the spot. Everything has accelerated, yet his thoughts move with agonizing slowness. He can not encompass the events happening with such speed in the tiny room.

Poncet plucks at his sleeve, grabs him firmly and propels him and the other musicians toward the tiny toilet cubicle. The black man who holds the sledgehammer stands by the bathroom door, holding it open after they jam themselves in, so they can see and be seen. He holds the heavy instrument by the end of its handle, and waves it around as if it weighs no more than a stick.

Meanwhile the other black man has plucked up Avian by the front of his shirt. Sheet music flies, instruments fall. The movement of the men's bodies in the small apartment brings chaos with each step.

Avian's feet are ten inches off the ground. As his shirt tears in the grip of massive fists, he is knocked sprawling by a swing of an open hand. He falls into the tape recorder, which comes down and shatters. The reels in the cabinet next to it spew forth in an unwinding mess of black and brown ribbon. Avian's tormenter picks him up again. Aaron tries to obliterate everything

from his consciousness.

"I want to forget this before I see it," he thinks. "It's a nightmare and I want to wake up."

His attention is fixed on Avian's face. The musician's features have gone slack with resignation. His eyes are clouded over, and he accepts his fate passively, limp as a doll.

"I thought I told you not to play!" the white man says, as his minion holds Coulter by his shirt collar. The fat little man slaps him with his open hand, back and across and back, and with each blow he repeats, "Not to play, not to play, not to play!"

Then he cocks his fist and with one blow knocks out half of Avian's teeth. The hapless musician lands in a pile of his own broken instruments.

"I PAID you not to play, motherfucker!" The man shouts, and gestures to his helper with the sledgehammer. With a few casual swings, the hammer man wields his weapon and destroys everything else in the room that is still intact: Eddie's drums, Charlie's eighteenth century double bass. With one whack the sledgehammer comes down on Donald's trumpet and twists it beyond retrieval.

Then they are gone, stepping high over the wreckage, kicking things out of their way.

Silence pervades the room. The entire apartment building seems as if it is listening in mingled pity and terror. The city itself seems to come to a momentary lull. There are no sirens in the distance, no accelerating buses, no honking cabs, no giggling fairy hookers passing beneath the apartment window.

Donald sits on the toilet seat, his mouth hanging slack, his eyes unfocused. Aaron is hunched in a corner of the shower, his hands over his ears, tears flowing from him without sound.

Eddie is first to move. He goes to Avian, who lays among his shattered reeds, face bloody. The drummer picks up his friend and carries him tenderly toward the pallet of his bed.

He snaps his fingers at Aaron. "Come on, man, we got to move. Get me some hot water and some rags. Charlie, clear out everything that looks like dope in here. Donald! Call emergency, we need an ambulance. Come on people, move move! We can't sit here like dipshits. Looks like his jaw's broken."

Aaron brings a bowlful of steaming water. He finds some peroxide and a roll of gauze. He is in shock but with Eddie's initiative he begins to think. After giving the bowl and bottle to the drummer, he begins to clear a path through the wreckage to the door.

Charlie bends over Avian, whose eyes are open. As Eddie cleans blood from his face, Coulter's tongue licks feebly at the stumps of his teeth. He says, "Graaah," but can not speak.

"Avian," Charlie says, "I'll hold your stash for you if the cops come. Is it behind the mirror?"

Coulter nods.

"You look like you can use a fix."

Coulter nods again. He smiles a ghastly toothless smile. "mmmfucker," he manages to say.

Charlie disappears and returns a moment later. "You want a snort? This don't seem like a good time to get the works out."

Just give it to me, Coulter's hand beckons. The bassist passes him the envelope. Shaking, Avian dips the wet end of his pinky finger into it and thrusts the heroin up his nostrils. He does that three times. Then he lays back. Eddie tenderly wipes Avian's nose with a Kleenex, then throws the Kleenex into the toilet and flushes.

Aaron has managed to fit the door back onto its hinges. It is nothing but a frame, ridiculous. People are gathering in the hall. A siren sounds.

"One of us will have to wait here, " Aaron says. "Anybody can come through this door, and take anything."

"You volunteering? You know what to say to the cops?"

"We got vandalized by some hoods, we don't know who they are or why they did it except to steal stuff. Avian got hurt and is on his way to the hospital. I don't know which one. I don't know anything at all."

"You got it. Play dumb. The rest of you guys, get the fuck out of here. You're all holding. Take everything with you."

Charlie and Donald head for the fire escape.

Eddie helps Avian to his feet. Holding a bloody cloth to his face, he totters down the stairs with the saxophonist to meet the ambulance.

Aaron is alone in the wreckage. The police arrive ten minutes later. They take Aaron's name, Coulter's name, desultorily write Aaron's description of events. They look in the medicine cabinet, lift the toilet seat and the top of the water cabinet, poke under the foam mattress.

Aaron doesn't know anything. He is a suburban kid hanging out with a jazz musician. After about twenty minutes the police depart. The neighbors peek around the edge of the door, gathering on the landing.

The scene keeps playing itself over and over again in Aaron's memory. From the knock on the door, the sledgehammer coming through the wood, to the expression on Avian's face of deep resignation.

He keeps hearing the words of the fat man. "I PAID you not to play, motherfucker!"

The amazing thing , as Aaron now pieces events together, is that Coulter wasn't surprised. From first to last, he behaved as if this was inevitable.

What the hell is going on? What does it mean?

Aaron will ask Eddie, later. For now, his confusion reigns supreme.

Chapter Twenty

One week later: Aaron's Retreat

Occasionally, Aaron can see the reflection of his face in the car window. When they pass through a small town, or when a truck comes up behind them and flashes its high beams, he can see the vague outline of himself. His eye will be thrown into relief on the glass, as he stares out the passenger window into the darkness. For a moment, when they stop to pay the toll on the Pennsylvania Turnpike, the light from the booth illuminates his reflection completely, and he realizes that he looks like Avian Coulter.

He picked up a ride off the 53rd Street Bridge, and he feels obliged to talk to the driver, a bald portly man in his fifties who teaches anthropology at some small college in Maryland. He is interesting, the hours pass pleasantly, and after a while they fall into comfortable silence. The talk serves to shut out the vision haunting Aaron: Avian's eyes as he slides to the floor, face bloody, teeth scattered.

Now those eyes rise up into the windows' glass whenever there is a bit of light. Even his beard, Aaron realizes, is a copy of Avian's. It is a solid block of hair, sculpted into a rectangle beneath his chin. He has no moustache. His sideburns descend and join the beard, and there is a little tuft of goatee under his lower lip.

He has absorbed an ancient mystery that Coulter elucidates in his music, something of Egypt, or even more ancient Nubian cultures, the sounds and visions of Meroe and Tostamoo. Whatever else Avian might be, there is no denying the power of his genius. He has tapped into the archetypes. His sounds go outside of time to some dimension of gods and spirits.

Mystery, Aaron thinks. Mystery. Yet the word is inadequate to express what I've heard and experienced. Beauty mixed with irony. Pain and the courage to transcend it. Initiation. It is about initiation. Life is initiation.

The driver, Mister Springer, turns on the radio to a classical music station. Aaron is glad to hear Bartok's Concerto for Orchestra. He doesn't know if he can listen to jazz right now, and pop music would be intolerable.

He is almost out of money. He is afraid to stay in New York. It has been too much. The town has opened to him in its way, he is becoming part of things. But he is afraid of the gangsters who control Avian. To watch Avian's torment is excruciating. It is all about heroin. Avian would not have agreed to take money to stop playing publicly if he had not needed it for dope.

He goes to see Avian at the hospital just before hitting the road. His duffel bag is heavy with the records he has bought. He has picked up every wild obscure label's recordings of Cecil Taylor, Albert Ayler, Archie Shepp and Pharoah Sanders.

The man who has pioneered the music lays in a hospital bed with half his teeth gone. He has a serious concussion. His jaw is broken, his eyes are screwy. He can barely talk. He will need a lot of dental surgery, and there is no telling how that will affect his playing.

"Don't worry man, I'll play, "Avian lisps. If he listens carefully, Aaron can understand. "I can write, I can play the violin, there are a thousand things I can do. The dental guy says I can handle reeds in about six months."

In his eyes there is an apology, a subtle emanation, as if he is trying to say, "Sorry kid, for all the shit I got you into."

Eddie is there when he arrives, and they are playing a recording of the Carnegie Hall music on a little tape machine. Aaron walks in and takes a seat. "You saved a recording?"

Eddie nods at Avian. "He stashed alternate tapes all over the place. We have the concert, don't worry. We got it with a Nagra, a nice machine."

A nurse comes in, and Eddie turns down the volume. "Medication time!" she says cheerfully, placing several pills and a paper cup beside Avian's bed. She raises him to a sitting position.

"Are you comfortable? Is there anything you need," She asks, as Avian takes his pills.

"Doin' juth fine." Coulter grins his toothless grin.

When she leaves, Aaron gestures at the empty paper cup. "Are they.....you know.... taking care of you?"

Avian laughs weakly. "Shit, they looked at my tracks, put me right on methadone. My own doctor's making sure they do me right. Rehab's the next step."

That is Aaron's last hour in New York City. When he gets up to go, when he says his goodbyes, Eddie accompanies him down the hall.

"You okay, man? You got enough money and stuff? You worked hard for us, if you need a few bucks I can..."

"I'm covered, Eddie. I can make it."

Eddie reaches into the pocket of his shirt. "Avian wanted me to give this to you. He says if you get back to the midwest, you should get a little drum kit and give this dude a call and drop his name. They both from Little Rock."

Zoot Prestige, the card says. Saxophone. Little Rock. A phone number.

Aaron laughs. "I got tons of Zoot's records. He was one of my first jazz heroes. This is great. Thank you. Thank Avian."

They go through the glass doors, out onto the driveway that circles the entrance.

They stand for a few minutes, silent. Finally Aaron says, "I don't understand, Eddie. What happened? I can't leave without knowing why."

"Let's set on this bench." They go to a concrete slab placed between two stunted evergreen trees.

"Avian didn't say anything, but I pieced it together. What it boils down to is that they are afraid of him, afraid of his music."

"Who? Who is 'they'?"

"People in the business. Record company people. A lot of the scene is run by mafia types. The clubs. Shit, man, the clubs are part of a corrupt system. Cabaret cards, payoffs. About five years ago these people were getting paranoid of Avian's influence on musicians, especially younger ones. They were afraid he would cut into the audience for crossover music, for this soul jazz they've been touting. You and I know this is crazy. Avian is far out. Avian will always be far out, he's never gonna have mass appeal. But his fame was spreading, people were imitating the way he was playing, kids were doing atonal riffs on their guitars, everybody was making saxophones out of plastic, leather, glass, all kinds of shit. And somebody in an office somewhere says, "okay, what's this cat's scene?" And somebody else says, "he's a dope fiend, he's strung out." Well no sweat, we know how to handle him.'"

Eddie looks at Aaron and his face is tragic. Aaron groans and puts his face in his hands.

"Yeah, you dig it. These people got to Avian's connections. They made sure he couldn't get no dope. They intimidated his doctor, they pulled his ticket. Now man, I don't begrudge Avian his dope. He functions fine on his medicine, but without it he's a mess. He's tried to clean up so many times. The sad fact is Avian needs dope. And these people got control of him. He gets so sick. He tries to kick but he doesn't sleep at all for twelve days and he just goes crazy for sleep. So these people say, "You don't play for five years, just in your apartment, no gigs, no concerts, and we'll take care of you. We'll give you thirty grand a year, we'll let your dealers wholesale to you. All royalties from your albums are still yours, and overseas rights, okay."

"Avian just broke. He couldn't take it. He thought after a couple years they'd forgotten about him. Even if they hadn't, he wanted to play a concert. He took a risk. He booked Carnegie Hall after he got his last royalty check. We didn't know anything about this stuff. We thought he was taking a sabbatical, like he said. And that it is over and we'll start playing with the Quartet again. No idea this shit is coming down."

Aaron raises his head, inhaling long and thoughtfully. The world is so different than he imagined it to be.

"What happens now?"

Eddie is quiet. Traffic sounds bounce and echo off the hospital facade. "I think they're going to leave him alone. I think the 'Avian Coulter Threat' has passed into oblivion and they're more worried about the Grateful Dead. Avian knew the time had come to make the break. He knew there might be consequences, just a formality, you know. He gambled that they wouldn't kill him. And they didn't. His rich doctor friend helped him stash money away and insure the band's instruments in case they got messed up. He thought of everything. He just bought Charlie a bass made by some Italian master in the eighteenth century. Cost him a fuckin' fortune. I got me a fine new set of Gretsch drums."

"Avian Coulter is an amazing man." Aaron says quietly.

"Yes, he is, " Eddie agrees. "A brave and determined man. One of these days, he'll get off dope. You watch. He'll find a way."

Aaron rises, decisively. "I sure hope so, Eddie. I have to go. Part of me wants to stay and part of me isn't ready to be here. But I'll be back. I hope I see you again."

The drummer shakes his hand with characteristic crispness. "You will. It's been a pleasure, man."

Professor Springer lets Aaron off somewhere on Highway Forty in Ohio. There are ramps going this way, that way, gas stations on every side, places to eat, stunted bushes in sandy soil in the little islands between concrete runways.

Cars slow a bit when coming from the ramps onto the main highway, and Aaron finds a strategic spot under the lights. He has barely put out his thumb when a Volkswagen bus passes, brakes, spews a bit of gravel and goes into reverse to pull back alongside him.

"Man, am I glad to see you!" the driver is saying as he leans to the right to slide back the window. "Come on, you want to go to Ann Arbor?"

"It'll do," Aaron calls, hefting his bag and trumpet into the van.

The driver, in his early to mid-twenties, has hair that disappears below his shoulders. He wears big wire-rimmed glasses and shows a happy grin. "What a goof!" he chortles, as Aaron gets in beside him. The bus reeks of pot smoke. "I just dropped off Lucy back at the Stop'N'Shop, or Pop N'flop or whatever that is, and here you are standing out there. How did you get here so fast? What a goof!"

The van has little acceleration and the driver inserts it into traffic without even a backward glance, forcing a number of cars to swerve and brake and honk horns in outrage.

"I...uh...don't think I..." Aaron begins to say, thinking he is being mistaken for someone else, but the driver stuffs a gigantic joint into Aaron's mouth and lights it with a lighter whose flame is adjusted so high it almost burns the vinyl ceiling of the van.

"Ho! Man! It's the same shit. Remember Danny? He copped this in some weird ghetto in Cleveland. I thought the spades were gonna stomp us!"

Aaron inhales deeply, then coughs.

"Hee hee! Whoa!" the driver commiserates. "See what I mean? It's worth that whole paranoid scene." He looks again at Aaron, his eyes straying from the road too long for Aaron's comfort.

"Say, you're not that dude from...you know, what's that place?"

"

No," Aaron chokes. "I'm not that dude. My name's Aaron".

"Oh.. Well, what the fuck. You're Aaron. I thought you were that dude from..uh.. you know...that dude. Whoa! For a minute you looked just like him. But now you don't look like him at all. Guess it's the beard. Whoa. Weird. You don't look anything like him. I better smoke some more weed. I'm Willie. They call me the Goofmaster. What a goof! You wanna go to Ann Arbor?"

"Yeah, that'd be fine." Aaron inhales again and passes the joint back. Willie crosses lanes, crosses back. He seems to struggle to think for a while.

"Wow shit, man,", he says. "I thought you were the dude with the speed. I woulda picked you up anyway. But I sure need some speed. I'm ragged. I thought you were, you know....."

"You want me to drive?" Aaron quickly volunteers. Willie has slowed to about thirty five miles an hour, and cars whiz by, honking.

"Yeah, that will be a goof." Willie pulls over immediately, no signal, no deceleration. The van fishtails onto the shoulder and comes to a rest. Willie seems suddenly enervated.

"Goddam, I sure am glad to see you. You going to Ann Arbor?" he asks again, as if he has just laid eyes on Aaron. He puts the van in neutral and begins climbing over the seat into the back, where there is a mattress and a few other amenities. The van keeps rolling, and Aaron slides into the driver's seat quickly, before they roll into the culvert.

Chapter Twenty One

Sarah's   World
1967: St. Louis

Every now and then, Sarah has the nightmare. A feral animal, a wolf, tiger, wild dog, will chase her. She runs, and her legs grow more and more heavy, until she is going nowhere, panting with terror, and the animal pounces, getting hold of her arm or leg.

She can feel the pain of teeth sinking into her flesh; can hear the snarling, and feel the grate of fangs on her fragile bones. Then she wakes up, sweating, screaming. Carlo, still asleep, swats at her in annoyance.

Sometimes the animal has Carlo's face.

She thinks about going to a psychiatrist. Her dad urges her to see Dr. Weiner, but she has seen the effect on her mother of clinical "soul tampering," has witnessed the corrosion of mind and body, of memory and intellect.

Instead, she discusses her dreams with Hattie Brown, the cleaning lady in her apartment building.

"Honey," the squat old woman says, "the sooner you get rid that husband of yours, sooner you stop havin' bad dreams."

Sarah admits the accuracy of the diagnosis.

"Tigers," Mrs. Brown, clicking her tongue, shakes her head. "Wolves and mad dogs. Mah lord mah lord, you're too young and too pretty to be havin' dreams like that. I tell you, girl, ain't really none of my business, but when I see a sin, I speak up. And a sin is what it is, you married to a man like that. oh screw, he ain't a man. He a boy."

Mrs. Brown pauses, thrusts her mop into the bucket and presses the wringing lever with hands that are almost black on top, and pale coffee-colored on the palms. Sarah leans on the coke machine in the hallway, one hand on her hip, balancing the weight of her advanced pregnancy.

Hattie has prophesied that it will be a girl. "I tell you that bee-yoo-ti-ful girl you got comin', don't want to be around no father like that. 'Course, it ain't none of my business."

"But Hattie, I love Carlo," Sarah protests weakly, knowing she sounds ridiculous. "And he loves me. He married me, didn't he?"

Hattie Brown waves a hand in dismissal. She straightens her body with a grunt, and looks into her young friend's eyes.

"Sarah, honey, you all of seventeen years old. I can tell you till I'm purple but you gotta learn it for yourself. What you call love is nothin' but you wantin' to hurt your mama. Now I don't care what your mama done to you, it just isn't worthy of you, girl, you have finer things in you."

Sarah's eyes burn and she wipes them with the sleeve of her blue sweat suit. The next thing she knows, she is crying into Hattie's warm, soft shoulder.

"Shh, it's okay," the woman murmurs. "I got five kids and all of 'em turned out fine. Tina got pregnant, Benny was in jail for dope, but they all fine upstanding people now, with families and jobs. It's just all the crazy things people do when they're young. And you're so young, girl, so young."

A week later, two weeks before her due date, she dreams of a tiger, awakes screaming, and Carlo hits her in the face. His arm rises from the blankets, impersonal, not attempting accuracy. His fingers connect with her forehead, and for a moment it seems that snowflakes are dancing before her eyes.

Then the snowflakes turn to hailstones and the hailstones are red with bloody rage. Sarah pulls the blanket from around Carlo's face, and, with her open hand, slaps him back.

"What the fuck!" He sits up, greasy black hair dripping over his forehead. Sarah tries to hit him again, but he deflects her arm. His pouty lower lip thrusts out with indignation.

"Fucking cunt, touch me again and I'll kill you."

In that moment whatever emotion Sarah has called love disappears. She laughs, as much at herself as at this ludicrous boy, this effeminate son of migrant workers who wants so badly to be a tough guy.

This makes Carlo angry, and he turns his body sideways to lunge at Sarah, reaching for her with his long, thin fingers.

Sarah has one over-riding thought: don't let him hurt the baby. They wrestle in the badly-sprung bed, and as hand grapples wrist, Sarah makes an amazing discovery. She more than matches Carlo's strength. Nine months pregnant, and she can control her husband's flailing arms.

She looks into his contorted, angry, increasingly baffled face, and it all falls away from her, the need to be with this moron. Hattie Brown's voice reverberates in her, and Hattie has been right.

Huge and burdened as she is, she leaps from the bed. When Carlo comes after her, she turns and raised a fist.

"Don't you dare touch me," she says coldly. When Carlo sees her eyes, hears her voice, he backs away.

As she recovers her breath, Sarah packs her things into a few shopping bags. Badly as it will damage her pride, she knows that her father will come and get her, and he will support her in her decision to separate from Carlo.

As she calls her father at the deli and blurts out her idea, she sees Carlo's face register the fact that she is actually leaving. He is buckling on his wide silver belt over his tight leather motorcycle pants.

The look on his face is one of unmistakable relief.

247

Chapter Twenty Two

The   **Gig**   **From**   **Hell**
1967: South Haven, Michigan

The gig has "wrong" written all over it. Zoot doesn't even have to go inside. As soon as he parks the Continental and looks up at the club's neon sign, he knows it is going to be a bad gig.

"Jason's Lounge," it blinks, and there is a neon cowboy roping a neon steer, over and over again, in pink, green and blue. Under the sign is a neatly lettered feature board. It says "ZOO PRESTIGE TONIGHT".

"Oh shit," Zoot groans, and reaches for an unprecedented fourth cheroot. "Remind me to never take gigs from a booking agent named Morrie Fink. What was I thinking?" He turns sideways, resting his forearm on the leather seat. He is wearing a white turtleneck sweater, a brown and white hounds-tooth sport jacket, white pants, gorgeously polished Italian shoes.

"I had a bad feeling about this maybe three miles back," Tyrone pops open his cigarette lighter and flames up the cheroot for his employer. "We turned right instead of left, and it didn't look like a barbecue and collard greens neighborhood."

They park in front of a redneck roadhouse, a big square barn near the shore of Lake Michigan. The area is a blue collar vacation resort, a dive-off-the-pier-eat-burgers-drink-beer-sleep-in-your-winnebago paradise.

"So we're Zoo Prestige," Aaron cracks. "Don't we have an album out on Mercury?"

"Are you shittin' me?" Zoot's left eye narrows, right eyebrow shooting toward his forehead.

"There IS a Zoo Prestige?"

"I didn't make the connection, even...I think they're a sort of psychedelic country and western band."

"Oh man, I'm gonna have to sue 'em. There are some wacked out probabilities in this frame. This is too bizarre, even for me."

"Money's good," Tyrone reminds his companions. "Eight hundred bucks. We're here. Zoo Prestige is probably down at the Esquire in Cleveland. And the Black Panthers is gonna love them!"

"The world gets stranger every day," Zoot murmurs, stubbing out the cheroot in the ashtray, then clicking the ashtray into the dashboard decisively. "Let's get movin'. And don't say anything. Let's just get through this."

"I'm not gonna say anything," Aaron pops the recessed door handle and steps onto the gravel parking lot, stretching. "We drove three hours from Detroit to play this gig. You think I'm some kind of smart-ass?"

Zoot lowered a sardonic gaze upon his drummer across the roof of the car as he emerges from the driver's side door.

"You have been known to be a smart ass. You have smart assed your way up and down the midwest and the south with me for a year and a half." From the corner of his eye he sees Tyrone get out of the back seat. "And you," he says, almost accusingly, pointing an index finger as long and broad as a breadknife, "you better know some country tunes."

looks outraged. "I don't know any country tunes, man." His hands are held out, palms upright, elbows bent, a 'who me?' gesture. He is wearing a beret, sunglasses, black sport coat over black T-shirt, pink slacks and brown sandals. A cigarette dangles insouciantly from his lips. A bit of ash hangs from his goatee. "Do I look like I know any country tunes?"

"All right, all right," Zoot concedes. "But we ain't smokin nothing tonight. We play it straight."

Aaron and Tyrone exchange a glance, a silent agreement passes between them. They'd sneak off somehow and get high.

It is seven forty five. They go into the cavernous interior of the club.

Zoot pushes Aaron ahead of himself, letting his white drummer lead the way. The jukebox is playing as people prepare for the evening. Steel guitar strains and boxy two-beat rhythms hang like crepe paper across the room. Aaron does a quick scan and knows the owner is the man at the far end of the bar, speaking to a truck driver with a Budweiser logo on his dark blue jacket.

"Can I help you?" the man asks, eyes passing Aaron and fixing on the two black men. He is chewing something, but his jaw stops working.

"We're the band, " Aaron chirps. "Where's the best place to unload our stuff?"

"You're Zoo Prestige?" One corner of the owner's mouth dips towards his chin, as if the other side of his face is paralyzed.

"Yep," Aaron responds. "I'm Aaron. This is Tyrone. And this is.....uh...The Zoo."

Tyrone kneads his goatee with one hand. Zoot looks solemn.

"Hmmm. I'm Jason." The man gives them a suspicious examination. He reaches beneath the counter and brings up an empty crisco can. He spits a wad of tobacco into it, then replaces it with a hollow metallic thump. "You guys can pull around to the side, there's a loading door over there, near the stage."

As they return to the car, there is a poster board on the left hand wall of the club, just near the door. On it is an eight by twelve publicity photo of the band Zoo Prestige, three men and a woman dressed in large cowboy hats. Each band member is cuddling or sitting upon a large stuffed animal. A Zebra, an elephant, a giraffe. The giraffe's neck is festooned with several feather boas and a cowboy hat sits upon each stuffed animal's head.

Zoot's hand strikes swiftly, like that of a biting serpent. The poster disappears into his jacket pocket.

"Aaron," Zoot hisses, "get the check up front, before we start playing."

"I'm one step ahead of you, man. I'll see what I can do."

"Tyrone," Zoot instructs, "leave the organ in the trailer. They got a Fender Rhodes in there, you can play that. Same for you, Aaron, use your Quick Escape drum kit. Leave the extra cymbals and tom toms in the trunk."

"Got it."

By eight forty five, they are set up and ready to go. Jason's Lounge is packed, there are people

pushing to get in the door.

From the back of the room, near the swaying kitchen doors, Zoot is watching Aaron haggle with Jason, at the bar. Tyrone is trying to screw the legs of the electric piano tighter. The hundred pound keyboard perches atop spindly aluminum legs that look like they will crumble as soon as the piano is touched.

There is not a single African American face in the crowd. The juke box is pumping out Hank Williams, and, on a tiny square dance floor, six couples dip and sway. The rest of the room is set in four-place tables, some moved together to accommodate larger parties. There is an abundance of towering hair-dos, baseball caps, Stetsons. Beer flows copiously, the laughter is boisterous.

Aaron squeezes his way through the packed throng , cups his hands and speaks into Zoot's ear.

"I got a hundred bucks. I told him my mother is in the hospital and I have to wire her money after the first set. He isn't buying it; he used the "N" word and the "C" word and even the goddam "J" word. I convinced him that the band has changed personnel but that we will play all the material from the album. Evidently, this band has a monster hit called 'You're An Animal But I Still Love You."

"Oh shit. You don't happen to know that tune, do you?"

"Heard it on the radio once, by accident. I think..." Aaron twists his face into a mask of revulsion.

Zoot leans over sideways so he can be heard by Aaron. "I'm gonna go kill Morrie Fink if we get out of this." He looks toward the stage. Tyrone has vanished.

"Where's Tyrone? We gotta start in about five minutes. I'll bet that goofball went out to get high."

Aaron stands on tiptoes and scans the room. "I'll go find him."

He starts towards the side door but Zoot puts a hand on his arm and forestalls him.

"No you don't. I'm not stupid. I'll go get him. Just wait right here. We got enough problems."

Aaron nods and watches Zoot's elegant figure disappear, parting waves of people like a black Moses descending from the shore of the Red Sea.

In a few minutes he returns with a grinning Tyrone. Zoot is fuming.

"Turn my back on you motherfuckers for one minute and you're like little kids; sheeee-it!"

Lights on the stage flash. The jukebox falls silent. The din of the crowd only diminishes slightly.

A woman with hair the size of a thunderstorm stands in a spotlight before a microphone. There are whoops from the audience.

"Alll riiiighttt!" She drawls. Her voice is amplified and boxy as if she is shouting through a megaphone. "It's great y'all can make it tonight!"

There is a collective "YEEEEE HAAAAAAA!"

Zoot puts his forehead into his hands and stares at the floor. "Oh shit," he sighs. Then he turns to his accompanists. "You know what we're gonna play tonight, don't you?"

"Hot Box, Bread and Butter, Fish Store......the whole act?" Tyrone rests his chin on the knuckle of his thumb, with his other fingers curled into a fist underneath. This makes him look thoughtful in a theatrical way. For Zoot, that is a sure sign he is stoned.

"That's right," Zoot affirms. His voice is smouldering with righteous anger.

The woman on the stage pirhouettes, lights glittering on her white cowboy boots.

"I'm not gonna waste any more of y'all's time, so let's git to it. Let's have a big hand for Zoo Prestige!"

"YEEEEE HAAAAA!" the crowd roars.

Zoot lets Aaron go first, to take his place behind the drums. Then he and Tyrone follow. The stage lighting is a weird shade of mauve. It blinds the musicians to everything but the front row of tables.

Zoot hangs the tenor saxophone from its strap so that it dangles against his chest. He counts off the tempo for "I Love Your Hot Box Baby". Aaron and Tyrone throw themselves into its Fats Domino-like groove. After four bars, Zoot steps to the microphone and begins the tune. His voice combines the perfect hoarseness of a blues singer, with a trace of the creaminess of Fats Domino.

He sings.

"I love your hot box, baby, keeps my sausage nice and warm

love your hot box baby, keeps my sausage nice and warm

when it gets time for breakfast

I got my sausage nice and long."

The volume level from the audience does not diminish, but changes in its tone and nature. There are whistles and howls. A few pieces of popcorn come onto the stage, some of them hitting Zoot.

"Hey!" Someone in the glare screams. "Play 'Lost Mama'. Another yells "You're An Animal, come on! When you gonna play 'You're an Animal?"

Zoot continues bravely.

"Love your toaster baby

put my bread into its slot

love your toaster baby

put my bread into its slot

when it's time for butter

it's gonna be nice and hot."

There are catcalls and the sounds of silverware banging on tables.

"Lost Mama!" Another voice in the crowd.

"You're An Animal!" Comes the refrain.

More popcorn strikes Zoot on his chest. One piece bounces from his forehead. He steps backwards to let Tyrone take a piano solo. His mouth is a tight round welt in the angry creases of his face. Then a large piece of meat comes flying out of the sickly pink light and hits Aaron on the neck. Its juices splatter his jacket, and it lands with a thunk in the center of his snare drum. Aaron spears it with his drumstick and puts it in his mouth. It seems the most efficient way to get it off his drum without dropping a stick.

Zoot lifts the saxophone very slowly from his neck and places it on its stand. A man in the front row is cutting another rectangular piece of steak. Before he can loft it toward the stage, Zoot points a finger at him and speaks into the microphone.

"You can fuck with me all you want, but you don't fuck with my musicians."

"Yeah, well fuck you, nigger," the man replies.

Zoot launches himself onto the table, trying to throttle the man in the front row. Plates and silverware go flying. Chaos erupts. Tyrone kicks at the piano leg and it comes toppling down with an eighty eight note crunch. Aaron hits someone on the head with one of his drumsticks, then feels himself go down as a press of bodies rushes onto the stage. He hears a fwunk! as someone kicks a hole in the bass drum. Aaron is only aware of a smothering weight atop him. There are so many people trying to beat him that no one can get in a good punch. A hole opens in the wall of bodies and he crawls through it. He sees Zoot swinging his saxophone and holding eight men at bay. The bandleader's motions are practiced and fluid, as if the instrument is an oriental martial arts device. The mouthpiece and reed look lethally sharp, and none dare pass through the twirling of the twenty pound hunk of brass. Tyrone has gotten to the top of the bar and is squirting pressurized seltzer into people's faces.

Women are screaming and beating their boyfriends and husbands with purses and shoes.

Zoot, Aaron and Tyrone head for the door, using the confusion. They go outside, where the cool air suddenly caresses their soaked shirts. Incongrously, the sound of frogs and crickets fill the night.

"Let's get the fuck out of here," Zoot says, pointing with his saxophone toward the car. They are inside the Continental with the motor running before anyone else can clear the door. Throwing a plume of gravel, Zoot backs out of his parking space, turns the wheel with one smooth stroke of power-assisted automotive skill and races straight from the parking lot without bothering to find the exit. He just puts the car and its towed trailer over the half-buried logs that border one row of parking spaces from the next, thump thump, thump thump, and finds the road.

For a while there is only the sound of panting. Aaron thinks ruefully about the drum set he saw being destroyed on the stage as he fled Jason' s Lounge. He's only had the kit for two months. It is his third drum set since beginning his work with Zoot.

Somebody has to say something. As their breathing returns to normal, as the lights illuminate the endless treadmill of road, there is a long silence.

Finally, Zoot glances sideways and backwards, just to make sure he has the attention of his colleagues. He reaches into the breast pocket of his sport coat and removes a cheroot from its red and white cardboard package.

"That was a good fuckin' brawl, wasn't it?"

Tyrone flips his lighter with a tinny little dink sound. Flame shoots up as he reaches forward over the seat to meet the tip of the cheroot.

Chapter Twenty Three

1967: Somewhere on the Road between Detroit and Chicago

"Why are so many jazz musicians heroin addicts?" This problem has beguiled Aaron for years. He wants Zoot's insight. There are different cultures, different compartments in the world of drug use. Marijuana is a staple of the music business: jazz, rock, blues, country, it is a universal unguent and lubricator. Aaron has never experimented with cocaine or opiates, but has seen the porosity of the soft/drug-hard/drug barrier and keeps careful distinctions in his own mind about what kind of drug use is permissible.

The road seems to slide beneath them like an infinite conveyor belt. Its perfectly measured white lines dash at right angles to the chrome front bumper as Zoot passes trucks and sedans, headlights blinking.

"Because they're weak and greedy," Zoot pronounces emphatically. He applies pressure to the gas pedal and honks his horn in response to the airhorn blast of a semi whose blinking headlights vanish in their wake.

Aaron waits for further discourse. When none comes, he asks, "Is that it? Weak and greedy? All of them? Bird? Dexter? Jackie? Elvin? Art Blakey? Gene Ammons? Sonny Rollins? Weak and greedy?"

"You ever see pictures of Bird?" Zoot asks impatiently.

"Sure, lots of them."

"Take a good look at that face. Have you ever seen a more guileful, deceiving face?"

"Now that you mention it.....yeah, Bird does have a kind of weasly expression."

"Naw, man, not Bird," Tyrone protests.

"Wait a minute, wait a minute," Zoot replies, "Look under the seat, I got a couple albums there. Turn on the light for a second."

Tyrone digs in the space under the front passenger seat. Aaron reaches up and clicks the little black rectangle that controls the inside light.

"Yeah, here's 'April in Paris'". Tyrone brings the record up and holds it close to his face.

Charlie Parker looks as if his cheeks are stuffed with fried chicken, he has just downed eight cups of coffee and is doing a mock 'Uncle Tom' mug for the white photographer, who will have no clue as to the mockery implied by the eyes-wide, toothy shucking smile.

"Yeah, I see what you mean," Tyrone concedes, "he look like one devious motherfucker."

"Okay, okay," Aaron leans over to examine the photo, then turns off the light. "But that's still not satisfying to me. How can such brilliance be merged with such flaws of character? How can Bird achieve the discipline required to become a virtuoso, how can he be dedicated, original, uncompromising and still be weak?"

"Man, you are very naive," Zoot says. His left hand is at the bottom of the steering wheel, resting languidly in the hard plastic ridges that are designed for grip in this top-end Chrysler product. His jade ring catches the glint from the sickly blue road lamps that flick by, every thirty seconds.

Zoot's comment makes Aaron a little angry. At twenty he is making a valiant effort to be tough-minded.

"Well, I fucking want to know. I still can't figure it out. Avian Coulter tried to explain it to me, but I didn't understand then and I don't understand now."

"Okay, I'm being harsh," Zoot explains. "Bird ripped me off for a horn. I was dumb, I was young, I was honored to be lending Bird a horn. He really betrayed me and it pissed me off. Think of it this way. An addiction is always a symptom of pain. Some people deal with pain intelligently, they cope, they find ways to comfort themselves, they learn skills from their parents, from being raised well. But there are some kinds of pain that are overwhelming. If you take a black man who has talent, deep sensitivity, who has worked for maybe thirty years diligently to become a tremendous musician, who has all the ambition and technique of the finest classical virtuoso, and you stick him in a funky nightclub where people talk over his deepest inspiration, where whores are making change at the bar, where booze and dope are being consumed in copious quantity, where the money he takes home is barely able to keep him and his family in a rotten tenement, where booking agents and club owners take thirty percent of his wages, where cops hassle him just for existing, where white musicians rip off his compositions and turn them into sterilized money makers, yeah, you might, just might, get consumed with frustration, you might have the makings of a teeeny little bit of self destructive impulse."

Aaron almost has to lean sideways to escape Zoot's sudden vehemence.

"Oh," he says, stupidly.

In the back seat, Tyrone murmurs something in Swahili.

Chapter Twenty Four

July 18, 1967

"This ain't no shortcut, Zoot". Tyrone is leaning out the passenger side window, trying to see road signs. "I thouht you were born and bred in this area, I thought you knew the backroads of Missouri like you know the chord changes to 'Round Midnight'.

Zoot is concentrating on his driving. A rain is slamming into the windshield so fiercely that the wipers are inadequate to push it aside. He slows the Continental to ten miles an hour as its tires geyser water in big fans to either side of the road.

"Close the goddam window," Zoot says testily, "I know where I am. I just don't see the Steelville Road, must have passed bout five miles back." He swings the vehicle into a slow turn, so that he is facing in the opposite direction. A bolt of lightning slashes into the ground nearby and the clap of thunder brings Aaron awake in the backseat.

"Holy Shit!" he says, blinking. "That is loud! We in Lawrence yet?"

The trio played a gig in Champagne the previous night, for the university crowd. Somewhat injudiciously, Zoot booked another campus gig the next night at the University of Kansas. They packed up their stuff after the gig, got into the car and started driving. Sleeping and driving in turns, they crossed Illinois and encountered a furious traffic jam near East St. Louis. Zoot turned north and crossed the Missippi at Alton, then looped south towards Jefferson City. A 'short cut', he called it.

At one oclock in the afternoon it is dark as twilight. The rain stops, abruptly, The wind dies down. Tyrone rolls the window up until it is just an open crack at the top. He lights a cigarette and blows the smoke towards the crack.

"We need a PissnGas," Aaron announces. He points at the gauge. "You're almost on empty and I'm almost on full."

"There's one at the Steelville turnoff, if I can find it." Zoot is unusually moody and terse. He feels stupid booking two gigs so far apart on succeeding nights, but he has a lot of people to support and the money is good. After all these years, he has learned how to pace himself, but now and then one of his wives calls or one of his kids needs school money and he is forced to push himself and his musicians.

Aaron leans forward and puts his face near Zoot's shoulder. "You're kinda gloomy, man. What's goin' on?"

Zoot steers with one hand and rubs his left-side bursitis with the other. "I don 't know. It ain't the weather and it ain't really the drive, we done this a hundred times. Somethin' spooky in the air, I can feel it."

"Yeah? Well what is that thing?" Tyrone is pointing across a landscape of ripening soybeans, toward the lowering sky in the southwest.

Zoot brakes suddenly and stops in the middle of the deserted back road.

"That," he says emphatically, "Is about to become a twister, it ain't quite touched the ground yet." Transfixed, the three musicians watch the sky writhe as it makes jagged blades of black cloud. The blades seem to fence with one another, dancing around a central core of towering dark moisture. Its beauty is at once staggering, menacing and inspiring. After a few moments, the dueling blades are sucked into this central darkness and they become a single stabbing dagger that connects with the earth. A skirt of debris rises from its intersection and surrounds its lower trunk with the red-brown and green of wet fields of soybean plants.

Zoot guns the car and starts racing down the road as fast as he dares. The twister reaches out towards them with a seemingly personal and purposive malevolence.

It knows we're here, Aaron thinks. It wants us.

The road is narrow but straight, and Zoot is able to get up to about fifty but the deep puddles in the ruts and potholes slow the car as it bounces and shimmies and slides.

"Motherfucker's getting closer," Tyrone says. His voice is loud but indistinct in the sudden roaring of wind.

Zoot looks for some protective feature in the landscape. He knows he has only seconds. They come to a covered wooden bridge fording a small creek, a deep notch in the otherwise flat terrain.

Zoot stops the car and opens the door. "Come on!" He bails out and heads for the side of the bridge, finding a path down towards the creek bed. Aaron and Tyrone follow, clothes flapping, hats flying.

"Down this way!" Zoot instructs, "get away from the bridge!"

The three men slap through muddy creek bed and find a big rock thirty feet from the bridge. They crouch under it like little children hanging onto a mother's skirts. Looking up, Aaron sees the base of the twister lashing back and forth, sees the sky whirling, sees leaves and limbs circling. The wind howls and he puts his face into his arms and holds the rock. His breath is sucked from his body. He has a moment of panic as he struggles for air. A sucking force is trying to pull him up, up, but his fingers find purchase in the rock face and he holds on for his life.

The wooden frame of the bridge explodes in the din and boards zoom into the sky, disappearing into blackness. The air comes rushing back into his lungs, and his breath returns. He hears voices in the wind, evil genies laughing, mocking, capricious in their power.

The twister travels down the road and across the fields and disappears back into the sky.

They climb back to the road, fearing for the Continental and their musical instruments.

The car is in the exact center of the road, pointed in the opposite direction in which it had been parked. Gingerly, Zoot opens the door. Nothing seems to have changed. Tyrone's cigarette butt still rests at the lip of the ashtray. The organist reaches in and takes the cigarette reverently, draws a puff and blows smoke into the still air. Aaron's copy of Downbeat Magazine is still open to the record reviews. On the road, piles of junk lay everywhere, clods of earth, wooden beams, uprooted plants. Trees are cracked a third the way up their trunks, all of their branches lying on the ground, pointing northeast.

Zoot shakes his arms and hands as if to disperse some unwelcome insect. "Man, I thought that twister was after me personally."

His voice shakes.

"So did I," Aaron agrees. His throat is dry. His heart is pounding.

Tyrone is so thrilled to be alive he is hopping from foot to foot. His pants are soaked with mud up to his knees.

"It was saying 'Tyrone, I'm comin' to git you'. I thought I'd open my eyes and be in Oz, with a bunch of little people dancin' round my feet."

Zoot walks to the now topless bridge. He looks at the steel superstructure and the remaining planks. He bounces around on them, hops across the gaps. "Looks okay. I ain't going back forty miles to get across this creek."

The men get into the car and Zoot steers it carefully across the bridge. "Still need a Pissngas?" Zoot inquires mockingly.

"I forgot I had to pee," says Aaron. "Now I got to pee really really bad."

"Well shit, get out and pee, we about fifteen minutes from the Steelville turnoff."

Aaron goes out behind a bush and relieves himself. He hears the sound of his own stream against a world that has gone supernally silent. There is no wind, no bird song. The sky is a weird shade of pink. As soon as he is finished the rain begins to fall again. The drops are huge, heavy, laden with silt. Covering his head, Aaron races back to the car.

After driving for ten minutes in silence, a black and white road sign appears. The trapezoidal shape of the state of Missouri encloses a number four. Fifteen yards past this sign there is a green board with white letters and an arrow pointing to the right. Steelville, eight miles, it indicates. At this one-sided intersection is a little gas station and a tiny grocery store skirted by a wooden plank walkway. Zoot pulls into the station. He gestures to Aaron to stay in the car. This part of Missouri isn't explicitly segregated, but it has the taint of old rebellion. Zoot asks a black attendant to fill the tank, and Tyrone jumps through the rain towards the store, looking for another pack of cigarettes. Aaron watches the Schlitz Beer sign flicker, rolls the window down to smell the storm-soaked earth. He knows this country, too. He has come here for vacations with his family. They have gone to Bagnell Dam, Lake of the Ozarks, Wildwood Resort. In a childhood with a paucity of happy memories, this country means peace, relief, respite, jumping from a pier into the lake, riding horses, mom on her best behavior, dad relaxed and having fun.

Zoot chats with the station attendant about the twister, informs him that the Willens Creek Bridge is no longer covered.

"Be damned," the man says, "twister blew the top the bridge away? No shit?"

"No shit, almost blew us away too, turned this here Lincoln Continental hundred eighty degrees backward but left a cigarette in the ashtray, still lit and ready to smoke." Zoot's dialects always reflect his circumstances. He pronounces "this here" as "thissheer".

Hurriedly finishing the transaction to get out of the rain, the attendant takes Zoot's money and rushes back into the shelter of the store.

A moment later, Tyrone comes walking out, holding a newspaper limply in his hand. His mouth is hanging open, his eyes have a staring and shocked quality, as if he has just survived a terrible battle. He opens the passenger's door , throws the newspaper towards Aaron in the back seat and slumps abruptly on the plush leather, one leg hanging out the side.

"You look like you just got terrible news," Zoot observes with concern.

Tyrone nods and points towards the newspaper.

"Coltrane's dead," he says mournfully. "It's in the paper. He died yesterday."

There is a stunned silence. Aaron feels as if he has just taken the first plunge on a roller coaster ride, his stomach goes up through his chest.

"No," Zoot says. "No."

Tyrone has the paper folded out to the entertainment section. It is the St. Louis Post-Dispatch.

There is a big article about Barbara Streisand, a review of the new James Bond movie, a review of the Led Zeppelin Concert at Kiel Auditorium. Down in the far right corner of the page is a two-paragraph squib. 'Jazz Musician John Coltrane Dies," it says. There is sketchy information about the jazz giant succumbing suddenly to liver cancer.

Aaron puts his face in the paper and squeezes himself with it, crumbling it around his cheeks. "He is forty years old!" He wails. "Forty years old! What is happening? Why are jazz musicians dying? Why Coltrane, of all people, Trane? "

Desperately, he claws at Zoot's shoulder. "We're all professional jazz musicians, Zoot. Is this my future? Is this Tyrone's? Are you going to die on us, too? Why can't we survive? What are we doing to ourselves?"

Zoot stares straight ahead, seeing nothing. He reaches across his shoulder and pats Aaron's hand, squeezing it.

"You're just beginning to see what it's like," the old musician says. "It's dangerous to be a genius. That's why I stay in this chitlin circuit groove, play the college campuses, keep my midstream profile. And this is hard enough. You think Coltrane can be inspired every night? You think he can get up there and reach down into his guts and deliver a brilliant set five nights a week, be a genius?"

A core of bitter reflection stains Zoot's voice. These are things he generally keeps to himself. As he speaks, his anger grows and his voice scrapes with frustration and old pain.

"You have to use something, like Bird, like Lester, you have to use something to get to that place where you even feel like playing at all, let alone be great. Then you raise the standard, people turn out and expect to be transformed, to hear an oracular performance, night after night. I smoke my weed, that's how I do it. And I don't ask too much of myself. That's why I'm sixty-three and still playing. I know how much I can give. Men like Coltrane, they don't know moderation, they can't know moderation, they have to keep pushing the limits or the critics jump on their ass, the fickle fans get restless, the talk on the street starts goin' 'round, 'Trane's lost it, Bird's lost it, Jackie's lost it, Prez's lost it, Bud's lost it! You have a couple bad nights and all these assholes who can't play a note go talking, he's lost it, lost it, getting' tired, man, runnin' out of steam, his great days are behind him, what a shame, used to be a great musician."

Zoot pauses for a moment, looking at his sidemen, at his disciples in the mystic art of music. Then he spits a long gobbet out the window and says, with a lengthy and contemptuous drawl,

"Sheee-it! Son of a fucking bitch!"

He turns backward to look at Aaron. Cobra-like, he shifts his body, glancing at Tyrone beside him. He is seething, indignant. "That's why genius musicians die. They have to die! Ain't no choice! Once they get a reputation as a genius, they have to be a genius every night. They use it up! Then they're gone!"

He turns on the engine and drives about a hundred yards down the road. He pulls onto the shoulder and scrunches the emergency brake with his foot. He puts his large hands in front of his face, then leans into them and begins to weep.

It is contagious. These three friends, of different ages, races, different backgrounds, are not afraid to show their feelings to one another. The three jazz musicians, on their way to a gig, taking a short cut through the back roads of Missouri, pull onto the side of the country lane and weap for John Coltrane.

Chapter Twenty Five

New **Worlds** **Calling**
September, 1969: Little Rock

"Looks like there's a Zoot Prestige revival goin' on, man."

Aaron sits on Zoot's front porch in Little Rock. Zoot, Tyrone and Aaron sip lemonade, taking the breeze from a small fan, nodding to neighbors as they walk past. Aaron reads the letter from San Francisco, and passes it to Tyrone.

"Didn't know I up an' died," quips Zoot, "didn't know I needed revivin." He tips back a tall clear cylinder of lemonade. The jade ring on his third finger glints in the late afternoon sunlight. "Now the hippies want me to play at the Fillmore, they want me to open for the Doors. Provide a little taste of au-then-TIC-ity"

Tyrone gapes. "They're gonna pay us this much? Shit, man, that's some good money. And airplane tickets. And hotel. You hit the big time, Zoot."

The saxophonist leans back in his wicker rocking chair and watches the comings and goings of his neighborhood. He owns a red brick three story house in a neighborhood of three story red brick houses. Built in the twenties, each house has a long narrow fenced back yard with apple and oak trees. In the front, twelve feet of concrete walkway lead from the porch to the street.

"I hit the big time every eight or ten years", says Zoot. "Don't mean nothing. Just do the same thing, play the music. Last time I was big was when I recorded that song, 'I Love Your Hot Box, Baby'. And that was in sixty one."

Aaron leans forward.. "You know I'm a hippie, don't you, Zoot?" He fingers his shoulder length

hair significantly.

Zoot laughs shortly through his nose. "You ain't a hippie, man. You're a hipster. Big difference. You're a working musician and a philosopher. If you're a hippie, how come you aint listening to the Jefferson Airplane and the Doors?"

"I smoke weed and take acid. I like Jimi Hendrix."

"Yeah, he one motherfucker," Tyrone agrees.

"What about the Grateful Dead?" Zoot inquires innocently.

There is a silence.

"You know that joke?" Asks Aaron. "What happens when the Deadhead runs out of drugs?"

No one says anything. They wait for the punchline.

" He Says, 'Gee, this band really sucks'."

They'd heard it before, but they guffaw.

"I still say you're not a hippie. A hippie is a young white person without a job, with a naive and shallow philosophical underpinning of hedonism, watered down oriental religion and utopian idealism."

"And what is the alternative?" Aaron asks. "Wouldn't you rather have a bunch of people running around naked, getting high, screwing, listening to music and having a good time?"

"When you put it that way, I agree. But I have a little more sympathy for the protestors, least they putting their skins on the line."

Aaron shudders when he thinks about how close he has come to being eligible for the draft. Only the family's extensive psychiatric history has snagged him a 1-F. The years he played mocking games with Doctors Weiner, Potts and Zuckerman have earned their dividend.

"You boys ready for supper?" Syreeta, Zoot's wife, comes to the screen door. She is an elegant, solidly built woman with a lot of Cherokee blood, mixed with plantation slave and a touch of the white master. She is about forty years old. When Aaron first met her, he was reminded of his family's maid, Vernice. He remembers how good he felt whenever Vernice came to the house. Every Friday, she spent four hours cleaning the place, while Esther stayed in her room watching television. Every hour Aaron's mother emerged to check on Vernice's work. She tried to criticize the woman for invisible faults, but Vernice just smiled, said, "Yes Ma'am" and kept her dignity.

Syreeta evokes the same kind of warmth in Aaron. He feels safe and comforted in her presence.

As they get up to go inside, Tyrone passes the letter back to Zoot.

"So we gonna play this gig?"

Zoot nods. "We gonna play the gig. Only we ain't flying. We drivin'."

* * *

Two weeks later they are driving down Haight Street. The Continental, like a parade float, glides through crowds of multi-colored human beings, a cream-colored royal barge, regally parting the waves.

"Holy Shit." Tyrone's eyes pan out the passenger side window.

"Holy Shit." Aaron's eyes pan out the window of the right back seat.

Zoot is smoking one of his cheroots. His chin is up like president Roosevelt's.

"This is why I don't read fiction," he says. The car stops at a light. A naked man with a painted face steps in front to peer in. He lips something inaudible. Behind him come four Hell's Angels in sunglasses. Then a ragged harlequin tiptoes through the intersection, followed by half dozen bleary eyed dirty teenagers.

"Looks like the Summer of Love is over." Zoot makes this pronouncement solemnly.

For a moment, to Aaron, the saxophonist looks weary of the world. The bags under his eyes are suddenly pronounced. They are like shelves of rock high up on a cliff face. Zoot's eyes peer over them as if from inside a cave. It is a sudden and startling vision. Aaron has grown up listening to the Master Tenor Player, the veteran Blues shouter. The man is as much myth as reality. Aaron lined Zoot Prestige records next to one another on his bedroom shelf. He owns the classic Zoot Prestige Meets Dexter Gordon. He has played "Mad Tenors" ten thousand times. Now he is sitting next to this man in his gigantic car, tooling down Haight Street in San Francisco, on the way to a gig.

Zoot looks over at him. There is a depth to his expression that seems to tap Aaron at the center of his chest. Then a glint comes to the older man's eyes.

"We gonna play like motherfuckers tomorrow night." He smiles, and his big beautiful front tooth, the one with the tiny crescent of gold at the crown, seems to wink at the two young musicians. "We gonna play I Love Your Hot Box, Baby. Hoooeeee!"

On the night of the gig, backstage at the Fillmore, Aaron sits in a large nondescript dressing room while various members of The Doors and their entourage indulge in adventures in psychopharmacology. At one point Jim Morrison approaches Aaron. "You guys are great," he says. "I can't wait to hear you. I got a couple of Zoot Prestige albums about ten years ago. Hey, you want some acid?" He holds a single finger toward Aaron. There is a purple tablet on its tip.

"Sure." Aaron licks his finger and touches the tip of Jim Morrison's finger, so that the tablet sticks to him. He hoists it into his mouth. "Got one for Tyrone?"

"No problem." As if by magic, there is another tab on the finger. The rock star hasn't seemed to move. Aaron looks into his eyes. Morrison looks completely mad, as if he is about to break into a maniacal jig. The eyes aren't really seeing Aaron. They are focused inward on some psychic riot that is happening in the singer's mind.

Tyrone is chatting up a foxy woman with heavy eye makeup. Aaron nudges him in the ribs. He looks over. "Oh. Oh yeah. It's San Francisco. It's LSD time at the Fillmore. Thanks, man." The organist swallows the tab, looks a little scared as the purple disk slides down his throat. His shoulders rise, then sink, as he swallows. At that moment Zoot comes in with Bill Graham. He has that look that says, "We just got paid, let's go play."

Aaron and Tyrone get up and follow their employer onto the stage.

They do the Rhythm and Blues Act. They minimize the jazz standards and play growlers and honkers from Zoot's Classic Book. Zoot sings Hot Box, then Banana Split Blues. He goes into his schtick, the falling down and collapsing, the raising of his legs in the air while the horn rests on his crotch. This is a prearranged signal for a stagehand to rush forward with a wet towel. Pretending to be injured, Zoot lets the stagehand help him to his feet. He staggers, and another stagehand comes forward with Zoot's purple and gold cape, draping it solicitously over the Master. Putting the back of his left hand to his forehead, Zoot blows a one-handed B flat, warbling over the rhythm of Aaron's drums and Tyrone's organ. He lets the stagehands lead him to the side of the stage like a martyred saint. "This man sacrifices his life to bring you the blues," the theatrical gesture implies. "He blows with so much soul that his very essence is ripped away from him, and he does it selflessly for you, the audience."

Aaron and Tyrone play a frantic shuffle beat while Zoot honks and duck-walks, kneels on the stage, waves his left hand in the air while his right rattles the keys of the horn, screeching. He feigns an inability to get back to his feet. Again the stage hands come running, put their hands under Zoot's armpits and help him rise as he continues to run his trilling note. It is only one note, which gives the two younger musicians freedom to modulate to a "strange" sounding drone. The chords search for resolution, and when they find that resolution, the result is an Eastern sounding mode, a Coltrane mode that retains its rooty vigor but brings intense drama to the music.

Zoot approves, Zoot knows he can do anything he wants, his musicians can do anything they want. There are no inhibitions at this gig.

The entire Fillmore audience is stoned on acid and thinks Zoot's act is completely marvelous, from note one to the rendition of "Gee Baby Aint I Good to You." As he plays the old classic song, Zoot leaves the stage, continuing to play, and he plays chorus after chorus, walking through the crowd. A line of people begins to walk behind him, and Zoot strolls right out the side exit, walks down the street, playing, gathering fifteen or twenty more people behind him like a Pied Piper, comes back in the front door, still blowing choruses from "Gee Baby," comes back up on the stage without losing a beat or missing a chord change. At the final climactic chord Zoot throws off his cape and slowly topples until he is laying in a pile atop his glittering saxophone. Stagehands rush out to attend his prostrate form. The lights go dark.

That night, in the hotel room, they sit around with about a dozen new "friends," watching the walls pulsate. Zoot looks indulgently at his young proteges. "I don't know what you get out of that stuff," he ventures. "You sure are some crazy motherfuckers. But I've never seen anything crazier than what's going on here. Shit, it's good crazy, don't get me wrong. Better than all the other uptight shit going on in the world." He is forty years older than most of the people in the room. Young ladies hang onto him, one at each side, but Zoot isn't lustful, merely amused. He rises to go to his own room. He waves his hand, indicating that he doesn't need company.

"I'm gone get some sleep, my young friends. You party on. Aaron, Tyrone…great

work tonight. You did me proud." He shakes hands all around, then saunters out the door and down the hall.

A reproduction of Van Gogh's painting, Starry Night, hangs on the wall. Aaron is standing in

front of it, transfixed. He is learning the true meaning of the art of painting. He will never forget what he is seeing in this painting. He thinks, with a pang, of his sister. It has been too long. He has not spoken to Sarah in months.

Later, he performs stumbling, inept sex in his own hotel room with a young woman called Genevieve. He doesn't humiliate himself, but he isn't covered in glory. Genevieve doesn't seem to care, one way or the other.

Things finally quiet down. Aaron gets the young lady out of his room and falls asleep. At about nine the next morning, Zoot knocks on his door. "You awake, man?" Aaron is awake. The curtains are drawn. The LSD is still active in his system. He has been watching fire come out of his fingertips, in the dark. He is watching the musical skill of his hands and thinking what a precious gift it is, to play the drums. He hopes with all his heart that he will never do anything to waste that gift.

"What's up?" Tyrone appears behind Zoot. His face looks as if it is floating two feet above his shoulders. His expression has a sweet innocence. Aaron thinks he looks like a young woman. He has never seen this feminine aspect of his friend.

"I want to talk to you guys." Zoot crooks his long index finger and beckons them back towards his room. They follow.

Zoot has scooted the room's easy chair towards the couch. Aaron and Tyrone sit facing their mentor. Zoot says simply, "I wanted to let you know that I'm going to die tomorrow. Or is it today?" He looks out the window. "I guess it's today."

There is a long silence.

"What the fuck you talking about, man? You're scaring me." Tyrone's face is metamorphosing into Zimbabwean masks. "Did you take acid too? You don't take acid...."

"I'm serious. I had a dream last night. God spoke to me. She said, 'Zoot, your life is over. You've done well. I love you. Tomorrow you come with me, you come home, to the Light of Truth.' Those were her exact words. The Light of Truth."

Aaron feels a terrible premonitory grief. He believes Zoot, absolutely.

"Oh man, you can't....." he chokes.

The tenor player leans forward and puts a fatherly hand on Aaron's shoulder. "I'm sorry, man. I know it hurts. I appreciate that you love me, that you've loved my playing since you were a little kid. Other than my wife, there's nobody I'd rather die around than you two guys. You crazy motherfuckers."

Tyrone begins to cry. Aaron's grief feels larger than his body, it is too huge to contain. As the waves of tears begin, Aaron feels such love that he understands how grief and love are partners of feeling, that they live side by side in this world and can never be separated. In life, the loss of beings that one loves is inevitable. It is the Law, and the Law is just and right no matter how much it may appear to be otherwise.

"You guys take care of shit for me, okay? I already called Syreeta. It was rough. She doesn't believe me, she thinks I was smokin something strong. I finally made her understand. Please keep an eye on her for me. She's young, she'll be okay. I cashed the check. Here's all the money. I signed over the car to you, Aaron, cause I don't trust Tyrone not to bang the shit out of it.." He passes a wad of bills to Aaron, along with an auto pink slip. "Everything else is with my lawyer. He'll take care of my estate. I got some things, stocks, properties, insurance. All my kids and ex-wives will come out okay."

Zoot massages his sore shoulder with the opposite hand. The three musicians feel a wind rising,

it is something interior, a wind of spirit. Outside, carpets of fog roll across the city.

"I want you to cremate me here and throw my ashes into the ocean from the Golden Gate headlands. It's really beautiful there, I love that spot. Syreeta will be here tomorrow." He plucks at the fabric of his shirt. "It's just a body. It's been good to me. Like a donkey I've ridden around for sixty five years. No big deal." He cups his right hand and drums on his breast bone with the tips of his fingers. It makes a pleasing, resonant sound.

"I got one thing to say to you, Aaron. Remember what I said before: when you get into trouble, ask for help. You have too much pride. Don't let it stop you from asking for help when you get in trouble. And you, Tyrone. You got bigger and stranger desires than Aaron. Try not to let them distract you from what you really do. You play keyboard, man, you got a special gift. Be grateful. Leave the other shit alone. I can see that you have to walk a strange path, you have to go someplace that not too many people go. It'll take courage, but I have faith in you. Now, I'm gonna smoke one last cheroot." He has the familiar red and white cardboard packet on the table next to the easy chair. There are two remaining cheroots.

With a transfixed expression, Tyrone leans forward with his cigarette lighter and lights the brown cylinder's tip. Zoot Prestige inhales gratefully and relaxes into the chair. He looks from one young man's face to the other. His right eyebrow rises slightly, his left eye narrows.

"As you can imagine," he says, after a few more leisurely puffs, "I've been considering what my last words might be. For a while I flirted with the vanity of uttering profound and memorable last words. A person's last words are powerful indicators of the nature of that person. Whether or not one has been true to one's nature can be revealed in last words. Stonewall Jackson said, 'Let us go across the river'. Socrates made a subtle in-joke about offering a sacrifice to Aesclapius. Charlie Parker, that estimable improvisor, laughed at a clown on TV, said, 'what a gas' and expired. At least that's the legend, the myth. Knowing Bird, he might have been referring to his own prodigious flatulence. As for Zoot Prestige, you cats can repeat this to anybody: Zoot Prestige's last words are simple." He hands the half-smoked cheroot to Tyrone. "Will you put that out for me?" he requests. He reaches for the cardboard cheroot container, unwraps a fresh one, and looks at Aaron. "Do you have a light?" he asks. He hands the cheroot to Aaron as if it is some kind of sceptre or talisman.

With that, he places his hands in his lap, leans back, closes his eyes, and departs this world. The breath leaves his body in a long, tranquil sigh.

Hands shaking, tears pouring from his eyes, Aaron lights the cheroot and shares it with Tyrone. Ritualistically, the young jazz men blow the smoke across the body of their mentor.

Chapter Twenty Six

Funeral   **Circus**
1969: San Francisco

The phone rings. Automatically, Aaron picks up the receiver. He is exhausted and numb with shock.

Aaron recognizes Bill Graham's voice on the phone. It is low and has a distinctive creaminess to it, the voice of a singer who has never tried to sing.

"Hi. I'd like to speak to Zoot Prestige."

"Zoot passed on this morning." It is hard to get the words out. They stick in Aaron's windpipe, squeezed by sudden grief.

There is silence on the other end. Then, "Passed on? You mean he died?"

Aaron can only murmur, "Mmmhmmm. Yes."

"My god. What happened?"

Aaron can't speak. He holds the phone and sobs. "Nothing happened," he says at last. "He died. Beautifully. Peacefully. No pain. He talked to us and he died. It was his time. The coroner and the police have been here. To them it's just an old black jazz musician who dropped dead, but it isn 't......it is......"

Tyrone utters a stifled howl. He sits on the fire escape landing, outside the opened window.

"I'll be there in fifteen minutes," says Bill Graham.

After that, the funeral is a Bill Graham production. Tickets are sent to everyone in Zoot's family.

Zoot would have enjoyed this, Aaron thinks. It's so goofy. Jimi Hendrix is in town and brings a bunch of gaudily dressed women. There are expensive cars and limos parked all the way down the access road from Fort Cronkite. The Doors, the Airplane, Jerry from the Dead, the weird speed freaks from Blue Cheer, Joe Cocker, agents, publicists, promoters, hangers-on, photographers from the Chronicle, photographers from Rolling Stone. Somehow the proceedings end up in the hands of Lama Tsangpo Rimpoche, dressed in his dark crimson robe with the slash of yellow at the throat and breast.

Syreeta has arrived on the evening of Zoot's death. She is with two of Zoot's Arkansas children, Christine and Paul, both in their twenties. They wait for three of Zoot's Chicago kids on another flight. Then the next day they pick up Zoot's St. Louis offspring, Cherie and Latifa. Zoot's ex-wives will arrive in the evening.

Syreeta is shocked by the tumult. They stand at the highest promontory of the headlands, looking out at the Pacific. The Golden Gate Bridge pokes out from a single tongue of fog that oozes into the Bay. The rest of the headland is drenched in sunlight.

"Who are all these people?"

"They're his fans," Aaron explains. "At least they are now."

"Well, where were they when Zoot couldn't work, five years ago?

How come he's so famous now that he's dead?"

A cool wind is blowing in off the ocean. Someone's feather boa lofts into the air, shrieks follow it, a giggling hippie woman chases it until it blows away into the sea. The smell of marijuana saturates the air, fumes of it drift over the crowd.

Syreeta is holding the urn. Lama Tsangpo Rimpoche, looking appropriately enlightened, crinkles his eyes wisely and intones a sutra in the supernaturally low Tibetan chanting voice. Jim Morrison passes out tabs of acid. Hendrix takes one. It doesn't seem possible for so many phosphorescent egos to occupy the same piece of land for more than ten seconds. Everyone wants attention. Everyone wants to be photographed as an important and integral part of the funeral of the now-legendary Zoot Prestige.

The Lama gestures to Syreeta, putting out his hands as if he has been assigned the duty of disposing of the ashes.

Syreeta clutches the urn tightly to her chest. "No way , man, you ain't tossing my husband's ashes!" The wind has turned so that her voice goes right back into the crowd. Someone laughs like a hyena. The laugh is so ludicrous that it makes someone else laugh, and its contagion spreads until hundreds of people are laughing hyena laughs.

Syreeta turns and tries to bull her way through the crowd. Aaron tugs at the sleeve of her jacket and catches up with her.

"It's a farce, Syreeta. Zoot would love it. I feel him laughing right now." Aaron smells a puff of Dutch Masters cheroot, but sees no guest smoking anything like it.

Zoot's wife sags against his arm. Tyrone holds her from the other side. Zoot's kids form a phalanx around her and lead her back to the promontory.

Aaron finds a milk crate brought by one of the photographers. He snatches it and stands up so that he can see and be seen above the press of bodies.

"Okay, people," he shouts. "My friend Zoot Prestige died two days ago. His wife is here. His ex-wives and children are here. If you're not here out of respect for him then you can go someplace else and get high and have a a fucking happening. Please!"

They quiet. Bill Graham stands nearby looking angry and embarrassed. The Lama folds his arms and nods benevolently.

Aaron looks at Syreeta for permission to continue. She nods, mouthing the words, "go ahead."

"I want to talk about Zoot Prestige, " Aaron begins. It is hard, for a moment, to continue. When he has composed himself, he goes on. "When I was ten years old I bought my first Zoot Prestige record. It is called 'Tenor Land'. I listened to that thing so many times I wore it out. I was just a little kid. I had to buy records from my allowance. When I could afford it, I bought another Zoot Prestige record, the one he made with Illinois Jacquet, "Tender Tenors". All ballads. All soulful stuff. I bought so many of his records. There are a hundred great jazz tenor players from Texas and Arkanasas, but he is my man, he is the one who grabbed me. I can recognize his tone in two seconds if I hear it blindfolded. He is always about one tenth of a tone sharp, that's his trademark. That and his rasp. He has one motherfuck of a rasp."

"Amen," somebody says.

"It's hard for me to separate the man from the music," Aaron continues. "There are a lot of talented people who are great in their talent but are not so great as human beings. Zoot wasn't like that. Zoot really took his talent as a gift from god and not as something that entitled him to special treatment. He never thought of himself as a genius. He was a working tenor player. He played three hundred nights a year for fifty years. He supported a large extended family. I feel incredibly lucky to have worked with him for the last few years. I've learned more about life and music from Zoot Prestige than any other human being on this earth."

He pauses and looks into the eyes of people. He sees, towards the back of the crowd, the faces of Sonny Stitt and Jackie Mclean, great jazz saxophonists, unrecognized amid the panoply of hippie celebrities.

"Zoot is my mentor, my father. I will miss him terribly."

Aaron looks to Syreeta and steps off the crate.

She steps onto it and opens the top of the urn. She waits for the swirling wind to settle. When it shifts seaward she turns the container upside down and Zoot's ashes flow in a silken ribbon on the wind, out from the promontory, away from the edge of the cliff. They begin dispersing as a side-wind picks them up and takes them parralel to the coast. In half a minute, they have vanished.

Syreeta tosses the urn into the ocean.

Jimi Hendrix is dressed in blue velvet bell bottom pants, a black cavalry hat with silver buckled headband, Hawaian flower shirt and a light blue fringed leather vest. As people filter back down the road from the headlands, he catches up with Aaron and Zoot's family.

"Excuse me," he says, quietly and politely. Syreeta turns. Aaron and Tyrone support her. "I want to tell you how deeply sad I am at the death of your husband. If there's anything I can do I will be very happy to help."

"Thank you very much," Syreeta replies. "What's your name?"

"Oh...I'm Jimi."

The musician is very stoned but seems to find this an ordinary state not needing further behavioral amplification. His pupils are utterly dilated, and Aaron can almost hear the buzzing of feedback guitar emerging from them.

"Mr. Graham has arranged a small reception at his house," Syreeta discloses. "My intention is to keep it private and discrete, but I'm touched by your sweetness and would very much like for you to come."

"That will be an honor, ma'am." The guitarist's voice is soft and melodious. Hendrix looks at Aaron. Their eyes meet and Aaron hears a majestic chord, as plainly as if the musician has plucked his guitar on the spot.

"We haven't really introduced ourselves," Hendrix says, extending a hand toward Aaron. "I'm Jimi. I watched your Fillmore gig from behind the stage; it just knocked my socks off. You know, I played with Zoot for about a month in, I think, fifty nine, when he had his rhythm and blues revue." Hendrix laughs fondly. "It was great. By the way, you really handled this mess here today beautifully. I wanted to punch some of these assholes."

"Thanks." Aaron flushes. He doesn't have many rock heroes, but Hendrix is one of them. He pulls Tyrone towards him. The organist, grinning toothily, is star-struck.

"Hey man, I'm Tyrone."

Hendrix makes a click with his tongue on the inside of his cheek, points at Tyrone and says, "Hammond B-3 man. You got some foot action on that thing!"

"Yeaahh," Tyrone's shoulders do a shimmy. Aaron sees, again, as he has seen so often, the body language of black men, black musicians, exchanging information about one another's hipness, adequacy, insight and fortitude. He can never truly participate in it; he can be close to it, he can measure up to it in his own way, but he will never bond as a black man to another black man no matter how many years he spends in the company of hip black musicians.

Tyrone takes Hendrix in tow and introduces him to all of Zoot's children and wives. The young ones know exactly who this person is named Jimi Hendrix. Zoot's wives are without the benefit of such knowledge and are more pleased by the musician's courtly manner and consideration.

The parties get into their respective limousines and drive fifteen minutes to Bill Graham's Corte Madera mansion at the top of Camino Alto Hill.

For those who have never been to California, the scene has a dream-like quality. Zoot's family gapes out the big picture window in Graham's living room at the vista of the city across the Bay, the Golden Gate Bridge, the cars whizzing past Sausalito on Highway 101. Aaron, Tyrone and Jimi Hendrix walk out onto the deck.

Aaron is aware, standing up close to such a famous person, that Jimi Hendrix is quite ordinary, his skin has pock marks, there are dark bags under his eyes and his breath smells of tobacco and marijuana.

"I wanted to talk to you guys about a gig," Hendrix states. "I need you for this one scene, because the guys in my band flew back to New York. There's a benefit we can play for the Haight Free Clinic that's gonna be this weekend. You wanna do it?"

Tyrone looks at Aaron.

"Yeah, we'll do it. Are you nuts? We'll do it." Aaron declares.

"Fuckin' A, man." Hendrix takes out a cigarette and extends the pack to Aaron and Tyrone.

Aaron shakes his head. Tyrone takes one. "We can rehearse at the Airplane Mansion, on Fulton Street. You know where that is?"

"We'll find it," Aaron and Tyrone say in unison.

"Allright. How about tomorrow night?"

"You're on," Tyrone says, and he and Hendrix do the palm-slide, hooked finger handshake with the thumb up at the end. Hendrix extends his hand toward Aaron. With perfect timing and smooth execution, Aaron slides his palm across Jimi's, hooks his fingers in the musicians' fingers, then ends with the thumbs up.

Chapter Twenty Seven

Troubles   In   Toyland
1972: Sarah, St. Louis

"Mom, I hate this!" Lisa pushes at her bowl of brown rice, turning it over so that sticky grains of it fall into the crack between the leaves of the expandable formica kitchen table.

Sarah's lips circle impatiently as if she is sucking on a straw that fails to draw liquid. "It's good for you," she says, fighting to control her anger. "It's macrobiotic."

"I hate Mark----mac---I hate this food!" Lisa kicks at the table leg, using the leverage to scooch her chair backwards until she is able to stand and push it over with her behind. "Why can't I have twinkies? I want twinkies. Everybody eats twinkies!"

Lisa begins to cry with frustration and runs from the room.

It is raining outside. An October thunderstorm rattles the building. As the wind rises and falls, vertical sheets of rain bulge the windows in their frames. It is six forty five in the evening. Sarah picks at the grains of rice with a butter knife until she has winkled each grain out of the table seam, then scoops them together and throws them into the trash. She takes what remains in Lisa's bowl and adds it to her own.

Have to chew sixty times each bite, she reminds herself. Her jaw works solemnly. The sound of television comes from the living room: an unavoidable vice for a single mother with an eight year old child. She never watches it herself. She reads books on Macrobiotics, Yoga, Philosophy and Psychology. She listens to Chopin, Bob Dylan and Dave Brubeck. She meditates and practices Tai Chi.

Having finished her unadorned rice, she washes it down with Mu Tea and cleans the dishes. She feels her body with her hands, running them down her front and sides. Still too fat, she thinks. Too full of pollutants. If I stick to the number seven diet for another twenty one days, I might clear myself. I know it's hard on Lisa. But if I so much as let a twinkie into the apartment, I'll start eating them. I can't do that. I can't.

She hears the bell ring, followed by the sound of the door opening. It is her dad. He comes to visit almost every night, sometimes for a few minutes, sometimes for hours.

Max puts his head around the eaves of the kitchen door. He takes off his raincoat and hangs it on the hook in the hallway.

"How are you?" The three words, as always, come as three notes, the first two identical, the third rising. There is a V-shaped wrinkle of concern at the top of Max's nose.

"I'm fine. Lisa just threw a fit."

"About what?" He takes one of the chairs and sits, while his daughter starts a pot of boiling water. She keeps instant decaf for Max's sake. Otherwise she will have no polluting product of plastic society in her kitchen.

"What else? Food. What am I supposed to do? She doesn't understand how important it is not to poison herself. She's just a kid, and all the other kids eat crap and rot themselves out from the inside."

Max knows he is going to sigh, and manages to limit himself to a movement of his chest and shoulders. Sarah looks so gaunt. Her eyes are black with strain. She has lost thirty pounds and her arms are beginning to resemble sticks. It is heartbreaking. Here she is, deliberately turning herself into a concentration camp victim.

"Don't you know how thin you are?" He asks. He can't help it. He can't just sit there and watch.

"Thin!" Sarah's voice arches with disbelief. "I'm a cow." She puts a hand on her belly. "Mooo! I'm huge."

"No you're not. You're losing weight so fast it scares me. Your color is bad. You're turning Lisa into a lonely child who can't play with other kids and can't eat normal food like normal people. Why do you have to do this?"

"This is an old conversation, dad. It's okay for you to eat meat and fat, that's all you've ever known. It's disgusting."

For a moment, Sarah looks so much like Esther that it gives Max a cold spasm of dread. So much craziness in this family, he thinks. So much craziness.

He takes the proffered cup of coffee. "I'll go see what Lisa's doing. I'm on my way to pick up some prescriptions from the drug store. Do you need anything?"

Sarah shakes her head.

"I'll take Lisa, " Max offers.

"Fine, " Sarah agrees. She knows he will buy twinkies for his granddaughter. She feels too weak to say anything about it.

As Max is putting on Lisa's rain gear, he is aware of the strain in the little girl. He examines her features, marveling at the utter and seemingly divine delicacy of her face, at the mixture of Jew and Hispanic that has united in this child to create such an imaginative and passionate creature. There are storms in her. How can there not be?

"You ready?" he asks the little girl.

She holds a finger to her lips. Her eyes gleam. "Twinkies," she whispers to Max. He is kneeling beside her in the hallway of the flat. He reaches forward and flips a lock of dark hair from Lisa's eyes and tucks it up into her clear plastic rain bonnet.

"Shhh," he responds, "it's our secret." Then, calling out to Sarah in the kitchen, he says, "We'll be back in a little while."

"Okay." Sarah's voice is muffled and indistinct.

They race from the building through the blowing rain and get into Max's car.

As he drives down the road, he hears Lisa singing a song through the roar of the storm.

"......and a hard rain is gonna fall..." she intones, her voice well pitched, sweet and full.

"What is that?" Max inquires.

"It's a Bob Dylan song, I think...."

"And who is Bob Dylan?"

"Grampa," she says, outraged, "don't you know ANYTHING?"

"I'm just an old square," he speaks indulgently.

"You mean a 'straight person', grampa. Not square. That's out. That's been out for a long time."

"Oh. I guess I'm a very straight person, then. What's that mean, anyway?"

"I don't know." Lisa's voice is full of juvenile impatience. "It means you eat meat and don't take drugs and don't care about getting enlightened."

"Oy, veyzmir." Max has a familiar feeling, as if he's about to find out something he'd rather not know.

"Does your mom take drugs?"

"Oh don't be silly. She doesn't take drugs. That's what uncle Aaron does. But she wants to be enlightened and that means not eating meat and not laughing and having fun and not doing all kinds of things."

This isn't quite the thing Max dreaded learning, but it makes him very sad.

When they reach the drug store, Lisa races to the checkout stand with a handful of Twinkies

packages. She wiggles her fingers at Max, demanding money. He gives her a dollar, lets her pay, then takes her in tow to the rear of the store where the pharmacist is located. On their way down the aisle, Lisa spots a toy she wants and slumps her body so that she is almost on the floor, hanging from Max's arm.

"I want that doll." Her voice is peremptory.

"We're not here to buy toys, Lisa. Twinkies, I'll get my prescription, then we go home."

"I want that doll!" she screeches, in a voice that charges the hushed air of the entire store.

Customers turn to look.

Max takes three breaths, then tries to pull Lisa upright.

"No," he says, firmly.

Lisa lets go of his hand and launches herself toward the shelf that holds rows of dolls. She pulls one down, then a second. Twinkies packages drop to the floor.

"I said no," Max reiterates. He smiles at a passing shopper, taking his eyes from his grandaughter. When he turns his attention back to Lisa, she is running down the aisle. One arm is flailing; she is pulling items from the shelves. In the other arm she clutches the doll. "I want the doll!" She screams, "I want the doll!"

A bottle of cough syrup comes from its shelf and crashes to the floor, breaking and spilling red fluid. Lisa runs to the checkout counter and thrusts the doll at the clerk.

"I want this, I want this, I want this," she insists.

The clerk looks on helplessly. Max hurries to the cashier and picks Lisa up. She pummels his thighs with the back of her boots. She is strong and heavy and capable of inflicting real pain.

"I'm sorry," he says, putting a twenty dollar bill on the counter. "I'd better get her out of here. Is

this enough for the doll and the broken things?"

The clerk looks around for her manager, but as Lisa's screams intensify, she takes the money and waves Max out the door.

In the car, Lisa is subdued, fascinated with the doll. Her face is full of Twinkies, white cream smearing her lips and cheeks.

Max is appalled. This is behavior never before witnessed, but it has a familiar tang to it, a familial scent. It should not have surprised him.

* * *

Max thinks things through, and by the time he reaches Sarah's building, he has made a decision. The storm has slackened. There is an eerie, mid-thunderstorm lull, the kind that sometimes heralds tornadoes. It is a green darkness, the hidden moon is illuminating the backs of the clouds and casting weird absence over the landscape.

Lisa is in a trance. She holds the doll close to her face and walks down the hall to the living room, completely preoccupied. Max finds Sarah where he left her, sitting and staring at the unyielding surface of the table. She looks as though she is wrestling an internal doppelganger, as though she is paralyzed by the equal strengths of her outer and inner selves.

He takes the chair opposite. Sarah gazes at him with dulled eyes. He recognizes this thing, this depression as an integral and malevolent component of his offspring, of his entire family tree.

"You're in trouble," he begins, cautiously.

"I'm fine," Sarah says wanly.

"You're not fine. Your child is not fine. As far as I'm concerned, you can do what you want, but Lisa is suffering and very frustrated. You have no idea what just happened at Glaser's......"

"Frustrated." Sarah shows more animation. "That's really good. What will you know about frustrated?" She considers for a moment what she has just said.

"No, that's not fair. You know from frustrated. You're married to it. Jesus, what a thing, to be married to frustration. You poor man....."

Max does not want to hear more of this, so he speaks before his anger can gather into enough cloud mass to create lightning.

"I think you should go into the hospital. Just for a while, to get things straightened out. Lisa will be allright. She can be with us, or with Aunt Violet."

"The hospital!" Sarah is astonished. "The hospital!? Is that your answer to everything, to put us in the hospital?" She rises from the table, her voluminous shift falling away from her body, covering her from neck to ankle in a gray shroud. It conceals her form, the body she is convinced is so fat.

"What's it like?" Sarah taunts, "What's it like to be the still center of all this everlasting trauma? Does it make you feel powerful? Does it give you a purpose in life?"

Max looks at his own chest. He adjusts his glasses, then clasps both hands in his lap. "I don't know," he says, after a long pause. "I don't know. I'm trying to help. I want you to be happy. Can you admit that you're terribly unhappy, that things aren't going so well, that you're depressed?"

"

I hate that word, 'depressed'. What's it mean? That I think I'm a piece of shit? That nobody will ever love me? That I have utter panic at the thought of being a mother, I mean I know I'm not raising her right, I know that, I'm a terrible mother. How can I know anything about being a mother?" Sarah's mouth quivers as if it is a leaf drowning in a downpour. She blinks and tears squeeze from the sides and bottoms of her eyes, forming a single large riverine streak that drains towards her lips.

She sits down hard in the chair with its little piece of broken naugahyde where the stuffing shows through. She cries as if she is coughing, a-hunk a-hunk, shoulders jerking.

Max would die or condemn himself to eternal hell if he couold alleviate his child's suffering. He

holds his impulse to crush her to his shoulders and comfort her. He can 't do that. It has never been his way to hug or hold people. He has quills exactly two feet long, and few people ever get through those quills.

"She's wrong," he internally asserts. "This doesn't give me any feeling of power or purpose. This just breaks my heart."

When Sarah composes herself, she takes a napkin and blows her nose. "All right, " she concedes. "I'll go into the hospital. I don't know what else to do, and I'm scared."

Chapter Twenty Eight

The Great Pyramid Of Frisco

1969

After the Hendrix gig, Aaron rents an apartment in the city with Tyrone. It is on Fell Street, just three blocks from the freeway exit. Cars and trucks downshift to climb the steep hill, growling in agony like caged and frustrated circus animals. The view from the back porch compensates for the noise and fumes. The bayward facing aspect of Downtown San Francisco rises like an ancient Egyptian city, translated into the modern world. The truncated dome of St. Mary's cathedral commands the foreground, white and gleaming against the pure blue sky. Attempting to dominate the further skyline, the Transamerica Pyramid's tapering spire somehow loses out to Coit Tower and the houses on Telegraph Hill.

For a week, Tryone and Aaron have little to do. They walk towards Golden Gate Park, stumbling into rock concerts in the Panhandle, observing the psychedelic madness as it slides inexorably toward amphetamine and heroin extinction.

Only now does Zoot's death feel like a real blow. To Aaron, it seems as if he has to devise a new method of breathing. Without Zoot, he feels unguided, unfathered.

He and Tyrone sit on the landing at the top of the stairs that go down the rear of the building. Five hippies live below them, on the ground floor. There is a constant stream of colorful people moving in the tiny back yard, hanging gorgeous tie-dyed clothes on lines. A supple, bare-breasted young woman smiles upward at the two musicians, who smile toothily back.

"Man oh man oh man, " Tyrone says, "lookee that."

"I lookee. I'm trying not to lookee, but I can't help lookeee."

"Why you trying not to lookee?"

"It's not polite to stare. Didn't your mother teach you that?"

"My mother," Tyrone says pithily, "taught me to wash between my toes but she didn't say nothing about staring." He inhales his cigarette, then blows a series of smoke rings.

Aaron waves his hand to dispel the smoke that drifts into his face.

"You know something?" Tyrone inquires rhetorically.

"What?"

"I think I'm a woman in a man's body."

"Keep the man's body," Aaron quips. "You'd be a really ugly chick."

"You think so?" Tyrone makes a moue of his lips, as if he is distributing freshly applied lipstick.

Aaron remembers the female face he saw the night of the gig, the night before Zoot's death. He looks at his friend and transposes a female body beneath the familiar face. He has to imagine an absence of facial hair. No flamboyant goatee, no double-spiked beard poking down almost to Tyrone's chest, no bushy moustache sitting beneath his nose like a squirrel.

"You know," he admits, "I think you'd be fine no matter which way you fly. It's just that I've related to you as a man since I've known you. It will be hard to switch. And, considering everything else…I mean you're a black jazz musician, so being a chick is not one of your better ideas."

With great deliberation, Tyrone reaches his hand out, takes Aaron's chin and forces his friend to face him. Looking into his eyes, he says, "I'm serious. I think I am a woman in a man's body."

Aaron regards Tyrone for a long time, before sighing. "Have I been colossally insensitive about something for the last couple of years?"

"No,"says Tyrone, returning his gaze to the woman in the yard. "I haven't been lettting out any signals, I ain't been signifyin' nothin'. But now Zoot's gone, seems like maybe you'll be gone too, maybe everybody be gone, so I think I better start telling my truth as I see it. It's WEIRD, man!" He flaps his hands around. They are almost winglike, they are so huge. "I aint a fag or nothing. I like women. Maybe I'm a lesbian. If that makes sense. Cause I sure don't feel like no man. All my life I been pretending, just so's to fit in." He starts crying. Aaron doesn't know what to do. Now, of all times, he can't embrace the man/woman sitting next to him. All he can do is listen. This is pure alien territory. "I want to dress like a woman, but I can't. I see the world like a woman, I feel things, I don't think things or analyze things. You know my music; it's so....so...feeling!

"Oh yes!" Aaron agrees. "Maybe...." he stumbles for a moment. "I read something in this book I have; you know the big book, 'Thinking and Destiny'? "

"God, I don't know how you can read that shit," Tyrone admonishes, with slight envy.

"It helps me make sense of things. Percival, the guy that wrote it, says that sometimes people reincarnate over and over as a particular gender. Then, because they need to have experience as the other gender, they start having transitional lives where they aren't sure of their gender, and after maybe twenty lives as a female, say, they turn up male, and they're confused, until they've lived male for a couple of lives. Or vice versa, you know? Maybe you're in a transitional life, and you're starting to think female but your body hasn't caught up, and you need to listen to that inner voice, and follow your destiny."

"Now THAT makes sense, " Tyrone agrees, "because I sure am confused. However totally far out wiggy your explanation is."

Aaron laughs, part of him knowing that it is indeed wiggy, part of him willing to entertain pure wigginess for the sake of having an open and speculative mind. After a few minutes of silence, while the traffic roars on the street in front of the house, and the young woman in the yard sings quietly to herself, Tyrone says, "I may have to go to LA in a month or two."

Aaron feels a pang of fear grip his stomach. Too many losses.

"No, Tyrone. Why?"

"Cause there's a doctor down there understands this shit, and he can give me hormones and counseling and help me figure this out. I can't find anybody up here. Don't worry, I ain't going right away. Let's make some friends here, first, play some music. This city's crazy, man."

Inside the house the telephone rings. It has only been installed the day before, so this is an occasion. "Who is that?" Aaron wonders. "Who will know this number, besides Bill Graham?"

"So? Maybe it's Bill Graham."

Aaron stands, patting paint chips from the rear of his pants, goes through the door, through the kitchen, to the living room with its three orange crates and mattress on the bare wooden floor. He picks up the telephone and looks out the front window. A huge Allied Van Lines truck is snarling its way up the grade.

"Hello."

"Uh, is this Aaron Kantro?"

"Yes. That's right."

"Oh good....this is Rob Weird."

"Rob Weird." Aaron tries on the syllables of the name as if they are a shirt just taken from a store hanger. "Am I supposed to know you?"

"Oh, sorry. I'm the rhythm guitarist with the Dreadful Great. Bill gave me your number. I saw you and the organist at the Free Clinic benefit."

"Oh, cool. So.....are the Great as Dreadful as I've heard?"

Rob Weird laughs. "They're pretty dreadful. That's why I'm calling you.

I'm splitting from the band, I've been writing some more jazz-like stuff. When I saw you and, what's his name, Tyrone? at the Hendrix thing I thought, yeah, that's what I need. You guys got a gig? You think you want to come to Larkspur and check things out?"

Tyrone is looking for something to sit on, settles for the windowsill, where he perches himself on half a butt cheek, extending his legs straight forward to achieve an uncomfortable balance.

"I think we can play some gigs," Aaron says, keeping excitement from spilling into his voice.

"This is pay-money-type gigs, right, not some volunteer thing, because we got one month's worth of rent on this apartment and a big ass Continental and not much else."

"Yeah, this is a money gig. I've made so goddam much money from the Dreadful Great and my one stupid hit song, you know that song."

"No, I don't, sorry."

"Well, never mind, let me give you the address. What you guys doing tonight?"

Aaron winks at Tyrone. "I think we're coming to Larkspur to hear your material."

Rob Weird laughs again. At first Aaron thinks it is a put-on laugh. It is a classic Snidely Whiplash villain's laugh, an evil and conniving chuckle with intermittent hiccups. Aaron realizes, as the laugh tapers to its inevitable conclusion, that this is Rob Weird's laugh, this is his real laugh. It's a laugh that you just have to laugh at. How does he get through life with this laugh?

"Okay, give me the address. Isn't Larkspur near Corte Madera?"

"Yeah the next town over. It's easy to find."

Chapter Twenty Nine

Hitting The Wall
1972: Jewish Veteran's Hospital, St. Louis

The orderly's name is Ellsworth Fish. He is a light-skinned black man with long eyelashes and delicate hands. After Sarah has been checked in, this aptly named creature leads her towards her assigned room. He is so tall that Sarah's eyes are below the bronzed name-badge pinned to his shirt pocket. He reminds me of a Fourth of July sparkler, she thinks. I can imagine his head being lit up and burning down his wire-thin frame.

"You're in Room 18 honey," Ellsworth lisps. "It's this way....." He looks up from his clip board, waves the middle three fingers of his hand with the thumb planted against the palm and the pinky sticking out sideways. The gesture is odd and quite distinctive.

"I know." Sarah sighs. "It's the same room my mother was in ten years ago."

"That's TERRIBLE!" Ellsworth's voice rises and falls in a perfect bell-shaped curve. He stops and looks with sympathy at Sarah. "We're completely full this week, but if someone gets discharged we can change you."

"Never mind, it's okay." Sarah is wearing a dark green sleeveless shift over a white turtle neck sweater. She clutches its volume at the knees with her left hand to keep from stumbling over it. In her right hand she holds her suitcase.

"You have a room-mate. Her name is Christine."

"That's fine, that's fine, whatever." Sarah is aware of several things at once. She is still hearing the sound of the wire-reinforced glass door that leads into the ward. It locks automatically with a ka-chunk, its tumblers sounding the irrevocable nature of psychiatric imprisonment. On the other hand, she feels a relief. There's no macrobiotic food in here, she realizes. No brown rice to chew sixty times each bite. It's going to be baloney sandwiches and beef stew, hot dogs, every sort of disgusting crap, and I'm going to have to eat it. Why does that make me so happy?

Room eighteen has an eight by twelve inch rectangle of reinforced glass, to give the staff a view of whatever transpires within. Ellsworth opens the door. Light spills wanly between the slats of the heavily wired south-facing window. A young woman sits on the bed closest to the window. She has short dark hair that looks as if strands of it have been glued together and arranged perpendicular to other strands. She looks up with bruised eyes as Ellsworth and Sarah enter.

"Christine, this is Sarah," the orderly explains with a patient voice. The woman says nothing, and puts her attention back to the celebrity magazine she is reading.

Ellsworth takes Sarah's suitcase. " Excuse me, honey. I have to search this, nothing personal you know. We just don't want razors or nail clippers or anything like that."

Briskly, he examines the contents of the luggage. He puts Sarah's nail clippers, files and a small scissors into a manila envelope attached to his clipboard. "You'll get these back when you leave, and I hope that's very soon." He touches her bicep with his long fingers whose cuticles are perfectly cleaned and manicured.

"There, that's fine," he says, when he is finished. He turns to Christine. "You behave yourself," he admonishes. "Be nice."

Christine thrusts her lower lip outward. "Fag nigger cocksucking putz," she hisses, and shows her upper teeth.

"I don't have to stay here and listen to you," Ellsworth speaks with finality. He looks once more at Sarah, checking, making an inventory. With a slightly fatalistic hitch of his shoulders, he leaves the room.

Sarah sits on her bed. Christine tears a strip from the magazine, licks it at one end, then sticks it to the middle of her forehead, so that it dangles from her hairline and drapes across her nose. She blows at it, making it rise and fall.

"I've had six hundred and twenty two acid trips," she announces. "I've fucked one thousand and eleven guys. I fucked Mick Jagger twice. I did a three way with David Bowie and another chick."

"I can see you're very proud of these achievements," Sarah responds.

"Well, don't tell anybody, but tonight I'm gonna make it six hundred twenty three acid trips, and I'm gonna fuck that orderly Charles who does the night shift."

She finds a photograph of Mick Jagger in the magazine, tears it out and pastes it to her chin. The strip on her forehead falls to the floor. The photo on her chin wags like a celluloid beard.

"Are you planning on having these adventures in this room?" Sarah looks around at the sparse chamber. She can remember her mother, lying on the very same bed, after shock treatments.

"Don't be silly, I'd get caught. I plan to lure Charles out on the deck and slip my hand down his pants before he even knows what's happening. He is so cute; he is cute cute cute, you should see him, you will see him, he's a doll, a doll doll. Y'wanna cigarette? We can't smoke in here. Let's go out on the deck."

"I don't smoke," Sarah demurs, "but I'll keep you company. What does everybody do here, all day?"

"Occupational therapy at ten, group therapy at one, individual therapy whenever. And a lot of time to plan escape in between." Christine neighs nervously. It is not a laugh, it is a compulsive space-filler that reveals the depths of her social unease.

The fifth floor locked ward is basically L-shaped, with two large community rooms at each end of the L. The long arm of the L ends in the TV lounge, where people spend a great deal of their day. The deck is outside the TV lounge.

Sarah is drenched in deja vu. She has not seen this ward since she was twelve years old. She can remember the view out over the park, through the brick wall with its fleur-de-lys patterned holes. An awesome cumulo-nimbus cloud rises above the city, its base rounded and layered like a cake, its top boiling with upward moving cauliflower stalks. Another big storm coming, Sarah thinks. She can feel its electricity in her bones.

There are six other people on the deck, sitting in various chairs and lounges. Two young men are playing chess across a round white metal table. An extremely obese woman with lank, patchy hair is rooting around obsessively in a paper shopping bag, taking out shapeless plastic objects, empty wooden boxes an inch square, hair curlers. When she has everything out of the bag, she will shake her head with frustration then return all the items to the bag and begin the process once more.

A middle aged man with two tiny pins of hair on his otherwise bald head is trying to play ping pong with himself. He keeps losing. An orderly whose name tag says "Bruce" sits in a picnic chair made of woven green and white plastic strips. Without stirring himself, he intercepts the wayward ping pong balls and tosses them back to the man, who stammers with servile gratitude and returns to his futile game.

Christine leads Sarah to the far end of the deck, where she takes two more picnic chairs and faces them so that their backs are to the rest of the people. Peeking through the holes in the decorative brick, Sarah can see the bridle paths in Forest Park. In the distance a boom of thunder sounds. She has always loved turbulent weather. She thrills at the immense mountains of cyclonic wind and tar-black cloud that rage over the midwest during the spring and summer.

Christine compresses her lips inward so that the red parts disappear inside her mouth and her cigarette is held between stretched white flesh over rows of teeth. She uses an engraved steel lighter that shoots a high flame. It's such a silly pose, Sarah muses, "bad girl lights cigarette and puffs rebelliously". Give me a break.

"You're not really going to take acid tonight, are you? That's just the delusional thinking, right?"

Christine leans sideways, closer to Sarah. She rotates her head towards the other people on the deck, checking the orderly named Bruce. Then she digs with her free hand into the pocket of her blouse, and brings out a little bindle of folded paper. She puts her cigarette back into her mouth and uses both hands to unfold the bindle. Inside the bindle is a little square of paper with the face of a purple Mickey Mouse stamped onto it.

"One of my friends smuggled it in." She puts the LSD-charged square of paper onto the tip of her finger and holds it towards Sarah.

Leaning forward to inspect this exotic substance, Sarah rounds her lips and blows firmly, lofting the paper square out through the view holes in the ornamental brickwork. The dose of acid disappears on the gathering wind.

Christine's eyes go round, her cigarette drops to the concrete deck. She gropes forward through the curtain of her surprise.

"You....you bitch!" She says, and one of her hands opens as if to slap at Sarah. "I don't believe

you did that!"

Sarah has been married to Carlo. Sarah knows fake toughness. She bristles and says, "if you even think of touching me I will beat the living crap out of you. I could have told the orderly, I could have turned you in. I know, we're SUPPOSED to be crazy, but if you think taking acid on a locked psych ward is a good idea, you're REALLY crazy. I don't want you bouncing off the walls of the room all night long, I really don't need this kind of crap right now."

326

Christine gets up, rigidly, overturns her chair, walks across the deck. She approaches two men playing chess and sweeps all the pieces from the board. As Bruce starts to respond to this crisis, the fat lady with the paper bag screams "All whores are in heaven!" and begins pelting the orderly with her bric-a-brac. The chess players overturn the board and spin their chairs crazily. The ping pong player jumps up on the table, which collapses under his weight.

Through the windows of the lounge the other patients see the riot breaking out and begin tearing pillows from couches and overturning chairs. Orderlies rush in and wave futilely at the accelerating chain reaction. In two minutes the frustration and rage are spent, and everyone sags as if they have just shared a powerful sexual experience. Bruce takes Christine in a thumb lock and hustles her to the Isolation Room. Custodians are called in to clean up spilt chocolate milk and fruit juice, and to put the furniture back together.

Sarah stands with her back to the bricks, watching this mayhem, astonished. She sees Ellsworth come through the door, towering over the other people. His eyes meet Sarah's and he comes across the deck.

"It happens about once a week," he explains, lighting a cigarette and putting it into a long onyx holder. "There's nothing we can do but to let it play itself out and try to contain it."

Sarah crosses her arms and clutches both breasts. "And this is a place where people are supposed to get better?"

"Sweetie, it's a warehouse for people whose families have good insurance." He winks at Sarah. "I didn't say that. You didn't hear it. Oh, by the way, its your meds time."

"Meds. What meds? I've only been here twenty minutes. I haven't seen anyone...."

Ellsworth examines his clipboard. "You have meds ordered. By Doctor Tannenbaum. It's right here."

Sarah's innards plummet with sudden fear. She has a horror of drugs, especially psychiatric medication. She has the ghoulish spectacle of her mother to demonstrate the usefulness of drugs.

"I want to talk to this Doctor Tannenbaum right now. Right now."

"She's only here on Tuesdays and Thursdays. You'll have to wait till tomorrow."

"Then I'm not taking any meds, I don't want meds."

Ellsworth flips the cigarette out over the park. "You seem like a pretty reasonable together person, I KNOW you're not crazy like some of the people in here. So I'm gonna tell you right now, we've got procedures for people who refuse to take meds, we can make you take your meds, so it's better if you just march right up to that window and take your meds."

Sarah acknowledges the logic of implied force. She lets Ellsworth accompany her to the dispensing window, where she is given two pills and a paper cup of water. The nurse watches as she puts the pills in her mouth. Sarah drinks the water and swallows. She turns away from the window, nods to Ellsworth, who nods back.

She goes to her room, where she takes the pills from behind her upper lip and flushes them down the toilet.

The next morning, after a breakfast of scrambled eggs, toast and sausage, which Sarah enjoys guiltily but hugely, she is taken out of the ward to the sixth floor, where Dr. Tannenbaum has an office.

The psychiatrist is a woman in her mid-forties, plump, well-coiffed, with long fingernails painted a teal color. Her glasses dangle from a chain just above her breasts. Their black plastic frames contrast with the string of pearls worn around the doctor's neck.

Sarah takes a seat in front of the desk. She finds the woman's smell of soap and perfume a bit overpowering.

"Well," the psychiatrist says, smiling without sincerity. "How are we getting along?"

"Okay, I suppose." Up to this point, Sarah has maintained some strength in the face of her new situation. She wilts under the gaze of this shrink. She knows, immediately, that she will find no human connection with this stiff basilisk of a psychiatrist. Her depression opens inside her chest like a trap door, and she falls through it into a place of utter vulnerability.

"You seem to be adapting well, you haven't made any problems."

In that moment Sarah understands the nature of the game: don't make problems and you'll be out of here. Participate in everything they ask you to do: meet with the shrink and make the appropriate noises, go to group therapy, occupational therapy. Participate. Don't isolate.

"I'm not planning on being a problem. There's just one thing I'd like to know. Why am I being prescribed medications when you've never interviewed me before?"

Dr. Tannenbaum flips through some papers. "I have your case history from Dr. Potts and Dr. Weiner. You were treated for depression in 1967, that treatment proceeded for a year. Then you were treated again in 1970. You're being given a standard anti-depressant and a standard anti-psychotic. That's our procedure for anyone who's admitted to a locked ward."

"Tofranil and Stellazine, right?"

The doctor nods, confirming Sarah's familiarity with the drugs.

This woman's an idiot, Sarah decides, and I'm getting out of here as fast as I can.

Chapter Thirty

It's
1973: Mill Valley, California

The fog comes over the ridge like hundreds of cupped fingers. It hides the tops of sequoia and manzanita trees and slowly whites out the expensive homes that nestle below Panoramic Highway. Aaron's house juts from stilts that balance and clasp it to the wooded hillside. He is sitting on its deck, still bathed in sunlight, reading the Koran and listening to the sound of foghorns as if they are giant sea-cows calling across the Pacific.

Aaron is taking Arabic lessons to better understand the teachings of Sufi masters. It is part of his ongoing education into schools of mysticism. He is convinced that the world is not what it appears to be and that his life is operating at deep levels that he does not understand. He wants to understand. He has a craving to understand. In his guts he feels that he is sick, that his mother has transmitted to him a disease of the soul. At sixteen he began his reading program: psychology, philosophy, Zen, esoteric Christianity, Cabbala. He hopes that somewhere in all this material he might find an answer to his abiding question: what am I? What is wrong with me?

His girlfriend Debra comes out onto the deck trailing the long wire of the telephone. She is just beginning to show her pregnancy. Aaron pulls on his marijuana cigarette and stuffs the roach out in an ashtray shaped like a serpent swallowing its own tail. He looks at Debra and feels vacancy, then dread.

"For you," Debra smiles. She is happy, pregnant, she feels secure. Aaron does not. Aaron feels trapped in a lie whose coils are winding around him ever more tightly.

He takes the telephone and smiles emptily back.

"Yo." he says.

"Hey man, it's Tyreeza."

"Tyrone!" Aaron yelps.

"No, it's Tyreeza. I did it. I got the operation. I don't care if I'm an ugly chick. At least I'm a chick."

Aaron is resigned to his friends' eccentricities, as he regards them. He has no clue about overwhelming gender dysphoria, it is a world hidden from his understanding. "All right, you do what you gotta do. If and when I see you I'm gonna have a hard time relating to you as a woman, so I'm just warning you now. How's things in LA?"

"I'm playing with Art Pepper."

"Holy shit, I thought he was in jail. Is it safe to play with Art Pepper? Is it even legal?"

"No, it's not safe. But motherfucker can wail. It won't last long. He'll be back in jail in a month, I bet you anything."

Art Pepper is a famous jazz musician and low-life. He has great talent, and a greater talent for taking drugs and getting busted.

"So what does LA think about you becoming a woman?"

"LA doesn 't care, L A is just one big sex change procedure anyway. How's Debra?"

"She's pregnant. You can ask her." He hands the phone back. "His.....I mean, her name is now Tyro....Tyreeza."

"Heyyyyy," Debra giggles into the plastic semicircle. "Now we can do chick talk. How are you, Madame Butterfly?"

Aaron sits back in the big wicker chair and looks around. He owns a house worth half a million dollars. It has a deck, a hot tub, a recording studio. His girlfriend is smart, gorgeous, a compact red-head, a wise-cracking comedienne who can dance, sing, tell jokes, act in serious drama, play a decent folk guitar. For reasons unfathomable to himself, Aaron is not in love. For reasons unfathomable to himself, he has agreed to Debra's pregnancy.

For reasons unfathomable, his heart feels empty.

That night, he takes his first taste of opium.

The Rob Weird Band is playing at The Lion's Share, in San Anselmo. It is an in-crowd night, all the Great Heads are there, all of Jerry's friends and Rob's friends and Phil's friends and Judy's friends and Tony's friends and friends of friends and people jostling at the front entrance, the back entrance, claiming to be Aaron's friends.

The definition of success, Aaron thinks, as he puts down his sticks at the end of the first set. People you don't know who claim to be your friends.

He plops down onto the ratty old sofa in the dressing room and accepts a huge joint from someone's friend. The room is crammed with people. Friends. There is so much hair that the bodies underneath seem to be mere appendages. The people yak to each other while the hair carries on its own ethereal communication. Across the room from Aaron there is a woman sitting on a sofa wearing a leather miniskirt. He can feel her staring at him, in the intervals when bodies part sufficiently to allow a view across the room. He looks, briefly, into blue eyes whose concentration and fixity on Aaron's person has an oddly erotic charge. Then his attention is drawn downward, where her legs are spread apart. Aaron's eyes follow the pale white curve of thigh, upward, to where he can see the lips of the woman's pussy, twin ridges of pink flesh barely concealed in a thicket of brownish blonde hair. He feels it breathing, exhaling in his direction, pulsing like a heart. He looks again at the woman's face. She smiles, and pokes the tip of her tongue at the corner of her mouth. She wiggles and pulls the miniskirt a few inches higher. She is positioned so no one but Aaron can see her offering.

"Holy Shit," Aaron groans, feeling the bulk in his pants shifting. He is hypnotized. He gets up and pushes across the room until he stands over the woman. I shouldn't do this, he tells himself, this is not how I operate, this is a devil woman and she means me no good.

Nonetheless, he takes her hand, as if asking her for a dance.

"Let's go outside," he says above the din. Languidly, the woman rises and goes with him out the rear entrance of the club, into the parking lot with its dark crannies. Aaron takes her to his Mercedes. He levers the front seats flat, turning the entire interior into a bed. He lets the woman into the back seat and follows her, shutting the door.

She smiles soundlessly as she lays herself out, pulling her skirt up to her waist. Aaron loosens his belt, unzips his zipper. The woman's knees are bent, thighs wide, high black boots contrasting with the ivory skin of her legs. Aaron puts his weight on her. She undulates once and lets him enter her, slowly. She is tight, like wet velvet sandpaper lubricated with olive oil. At that moment she is the sexiest animal Aaron has ever encountered. He thrusts all the way into her.

"Ah," she says quietly. "Ah."

He pulls himself almost all the way out, then thrusts again.

"Ah," she says again. Aaron looks at the misted eyes. She is far away. He thrusts again. Her hands grip the back of his shirt, her legs fall across his buttocks. He thrusts and the orgasm builds with each thrust until he explodes, bellowing.

"Ah," she says.

From the trembling precipice of orgasm, Aaron falls into a chasm of self-contempt. He has betrayed Debra. He has fucked this total stranger without even knowing her name. He has lost control of himself.

He puts his pants back on. The woman sorts herself out, then digs in her purse until she finds a little clear plastic envelope that contains what appears to be a bar of sticky licorice. "Want some?"

"What is it?"

"Opium." She licks her lips and tears a chunk of the piece. "Real opium, not that stupid stuff that's incense and miso paste. Really beautiful, really really beautiful."

"Addictive as hell," Aaron says.

"It's not like heroin. Kicking opium's a breeze, like having the flu."

Aaron is numbed by his weakness, by his own capacity for evil. He has fucked Debra and got her pregnant and told her he loves her when it isn't true, and now he is going to have to marry her and become a father, and he doesn't want these things at all. He wants to be a free rich rock star with a big house in Mill Valley and be able to fuck women like this groupie any time he feels like doing so.

He has lied about his feelings for Debra just because he is too cowardly to hurt her.

He continues lying, even when the pregnancy happens, and he doesn't know why. Then he watches the lie grow around him like a mossy plant with a grip of deceptive power. It seems that he can break out of it at any time, but when he tries, the plant puts him in a cocoon's embrace and he can't go anywhere.

"Yeah, I'll try some," he agrees. The woman coquettishly puts a little piece of opium on her finger and slides it into Aaron's mouth.

Chapter Thirty One
Eating Is Good For You

1973 : Jewish Veteran's Hospital, St. Louis

The meals come up from the hospital kitchen in two giant slotted carts, just like on an airplane. There is also a little kitchen nook on the ward, opposite the Isolation Room, where a refrigerator contains snacks, cold cuts and soda. Eating is a time-passer on Fifth Floor South. It is encouraged.

Sarah lays in her room, aware of the food available to her. Plastic food, pre-packaged junk, full of nitrates and other preservatives, the leavings of dead animal entrails or compacted glutens and polyunsaturated fats, factory produced empty calories, white sugar toxic carbohydrate slush.

God, she wants some. She has eaten the served meals out of necessity, has even secretly enjoyed them, her entire body goes "slurp!" with the ecstasy of ingesting animal fat. But now she is not hungry, yet she is hungry, she craves a baloney sandwich on white bread, her mind will not relinquish the picture of baloney sandwich on white bread.

Christine comes through the door, gives Sarah a resentful glance and dumps herself on the other bed. The springs bounce her weight, then settle. Lying face down, Christine reaches for the box of kleenex, takes two tissues, wets them with saliva, twists them into long strands, then places one in each ear.

She waves her new pink appendages back and forth. "Huh huh!" she demonstrates to Sarah. "Huh huh. My ears are inside out, I can hear every thought in your head."

Sarah gets up and goes wordlessly to the kitchenette. The baloney sandwich will not leave her mind.

"This is against everything I believe in," she thinks, as she spreads thick mayonaisse on slabs of Wonder Bread. She puts the sandwich on a paper plate and takes it to one of the tables in the east lounge. She chews it quickly, then washes it down with Seven Up.

"What am I doing? What am I doing?" she wonders with utter dismay as she gets up and makes another sandwich, this one from pressed turkey meat. She finishes the Seven up, gets a second, then stands in the kitchenette eating the sandwich.

"I am insane," she decides. "I am truly insane. I can't do anything right. I can't stick to anything, I have no discipline or will power, I'm just worthless worthless worthless."

With insight as sudden as a lightning bolt sizzling down her spine, she hears her thoughts change in tone, as if another voice is speaking them, a voice not her own but Esther's.

"She's inside me, talking to me, destroying me," Sarah recognizes with terror, "she's controlling me, she's thinking for me and I can't get rid of her."

She dumps the food into the trashcan and runs towards the deck, holding her hands over her ears.

"Stop stop stop!" she screams mentally. "Get out of my head, you bitch!"

She pushes the hydraulic door bar and fleees to the farthest corner of the deck, against the bricks, where she clutches with her fingers in the ornamental openings, each digit wrapped like a tentacle around the abrasive surface. She would throw herself off the deck and drop five stories if she was able. She looks through the niches at the park and tries to conjure an image of happy childhood outings. What surfaces instead is a vision of a baloney sandwich on a picnic table and Esther stuffing it into her child's mouth, screaming, "Eat this you little cow, eat every last bite! How dare you defy me! How dare you!"

Sarah knows that if Esther entered the ward at this moment and stood before her, she would kill her. Sarah would tear her mother's eyes out, claw chunks of flesh from her face, throttle her throat with fingers like steel wires, stab her with the plastic knives until one of them pierced her evil black heart, then she would kick her mother's body until every bloated inch of her rotten corrupted flesh is bruised more purple than the most marinated piece of dead meat.

She squeezes her face against the bricks and resists the impulse to bash her own head to a pulp. Tears stream down her face. Her entire body is rigid with murderous rage.

A soft voice comes from behind her. "Sarah."

It is Ellsworth. He has the presence of mind not to touch her. "Sarah, are you okay?"

"No, no! I'm not okay," she manages to say, without turning around. Her eyes are fixed on the park, on the picnic, on the punishing baloney sandwich.

"Is there anyone on the ward besides Doctor Tannenbaum? I'm about to explode, I need to talk to someone, a real human being."

"I can take you to Serena Steinberg, she's the intern, she's a therapist, not a psychiatrist. You might like her," Ellsworth says gently. "Come on, it's okay, you'll be okay."

Sarah manages to ungrip the bricks, finger by finger. She can not meet Ellsworth's eyes. She is afraid he will see the murder in her.

Chapter Thirty Two

BeteNoir
1973: San Francisco, California

Her name is Lucinda Cole. Her grandfather owned paper mills in Connecticut, her father has branched out into publishing. She has brothers named Boothe and Harrison. She receives five thousand a month from a trust fund, on the condition that she stays out of Connecticut.

She is a drummer-groupie. She follows her favorite bands from gig to gig, screwing the nutcases who play giant drum kits with two bass drums, a dozen tom toms and every gong and cymbal made since the fall of the Ottoman Empire.

She has a lethal exoticism for Aaron, she is a bad Shicksa from a rich New England family with a Peter Pan haircut and pale smooth skin.

She is a speedballer, a jack flasher, she likes cocaine and opium, or, better yet, freebase coke with Persian brown heroin, a Brown Bash, two melting substances merging in the glass bowl of a pipe. Take a hit and simultaneously feel your body melt and your head explode.

She has slept with Mick Jagger twice. He isn't a drummer but no one refuses Mick.

Aaron inhales one more mix of heroin and freebase cocaine from the bulbous glass pipe and lays back on Lucinda's bed. It is a covered four poster, lace scallops hang from its frame, amber colored in the light of muted tiffany lamps. The bed is antique Italian oak, black with age. Cherubs smile from the baseboard, holding little bows.

"I ought to go home. Debra's due any second now."

Lucinda is dressed in a pale blue slip. A necklace of tiny gold links holds a delicate crucifix above her breasts. "Let's play some more, don't go home." She puts the tips of her fingers on Aaron's lips, then scratches the stubble of his unshaven chin. "Come on, cutie pie." She takes one of his hands and places it on her thigh, inches from her pussy.

Aaron takes it away and sits up, his body tingling with the rush of the two drugs, one a powerful stimulant, the other a deep analgesic. Together they make a single drug, a perfect hybrid that keeps him precisely balanced on a tightrope of alert relaxation and sensual pleasure. It is almost enough to numb the ripping sound of conflict in his soul.

"No, I've got to leave." He pushes himself up, swings his feet to the floor. He reaches down to retrieve his pants.

345

"I don't want you to leave," Lucinda states, in a tone that warns Aaron of impending trouble. He sighs.

"You've got plenty of heroin. Steve will be here in what, an hour? with more coke." He looks at the clock. It is two twenty in the morning. "You don't really want sex, that's just a tool for you, it isn't something you really need, not like you need drugs. So what do you want with me?"

"I'll be lonely," she says, lifting the slip above her hips. The word lonely is drawn out, low own ly. "I want some company." Cuh ump any.

She is playing Baby Doll. Aaron lacerates himself for finding it sexy, but he does. He is just a Jewish boy from the suburbs. He has no defense against this onslaught of forbidden folly.

Before Aaron can pull his pants up, Lucinda reaches out and strokes his penis, cupping it between her thumb and fingers.

In spite of himself, Aaron responds. How can she do that, he wonders. How does she know how to make my blood flow? He looks at her and looks at himself at the same time. There she is, lips full and inviting, shoulders as smooth and pale as a statue in a museum. Her face is not so symmetrical as to be boring, like that of a model's. It is slightly freckled and perhaps a little too round and chubby to be considered ideal. Through the V-cut of her slip, her cleavage is perfect, not large, not small, rounded and firm. As she moves around to display her legs she smiles up at him with wicked innocence.

Okay, okay, Aaron thinks, I've had great looking women, I've fucked models and superstar groupies, what's the big deal?

She strokes and his penis stands at attention, jutting its angle from his abdomen. Lucinda sits up and slips to the side of the bed. Looking into Aaron's eyes she puts her mouth around him and slowly lowers her head. He looks back into those blue eyes. Their gazes lock.

"I'll stay, I'll stay," he whispers. "I'll stay."

Chapter Thirty Three

Therapy
1973: Jewish Veteran's Hospital, St. Louis

Sarah sits rigidly in the anteroom outside Serena Steinberg's office. Ellsworth's voice attempts to soothe her with meaningless but necessary reassurances.

"It'll be okay, honey, don't worry, you'll be all right."

Sarah's body is hunched forward like a bow, as if a string is running from her forehead to her knees. Breath comes through her nose in quick little snorts. She is aware of Ellsworth's sounds, grateful for them at a subliminal level.

Finally, the inner office door opens. Sarah is not looking up, but hears her name being called.

"Sarah?"

"Yes," she raises her eyes. At first glance, Serena Steinberg's appearance conjures two words, two arrogant, presumptive and annihilating words: Fat Woman.

She must weigh at least two hundred, two twenty, Sarah thinks, as her eyes do the lightning-fast evaluation of a food-compulsive woman meeting another woman. It gives her an immediate internal sense of leverage, of comfort. The therapist isn't huge, she isn't waddling and jiggling. Rather, she is rounded and soft. She has a young pretty face with a bit of neck wattle and a pair of breasts that make her look like an ancient mother-goddess dug up from an archeological site.

Then Sarah meets the therapist's eyes and does not see what she expects to see in a Fat Woman. She does not see shame, discomfort, apology, and victimization. She sees an easy and compassionate smile. She sees security.

"Come on in," Serena Steinberg says, extending a hand towards her office.

As if a magnet is pulling her, Sarah goes toward the door. She looks back to Ellsworth and mouths the word "thanks".

There is no desk in the office. There is a couch, to the right of the door. Flanking a large window that looks out over the park are two well-upholstered grandma chairs. The therapist gestures to one of them and takes her place in the other, gazing at Sarah with obvious concern.

"I can see you're having a really hard time. Can you tell me about it?"

As if the bow string that keeps her body in correct equilibrium has just snapped, Sarah hunches forward and puts her face to her knees and begins weeping convulsively.

"I can't tell where I end and my mother begins," she howls between sobs. "Or where my mother ends and I begin, or whose thoughts I'm thinking, if they're my own or if I'm just hearing an endless tape recording of things I heard in my childhood."

She wraps her hands around her chest as if she is cold, and coughs hoarsely.

"All right, all right," Serena Steinberg encourages. Sarah looks up into the face of the therapist. She sees an emotion that startles her. She sees sadness. She sees genuine compassion, a compassion made not of pity or superiority but of true equality. Compassion MUST come from equality. Serena Steinberg has wrestled with her own devils and has found a way to make peace.

I can do that, too, Sarah thinks.

Taking an immense risk, she voices her thoughts.

"I don't want to offend you, but you're a pretty big woman."

The therapist laughs, throwing her head back. It is a good laugh, it peals with a crystalline tone, ding ding ding, as if three different sized fine goblets have been struck with a fingernail.

"My secret weapon," she says, eyes gleaming. "The world is full of different shapes and sizes and tastes, and being 'big', as you put it, is something I was born with. Are you suggesting that I can't help you because I'm fat?"

Sarah puts up her hands. "No no no no, just the opposite. I think you may be able to help me because you are, uh, excuse me, 'fat'."

"Well," the therapist says with satisfaction, "we've got the word 'fat' out in the open already, don't we? See what I mean about my secret weapon?"

"Fat," Sarah reiterates. "Fat fat fat. Fat fat." She smiles, for the first time in weeks. "Fat fat fat."

Serena joins the recitation and both women are saying "Fat fat fat, fat fat fat,"

and it acquires a rhythm, like they are a doo-wop band singing nonsense syllables. "Fat fat fat, fat fat fat."

The women begin to giggle, and then to laugh until they are holding their sides.

The word "Fat" has been utterly drained of its destructive power.

Sarah feels a lot better than she had five minutes ago.

Chapter Thirty Four

1973: Mill Valley, California

Aaron knows that he will remember this moment for the rest of his life. He is looking at his reflection in the bathroom mirror. It is a moment of decision.

"I can't keep doing this," he tells himself. "I need to decide; to be one thing or the other. I'm ripping myself in two."

There is a ball of opium in his hand. He is trying not to bring it to his mouth. One of the two people that are Aaron Kantro will swallow the opium. The other Aaron Kantro will toss it down the toilet, open the door and return to his family. Beyond the bathroom's closed door he can hear the playing sounds of Debra and Stefanie.

"Who's Mama?" Debra asks. A brief pause; the adorable toddler that is his own flesh and blood responds jubilantly. "YOU'RE mama!"

Laughter. Mother and child. Aaron wants to be part of this family, but that is the lie he's been telling himself, the lie he tells Debra.

He doesn't want to be part of this family. He wants to be free from it. He is not, in fact, part of this family, he has taken himself out of it to be part of the family of opium, cocaine and all the other drugs in the world of Lucinda Cole.

The musician's life and domestic life are not well suited to one another. Aaron's initial strategy had been to take opium at gigs or with Lucinda, then come home and become "normal" Aaron, Daddy Aaron. But Lucinda keeps beckoning him like a ghost, calling to him to come see what lies in her garden, what surprise and delight wait behind the door. Through the door is another door, and he keeps following through each door until he is enclosed in a labyrinth beyond solution.

Lucinda is a one-woman plague. She wants everyone to try opium. She may have been fucking Aaron but she is giving sticky black marbles to every musician in the scene.

It is a transitional phenomenon and this little woman is its avatar. Smoking weed suddenly seems tame. A creeping tide of white powder, smokable cocaine, opium and its cousins starts appearing in the dressing rooms of clubs, auditoriums, festivals and charity events.

Aaron starts taking opium three days a week. Don't let the body get used to it, he tells himself. Avoid addiction. Hold tight to Daddy Aaron. That way is the right way, the safe way, the moral way.

Then the demon-woman beckons with seductive charm, come see what's in here, in this treasure room, inside this scented chamber. He looks back at the Daddy Aaron world but it seems flat and lifeless compared to the ever-more substantial ministrations of the wet mouth, the warm vagina, the inside-out rush of opium and cocaine ecstasy that comprises the world of Lucinda Cole.

He compromises by taking opium every other day. He goes on like this for a couple of weeks. It is a self-deceiving strategy, an "I'm not an addict" game he plays with himself.

Which brings me to this moment, Aaron thinks, staring into my bathroom mirror trying not to take opium on the 'off' day. But I can't stand the on/off, on/off tone of my existence. I can't stand the off day. So I need to make a decision. I either quit now or I become an everyday opium addict. That's what you're called when you take a narcotic substance every day: an addict. It isn't complicated. At some point in your life you make a conscious decision to become an addict.

This is that moment.

The tendons of his wrist contract. His bicep clenches. The ball of opium comes toward his mouth. Don't do it, don't do it, something screams, it's not too late, walk away! But it screams like a man falling from a high building, its voice receding into a fatal distance, downward, down.

The hand is no longer connected to the rational mind. It zooms towards his face, inexorable, and deposits its tar-black freight onto his tongue. He swallows it, then bends to the sink, washing the bitter stuff down with cold water.

Chapter Thirty Five

1973: Jewish Veteran's Hospital, St. Louis

Occupational Therapy is a long room with round opaque white skylights and tall rectangular windows. For residents of the locked ward, OT is a voluntary activity. On any given day ten to fifteen of its patients will be accompanied by two psychiatric nurses to this haven of arts and crafts, to mingle with the general hospital population and encouraged to engage in healthy embroidery, sculpture, drawing, painting, pot-holder weaving, popsicle stick utensil construction and other creative pursuits.

Sarah makes a beeline for the lone unoccupied easel. "This is ironic," she thinks, "I have to get locked up in a loony bin to find time to paint."

There is a full range of acrylic paints available, no oils, some tempera, and lots of crayons. A little cartoony to Sarah's eyes, hard to layer or build, to get the impasto, but good enough.

She obtains a canvas board, two feet by three feet.

She puts it on the easel and immediately covers the board with sky blue paint. Then she uses other shades of blue, from powder, to cerulean, to indigo to graduate the sky's color so that it is lighter at the top of the frame than at the bottom. Then, at the bottom, she draws with a pencil a rough city skyline, sooty and grey, as if it is a caricature of an American city from the 1930's. She can almost hear the Gershwin-style melody, the trumpets and saxophones, the wah wah of film noir music. Then, erupting from the far right corner of the painting, a chimerical creature with a long sinuous neck comes undulating out from behind the facades of the skyscrapers. It rises into the sky, arching from right to left, as if it is about to take a bite out of the urban landscape beneath it.

Sarah draws very quickly, and, when she is satisfied, begins to apply paint to the basic structure she has drawn. Before long, the creature takes on aspects of her own environment. There is a Christine-face, an Ellsworth-face, a Serena Steinberg face, a demented paper-bag shuffler Carolyn face, a frustrated futile ping-pong playing George-face, yet all these faces bleed into one another so that a single wolf-like face hovers menacingly over the cartoonish city.

There is a silence in the room that has a palpable substance to it. The absence of noise suddenly makes Sarah aware of her surroundings. She looks up and away from the easel, then turns to see behind her.

Twenty two people are arrayed in a wide semicircle, watching Sarah paint. Several patients are craning to the right or left, to see past Sarah's body to the contents of the canvas board.

Sarah steps aside. There is a whoosh of air from the gathered patients. No one utters a word. One of the locked ward patients, slack-jawed Roger Kulick, shuffles forward and puts a finger to the wet paint. Sarah does nothing to deter him.

Gingerly, respectfully, he takes his little bit of blue paint and puts it in his mouth.

This guy has the right idea, Sarah realizes. Paintings should be eaten. Music should be smelled. Writing should be pissed on. Sculpture should be excreted. It is a kind of illumination of the profound irrelevance of Art, yet of its utter necessity.

She bows silently from the waist, holding her shift with one arm. A paintbrush is clenched between her teeth, like a flamenco dancer's rose.

The crowd claps and cheers, genuinely thrilled, truly understanding the meaning and import of Sarah's work. At last, they disperse. Sarah, tingling from abdomen to forehead, resumes putting the finishing touches on her painting.

* * *

"So....how much psychotherapy do you think I'll need?"

Sarah is sitting in the large chair as if she is trying to disappear into one of its corners. Her body is curled like a question mark. She is holding her elbows with hands that seem like winter-blasted twigs at the ends of old tree branches.

"Before?" Serena Steinberg prompts. "Before......before what?"

Sarah doesn't answer for a moment. She releases her protective grip on her elbows and puts her hands in her lap, palms up. She cocks her head and looks at the therapist as if the question is stupid. She knows it isn't. It is a question so huge that she feels stupid for not being able to answer.

She expels the breath from her body in one long whoosh and just lets her mind go blank.

"Before I'm throbbing with vitality," she says in a withering tone. Her hands twitch and the fingers open just a bit. "Before I'm able to have five body-wracking orgasms a night with a man I adore who won't want to beat me."

She shifts her weight from the side of the chair towards its center.

"Before I can live a single week without depression so overpowering it's like a four hundred pound python squeezing the life out of me. Wait....." she puts a finger into the middle of the air, then looks at it. "Oh jesus, I'm really emaciated, aren 't I?" She considers her finger, then the rest of her hand, then her wrist. She pulls back the sleeve of the white cotton turtleneck blouse and looks at her arm. Then she looks at Serena Steinberg, her eyes like birds that are exhausted from flying too long.

"What have I done to myself?"

The therapist sits with seeming composure. She is at a loss for words, but that is not a problem of itself. She knows that Sarah will find the words.

"That's not the first time I've asks myself that question," Sarah finally admits. "Nor will it be the last." She crosses her arms again, this time placing her hands on her ribs, unconsciously counting the spaces between each of them.

She gives the therapist an accusing look. "You look like a goddam cherub, you're so pink and rosy and plump. How many kids do you have?"

"Two." Serena does not amplify. She has long ago decided how much to divulge about her personal life. She will answer certain questions if asked. This is one of them.

Sarah grasps the lack of forthcoming detail.

"Your personal life is not my business, is it? The less I know about you the better. You're supposed to be a Tabula Rasa, a blank slate, upon which my projections can be made visible and tangible. Jeez, isn't psychotherapy bullshit?"

Serena laughs. "It's necessary bullshit. Sometimes it's all we've got."

"Damn straight, sister. As long as we both know it's still bullshit." A bit of color has come to Sarah's face. She has relaxed into the chair, her back now touches its soft upholstery. "So let's go back to 'before what?' I was on a roll there, until I looked at my pathetic bony finger."

"Let's do that," Serena agrees. "How much psychotherapy do you need before what?"

Sarah moves her weight forward again, curling her fingers into claws.

"Before I can kill my bitch of a mother," she says defiantly. She looks for any registration of shock in her therapist. There is none.

"Okay, we're going for the sick and the twisted here, right?" She pounds her fist into her open palm.

Serena pounds her fist in response. "Right! Sick and twisted!"

"There is something in me that wants to kill Lisa, too." Her voice grows suddenly cautious. "I mean, anybody would want to kill Esther. But I have fantasies of killing my own child. Isn't that horrible?"

Serena considers this statement with the sobriety it deserves. "Yes," the therapist says at last. "It is horrible. But it's true, and sometimes what's true is horrible."

"Do you think I'm a monster?" Sarah asks weakly, imploringly.

"No, you're not a monster. If you were a monster you wouldn't be here, you'd be taking out your monstrosity on other people instead of taking it out on yourself. You have a conscience, Sarah. You have a real sense of personal responsibility. That's part of your predicament."

"But I know monsters, I have them in me and I can't separate myself from them." Sarah is almost wailing. "My mother is a monster! I was born from the womb of a monster! And I'm afraid my child is a monster, too! Where does all this monstrosity end? How do I find sanity and gentility in myself, goodness and strength and virtue? And how can I save Lisa from all this violence?" Her right shoulder twitches as if she is inwardly restraining herself. Her hand jumps up and down on her thigh.

"You can, and you will, because you want to." Serena knows the words she speaks are just words. They might be remotely comforting. She admires and loves the tormented woman sitting across from her. In moments like this, moments of psychic desperation, the silent force of love is the only remedy, even when it can not be felt by its recipient. Without the love there is no point in endless years of therapy. She has the love, feels it in the core of her being, as for one of her own children, or her mother, or her sister. She knows that the vulnerable clay of Sarah's psyche will take the impression of her love as if molding itself to a new and unknown shape.

Sarah takes a kleenex from the box on the shelf next to the window. She blows her nose into it, more to break the strain of her own inner confrontation than to remove the trace of mucous from the end of her nose.

"Desire is the ultimate force, the shaper of everything," she says, when she has calmed herself. "My desire to heal my own soul is more powerful than life itself."

The two women breathe in unison.

"I know I'm talking in silly generalities," Sarah continues. "Words like 'soul', 'desire', 'healing'. They don't mean shit. But they're the best I can do right now."

As usual, the therapist says nothing. She looks on with calm affection.

"At least," says Sarah, "I feel like I'm coming un-stuck. Just a little."

"You are correct, sir," Serena mocks a catch-phrase from a popular television personality. "You are correct."

Sarah snorts, then dabs snot from her nose with a piece of tissue paper.

Chapter Thirty Six

Thwok! The house shakes as if some brawny lumberjack has taken an axe to the front door. Thwok! Again, the rattling impact vibrates through the home's studs and bricks.

A groan curls from Max's chest as he turns to look at the blue dial of his alarm clock. Eleven o'clock. He'd been in bed for an hour; dropped to sleep like a stone. Now he knows sleep will elude him the rest of the night.

Esther rolls, and her weight squeezes his elbow so that his ulnar nerve sends shock waves down his arm. He pulls free. He knows she is awake, her snoring stops and what passes in her melted frame for alertness manifests in raised head and turned ears.

"Max, f'god's sake, stop that monster. Do something about him!"

The load of Thorazine, Mellaril and Percodan in her bloodsream dries her lips and tongue, so that her last words sound like "do shumshing 'bout hi…"

Max sits up. Air comes into his lungs audibly, a long hiss of inhale, followed by the reverse exhale, "uhhhhhh." Weary and resigned, he throws his weight forward so that he can get upright.

He tracks his aging process by his difficulty in getting out of bed. Now, at forty-seven, his abdominal muscles have grown lax, so getting up is no longer a simple unconscious task but a combination of movements and a use of momentum. He grabs the side of the reading table and gets to his feet. He dons a robe, covering his scrawny legs and boxer shorts. He opens the bedroom door, shuts it behind him. Switching on the hall light, he hobbles on aching feet down the corridor and through the kitchen.

Over the years, the Kantro house has grown. This second, larger home has acquired a garage conversion, enlarged bedrooms, and, finally, a bedroom at the opposite end of the house, off the one-time garage. This essential separation of Mark from the rest of the family had occurred two years previously, when some of Mark's habits became unendurable.

When Mark asked to learn Karate, Max saw it as a potential blessing. "It will aid his concentration," he thought, "give him goals and discipline."

Max has to admit, it has succeeded. Mark has acquired discipline and goals. Now Max's son is a martial artist without feeling or compassion. He is armed with dangerous knowledge, an inflated ego and ruthless criminal ambition. All he needs is a few more years to hone his skills, get bored with living at home and go out into the world. He will never be anything but a mediocre martial artist, but he has a certain dedication to his sense of self importance. Hence, he practices. He improves.

Max shudders.

The room that was a garage is now a rumpus room. At the far end is the television set. Beyond that, a door leading to a storage area seals what remains of the garage, an area stuffed with boxes and files. A couch sits against the wall that lets out onto the back patio. Past the couch is the door to Mark's room.

Thwok! The sound curdles in Max's stomach. He looks at his fingernails in the dim light, then uses his knuckles to rap gingerly at the door.

"Mark," he says, "It's late. Enough of that, now."

Thwok!

Max's chin goes up slightly. He pinches the skin between his two nostrils, almost sealing off the air going through his nose. Then he lets go, rubs a bit of moisture from his fingers. He taps harder at the door.

"Mark!" his voice is now definite. "Open up. Let's talk."

Thwok!

For a moment, Max's fingers curl as he fantasizes the throttling of his youngest son. The little shit has given me nothing but grief, he thinks. Then, as he considers the totality of his children, he realizes that ALL of them have given him nothing but grief. That does not change the fact that he likes and loves two of his kids, and, well…. loves the other two. He can not stifle the revulsion he feels for Mark. Whatever human traits he respects and values, things like loyalty, integrity, courage, honesty, kindness….he can not find a trace of those attributes in Mark. He finds, instead, a magnification of his wife at her most dreadful. Unconsciously, he excuses himself from blame for the monster that is his younger son.

Esther is a shambles. Drugged out of her energy and intensity, she stumbles from day to day, thinking a few tired thougts, talking the same talk. Mark is some souped-up version of Esther in youthful male form, a hot rod maniac whose brakes are always smoking.

"You know you're going to open the door," Max says. "We both know it. So why don't we negotiate something. Your brakes are about to go. You don't have a dime. I can tell Fred it's okay for you to make one visit to the junkyard. You and your friend."

Max has embargoed Fred Silverstein's auto yard. Fred, one of Max's old high school buddies, knows what strings of bribery and destruction lay in his yard. Mark Kantro has obsessively spent most of his sixteenth year dragging pieces back and forth, "working" for Fred in order to assemble a beaten-down black Chevrolet. The nature of Mark's work ethic is reflected in the primer-blotched automobile at the back of the Kantro driveway. It functions, with a menacing gurgle and clouds of vile fume. Mark seems to regard it as a battering ram, drives it with defiant shame, looking always for reasons to dent Jaguars, Cadillacs and other expensive vehicles belonging to arrogant seventeen year old boys.

Thwok! Max recoils from the door, then moves closer once again. He knows it is the last "thwok". He hears the shift of his son's weight, a slow pad pad as he approches the door.

Snap! A lock flies back. Clack. Another lock. A turning sound indicates Mark's work on his third lock. There is a drag, grunt, drag, as Mark pulls furnishings out of the way. The door is seldom used. Mark climbs in and out the window. The family seldom knows when he comes, when he goes, where he is. It is better that way. Better not to know.

Max has to look up to meet the turbulent green eye that peers out from the cracked door. Satisfied that no one else accompanies Max, the young man unlatches a chain and allows his father entry into his sanctum sanctorum.

"Hey, dad," Mark's voice is unctuous. "What's up? How's it hangin'?"

Max can never quite get over the size of his son. This towering hulk isn't finished growing yet, and he tops six feet four, with breadth to match. A slightly elongated belly hangs below a black t-shirt. He wears loose khakis, mis-matched socks and mocassins.

Mark seems genuinely unaware that anything is wrong. He smiles sweetly, his eyes amazingly and apparently guile-less. This, Max finally understands after years of denial, is the charm of the sociopath. Mark is a quintessential calculator. If honey works better than bile, he has loads of honey to spread.

"Mark, do you know how late it is? We're asleep. What are you....?"

Before he can finish his sentence, Mark whirls away, toward the back of the room. "Hey, dad,

look at this...this is SO cool! Watch."

The boy is wearing fingerless bicycle gloves. The room is spacious, big enough to accommodate this large reckless young male and all he collects. There are pegboards all around the walls, and shelves of objects whose purpose Max can only guess. Mark picks up a piece of black metal and goes into a crouch. "Watch," he commands again. Then, as an afterthought, he says, "better step back. You're right in front of the target."

Max decides it is more prudent to move behind his son. Mark coils into himself, does some kind of wind-up and throws the metal object toward the mouldings next to the door.

"THWOK!" The thing sticks into the doorframe, vibrating. Max sees that it is some kind of weapon.

"It's a throwing star, a Shuriken!," Mark triumphantly explains. "BAM! Did you see that? Wow, is that cool, or what?"

"Mark," Max begins, but his son forestalls him.

"This is one of the ninja's most deadly weapons," he says, bouncing on the balls of his feet. He strides purposefully towards the door and pries the weapon out of the woodwork. He shows it to Max, excitement animating his face. It is a heavy black iron disc with five sharpened points jutting from its lethal circumference. "I've been practicing, I'm getting pretty good with it. Sensei Ioki tells me if I can pass the fourth degree black belt, I can study using these in his Monday class."

There are pock marks everywhere in the room, on the woodwork, on the ceiling. Wooden splinters litter the floor. The chamber is a martial arts exercise gym, with poles, racks, targets. There are crosses, X's, bull's eyes, painted everywhere, each one almost obliterated with blows of knife, sword, sticks, spears, god only knows what else Mark posseses in his arsenal. His collection of Oriental weapons occupies the pegboards. Max has no clue how his son can have purchased such things. He holds no job, at least none Max knows about. He receives no money from his family, just a rent-free room and occasional meals. The weapons are not impressive looking. Mostly, they seem to be cheap versions of authentic Japanese metal and woodwork. There are also pistols, rifles, bows and arrows, a crossbow, police-issue clubs, handcuffs, restraints.

Max feels cold. What have I wrought? he wonders. This is my son.

"Very impressive," Max speaks with feigned conviction. He doesn't know what works anymore, with his son. He knows anger, force, coercion, all are useless. Only negotiation, bribery and appeals to Mark's self interest hold any hope of gaining a response.

"Yeah yeah," Mark paces the fourteen steps that the room allows. His fingers drum impatiently on his thighs. "I'm done, are we done here, dad? I won't keep you awake.....I think I'll go to bed, okay?"

Max is aware that sleep is the farthest thing from Mark's thoughts. He'll be going out, getting into mischief. Max can only count the days before the other shoe drops, before his son graduates from teenage thug to the status of true criminal.

"Fine," Max concurs. "Get some sleep. You're all wound up."

"All wound up," Mark repeats. "I've been hearing that phrase my whole life. I'm 'all wound up', and, you know, it's true, I AM all wound up. Somebody twisted my head round and round and round," he casts a lethal look towards the other end of the house, indicating his mother's decayed soul. "Somebody wound me up, wound me up till I'm so tight inside, I can explode." He fingers the black anodized throwing star, and Max takes a step back, feeling a real apprehension, as if his son can randomly murder the whole family in their sleep, beginning right now, with himself. This is just a fantasy, he tells himself. Mark isn't that far gone. He has a few more steps along the road, he's still got a greed and a need, for power in the world, for status, for aggrandizement. By pure calculation, he won't do something as crazy as murder, because he sees himself as a major player, a kingpin, someone who will tell other people to do his dirty work. No, Mark isn't 'there' yet, but someday, after repeated failures, he will get to that point, and he will be truly dangerous.

A cold feeling dwells in Max's heart, a fatal sadness that it is his own failures that have led to his childrens' misery. He is used to that cold feeling. Being used to it doesn't make it better, it just makes it familiar.

"Okay then, good night," he says. He has run out of ways to communicate. He can only stay on the surface of things and observe his son with as much detachment as possible. He backs out of the room, closing the door behind him. As he pads back towards the master bedroom, he hears the locks being clicked back into place in Mark's room.

When his father is gone, Mark puts on a pair of tennis shoes and a black hooded sweat jacket. He opens a drawer and removes a nan-chak, an oriental weapon consisting of two burnished pieces of foot long wood connected by four inches of chain. Mark is good enough with them that he won't hurt himself. He isn't good enough to hurt anyone else, but he fancies himself a master of this subtle and ancient instrument of combat. He tucks it into his waistband and zips up his jacket. From another drawer he gets out a lock box and from it removes five one hundred dollar bills. These go down his sock.

His window is only waist high. It's easy to open it, and step over. He lands behind a hedge of six foot high juniper bushes, all neatly trimmed to perfect ovals. He squeezes through them and turns to the left, walks along the backyard path and goes to the driveway, where his car sits, over to the side, half on and half off the grass. He always leaves his car just down the lip of the driveway slope, so that he can roll into the street without starting his engine. He gets in quietly, shuts the door, puts the key in the ignition. He lets out the emergency brake, puts the car in Neutral and rolls onto the street. As he reaches the curb he starts the car, which rumbles satisfyingly. He turns on the headlights and drives sedately up the hill. When he reaches the end of the street, he looks both ways down Old Bonhomme, sees no oncoming cars. He turns onto the road and floors the gas pedal so that he squeals off into the suburban night. The car is tuned and loaded. He isn't a very good mechanic, but he has the help of Tony Reltz. Tony loves amphetamine and Mark knows how to get amphetamine from a nurse he woos at University Hospital. Tony periodically shows up at Silverstein's junkyard, crashing and all bummed out, and Mark feeds him pills and watches him work on his Chevy, watches him prowl the junkyard for the good parts. What he has under the hood of this beat up looking Caprice is a 454 litre engine with a lot of big bad horses.

On nights like this one, Mark likes to drive and look for opportunities. He can go anywhere in St. Louis, down to the south side, or across the bridge to East St. Louis. He needs to find some speed, because Tony has eaten up his supply working on the car, and he has customers who will give him five bucks apiece for black beauties and white crosses. It is so easy to sell. He has the whole town wired, he knows the drive-in burger places where kids go to find and sell dope. He doesn't know quite how much money he makes, but he estimates that in the past year, twenty or thirty grand has passed through his pockets. Fortunately, he doesn't do dope. He knows he is too crazy to do dope. He knows he is wired up anyway, of what use can drugs be to him? He'd taken all those fucking shrink drugs when he was a kid and the idea of putting some pill in his mouth is repugnant. It's better to deal dope for profit. That's the smart way to do things.

He heads vaguely south, picking up Olive Street Road into University City. Down near Heman Park there is the old Hamburger Heaven, the place with the amazing sauce. Lots of people wind up at Hamburger Heaven after midnight, sitting on the hoods of their cars, opening and closing doors, laughing, whooping, exchanging girls, buying, selling.....

The streets here are almost empty. Orange sodium vapor lights cast a pall over everything. Neon flickers light car lots, closed furniture stores, pharmacies, empty gas stations. Mark reaches under his seat and turns on his police scanner. Chaotic chatter fills the car, voices, numbers, locations. Some of the voices are familiar, cops he knows by sight, by name, dispatchers about whom he fantasizes. The one in Overland has a sexy voice.

He likes to know where all the cops are cruising. He fancies that he can form a coherent picture of all their locations, but the chatter is confusing and in fact he gleans only the most cursory information.

Chhhhh! The U-City dispatcher is talking to a squad car. "Dave 38, we have a disturbance, some kind of domestic over corner of Hanley and.....chhhhhhhh!"

Okay. This is useful. That will pull two or three cop cars on a night like this. Mark turns right on Price and then left on Ladue, to make a loop around the disturbance. This is a long dark stretch of road, straight and smooth and a great place to let his 454 do its worst. He ratchets the gear shift into second and accelerates, feeling his weight forced back against the sprung seat. Third gear, fourth, fifth, the sound of the car's engine shifts into a lower register as the overdrive gear roars the rpms. Sixty, sixty five, seventy.....a pair of headlights appear behind him and he slows.

The police chatter continues from the tiny speaker beneath his seat, but he doesn't make out any Ladue cops, but just the same....

The headlights grow like owl's eyes, and as the car closes the distance, Mark can tell it isn't a

police cruiser. He is about to hit the gas again when he sees, thirty or forty yards ahead, in his lane, a lone bicyclist, just then passing under the wan orange glow of a street lamp. Mark slows way down, to about twenty, until the driver behind grows impatient and passes him. Lincoln Continental. Typical Ladue rich person, Mark sneers. He is slowly coming along to the bicyclist. Who will be out at this time of night on a bicycle? A red tail light shines dimly from the back of the seat, and evidently some sort of flashlight has been taped to the handlebars, as it glows feebly ahead of the rider. From about twenty feet, Mark can see the bags hanging off the bike's handlebars, can see a middle-aged black man laboring along, going home from serving at some party in this ritzy neighborhood, or cleaning windows, mowing lawns. He will have one hell of a long ride!

I wonder how close I can get to him without hitting him, Mark asks himself. He changes his trajectory so that it will take him towards the road's shoulder. Out here in the western suburbs there are no sidewalks. Tall trees line the road, concealing houses worth millions of dollars, houses at the ends of long driveways. Mark accelerates to about forty and swishes alongside the rider, missing him only by inches. In his rear view mirror he sees the man go down, bags flying.

"Haha! Whoo!" Mark pounds the knurled steering wheel in exhiliration. This is the best rush he's has in weeks. "You are one mean motherfucker, Kantro!"

He congratulates himself. He doesn't wonder why he does these things. As a child, he was told often enough that harming other people is morally wrong. He doesn't care. It makes him feel good, makes him feel powerful. It makes him.....well, just feel.....He crunches down on the gas pedal, feels the car roar, feels the wind whistle in through the badly patched window, feels the road melt beneath his wheels, it is great! As he passes Ladue Estates going south, a police cruiser comes out from behind the concrete marquee of the subdivision and lights him up. Whoop whoop! the siren honks, red and blue lights flash. A search light comes on, silhouetting Mark. Quickly, he reaches down and turns off the police scanner. He pulls right, stops the car and waits, looking in his side view mirror to see if he has caught a break.

The cop saunters forward, waving his flashlight. "Mark," he says as he reaches the car. "I clocked you at eighty seven; ain't that pushing things a bit?"

He has indeed caught a break. Mark looks up at the face of the officer. "Phil," he says, "how's it hangin? How's your kid doing on the swim team?" He smiles his crinkly, guileless smile. The policeman squats so that his face is on the same level as that of Mark. He is a burly young man, about thirty years old, wide and powerful with a weight lifter's body. He looks immaculate, as though he has washed every inch of his body and has gotten a hair cut that afternoon and sent his uniform out to a classy dry cleaner to have it pressed perfectly.

"Eighty seven miles per hour," he repeats. "In a forty five mile zone. You know how much a ticket like that would be?"

Mark hears the word "would," not "will," and he relaxes. He knows there will be no ticket. He knows how to handle cops. Never argue, always be polite, get to know each and every policeman in the city, talk the police lingo. He has hung around with this guy off duty, at the local donut shop. He has been stopped three, four times by the same cop, on duty. "I was just thinking about my girlfriend, Phil, we had a fight. I forgot for a second, that's all. I know this is your turf. I wouldn't speed down here on purpose. You're a good law enforcement officer, and I respect your turf."

"I've heard all your lines before, Mark. I won't warn you again. I see you speeding here one more time, I'm gonna write you up."

"Thanks, Phil. You're a good man. You know I want to get into the academy?"

"You want to be a policeman, Mark, you have to straighten out and fly right. You don't need a lot of history following you around."

Mark is about to ask, again, about the officer's son, whose name he now remembers. Stephen. But a black man on a single speed, wide-tired bicycle pulls up behind Mark's left fender. "This man just tried to kill me, officer," he says. "Run me right off the road, almost squished me like a bug."

Officer Phil swings his flashlight at the newcomer. "Step back from the car, sir," he says firmly.

"He come within an inch of me, man, if I din't see him comin' for me I'd be dead right now."

"Step..back..from..the..vehicle......Sir!" Phil's voice brooks no nonsense. The black man is panting with exertion and rage, but he moves away, dragging his bicycle two or three steps, retreating towards the police cruiser.

"Stop right there, sir, I want you where I can see you." He turns back to Mark. "What's he talking about?"

"I haven't the slightest clue," Mark replies.

"You LYIN'!" the bicyclist screams, "You lyin' sumbitch! Look at me!" He gestures at his torn clothes, his bloody arms, the bent wheel of his bicycle.

"It isn't me," Mark reiterates. "Somebody else, maybe? I saw a pickup truck just a few minutes ago, doing weird things down on Price Road."

Officer Phil, making a quick mental equation, decides that a white man, one whose family is known to him, trumps a black man in this neighborhood at this time of night. The question of guilt or innocence is irrelevant. He turns away from Mark, reaching for his handcuffs. "Sir," he says, "please step over to the police vehicle and lie flat on the ground, on your stomach, and put your hands behind your head."

"Oh fuck that," the man says, and with the speed of a ferret he dodges under the policeman's arms and half jumps into Mark's car. He gets his hands around Mark's throat for a moment, and then the butt end of Phil's long black flashlight smashes hard into his ribs, once, twice, and then he lets go. The policeman pulls him out of the car and begins wrestling him to the ground. The man is a mere five six, five seven, wiry and small, but he fights with aggression and determination. Mark gets out of his car and goes to aid the officer, and the three men fall in a scrum of writhing limbs.

"Lyin' sumbitch!" the black man screams, and the men tangle for half a minute before he succumbs from exhaustion, unable to fight off the weight of two large men. Momentarily, he is handcuffed and sitting in the back of the cruiser. Within seconds, another two squad cars from the Ladue Police Department and one St. Louis County Sheriff's car roll up, lights blazing. It is the way things work on a Thursday night at eleven forty five, when not much else is happening. Cops follow the action, gather at the scene to shoot the shit.

"We're not gonna say anything about your part in this, right Mark? I don't think I'll need you for a witness; assaulting a police officer, y'know? That little black fucker, he is strong!" Officer Phil tucks Mark back into his car, gesturing for him to go. Before he puts his car into gear, the policeman leans down and puts his face close to Mark's, just a few inches from his nose, so that he can feel the breath warm on his cheeks, smelling of some kind of mouthwash.

"You didn't try and run that guy down, did you, Mark?" The policeman's eyes glitter with a cynical light.

Marc has a powerful urge to giggle. His blood is pumping so hard with excitement that he has to clamp an internal fist down on his temptation to guffaw. Even so, his lips twitch upward at the corners, just slightly, and his eyes wrinkle.

"No way, Officer," Mark answers. "No way."

"Crazy old nigger," says Officer Phil. He looks hard at Mark, telling him with his gaze that he isn't fooled.

"Crazy old nigger," Mark agrees, and starts his car.

Chapter Thirty Seven

1975: Mill Valley, California

Aaron is having an opium nightmare. He is in a forest, and strange creatures are leaping through the undergrowth. They look like wild boars but they have elephant trunks and a third tusk protruding from their foreheads. One comes charging toward him and he jumps into a tree, clinging to it for protection. As he settles into the nook between branch and trunk to let the stampede run below, the tree opens its eyes, he is staring into a round chartreuse face, the bark comes alive and feels cold and evil to his touch. Aaron scrambles out onto the end of the branch and the tree's eyes follow him. Every tree in the forest is weaving and swaying and staring at him. The end of the branch clutches at his arm and the tree screams "Aaron! Aaron Aaron Aaron Aaron!"

He opens his eyes. Debra's fingers are around his bicep, she is pulling him from his drug-saturated sleep. "Wake up! Someone just had an accident in our driveway!"

"Okay, okay," he mumbles. He is confused. He remembers the dream. A glance at the clock tells him it is five twenty. It is still dark. He only got home three hours ago.

He pulls on his pants and goes towards the front of the house. He flicks the outside lights on and peers through the front window. He sees a patch of blue toward the end of the driveway but can see nothing else. Taking a flashlight he goes down the steps, down the long curving driveway towards the street.

A blue Porsche is angled across the driveway as if it has spun into the turn and wound up almost backwards. Its rear fender has hit the light post, and its driver side wheels hang off the concrete.

It is Lucinda Cole's Porsche. Aaron approaches the car and sees Lucinda slumped unconscious across both seats. A syringe is still dangling from the vein inside her arm.

He knows that something is ending, right here, right now. Debra is a foot or two behind him. She stops as Aaron opens the car door and lifts Lucinda from the clasp of the bucket seats.

Debra points with horror. "That's.....that's yours, isn't it? You brought that here."

Numbly, Aaron nods. He takes the syringe from the vein and drops it to the ground, where he crushes it, then digs a little hole with his shoe and covers it over. All sounds are absorbed by the creek that is crashing down the rocks beside the house, full of winter rain.

Lifting the woman's loose-limbed form, Aaron caries it up towards the house. She is thin, she seems to weigh no more than a slice of toast. She smells like a skunk, an odor of metabolized heroin rises from her armpits and from the sweat oozing from her pores. "I never meant for this to happen," Aaron stammers, " I never meant for the sickness to reach here."

Debra laughs bitterly. "You're way too late, buster. Way too late. The sickness has been here for a long time." She runs up the steps and holds the door open.

Aaron puts Lucinda on the Persian rug in the living room and begins mouth to mouth resuscitation. After about thirty seconds she vomits into his face and begins to breathe. Only now does Aaron notice that Lucinda is wearing nothing but a flimsy black negligee and stilletto high heels with straps.

She has thrown a bomb into his life. The fuse is a delayed detonator, it has been ticking away for a couple of years. It has just gone off.

Debra is hanging from the door, neither in the room nor out of it.

"Is she going to be okay?"

Aaron wipes vomit with his t-shirt. Debra throws him a terry cloth towel and he cleans Lucinda. Color is returning to her face. "For now. It's just a matter of time."

"Is this the.....the....thing, you've been spending all your time with? Is this why you don't come home? Is this why you don't have time to play with your daughter? Or make love to me?"

Aaron kneels abjectly. His hands go together as if he is praying, the filthy towel dangles between them. "It's not her. It's the drugs."

Debra comes into the room. Her fingers are spread wide over her heart and her mouth is open as if she is terrified. "How bad is it?"

Aaron bows down, touches his head to the floor. "It's really bad." His voice muffles into the carpet. Lucinda stirs, opens her eyes, raises a languid hand to Aaron's face.

"What time's it?" She asks. "How'm I doin? Zit okay? Everything's okay."

"I'm leaving with Stefanie," Debra says. "I'm not going to expose her to things like this. Not ever. I have felt like a ghost in my own home, you've treated me as if I don't exist. I can't wait around for you to get yourself straightened out. You have everything, Aaron, everything. Why can't you just.....just.....not be so hollow?"

Here he is, sandwiched between two women. One is standing up, one is prostrate. One wants to leave, one wants to destroy him. This isn't about either one of them, Aaron understands. It's me. No one is doing this to me but me. I don't know how to love.

Somehow, that part of my brain fails to function. There's some essential piece of humanity that I don't possess.

He helps Lucinda to a sitting position, then lifts her onto the couch. Debra backs away, as if the smell is overpowering. "I can't even watch this," she says, "I'm going to start packing."

"No!" Aaron says. He squeezes his face between his fingers, pushing his cheekbones, willing the pain in his eyes to go away. "I'll leave. The house is yours. I'll call Bob Leavitt as soon as he gets into his office and make sure the title is transferred. If I don't do this now, you and Stefanie will have nothing, I'll have nothing. I want you to have a home, I want my daughter to have a home."

"Wanna go home?" Lucinda giggles, her arms flailing around. "I got some more SHIT there."

Chapter Thirty Eight

Envelopes
1977: Olivette, Missouri

Marilee's wedding is a nightmare. Max has pride. He is going to pay for everything. But how on earth is he to keep up with the insatiable demands of his daughter? How is he to throw an affair that will be of sufficient scale to impress his in-laws-to-be? He has never expected anything less from Marilee. She has found her rich lawyer. His name is Irv Josephson, and he is the son and grandson of prominent St. Louis lawyers, society people. Manny Josephson, Irv's father, is THE first Jew to have a daughter enact her debutante 'coming out' at the Veiled Prophet Ball, the annual ritual of St. Louis society money.

At one of the preliminary dinners for the planning of the wedding, Irv's father takes Max aside. When he reaches into his sport coat pocket, Max knows what is coming. He has seen the gesture many times, he has made it himself many times. Manny Josephson is stout, short and exudes an air of power and cigar smoke. He begins by leaning, tilting his body from the hips: there, in the alcove leading back to the restrooms, he gets close to Max, as if about to whisper a secret. Then the hand goes to the inside sport coat pocket.

"Max," he says, "this is strictly between you and me. This has to be a big affair, the kids want it. Why be meshuggeneh? Here."

The envelope is in the air, now, like a missile just out of its silo. It is lofting its deadly way to its target: Max's pride. It touches his hand, and Manny Josephson begins to press with his other hand, solicitiously. The only problem is that Max has withdrawn his palm, there is no place to press.

"I can't, Manny, " says Max, backing away just a few inches, just enough to cancel the air of fake intimacy the other man has been trying to foist on him. The two men don't like each other, don't respect each other.

Josephson's expression is patient and condescending, as if he knows that after a refusal or two, just for form, this new relative-by-engagement will take the money. The message in this little man's face sickens Max.

"There's no way I can take it, Manny. I'm not going to change my mind after you insist. The kids will have to make do with what I can afford."

The next day the trouble starts. "What do you mean, we can't afford La Chateau?" Marilee is apoplectic. La Chateau is the ONLY place to hold a wedding reception. They do all the catering on-site, their staff is impeccably servile, their rooms lavish with mirror, marble, chandelier.

She is her mother's daughter: she throws plates across the kitchen, storms out, goes into her room and tears up half her own clothes.

This is normal life to Max. He will listen but not hear, he will register the shock, the outrage, the thwarted tantrums without much comment. His face, after all these years has set into a numb but long-suffering mask. He has become, in his forties, like the Eternal Jew with his hands spread, palms upward, as if to say, "Why me?"

Marilee has a good job with United Airlines, seems to have all the things required for a successful Jewish girl. Rich fiance, nice car, friends, clubs, jewelry, clothes. Max has stopped wondering why he dislikes her so much. He just wants her to get married and move out. She is the only child left under his roof. Aaron is god only knew where, playing music in some bar in Chicago or Detroit. Mark is in Las Vegas living a life of total fantasy. Thank god for Sarah. She, at least, has finally gotten her head screwed on right.

That night at dinner, the tantrums start again. "I want The Jack Pacer Band, daddy. Can you book him, please please please?" Marilee's voice goes up into a plaintive squeak that is supposed to be cute but is just annoying. Her eyebrows hook upward above the bridge of her nose as she molds her face into a little-girl plea.

Max looks at Esther, who is staring off into nowhere. It is her Thorazine stare. Max has learned it is better to leave her medicated. He tries to explain reality to Marilee. "Honey, I have five thousand dollars to spend on your wedding. No more, no less. Jack Pacer costs a thousand. The Island Room at the Rosemont costs eight hundred. Caterers, food, gowns, it's gonna be tight. I thinks maybe Ross Rose and the Cavaliers will be a good band."

"Ross Rose! They're creepy!" Marilee bangs her dainty fist on the table so that the knives and forks jump. Esther watches from afar, like a snake entranced by a fakir's moving flute. Marilee's voice is so much like her mother's, but even more shrill and nasal. "You can get more money. Manny offered you money. Why are you so damn stubborn? He can afford it. If you take his money, just as a loan, we can have a proper wedding instead of some shmata shlepper piece of shit!"

Max opens his mouth, but nothing comes out. There is no point to saying anything. He is on this roller coaster ride until it is over or the tracks underneath rot away and it all comes crashing down. Marilee picks up the serving bowl with the peas in it and tosses it at Max. She storms from the room.

"What kind of a man are you?" she calls back over her shoulder. "Useless. You can't make a decent enough living to properly pay for your own daughter's wedding!"

The door to her room slams. Esther stirs. "Are we going to eat? Where did Marilee go?"

Max sighs heavily and reaches for a towel to clean up the mess.

Everything is downhill from there. The wedding duly takes place on June Nineteenth. The limousines are late, the wedding party stands like fools at the door of Temple Beth Israel for ten minutes. Ross Rose has strep throat and sends a tuxedoed accordian player. The band's drummer is smoking something smelly behind the kitchen and saunters in lopsided for each set. Instead of an ice sculpture in the shape of a leaping dolphin, the guests are greeted by suggestive abstract shapes that dominate the long reception table and leave people bewildered and uncomfortable without quite knowing why.

On the wedding cake Marilee's name is mispelled. The bride herself is hiding in the lady's room , hysterical with sexual anxiety and social shame, while the groom smokes endless cigars, becomes more and more drunk, and associates only with his old college cronies as if this is still the bachelor party that took place last night.

Esther wears a hat that looks like a skunk with an arrow through its rectum.

Manny Josephson smirks. Leah Josephson looks appalled and ashamed. Everyone else seems to have a fine time, but there hangs over the reception a heavy air of wrong decisions, missed opportunities, poor planning, poverty, embarassment and anxiety. Fortunately, the accordian player is a great comic, a real find, and with a keen and compassionate eye tells stories that have everyone in stitches. The goddam accordian player saves the whole goddam affair. Afterward, Max presses an envelope into his hand, in addition to the check.

Chapter Thirty Nine
The Bottom Is Hard

1978: Aaron at Thirty Two, San Francisco

"How did this happen to me?" This question, iterated thousands of times in Aaron's mind over the past few years, might as well be on the billboard across the street from where he sits. Instead of the svelte model pushing Virginia Slims, there should be these words, in letters twelve feet high: HOW DID THIS HAPPEN TO ME? Aaron sits in the doorway of an abandoned building. Half a block down, the freeway overpass roars like a jet engine. Cars grind to a stop at the light immediately to his left, idle, then spew their fumes into his face as the light turns green.

There is an old wino puking into a concrete planter containing a withered tree. As soon as he is finished, Aaron has to get up and puke into the same planter. Seeing the wino is like seeing his future.

His possessions are in a black plastic garbage bag. His only friend is his dog, Diz, who is curled patiently against his thigh.

"How did this happen to me?" As he sits there with his back against broken tilework, just barely out of the wind and the rain, he makes an inventory of himself. What is his life? What are his dreams? How did his life get so completely derailed that he sits here with his heart like a concrete block tied to his ankles by his own demons?

He has an IQ of a hundred and sixty. Five years ago he was the premier new drummer, straddlling the worlds of rock and jazz, an innovator, a creative force. He was in demand, he was recording with other musicians, releasing albums under his own name. In his free time he wrote fiction, and his first novel was being read with interest by top publishers. He was with a woman he thought he would marry. They had a beautiful baby girl. It's true, his role as husband and father made him nervous. He had accomodated himself. He would be responsible to his family, provide for them. He planned from the start to be unfaithful. He is a rock star! What can he do?

He had everything he ever dreamed about. There were a few blemishes, but this is life. Nothing is ever perfect.

He separates from Debra and the baby. He was emotionally hollow, so Debra said. He didn't feel emotionally hollow about music, about creating art. He feels hollow about that particular relationship, it is true. He loved the baby but she terrified him. When he held her he feels anguish. He feels prison bars of responsibility rising from the ground, growing fast like rampant bamboo. He couldn't be a father! It feels so wrong to him!

His lack of love, his lack of giving made Debra miserable. Everything began to slide. At the gigs, people gave him weed to smoke, coke to snort. Then Lucinda Cole appeared with her opium, heroin, cocaine and crack. He made a very bad decision. He had conjured Lucinda Cole out of the aethers. If she hadn't existed he could have built her like Frankenstein's Bride, out of parts of his own mental universe. Lucinda didn't destroy him. He destroyed himself.

When he was young and innocent, he swore he would never use hard drugs. He broke that promise. He has broken so many promises. His words have lost their meaning and weight from the number of lies he has told over the last five years. Every time he says he will do something, and doesn't do it, every time he makes a commitment and fails to keep it, power drains out of him.

Now, he is sitting in a doorway between Brannan and Harrison in San Francisco. He has fixed with some low grade Mexican dope last night before sleeping in the back of a truck he'd found unlocked. Now he is sick, scared, in utter despair.

His last dope connection has cut him off. He has no money, no job, no home, no friends, no car. He has a little white dog and cravings for heroin and cocaine that are roaring towards him like tornadoes.

Aaron gets up, looks around, then sits down. Diz stirs, looks at him hopefully. The dog has put up with everything for five years. The dog has followed him from the house in Mill Valley that he bought after the separation. The dog followed him to his not- so-nice apartment in San Rafael. The dog followed him to his even less nice apartment in the city. The dog followed him to a crash pad with five or six people crowding their drama into a small dirty space. The dog followed him to a few more crash pads with dozens of people drifting in and out, ever dirtier and more dramatic, then to his crummy hotel room, then to his filthy motel room. The dog stayed with him in his van, and now the dog stays with him wherever he finds a place to sleep.

Aaron gets up again, and sits down. The wino has stumbled away. It starts to rain, and he pulls his stocking cap down over his face to ease the bite of the wind. Diz shivers. Aaron rummages in his plastic bag and gets out a sweater and spreads it over the dog.

He gets up a third time, looks left, looks right, looks up at the windows of the warehouse across the street. Diz gets up, then sits down again as his companion subsides once more onto the cold concrete step.

Aaron hasn't been able to cry in a long time. He begins to cry now, long sobs that make his shoulders move up and down, sobs that twitch in his abdomen. Diz whimpers; he doesn't understand.

"I can die," Aaron thinks. "I can die today. I can go down to the junkie camp in China Basin and trade my ring for one last big fix, and I can die."

Finally, he is able to get up and move. He has motivation, he has a purpose. He uncovers the dog, removes his coat and puts the sweater on himself, then replaces the coat. He emerges from the doorway and goes left, down Brannan Street. Diz, glad to be walking, tugs joyfully on his leash.

Aaron looks at his dog, prancing. Diz is an American Eskimo, like a miniature Samoyed. His ears are pointed and upright, his face fox-like, his white coat thick and rich. Diz eats before Aaron feeds himself. If there is only money to feed the dog, Aaron goes hungry. Aaron has lavished all his love on this single creature.

He has gone half a block when he stops, abruptly.

"If I die, the dog dies," he realizes. Unless he wants to abandon the dog to his fate in this miserable district, he will have to kill Diz.

He picks the dog up and cradles him in his chest. "I can't do that to you, Diz. Just because I fucked up my life, it doesn't give me the right to take yours. I can't do it. I can't....can't do it!"

Aaron finds another of those useless civic planters and sits on its rim. He puts the dog into the dirt. Dutifully, Diz lifts his leg.

The weeping comes back, and Aaron sits there, feeling himself to be at the bottom of a deep dark well. The sides of the well are slippery with algae and slime, and there is no way he can lever himself back up, back to the light of life.

He has prayed to god many times before. He has a sophisticated concept of God, he is an educated mystic. He doesn't believe in a deity personally involved in his life, ready to intervene on his behalf. It is possible, he admits. Anything is possible. He has always had the habit of prayer, even as a child. He prays because he is lonely, confused, and it helps him to focus his thoughts and his desires.

Wouldn't it be comforting to think that God or some angel watches over him, personally? He fiercely wishes he can believe it. He can't quite make that leap.

Now he prays from a different place in himself. He is at the lethally sharp cleavage where only two concepts exist. There is meaningless death. There is God.

That is it. No other choices, no other ideas have relevance. He has to chose, and it isn't difficult. He choses God. He can still die, but he isn't going to invite death into what is left of his house. He isn't going to make it easy for death.

"Dear God, don't let me waste myself," he prays. "You gave me many gifts, and I tried so hard to be worthy of them. In spite of all my efforts, I failed miserably. I practiced Yoga, I meditated, I did good works and helped people. I know I was a selfish person with my family but I couldn't help the way I was. I did everything to be a spiritual man. I betrayed you, betrayed my gifts and betrayed myself. I know what it is to be utterly crushed. I have nothing left; I am empty and without a single resource. Please, God, I am willing to help myself if I can find a way. I don't know where to turn. Help me, God, I don't want to die. I don't want my soul to die."

He emerges from his prayer, shriveled and exhausted. He expects nothing. He takes Diz, puts him back on the ground, and starts walking in the opposite direction. He has some vague notion of attempting to talk his way back into one of the Methasone clinics that he has passed through on his way to his current dilemma. He turns onto Third Street and walks up towards Mission.

As he walks, he begins hearing a car honk behind him, insistently. "Shit," he thinks, "I'm busted."

He turns, expecting to see a police car, but there is a shiny new maroon BMW, pulled to the curb and edging alongside. There is a man at the wheel and a woman in the passenger seat. The woman slides her face out the window and says, uncertainly, "Aaron? Aren't you Aaron Kantro?"

Aaron hasn't the energy to wipe his tears or summon a pleasant face. He stares into the woman's eyes from his utterly naked soul.

She holds his gaze. "Remember me? I''m Sheilah Price. The singer. You played on my record, my first record. You got me the producer, the engineers, you did everything. You were great. Without you that record would have been nothing. I wouldn't be where I am today."

Aaron sinks to his knees next to the passenger door, taking the dog into the crook of his arm. The words Zoot Prestige had spoken, way back on the highway between Detroit and Chicago, come back in his memory as a prophecy that Zoot had held, had known about Aaron's future. "Ask for help, babe," Zoot said. "don't be too proud. Ask for help when you need it."

Aaron had blanked out that memory in his success, in his grandiose but empty achievements. Now he truly needs to take Zoot's advice.

"I need help," he croaks. "I really fucked up my life."

Sheilah Price looks once to the man, whom Aaron now recognizes as her husband, Victor. He knew them in better places and better times.

Victor puts the car in park, gets out and comes around to where Aaron is kneeling. He takes Aaron's garbage bag and puts it in the trunk. Sheilah leans back to open the rear door of the car. Diz jumps in and sits comfortably on the leather seat, his tail thumping.

"Thank you," Aaron whispers. "Thank you." He follows the dog.

Chapter Forty

WeddingNightPlusOne
1972: Waikiki

Irv Josephson tips the bellboy with a twenty and shuts the door to the suite. "Jesus. I'm exhausted." He makes a goofy face, sticks his tongue out the side of his mouth like a dead animal. He loosens his tie and kicks off his shoes.

Marilee, sitting on the bed, manages to look both wilted and rigid. Her white skirt has wrinkles going at oblique angles against the line of the pleats. Her hat is a little black thingie with a funny half-veil that never gets below the hairline. It hangs crookedly, almost falling from her pinned-up hair.

Pushing through a curtain of jet-lag, Marilee gets up and walks to the glass doors that lead out to the balcony.

"Why don't you get some sleep?" she asks. Irv hears that and registers the word "you," singular, that is, he can take a nap by himself so there is no chance to take another crack at Marilee's virginity. She'll come around in time, he tells himself, dismissing his own inadequacy in a sweeping gesture of unconsciousness.

Marilee tosses her wreath of Hawaiian leis onto a chair and opens the double glass doors that look out onto the beach. "Waikiki," she breathes. "Oh my god, It's gorgeous." The vista gives her some energy, it is a costly vista, the suite is a costly suite. On the beach, rich people swim and lay in the sun, and rich people's boats gently rock on the expensive waves.

Irv disentangles himself from his batch of guest-plumage and tosses it atop Marilee's discarded mess. He joins her on the balcony, putting his arms around her wiry petite body from behind, enclosing her in his embrace. He is considerably broader of build than his new wife, though his youth prevents that plumpness from becoming fat. There is still plenty of muscle tone on his body, tone that is beginning to forget itself now that Irv has passed the Bar and is in practice with his father. He so resembles his father: it will be a couple of years before he assumes Manny's pear shape. There is little doubt that he will achieve even greater corpulence. He has bigger appetites. He likes food, he likes sex, he likes to drink. He is bottom-heavy. His neck is of average proportion, his shoulders are broad. His stomach seems to lurch forward horizontally, giving his upper body the shape of a ski slope. His butt cheeks are large, equal in girth to his legs, which are extraordinarily wide and strong. On his face there seems always to be an expression of slight confusion, as if he has awakened from an incarnation where he is a great prince, and can't understand how he got into this poky Jewish identity where everyone bosses him around.

Marilee makes an effort to lean back into her husband's embrace. It doesn't come easily to her, touching, intimacy, the necessary looseness for sex. Irv's penis, now that she has seen it, looms in her imagination like some fleshy atomic bomb. "Fat Boy," she calls it, remembering photos of the Nagasaki bomb. Her husband's organ is not overly long, but it has girth, like the rest of him.

Last night, after the reception and before today's flight, they had booked into the Chase for a honeymoon night. Marilee was unable to get that thing into herself, and Irv finally just made a mess on her thighs, a disgusting spectacle that took half a roll of paper towels to clean up.

She breathes in the sea air, praying it will relax her. She has thought about the challenge of her wedded sex life at some length. She doesn't dislike sex but she is very particular about certain aspects of it. Her ignorance of sex is fairly comprehansive. Irv is crazy for sex. Of course, he is a man, they all like sex, that's all they think about.

"I'm not sleepy," Irv says, nuzzling her neck, just beneath her ear. She can feel Fat Boy like an ingot trying to wedge itself between her ass cheeks. "We can try again, honey," he says with a pleading note in his voice. "I'm not so drunk, and you're not so sober. Maybe we can figure out the formula, whattayou say?"

She forces herself to be nice, against all her insticts of revulsion. "Give me a few minutes, baby, okay?" She turns around within the warm cylinder of Irv's embrace and pecks him on the nose with her lips. Her hands are more or less pinned to her sides, albeit gently, and she is aware of the natural animal strength in the male body to which she is wedded. Her right hand rubs Irv's atomic bomb, and he sighs, and in that sigh, Marilee feels her sexual power and that gives her some position, some strength and joy, and she might be able to use that feeling to go through with this act enough times now and in the future that she can keep this rich man until she has thoroughly infiltrated his financial world.

"You know," she croons, "you're so…..so big! I was surprised! My poor little Miss Peekaboo wasn't ready for such a big visitor." Her voice has gone up two octaves, all googoo squeaky, a little Sandre Dee, a little Marilyn Monroe, and just a touch of Annette Funicello. She knows her prey. She knows what Irv likes.

She can feel Irv expand with gratification at her comment on his penis size. Men are so primitive, she thinks. "Let's have a drink together, sweetie, let's get all comfy and we'll try it, okay?" It is a sacrifice she is prepared to make. On the plane, she has taken 15 milligrams of Valium. It is hitting her now, and with a little Vodka and tomato juice, she might be able to relax enough to let Fat Boy come into Miss Peekaboo in a fashion that will gratify her husband. She knows she has to gratify her husband. It won't do to have him sniffing around other women if he can't get what he wants at home.

"You pour the drinks," she instructs, her voice getting soft with the flush of the valium, "and I'll go in here and slip into a nice nightie. Why don't you turn down the lights, honey?"

She can almost see Irv pant like a puppy. She has 'saved herself for marriage' and that has kept her power at a high level. Now, she thinks, I have to give him something, or I won't keep my power over him. He has to enjoy having sex with me.

She ruminates on the dozens of magazines she has read, giving her tips on ways to keep her man happy. A tumbril of anxiety races down the cobblestones of her stomach. There is an inward lurch of pure terror, and she closes her fists tightly, applying her considerable discipline, aided by a strong pharmaceutical, to conquer her misgivings. "I can do this," she affirms. "I can act all hot and sexy. All I have to do is think about the Forbes 500 list. Yes, Irv's dad may be ranked at number four fifty six but come on, this is the Forbes 500, this is THE LIST! And my father in law belongs at the table...MY father in law as of the day before yesterday. Or was it yesterday? I'm not sure what day it is at the moment, but it's Hawaii and it will do, it will do just fine."

Irv goes to the suite's wet bar and begins making drinks, clinking ice cubes into long-stemmed saucer-shaped glasses with a pair of tongs. Marilee gets her night case from the pile of luggage at the door, and walks into the bathroom. She takes out a black nightie, selected for this occasion, slips it over her head, and then flings a kimono over herself, tying it with a matching wide belt. It is white silk with pink chrysanthemums embroidered into it, each stitch made with painstaking attention. The cloth is a bit stiff and papery, having never been worn, but it makes no difference.

Outside, night is falling rapidly, and luau music wafts up on the smoothly modulated winds, drifting through the newlywed's suite at the Waikiki Hilton.

Marilee examines herself in the full-length mirror. She flings open the kimono, showing herself the effect it will have, as it reveals the black nightie. Holding the kimono wide, she examines her hair, her body. "Even after twelve hours of jet travel, I look good," she assesses. The Valium is smoothing away her fatigue. She paws through her night bag and gets out a bottle of Percodan. Taking two, she chases the pills with water.

"That ought to do it," she decides. " That and the Bloody Mary. I have to stay married for ten years, have to keep Irv happy for ten years. I'll have one child, hopefully a boy so we can name him

Manny. Ten years, one child, and I'll be set for life. What else can a woman do in this day and age? Work like a dog? For what? A schmatte house in a schmatte neighborhood with three or four bratty kids? And then, she gets old, the husband leaves, she's got no money, no looks. Screw that."

She has refused several suitors, one of whom she liked a great deal, to be with Irv and bask in the reflection of the Josephson family fortune.

Under the black silken garment, her body is taut from regular workouts at the gym, her breasts just big enough to appeal, not so big that they sag. She knows she has a great body, and the nose job she wheedled out of her father took care of the one major flaw on her face. She is a good looking woman, she decides. A damn good looking woman.

Taking a deep breath, she re-ties the kimono, feeling the air currents moving as she wraps the garment's great wings around herself. A dangling piece of toilet paper rocks back and forth on its holder until the little self-generated wind subsides. Applying the final touch, the coup de grace, she unzips a shoe bag. It contains a pair of black stiletto heels. Languidly, she sits on a wicker stool and puts the shoes on her shapely legs. Then A squirt of perfume in her armpits and at her shoulderblades punctuates and defines her sexual design.

Marilee opens the door and steps out into the suite. Irv has taken off his jacket and shirt, and stands at the bar in his slacks and T-shirt. His mouth falls open.

"God, Jesus…holy mazoley!" he erupts. His face is filled with genuine awe. Marilee feels lifted by her husband's adoration. "You look…in..cred…ible." These last words are drawled so that each syllable divides in two. The words are sung more than spoken.

He turns for a moment and puts the drinks down on the dark mahogany bar. In three steps he is at her, lifts her up, staggers five more steps to the couch, and throws her down. He is atop her with a graceless plunge, snugging at her face, neck, arms.

"Whoa! Whoa, King Kong!" Marilee pushes him away firmly. "Remember last night? I can't do this so fast. I'm a lady, I'm not a side of beef, for god's sake, Irv! Get a hold of yourself!" Fat Boy is pulsing in Irv's pants and she does not want an unplanned ejaculation to ruin any of her clothing.

Shame-faced, Irv sits up. "Sorry honey, you just look good enough to eat…I mean… you're not beef, y'know, but still, you're pretty fuckin' edible, yummy yummy yummy!" His cheeks are flushed vivid pink and little sweat beads gather at his receeding hairline.

"Language, Irv, language! There's no cursing in our house," Marilee admonishes. "We have to do this like civilized and sophisticated people. Now brng me that Bloody Mary." Irv crosses the suite, stumbling slightly where a pair of steps divide the room with an S-curve into distinct segments: the bar on one side and a dining table, then, up the steps to the plush couch, the television, a mahogany cabinet for hanging casual clothing, topped by a tall dark turquoise vase filled with Bird of Paradise flowers. Next to the sliding glass door is a desk. The master bedroom is behind a slatted double door decorated with a wicker Tiki mask. In the master bedroom another balcony juts from their eighth floor promontory. Reproductions of Gaugain's paintings augment the suite's Polynesian motif.

Marilee gathers herself together and goes into the master bedroom, opens the sliding doors and steps onto the balcony. Irv follows her with two Bloody Marys. There is a large contraption on rockers, supplied amply with cushions so that two people can sit together and watch the ocean, sipping cocktails. The newlyweds sit on this divan, Marilee facing forward with her drink, Irv sitting sideways to face Marilee, his right leg tucked under his rump, his left leg sprawled out so that his foot rests on the deck. His body leans towards Marilee's as if she is a magnet, his head groping forward on inexorable waves of attractive energy. Though he can barely control his lust, Irv magnanimously raises his glass and says, "Let us toast our long and happy marriage."

Marilee raises her glass, clinks it to Irv's, and concurs. "A toast. May our marriage be long and happy." As she drinks, she keeps thinking, "Ten years with the schlub, ten years. That's nothing. I'll still be young when we get divorced."

Quietly, each to his or her own thoughts, the couple sips their vodka drinks and watch the twilight descend on a beach as perfect as any in the world. Couples walk hand in hand, silhouetted against the bright sea. The sound of the surf gathers and grows loud with its inward surge, then quiets as it leaves the sand damp, glistening and black as it withdraws into the sea. Hypnotized, Marilee feels the Percodan enter her pharmacological mix with a warm rush and knows that it is going to be now or never.

She finishes her drink in a gulp, then takes Irv's drink away and sets it down on the nearby table.

"Come on, Jungle Man, I'm drunk enough and you're sober enough." She takes his hand and leads him into the bedroom. He stands with his back to the sea, and watches his new wife slowly unwrap her kimono, to show him the body beneath in its silky black container. Marilee finds enjoyment in the expressions of Irv's face as she performs a not very sinuous strip tease. The drugs and booze have taken away most of her inhibitions. She isn't expecting to love anyone, but the concept of being loved has a certain fascination. No question, Irv loves her. He adores, worships her. It isn't the first time she has been adored by a man but it is the first time it is going to be taken to a serious conclusion. So she hopes.

The sun dips into the ocean and spills its light through the windows of the bedroom. Shadows from gossamer curtains undulate on the carpets. Marilee lays on the bed and gestures to Irv with both hands, her palms facing inward in front of her face. She waves her fingers from the pivot of her wrists, inviting her husband as seductively as she knows how. In spite of the lovely cocktail coursing through her veins, she is still frightened. "I'm in command of this situation," she tells herself. "I call the shots."

Eagerly, Irv hops out of his pants, one leg at a time. He tears his shirt off, popping buttons. His atomic bomb sticks out from the opening in his boxer shorts, and Marilee averts her eyes from it. The room is somewhat chilly, and she jumps up, pulls the blankets from her side of the bed and slips under them. Wearing his tank top t-shirt and one sock, Irv gets halfway under the covers beside her. He slips one arm under her neck, kisses her hard, too hard, his tongue seeming like a glutinous creature invading her mouth. Then he rolls over on her like a flopping fish. Between his groping mouth and his weight, Marilee is nearly smothered.

"Irv, Irv!" she gasps. "Slow down! Haven't you ever heard of foreplay?" She pushes her husband away, forcing him onto his back. She is strong enough to handle him.

"Oh!" Irv says stupidly. "Yeah. Sorry babe, I'm just so hot for you."

"You might be hot for me, but Fatb....uh, Atomic Bomb won't get inside Little Miss Peekaboo unless you're gentle with her. Come on, Irv." She takes his hand and puts his index and second fingers on the lips of her vagina. She has an immensely powerful urge to call Irv an idiot.

God, she thinks, you're an imbecile! Don't you know anything? She clamps down on the urge to say these words aloud. Calling him names won't enhance his delusions of manhood. She has to exert self control.

Irv gamely explores the hair around Marilee's labia. He has no concept of a clitoris, no idea of the complexities that lay at the heart of a woman's mystery. He puts a finger partway up her. She is dry. She wriggles and says, "Ow! Easy! Here, let me show you." She spreads her legs wider and guides his two fingers to her clitoris. "Feel this thing?" she asks.

"Uh, I think so."

Marilee rotates his fingers just so, the way she masturbates herself. She thinks of Myron Goldstein, the man she likes the most and would have married, had he not been a plumber. Myron has a cherub's face and sweet puppy dog eyebrows. Always, his blue eyes pleaded with her, oh love me as I love you, Marilee. Love me, love me. Myron is destroyed by Marilee's rejection. She feels badly but what would she do as a plumber's wife? Impossible.

The room grows subtly darker. Surreptitiously, Marilee wets her own fingers and spreads saliva around her opening. Irv is impatient. While he explores with his fingers, he is humping into her side, his penis bumping against her hip. She'd better try to get him in her, before something happens.

"Come on, big boy, get on top." Eagerly, Irv obeys. He moves his legs and hips, groping for the right place. He is near that place, but Marilee is small and dry, and even with her help, the entrance seems impossible. "Ow," she cries again. He has pushed at her with energy, and his penis rasps against her passage without finding its destination.

Again, Marilee tries to guide him, but she is becoming frustrated with herself as well as with Irv. This is a nightmare, she thinks. It isn't working. He's just too big for me. Down there, where their hands and genitals mingle, where hips work and legs bang into each other, it's chaos.

"Okay okay!" Marilee gulps, moving away from Irv. She intends to start over again.

"Irv, sweetie, it will help a lot to get me going if you will try licking it, you know… using your mouth."

Irv's usual look of surprise now mingles with a look of distaste. "Wha…what? You mean……..down there? Little Miss Peekaboo?"

Marilee works hard to suppress her impatience, because she knows from Irv's expression what he is going to say.

"Eeeewww," he almost squeals. "That will be, uh uh, gross!"

"But you wouldn't mind it one little bit if I, uh, pay a little attention to Mister Atomic Bomb, here, will you?" She gestures with her chin at the now-flaccid organ. As Irv indulges in the fantasy of a long-sought objective, the very possibility of it causes his penis to twitch and grow.

"That's different!" he says, almost happily. He isn't entirely stupid. He knows that Marilee is about to attempt to point out the hypocrisy of his position, and he has already marshaled his arguments, as any good lawyer would.

"My thing, my 'Atomic Bomb', it's…well, it's outside, it's right here, it's clean, it doesn't smell or anything, it doesn't have a period once a month." Raising himself to a full sitting position he looks down at his half-erect genitalia. "It's more hygienic!"

Marilee considers. Instead of attacking her moron of a husband, she needs to gratify him, and she considers the size of his penis, measuring its width against the capacity of her mouth. Maybe with a little practice, a little trickery, she can fulfill Irv's fantasy. It is better than having him tear mindlessly at her vagina and spilling himself all over her expensive chemise.

"Okay, you gorilla," she forces herself to say. She pushes him back down onto the bed with two fingers on his breastbone. "Relax and enjoy yourself."

This will be her first attempt at oral sex. She has talked to friends about it, and she has studied a little pamphlet from an organization called "The Houston Center for Sexological Research". It is all very respectable. Photos of clean, middle class couples in various positions are accompanied by text written by doctors on the benefits of sexual education in furthering harmonious marriage.

"Just relax and fantasize for a minute, Irvy sweetie," Marilee oozes without sincerity. "let me prepare myself. It'll just take a second."

She scoots into the little second bathroom, where she sheds her expensive black chemise and replaces it with a less expensive mid-length slip. She grabs a handful of paper towels from the dispenser. In half a minute she is astride Irv's body. She finds that he is too big to enclose between her knees, so she shifts to one side and slides down the bed so that her head is near Irv's 'bomb'.

He is already erect. Experimentally, Marilee licks the thing. It throbs, and Irv groans. Marilee raises her head and begins to insert Irv's penis into her mouth. It isn't impossible. It makes her jaw sore, and she manages to get about a third of the way down his length before she gags.

"Oooh," Irv sighs. It hardly matters how Marilee performs. The fantasy has the ultimate power. This is the third blow job of his life. The first two were from prostitutes and they were memorable only in their context. This is a blow job from the adorable and exquisite Marilee, his new wife. This fantasy has been rolling around in his head for almost two years, and he can barely contain himself. He does not hear Marilee's gag. He is trying to slow down the rising tide of thwarted lust that is boiling up from his loins.

Marilee makes a second attempt to get Irv into her mouth, and she does a little better.

"Oh oh!" Irv cries. "I can't hold it any longer, oh Jesus!"

Shit! Marilee shudders inwardly. She feels two powerful throbs from Irv's penis and she moves her head away from him as quickly as possible. Irv is spewing himself all over her slip. Some of the sperm gets on her lips, and she swiftly grabs a paper towel and pats the stuff away. Irv screams and bucks a few times, then subsides with a long exhale of relief.

She jumps from the bed and runs to the bathroom.

"Im sorry, baby, I just couldn't help it," Irv calls from the bed. He is dabbing at himself with kleenex from the box on the bedside table.

"Oh honey, that was great," he adds, "that was incredible."

"I'm glad you liked it," says Marilee, as she wets the paper towels and wipes drops of sperm from her Saks Fifth Avenue silk slip. It cost seventy five dollars and she doesn't want to throw it away. She feverishly hunts through her night case and finds a small bottle of Listerine. With this she rinses her mouth, dabs her lips, gargles repeatedly. Between gargles she gets herself into a clean slip.

She runs the tap water in the bathroom sink until it is hot. There is a little squeeze bottle of soap in her nightbag and she pours five or six drops into the water. Then

she bundles her stained slip and submerges it in the sink, wringing it a few times. It will have to do. She leaves the slip in the soapy solution, hoping it can be saved.

She returns to the master bedroom to find Irv snoring contentedly, lying on his stomach with his face turned in her direction.. His mouth hangs open and a bead of spittle has formed at the corner of his lips. His snore is an inhale with a high pitched buzz, followed by an exhale that is a whistle punctuated at the end by a little hiccup.

Marilee snorts with contempt. She feels agitated, hyped up. Percodan acts paradoxically on her as a stimulant. Blended with the valium and a little bit of alcohol, she has a fine buzz and is in no mood to waste it. Irv will be out for hours. She has no inclination to sit in the suite and watch Huntley and Brinkley. No indeed, she is in Hawaii at the Waikiki Hilton and dozens of excellent shops are no farther than the lobby.

The bellboy has brought the large suitcase into the bedroom. She opens it and hangs some things in the closet, then organizes a few drawers of the dresser with her underwear and cosmetics. She makes no attempt to be quiet. Irv sleeps like a bear. Tufts of back hair show over the top of his t-shirt. His arms are hairy. The blanket covers the lower part of his body; the rest of him is a sprawl, left arm hanging off the side of the bed. Marilee looks at her husband's sleeping face for a moment, winces, then returns to her unpacking.

Enough of this, she thinks. Let me see, what can I wear? I have this cute little emerald pant suit from Nieman Marcus, a string of pearls, a pair of pumps by Ottolini. Nice. She applies make up carefully to her face, choses a lipstick that goes well with the pant suit. She brushes and poofs her hair with some spray. All dolled up, she casts one more look at Irv. His pants are still on the floor, and she picks them up, finds his wallet and checks inside. In her own purse she has two credit cards with twenty thousand dollar limits. She is angry with Irv, angry for his clumsy attempts to penetrate her. There are traveler's checks in his wallet for five thousand dollars, and three or four thousand in cash. She takes a handful of hundred dollar bills, just for spite. She walks from the room and out the door.

A couple in their forties are coming down the hall towards the elevator. Marilee smiles distantly. The woman has really let herself go. No amount of hair spray and pancake makeup can compensate for the sagging cheeks, the slack belly. I'll never let myself get like that, Marilee smugly vows. It takes work, but it can be done. Forty doesn't scare me. Fifty doesn't even scare me. By that time I'll have enough money for the best plastic surgeons.

The elevator dings and the three people get on. Uncomfortable silence and avoided eyes mark the downward descent. Marilee thinks the woman is glancing at her jealously when she isn't looking, and the husband is studiously avoding letting his wife know that HE is looking. Let them steal a peek! I've got it!

In the huge lobby, a number of activities are in full swing. Outside, in a little courtyard, a fire twirler spins his burning torches, while drums pound. Pretty young Polynesian girls are at the stations near the entrances, handing out leis and kisses on cheeks.

Corridors of shops run in two directions off the hotel's mezzanine. Lighting is provided by faux electric torches in wall sconces. Wicker furniture and Tiki gods, effigies of Pele are on offer. Marilee stops at an antiques shop and looks through the window at price tags. Fifteen hundred dollars for a chair. Thirty five hundred for a set of eighteenth century wrought iron fireplace tools. Marilee moves on. Her antennae are set on clothing, her radars are tuned to the frequency of Italian shoes and handbags, Paris dresses, hats and scarves. She looks down the corridor but her heightened senses are telling her that the clothing boutiques are in the other direction, so she backtracks, again passing through the lobby.

At that moment, she sees a face approaching her, a man who looks oddly familiar. She knows him. The context is different and she can't place him because he doesn't belong here, at the Waikiki Hilton. When the man catches sight of her his eyes grow in his face, his mouth opens, and suddenly she realizes that it is Myron Goldstein. Myron! Her heartbroken suitor. The puppydog eyebrows, the cherubic face with its blue eyes and sprinkling of freckles. There he is with the same pleading expression: Love me, Marilee, love me as I love you!

She stops and her hands fly up to her cheeks, fingers spread taut with astonishment. Myron runs towards her, his arms extended tentatively, as if he knows and acknowledges his rejection yet still nourishes a desperate hope.

He stops a few paces away when Marilee's hands come away from her face and move forward, blocking, blocking. "Myron!" she squeaks. "What in God's name are you doing here?"

"Marilee, Marilee," he tries to get through the blockade of her hands, and then finds himself grabbed by the front of his shirt and thrust sideways into the lee of a large plant, a place of concealment.

"Goddammit Myron, you're following me on my honeymoon, you bastard!"

The misery on his face is so abject it is almost cute. "I can't help myself, Marilee. I have this compulsion, I don't know what made me do it, I just can't believe that you married that...that....fat lawyer for his money. You want to marry me, don't you?" His voice rises in pitch as he repeats, "Don't you?"

Marilee's eyes turn in all directions to see if anyone is looking at them. No one is paying attention. The hotel bustles with its business, the drums beat, torches whirl, the strolling singers serenade. Bellboys rush here and there with dollies full of luggage.

Returning her gaze to Myron's face, she says, "No I don't want to marry you, Myron. You're a plumber. Don't you understand? I like you....I almost love you if I can love anybody, which I can't, of course. Love isn't in me, it isn't in my soul. Im just like my mother, I'm completely heartless. I love you the only way I can."

"I know that, Marilee. I don't care. I love you anyway, I love you the way you are. I think deep down you're good and you're searching for goodness."

Marilee laughs a brittle laugh, each note like someone crushing a box full of tin foil. "No, Myron. No goodness. I'm not really so bad, either, Im just out for myself, that's all. You're too good, you don't deserve the hell I will put you through."

Tears are streaming down Myron's face. "I don't know what I'll do, Marilee. I don't know how to erase the image of you inside my heart. I came here just to see you from a distance, to protect you if you looked unhappy...I don't know...I really don't know why I came here...."

Something in those boyish blue eyes affects Marilee, and her hands change positions and she pulls him towards her body until man and woman join in a sweet soft kiss. Suddenly, Marilee's dry female parts fill with warmth, a surge between her thighs almost crumples her to the floor. She reaches to stroke Myron's powerful shoulders, run her hands down his arms. He is wearing a Missouri University T-shirt and his muscular biceps fill its sleeves, his sinewy forearms grip Marilee's hands. He's so handsome, she thinks, Jesus he's a good looking guy, and he's sweet. What am I doing? What the hell is gong on here? Oh fuck it, I don't care.

"Myron, where are you staying? Are you here at the Hilton?"

"I..I…are you kidding? I have a motel room down the road a couple of miles."

"Then take me there. Did you rent a car?"

Myron nods yes.

"Don't ask me any questions, don't demand anything of me, don't make plans, don't fool yourself about the future. Don't don't don't don't. You understand? Just take me to your motel room for a while."

His eyes betray confusion, hope, lust and a barely perceptible sunrise of promised satiation of a long, long obsession, the gratification of a desire delayed almost to infinity.

"There's an exit down this way, and the parking lot's right out there." Myron takes Marilee's arm and propels her along the corridor. The hubbub of the hotel's lobby fades away. Panting, Myron and Marilee make their escape.

All the way to the motel, Myron and Marilee are stroking one another. She reaches inside his pants, and he has his hand gently rubbing her everywhere, fondling her nipples, reaching down her waistband, stroking her neck. They reach their destination and tumble into Myron's room. Marilee's drugs have worn off, and she doesn't care, she is glad, she feels more sensitive, more alive and that's what she needs to feel.

Myron's kisses are sweet and he puts her on the bed and kneels on the floor so he can put his head between her thighs. Marilee pulls at his hair and moans. Myron slithers his way up her body and enters her effortlessly. They rock their way to a staggering climax that is heard up and down the motel's corridors.

Myron drives her home. He is quiet, sad, happy, forlorn, confused.

"Will this happen again, Marilee?"

"No," she says firmly. "No. NO. NO NO NO!" Each syllable is a brick and each brick builds a wall. "I'm married, Myron, and I have to stay married."

As she says this, she feels a chink in the wall, a little hole where the bricks aren't quite cured solid, where her resolution feels a little crumbly. This kind of pleasure will never come from Irv Josephson. She takes her hand from Myron's hand and puts it in her lap, determined. Myron puts his hand over hers, and she does not push it away.

When she returns to the suite, Irv is still sleeping, exactly as she left him. She begins to put the money she has taken back in his wallet, because Irv is an obsessive counter, he will know to the dime exactly how much cash is in his pocket. She reconsiders. "What the hell is he going to do with me? We better get this kind of stuff straight, right now. Your pocketbook is open to me, Irv Josephson, full time."

She puts the bills back into her own wallet and clips it shut, decisively. Then she showers, washes her thick black hair, puts it up in a towel, and wraps a towel around her body. As she emerges from the bathroom, Irv is standing bleary eyed in the middle of the room.

"Jeez," he says, "I needed that nap." His eyes clear a little bit as he beholds Marilee. "You look good, you look really beautiful. You want to try again? You want to stay a virgin your whole life?"

Marilee drops the towel and lets her husband see her nudity. "No, honey, I don't. Let's try again. I think this time things might go a little better."

To Irv, Marilee's expression looks soft and inviting. Marilee, however, is feeling only a steely determination to see her task through and get what she wants out of life.

Chapter Forty One

1980: Aaron 1980: Aaron Returns To The Poisoned Nest

As he drives home from work, Aaron takes a dryly ruthless self-inventory. He is thirty two years old, with a dead end job frying donuts at a franchise donut shop. He has returned to the place where he grew up. Life has beaten the crap out of him and he feels there is nowhere to go but back to his sister and his father.

Aaron has a rent free suburban home with his Uncle Jack. Max's brother has an empty house, his kids are gone, his wife has died, and he is happy to have his nephew Aaron taking up some space..

Aaron sees his mother infrequently. It is an experience of confusion, grief and revulsion. Though Esther is a spent force, she still makes his skin crawl, makes him want to pick up a butcher knife and sink it into her brain.

He has been clean for five months. It is an uneasy, tormented sobriety. He experiences a continual craving for dope. He fights the craving. He remembers what Avian Coulter said. Will power isn't the answer. White-knuckling ultimately backfires. What he has to do is heal the pain. And he doesn't know how to do that. How do you heal a childhood of terror and torture? How does the child who nursed on cold sharp stones, on shards of crystal glass, recover from that trauma?

He isn't indulging in self-pity. He is literate in psychological theory, he has read voraciously in an attempt to find some bit of information that will be useful. In all these thousands of pages he has devoured, there is one thing he has learned: it can't be done alone. He needs help but he doesn't know where to turn.

It is eight in the morning. Aaron is exhausted from a shift of lifting trays of raw doughnuts, dipping them into boiling oil, turning them in a trough full of sugar glaze. All night, over and over, he repeats this procedure, repeats it until his forearms ache and blisters pock his skin where drops of hot oil have splashed and sizzled.

He is driving back to Uncle Jack's house when he thinks about his mother. She is there in that big house, alone. His dad finally made his move, he separated from Esther, bought a house just a mile away from the old house. He goes by there every day to check on Esther, to see that she is fed and clothed, that the utilities are paid. It is supposed to be a big secret that he has a girlfriend, but Aaron knows, Sarah knows.

He is afraid to go to the old house. He knows the place is full of drugs, sickness, tempation, insanity, depression. Something in him finally gives way to pity. What can it hurt to go see his mother? He feels genuinely sorry for her. Forlorn, she wanders the house in a daze or loses herself in TV soap operas. She is immensely fat, profoundly deteriorated. Yet, on this day, Aaron feels no rage, no bitterness, just a deep sadness that this person, this mother of his flesh, has fallen so low. And he who is so low himself, can not blame it all on his mother. He has been totally culpable in the destruction of his own life.

He shifts the car into the left lane and turns onto Olive Street. In ten minutes he rolls up into the driveway of the house where he spent the last few years of high school. Just up the street is Katherine's house. She is long gone, moved to Oregon with her third husband.

He doesn't knock. The door opens quietly. Plastic runners go from the foyer to the dining room, across the still-pristine carpet of the never-used living room. There is the sound of television coming from the master bedroom

"Mom? It's me. Aaron."

The door is slightly ajar. "Aaron? Let me get up."

She comes from the bedroom, dressed in slippers and a yellow checked house coat. Her eyes are dark and fixed. Around them, wrinkled grey sockets and wattles of fat distort the original shape of Esther's face. Aaron can never look at his mother without dismay. She looks like a dead chameleon.

"Did you come to visit?" Her voice has no life, no air and no resonance. It is that of an old woman. She embraces her son perfunctorily. She smells of the same old perfume, sweat, and the stench of inner decay.

"I just got off work. I thought I'd drop by and say hello."

"That is very nice of you. Your father moved out, you know. He can't stand me anymore."

A

aron doesn't know what to say to that.

"I've done the best I know how, " Esther explains. "I loved everyone the only way I could. I meant the best, believe me."

"I believe you, mom."

"Here, let me fix you some breakfast. What time is it? Is it breakfast time or time for lunch? Oh…doesn't matter." She gestures him into the kitchen. "You want some fried matzoh?"

"That will be fine, mom. I can do it, you know."

"You sit. Let me make your breakfast."

She fumbles at the utensils. Her legs are huge and veined with nasty red networks, bruised and bloated. This is my mother, Aaron thinks. This is the creature that gave birth to me. How can I have become anything? How can I know or do anything? I was born already up to my eye sockets in misery and alienation. The past thirty-two years have been an attempt to fill in the hole so I can stand even with normal people. I haven't gotten there, I can't function any better than she can. I've been shoveling and throwing dirt back in at the same time.

Esther manages to get a skillet with some hot butter on the stove. With confused and sluggish movements, she bangs a steel bowl and a mixing fork and struggles to get eggs, milk, crumbled Passover crackers into the same container. Then she splashes it onto the butter and turns it over, stirring slowly. The fork stops and rests in the midst of the sizzling mixture as Esther's gaze goes blank and her body halts as if it is a machine that has run out of fuel.

Aaron gets up and takes the fork from his mother's hand. She starts up again, but she is sagging, barely able to know her location or purpose. Aaron gently moves her aside and stirs the eggs and matzoh.

"I'm tired. You finish up." Her face is expressionless. She pads robotically back to the bedroom, where a game show is on television.

Aaron takes a spatula and turns the mixture. When it is brown and crispy he puts it onto a plate and slathers it with grape jelly. After he has eaten, he is immensely sleepy.

428

He fights the temptation to scout through the bathroom cabinets for
drugs. He knows they are there, but that isn't why he has come to
this place. He might sleep. It is hard to fall asleep; his bodily
rhythms are still disturbed from withdrawal. He is so exhausted.
He passes his mother's room, through the rumpus room and enters
the sanctum that has been Mark's. His own room has long since
been turned over to storage.

The pegboards are still on the walls. Mark displayed weapons here
when he was a kid. Now they are empty, just hooks and dusty
sillhouettes of pistols, rifles, swords, martial arts weapons,
throwing stars and nanshaks. Mark. Where the hell is he, anyway?
Nobody knows. Nobody wants to know. He might be in jail. He
might even be dead and the family hasn't been notified. Aaron can
see that: Mark's corpse dessicating in some hole in the desert
outside Las Vegas.

Max will know. Max will always know the locations of his
children. Max has turned responsibility and courage from virtues to
vices. He has forgotten to live. He has not shown his children how
to live, how to be joyous. That is what Aaron wants from his
father. He wants a father with a big spontaneous laugh. A father
who plays silly games with his kids. A father who knows how to
use his dick for pleasure. He is pleased at the idea of his dad
getting laid, he is happy his dad has a girlriend. For Aaron, it is too
little too late.

He falls asleep on Mark's bed. He sleeps deeply, dreamlessly, for
at least an hour. Then he has to pee and he gets up to go to the
bathroom. The TV is off in his mother's room and he can hear her
snoring, stentorous, elephantine. He returns to Mark's bed and falls
alseep again.

The next time he wakes, it is one oclock in the afternoon. Good sleep. A blessing. The house is silent except for the ticking of clocks. No snores come from Esther's bedroom. Aaron puts on his shoes and goes down the hall. The door to Esther's bedroom is slightly ajar. Something about the absence of snoring disturbs Aaron. He pushes the door open. Esther lays on the bed, sprawled almost sideways. Her lips are purple-black. Aaron knows immediately that she is dead.

He moves her back and forth. She is so inert, so heavy. She has been dead for a while. He has no impulse to call for paramedics. He has no desire to save her life. He sits next to her body and begins reciting the only Hebrew prayer he can remember.

"Shemah yisroel, adonai, elohainu, adonai echad."

Over and over he sings this ancient hymn. It is the only way he can honor his mother's soul and send her to wherever she is destined to go.

After about fifteen minutes of this, he begins to look around. Esther hasn't died of natural causes. Esther has killed herself. He finds the two empty bottles of barbituate in the trash can at the side of the bed. She has taken sixty Nembutal. She wasn't fooling around, not this time. Aaron crushes the plastic bottles under his shoe, until they are hundreds of little shards. Then he sweeps them up with his hand, and flushes the shards down the toilet. He follows that by a careful vacuuming of the carpet.

He calls 911 and then he calls his father. "I have some news, dad, some terrible news. I hope you're sitting down." He pauses for a long moment, because he intuitively knows that his father knows what he is about to say. "Uhhhh.....Mother's dead."

Max is silent. Then he says, "Oh my god. Have you called paramedics? The police? Someone?"

"Yes."

"I'll be right there. Sarah's here. We'll close up. Oh my god." His voice is like paper tearing. It shakes and rasps.

As he waits for his father, for the ambulance, for the coroner and the paramedics or whoever is going to show up, he opens the top drawer of the large file cabinet that is against the wall of the bedroom, next to the closet. It is filled with plastic prescription bottles. Most of them are full or only partially empty. There are hundreds and hundreds of prescriptions. There is every imaginable category of drug. Bennies, ludes, tranks. Valium, Melloril, Preludin.

"Ohhh, shit." Aaron groans. He finds one bottle. It must have contained a hundred Darvon. He swallows three, taking water directly from the carafe at his mother's bedside, then empties the rest into a paper sack and runs the sack out to his car, where he puts it into the trunk. He runs back inside and opens the bottom file cabinet. More of the same. He is only interested in the opiates. He finds Demerol, Percodan, more Darvon, lots of codeine. The more he digs, the more he finds. He comes upon the REAL stuff, the quality dope: morphine, dilaudid, fentanyl. Hurry hurry hurry! he tells himself. His sobriety is over, definitely and conclusively done. His heart is pumping so fast he thinks he will have a seizure. He knows he has somewhere between five seconds and five minutes. He can stay high for months. He shovels about fifty bottles of the powerful opiates into one of Esther's purses and runs them back out to his trunk. As he closes it he hears a siren in the near distance. The first ambulance comes zooming down the street, its lights flashing, its diesel engine roaring. Aaron raises his hands to guide the paramedics into the driveway. Neighbors are spilling out of their front doors.

"She's in the bedroom, turn left and go down the hall." Aaron steps aside as two technicians enter the house, carrying yellow cases of gear.

There is nothing to be done. The paramedics run through the formal resuscitation protocols. None work. They finishe their job and tell Aaron that his mother has "passed on".

A police car arrives. "You the son?" the cop asks.

"Yes."

The policeman huddles with the paramedics for a moment. He returns to Aaron.

"I'm sorry. There's nothing anyone can do. Looks like a heart attack."

"She has a bad heart. She has diabetes, kidney disease. It's not unexpected."

To his surpise, Aaron begings to cry. He hasn't cried in years. He can't remember the last time he cried. It is nameless inchoate emotion. It isn't grief, shock, sorrow. If anything it is relief. She is gone. At last at last. She is gone.

Max and Sarah arrive. There are people passing each other in the cramped hallways. "Let me see her!" Max cries, pushing through all the officials on the scene.

They part for him. He throws himself on the cold body on the bed. His hands are shaking like frail autumn maple leaves, dried and waiting to drop.

"Don't do this to me, Esther!" he implores. "Don't don't." He looks at the ceiling, opens his mouth and howls. He sounds like a wolf calling to a lost mate.

Electrified, Aaron and Sarah stand at the doorway to the bedroom. They have never seen emotion like this from their father.

It is impressive. It is sickening.

Sarah finally pries the wailing Max off the body of his dead wife.

F

orty five minutes later a funeral home employee, a corpulent man who must weigh at least three hundred pounds, wheels Esther's body on a gurney. He is so large that in the hallway he almost jams against a man from the coroner's team. They rearrange themselves, moving the gurney so that one man is on each end. They manage to get Esther into a waiting black wagon.

The Black Truck has come, has finally come, for Esther.

Book Two

Chapter Forty Two

War   **Inside**   **and**   **Out**
September 1982: Konar Province, Afghanistan

There is one vulture, sitting on a thermal as if it is a mattress of hot air. It is at eye level with Aaron, as he painfully negotiates switchbacks in his rented burnt-orange Land Cruiser. The bird circles towards him and lowers its head so that it can regard him with one eye. It seems a bored eye, floating at seven thousand feet between two mountains, watching a man in a vehicle. Aaron feels as if he is a tick crawling up the side of an elephant. He has no idea whether or not he has crossed the border from Pakistan to Afghanistan. He is following the map, given to him by a man in Peshawar, that takes him around the border posts. There is just the trail, the mountain on which he drives, the mountain across the valley. Blue sky above, brown and grey everywhere else.

He is glad for the company of the vulture.

"So....how's business?" He asks.

The vulture tilts its left wing and soars away from the cliff, then slides back to its previous position.

"You know, it's all about location, location...... there doesn't seem to be anything here. Of course, you might know something I don't. Maybe there's a good rush hour. I should think

Afghanistan would be an excellent place to be in the vulture business."

He stops the car's motor and wedges himself out the door on the mountain side of the trail. It is hot. He pulls his voluminous shirt out of his rope-tied pants and flaps it around, to cool himself. He is dressed in local clothes: they suit him, comfortable, inconspicuous. His hat, called a pakol, is shaped like a pancake on top with a cloth ridge that runs around its bottom, to grip his head. A wind gusts up from below and the vulture suddenly rises twenty or thirty feet. Aaron pisses onto the rocks and then gently eases himself out toward the precipice. Way below, a polished-steel ribbon cuts its way around the mountain bulges: some river, a tributary of the Konar Darya.

The vulture adjusts its height and comes within feet of Aaron's outstretched hand.

"I'm lost, " Aaron tells the animal. "Do you know where I can find the village of Kamchi?"

The scavenger's head is smooth and iridescent blue. It blinks once, bends its wing and circles away.

"This is the perfect symbolic situation for what my life has become," Aaron states. The vulture turns back in his direction.

There is some elemental attraction between the two living creatures in the midst of vast desolation. "You mind if I talk to you? I won't anthropomorphize. You're a vulture, I know. You're only interested in finding something dead to munch. You see anything down there?" He pushes some gravel off the edge with his toe. It tumbles, gathers momentum, dislodges minor debris as it falls.

"Rabbits? Mice? Dead Afghans? Dead Russians?"

Aaron is talking because he doesn't want to be scared. In the back of the Land Cruiser and lashed to the roof rack are forty green wooden boxes of ammunition and twenty five brown cardboard boxes of medical supplies. He is supposed to deliver them to a man named Murid in the village of Kamchi. In return, he will take sixty pounds of opium back to Peshawar, from where he will smuggle the drugs into the United States, packed into the tubing of Pakistani-made bicycles. He has it all figured out. Twelve hours ago it seemed a reasonable plan.

He reaches into his pocket and takes out an object the size of a large Hershey bar wrapped in wax paper. Opium, otherwise known as Kandahar Kandy. He unwraps one end of the bar and pulls at its taffy-like surface until he has prized loose a ball the size of a small marble. He pops it into his mouth and lets it sit under his tongue.

To Aaron the bitter red-black earthen taste of opium is like honey. He lets it dissolve in the heat of his mouth, feels its warm numbing juices go down his throat.

There's nothing to fear, nothing to fear, nothing to fear, Aaron mentally recites. I'm in a country at war with the Soviet Union, smuggling dangerous contraband among desperate people I do not know, do not trust, on a road that can throw me five thousand feet into a river at any moment, without any way to turn around. I'm addicted to THIS stuff, but everywhere I turn someone has it for sale, or as a gift, or a sample, or it's just laying on a table, forgotten, there's so fucking much of it here in War Land. There's nothing to fear. When you strip everything away, I am the fucking scariest thing in this place. I AM!

"Perfect symbolic situation," he reiterates to the vulture. He walks ahead of the car until he rounds the face of the mountain. There is nothing ahead but more curves, more trail that looks too treacherous to bear the weight of the Land Cruiser.

He gets back in and turns the key in the ignition. The Toyota stutters, won't start.

"Oh Jesus." Aaron lays his head on the black steering wheel. It sticks there. He pulls it back up and tries the engine again. The car starts.

He drives ahead, slowly, eyes darting from side to side, gauging his distance to the edge. Once in a while he will overcompensate and grind the fender into the mountain face. The Cruiser is a cosmetic disaster, scratched, bumped, dinged, flaked and rusted. But it runs. It keeps running.

The opium comes to him in a sweet rush. He stops again, to savor it. All he wants to do is get back to California with a whole LOT of opium, luxuriate in it, stop worrying about scoring, end the chaos for a while. He can both consume it and live off of it for a couple of years. So he figures. He has arranged to sell the bicycles to a local shop. It is all wired up with a customs broker. It is a tight plan.

Without emotion, he takes a hard look at himself.

I don't like who I've become, he thinks. I don't like where I am. I don't give a shit about anything but getting high and staying high. I'll do anything to achieve that end. I've tried to quit and I can't. What is this, my sixth relapse? My seventh? What happened to all my dreams, ideals, hopes? My music, my writing?

"Fuck it, " he says aloud. "Fuck it!" he yells back at the vulture. That is what the opium is for: To feel nothing. No remorse, no shame, no grief for lost opportunities, for wasted talents, for broken relationships. It is possible to acknowledge, with his mind, that his character has deteriorated. He has become dishonest, unreliable, ruthless, a thief and a dealer. He can't accept that reality in his guts. There is still a spark of hope in him. He can't let go of a vague dream that some obscure angel will hear his prayer and guide him out of this mess. In the real world there is nothing ahead of him but a stupid wasteful death. He hasn't let go of everything. He hasn't let go of a desire to untangle this snarl of his life and repair things. He had once been something. Maybe, maybe...he can be another kind of something. He rounds the next curve and to his relief sees that the trail opens out a bit, the contours of the landscape change. Ahead, he can see some stunted growth, a few gnarly trees, big boulders covered with lichen.

He hears a cough-like sound. It echoes once or twice against the walls of the valley. Directly ahead of him there is an object, bright yellow-red, growing larger. In the second it takes for him to realize that it is a projectile heading towards his windshield, he throws himself to the floor of the car.

Bam! The thing hits the cliff face behind him, raining down bits of rock onto the Land Cruiser.

"Shit!" he screams. When the debris stops falling he peeks out through the windshield.

There is another cough, another shell is hurtling towards him. Again, it strikes somewhere above him and throws dust and stone all over the vehicle.

There isn't any way to think or make decisions. Aaron jumps out of the car and begins running back along the trail. He gets about twenty feet when a grinning bearded man materializes out of nowhere. Then there are others, all over the trail, all over the car. They are carrying assault rifles, grenade launchers, bolt action Lee-Enfields. One has a mortar base plate, another the tube.

Mujahiddin. They are filthy, dressed in loose trousers and tunics of grey or faded green. They wear pakols on their heads, or yards of cloth wrapped around white skullcaps with a foot or so dangling to their shoulders. On their feet are shredded Nike tennis shoes or sandals made from rubber tires and fixed with electrical tape.

One of them shouts down the valley and another Afghan emerges from the rocks. Now Aaron can see the barrel of a fifty seven caliber all- purpose gun. Russian made, Degtyarev, the famous

DSHK. It has been a standard weapon of the North Vietnamese, Khmer Rouge, Kashmiri rebels, Kurd separatists. That's what has been shooting at him.

He stands like a paralyzed point in a shifting circle of men. They are laughing. The front of Aaron's pants are wet. When, at last, his wits settle, he recognizes Murid, his contact from Peshawar.

"He wasn't going to hit you, " Murid says in a cultivated voice. The gunner joins the circle of laughing men. "He just wanted to put the fear of Allah into you."

For a moment the whole world turns red before Aaron's eyes. With the palms of both hands he pushes Murid in the chest, sending him sprawling into the gravel of the desolate trail.

"You motherfucker!" Aaron screams. His voice splits with rage. "You wanted to scare me? That's your idea of funny?" He jumps on Murid, livid with the intent to annihilate this smug grinning person. He has not felt such a rage since he was a child. He can only think of killing, pummeling, beating. His body pulses with malevolent intensity.

Murid scrambles backwards. There is a series of clicks, all around Aaron . The noise is so ominous that his rage flees as suddenly as it has come. The barrels of eleven rifles are pointed at his head. He is on his hands and knees. He looks around, slowly. There is a black steel hole every eighteen inches. At the bottom of each is a bullet, seven point six two millimeters, or thirty ought six, or two two three. He can see the spiral rifling grooves going down each barrel. Very reliable gun, the AK-47. Never jams, withstands abuse, water, dust, sand, mildew. Chromed ejection chamber. These are of Chinese manufacture.

"Fuck you all," Aaron says. "Shoot me. My life is shit."

Under the rage lays another terrible and irresistible feeling. His desire to kill Murid has acted as a hammer on a chisel. It has jarred loose a deeply hidden emotion. He feels like a child suddenly bereft of its mother. He fights this upwelling. No way, he thinks, I can't do this here, I can't do this now, in front of these savage men. He tries to control himself but it's too late. He is in the grip of something overpowering. He curls up into a ball and cries with desolate anguish.

He goes on like that, not thinking, knowing or caring about his fate. For him, the world ceases to exist. He returns to awareness when he hears a sound. It is another sound of weeping. He looks up and one of the Mujahiddin has crouched onto his haunches, slung his gun over his shoulder and begun to weep. His closed fist is banging into his heart, as if it hurt, there, there, right there, at the center of his life. Then another, and another, until all the men are crying into their hands or the loosened ends of their turbans, or pounding their fists into their hearts.

A vulture comes up from the depths of the canyon, paying scant attention to the group of weeping men. Murid touches Aaron gently on the shoulder. The man's tears have cleaned gullies of dust down his face. The tears drop, black with the soot of war, from his chin.

"My brother," he says. A bubble of snot turns into a rivulet under his nostril. He wipes it with his hand and wipes his hand on his baggy pants. "My brother," he repeats. "All our lives are shit."

Konar Province, Afghanistan

Eleven heavily armed Afghan warriors glue themselves to various places in or on the Land Cruiser and it proceeds down the trail to Kamchi like an orange porcupine with grey-green quills. Murid sits in the passenger seat next to Aaron. One of the Mujahiddin insists on directing the car from the left fender, making flamboyant gestures that Aaron ignores.

"Ho!" The man will point with his rifle. "Nah!" he will say, indicating that Aaron's driving is somehow defective. Aaron can barely see anything through the pressed and clinging bodies of dirty bearded men.

The man on the right fender studies the sky intently.

"Can the Russians come this close to the border?"

"They can and they do," Murid answers, peering upward with creased eyes. The man's nose is a great noble jut. His beard is yellow with dust and there are dark stains on what was once a gorgeous beaded vest.

"Where did you learn such good English?"

"At Stanford. I've been in the U.S. for the last nine years. I was studying to become a molecular biologist."

Aaron digests this information.

"Then why did you.....no, wait.....that's a stupid question. This is your country."

Murid studies the man next to him. "I am a prince of the Yusufzai, the most ancient Pakhtun tribe. My father and grandfather and greatgrandfathers have been emirs of the Kamchi Valley. When our land is invaded we fight. We return from wherever we might be. It's that simple. There were sixteen other Afghans at Stanford, men and women. We all came home."

That silences Aaron. He feels like some kind of base fool. He is, in fact, a base fool. He has grown up in material comfort, has evaded the Vietnam draft, has run away from the responsibilities of his marriage and his child and has become a drug addict.

The car sways and sags with the weight on its springs. The trail begins to descend. The man on the left fender cries "Ho!" and points to his right. Aaron sees the fork at the last second and obeys. The air is suddenly cooler. The land begins to show green. There are little scatterings of bunched trees, sucking water from deep in the ground.

Aaron drives ahead, keeping his speed to that of a walk so no one will be thrown from the vehicle. Sometimes men jump on and off, walking alongside, switching places. The Land Cruiser bobs, shimmies and sways as it traverses the rutted uneven terrain.

The ride stretches on for another hour, then another. Occasionally someone will pound on the hood and Aaron will stop for a piss break, or allow his passengers to uncramp their grip or get a fresh seat on the roof rack.

At length, Murid breaks the silence. "Why do I like you?" He asks . "I don't understand it. You're an American drug addict come here to get opium and make money and get high off our tragedy."

Aaron looks briefly at Murid, and thinks about the experience back on the cliff face. He had broken down completely in the presence of all these men, and they had joined him. It made a strange bond across a vast social and cultural gulf.

"I don't know," Aaron replies. "I don't like myself very much."

"Maybe you are fighting a war, too. Maybe you don't understand that some things are worth suffering and dying for. Maybe that's why you are here."

Before Aaron can even consider this statement, Murid emits a grunt and thrusts his head out the window. There is a sound like distant thunder, rolling through the valleys. The Afghans fall silent, tense. Aaron drives on, apprehensive. The land is descending in gentle waves. Long meadows stretch ahead and the trail has become a road, running beside a small swift river.

Murid spits an epithet in Pakhtun. Now Aaron sees what Murid saw moments before: a column of smoke rising in the distance. With half his body hanging from the window, the man curses. Aaron needs no translation. He knows what the man said.

"They are bombing Kamchi!!"

Aaron stops the car. A realization streaks through his head like lightning and creases his innards with fear. "The opium," he thinks. "Now I won't get the opium."

Then his mind stops dead as if braking for some fleeting animal in its path.

"These men are seeing the devastation of their homes and maybe the death of their loved ones. And my first thouht is that my drug stash is gone."

The Afghans spring from the car and head at a run towards the smoke. Aaron sits in the car in complete despair.

"I have to become another person," Aaron decides with terrified finality. "I have to start right now. I've always postponed this until conditions are right, until I have enough support, until I have help,until this or that comes about. And it never comes about. So I have to start now."

He reaches into his pocket for the bar of opium. Before he can think, reconsider, be frightened or otherwise lose resolve, he tosses it into the river. Then he runs after the Mujahiddin, his long shirt flopping in the wind.

* * *

There are fields of planted wheat. Some are yellow, others are green. They alternate in tight rectangles, going down the slope and neatly framing what has been the village of Kamchi. Trees line both banks of the river, and as Aaron runs he can smell a fragrance like that of honeysuckle. Then the wind shifts and the smell of smoke and exploded ordnance fills the air.

Kamchi lay like rows of broken teeth in the jaw of a colossal bleached skull. The mountain ridge rises behind the village and juts of high crags enclose it on three sides. Smoke rises like the robe of a vengeful spirit. As it gains altitude, the wind takes it and smears it across the sky.

Murid reaches the ruins first. The remains of rammed-earth and brick houses lay in what has been Kamchi's streets. It was a village of more than seven hundred people. There is no sign of animate life. A dead dog slumps atop a fallen support timber. The leg of what may have been a donkey is jammed into a flower pot.

Murid plunges over the brown piles of debris until he comes to the highest point in the town. There is half of a two story house, pulsing with heat. All the mujahiddin converge at that point. Not knowing what else to do, Aaron follows. He is now a completely will-less mote flowing on the streams of circumstance.

There is shattered crockery, burnt photographs, a finely engraved serving platter, bent and melted silverware.

Shouting in Pakhtun, Murid begins digging through the rubble with his hands. The others fall to their knees and help. Aaron finds himself at the end of a line of men, tossing ancient baked-mud bricks onto a heap. They work quickly and tirelessly. After about fifteen minutes, Murid snaps his fingers impatiently and one of the men passes him a folding tool, a combination shovel and pick that has Russian letters on its handle.

Murid has uncovered a wooden door leading into a cellar. It has a recessed metal handgrip, and he pulls at it now with all his strength. There are still hundreds of pounds of brick dust and shards atop it, but he prises it open a few inches and the other Mujahiddin ram tools and brick shims into the opening. Grunting in unison "Allaho Akbar, Allaho Akbar," they finally lift the wooden slab. It falls backward with a crash and raises a giant cloud of dust and ash that flies into everyone's faces.

Waving his hands about, Murid disappears into the hole in the earth. Everyone waits without breathing. At length, Murid emerges, staggering up the earthen steps, supporting the weight of a woman whose face, clothes and hair are covered in soot.

She gasps for air, then puts both hands to the sides of her head when she looks around at what remains of her home, her village.

She cries something in Pakhtun, her teeth showing white in her blackened face. Murid lifts her and stumbles down the piles of rubble, out into the relative clearing of the street. All the Mujahiddin follow like a bacterial clot of benevolent cells surrounding a wounded corpuscle.

Not wanting to intrude, Aaron follows until they reach the banks of the river.

Murid removes his turban and soaks it in water and solicitously washes the woman's face as they sit atop an ancient rampart where generations of Kamchi's inhabitants have stooped to draw water.

As the soot goes from the woman's face to the turban and thence into the river, Aaron sees that she is about fifty years old. Finally, she waves Murid off and dips her entire head into the water, then throws her hair back in a thick cascade of black glistening strands.

Aaron is struck by many impressions at once. The woman has a timeless, ageless beauty that flows from a sense of inner authority. He can feel it, as he sits helplessly on his haunches outside the circle, feeling so alien, so strange, so frightened. He is almost impaled by a pang of envy. I want to have that kind of dignity, he thinks. I want to have that kind of wildness.

She drinks from a cup offered by one of the men. Her hands shake and she grips the tin vessel with long fingers that seem to contain incredible tensile strength. They are like a concert pianist's fingers. Aaron can see them disappearing up the long flowing sleeves of the woman's clothing, cords of muscle and cartilege vanishing into what remains of an emerald green robe.

Exhausted, the men sprawl on the ledge and the road. Murid puts his head in the hollow of the woman's shoulder, and she pats his hair tenderly.

With half an eye, Murid notices Aaron. He raises his head and points from the woman to the American man sitting outside the group.

"This is my mother, Fatima," he says.

Then he says something in Pakhtun to his mother. She looks at Aaron with a full and vivid gaze that lances him with comprehension. Aaron feels ashamed. He wants to be a real and complete person.

He looks around at the devastated village. "Where is everyone else?"

Murid points with his chin to the east. "They've gone to Pakistan. We usually get tipped off about Soviet operations. Something screwed up, this wasn't supposed to happen till tomorrow. Praise Allah, the last ones left a few days ago. All the women, children, old people; most of the animals. They will wait there until this is over. Then we will rebuild Kamchi."

"It's a beautiful place," Aaron says. "It must have been a great place to live."

"When I was a little boy it was very isolated." Murid points to string of toppled steel pylons disappearing through a notch in the far ridge. "See those? We got electricity ten years ago. The oil pipeline is coming here, following the electrical grid. We blew up our own towers. We don't want to be a waystation between Tehran and Moscow."

Fatima rises and looks at what remains of the village. In perfect English she says, "It won't be over in my lifetime, or your lifetime or your grandchildren's lifetime. There will be war in Afghanistan for a hundred years." She sighs and dusts ash from her hands. "Fucking war, I hate fucking war!" Her right forearm comes up and her hand covers her face, the fingers digging into her forehead, just below the hairline. The other hand clutches at her heart. Her shoulders rise, and her whole torso trembles silently, swelling with a grief that she somehow contains, allowing no cry to escape from her lips.

She turns a virulent gaze upon Murid, but she is speaking to the entire group.

"If you think I'm going to cover myself up from head to foot because we have men outside the family here, you don't know me. I won't do it. I won't!"

Some of the other Mujahiddin have averted their gaze from the sight of Fatima. They look intensely embarassed. Murid's mother says something in Pakhtun to her son. He digs around in the folds of his clothing for a moment until he finds a long piece of cloth that is dyed a deep purple. He hands this to Fatima.

The woman ties it scarfwise around her head, wrapping it beneath her chin with a delicate knot. Her beautiful hair vanishes. Aaron is sad to see it go.

"That's it," Fatima speaks again in English. "My concession to your bullshit woman hating paranoid culture." She speaks in Pakhtun to all the men at once. Their demeanor hardly changes, but it seems as if some spring has been released. Their embarassment abates. Still, they do not cast direct glances at the woman.

The sun has been lowering itself onto the mountain crags, so that a dagger of shadow now thrusts at the landscape. A man in the group of Mujahiddin speaks, and holds both hands open at shoulder level. He is clearly the oldest man of the group. His beard is white, creases run down the center of each cheek and across his forehead.

The warriors sort themselves out. They line up in two rows, with the old man at the center of the group, facing away from the sun. Fatima takes herself to a discreet distance of about five yards and sits on her knees with her legs tucked under her.

"

Allaho Akbar," the old man intones. The group echoes him.

"La Illahah l'allah. Bismillah Rachman Rahim".

Aaron knows the words and the gestures. He studied Sufism, way back in another life, in California. He immersed himself in the world of the poet Jelalladin Rumi, learned the Arabic alphabet. After all, he had mastered Hebrew before the age of thirteen. It wasn't that difficult.

It feels easy and natural to sit behind the other men and join them in their prayers. He bows forward and touches his forehead to the ground, with the others.

The moment of quiet and contemplation gives him time to think, for the first time in many hours.

He is terrified. He has thrown away his drug, his anesthetic. He knows what lays ahead: days of agony, weeks of sleeplessness, months of depression. It only now occurs to him that he might be a ridiculous burden on these people in their crisis of war. It is too late. He has made a symbolic gesture and it is too good to waste. He will find a way.

As he sits there listening to the mullah, his heart begins to pound, his mouth becomes parched, his thoughts race. It's too early to be sick, he tells himself. I have hours yet before I'm sick. It won't start till tomorrow. I'm so full of opium I'll be pissing poppies for days.

It is a familiar terror, one with which he has lived for years. Get some dope or suffer agony. Get some dope or suffer agony. This is the stark and obsessive reality of his world. Get some dope. Get some dope. It is like being sliced in half; the heaven of being high alternating with the hell of being sick. He is in this place in Afghanistan because he needs desperately enough dope to achieve some sort of stability. He has acquired the money for the venture by selling a pile of silver dollars left to him by his mother. It seems a fitting and ironic way to spend Esther's suicide legacy.

He hears feet crunching on gravel and opens his eyes. Murid crouches before him, looking earnestly into his face. The sun throws a final ray over the mountains and it crowns Murid's head.

"You are Muslim?"

Aaron can not see the man's face, he can see only the crimson rays. He laughs, weakly. "My parents are Jewish. I acknowledge all religions and philosophies. I am a Sufi. I was a student of Sufism for three years. My teacher is Dr. Ali Korsagian, of the Mevlevi lineage."

"You are a very strange man. I truly do not know what to make of you. I won't tell my cousins about your being Jewish." He made a small covert gesture toward the other Mujahiddin.

"They've never met or seen a Jewish person, and they're already tempted to kill you. I told them you might be with the CIA and supply us with missiles."

"I won't mention it again," Aaron says carefully. "And I'm not with the CIA."

"Too bad." Murid stands up. "We must eat something. We have many things to do. We can't stay here in the open, in case the Russians return. I suggest we finish our business and get you on your way out of here."

"The opium?" Aaron chokes. "It's still here?"

"I will assume so....it is in the cellar where my mother survived the bombs."

Aaron feels the two parts of his identity open like a chasm. One part oozes like molasses toward the promised warmth and relief of the opium. The other part stands rigid and unyielding, determined to correct the awful crimes he has committed against himself and his family. For a long, long moment, he is utterly unable to think or speak. Then he pulls at the depths of himself, howling inwardly to some dim and echoing cavern where there might be redemptive strength. He can not see it, but he remembers something about himself. He remembers defying his mother on an autumn evening, decades ago. He snatched the letter with the music test results out of the garbage and ran into the little copse of trees across the subdivision.

That took something, he told himself. That took some courage. I'm still that boy. I still have something of determination in me. It isn't all corroded away by my addictions.

"I don't want the opium. You can have the supplies I brought, and you can sell or trade the opium to someone else. I'll go get the Land Cruiser."

It is now almost dark, and the Afghans are sorting themselves out preliminary to moving back into the hills. Aaron stands up. Murid also rises. He is a few inches taller than Aaron. "What is going on here?"

"I threw my opium in the river, back when you first saw the smoke of your village. Something happened to me.....it's hard to explain. I...have to do something right, to begin to do something right, to live a different way. I know you trade opium to survive and to wage war on the Russians. But I take opium to escape. And it isn't possible to escape any more. So, I've kind of set a trap for myself."

Murid sighs. "Your timing is ridiculous. You'll be sick. How will you drive back to Peshawar?"

"I don't know, but I will."

"You're not what I expected. You are a truly surprising man."
Murid inspects him carefully. "You're sure about this? Really
sure?"

Aaron swallows, nods his head. "Yes, I'm sure."

Murid turns and speaks softly to the group. Some of them grunt in
acknowledgment and move off into the darkness.

"Let's get the car, " Murid tells Aaron. "I'll show you where to go,
and my uncle and my cousins will help unload."

They walk back along the river to the place where the car has been
left. "Keep your lights off," Murid instructs. He directs Aaron
across the fields and along another barely visible track that passes
through several irrigation canals. The car splashes across them in
the dark. Once in a while, Murid shines a flashlight to keep Aaron
from going into a deep ditch.

At length, Murid grunts "Stop here". The others materialize out of
the darkness and unload the vehicle, putting the supplies and
ammunition down a dry well, then covering it with a wooden top,
followed by stones, dirt and wheat chaff.

When it is done, they drive the Land Cruiser back to the other side of the village, under a copse of trees, and camouflage it with the same materials. Murid pushes Aaron gently into the line with the others and they begin to walk. They leave Kamchi behind and begin winding their way up into the mountains. At first Aaron stumbles and falls, cutting and bruising himself on the stones. After a while, his eyes adjust to the night, and he follows the color of the vest of the man in front of him. He gets his footing and his wind. He is still a drummer, an athlete, lithe and strong. A strange fierce joy fills him as he climbs.

When they have climbed for many hours, they come to a cave. Breathing hard, the twelve men and one woman fall onto the floor of the chamber. The sound of puffing is all that can be heard for about three minutes. Then someone laughs. And someone else laughs. It isn't necessary to explain or define what is so funny. Life is so tragic and horrific and difficult that it becomes funny by sheer default. There is no other way to remain sane but to see this hard breathing, this climbing, fighting, losing, destroying and being destroyed as anything but total farce.

Everyone laughs. Aaron laughs till he is banging his head against the cave floor. Tears pour from his eyes.

After a while, a small fire is built, blankets are pulled from packs, and tins of dates dipped in sesame butter are distributed around the group.

Almost immediately upon finishing the food, there is another prayer. Aaron sits behind the men, but one of them turns and beckons with his chin. Aaron shuffles forward on his knees so that he is part of the line of Mujahiddin. His heart expands so suddenly he nearly chokes with emotion. A fragment of his personality, like a seed, takes root in the worship of God. He feels as though he is part of a garden. The acceptance in the Afghan's gesture, the invitation to be part of their community, creates something completely new in his soul.

Then, with the exception of Aaron, everyone falls into profound sleep.

Aaron has to stay awake with his terror. It is a portal through which he must pass. He goes to the mouth of the cave and looks at the sky. There was a quarter moon, earlier, but it has now set, leaving the vault of stars blazing in profuse and unspeakable beauty.

Aaron puts his knees tightly into his chest, banding his arms around them, as preliminary pain

begins to sting his nerves.

Someone has given him a blanket. He wraps it around himself and passes the time picking out constellations. There is Cygnus, the Swan, flying down the Milky Way. Just over the lip of the the ridge on the opposite side of the Kamchi Valley, he can see the claw of Scorpius, and the baleful red star Antares.

He feels a human presence beside him. He smells the odor of a woman, Fatima.

"Murid explained things to me, " she says quietly. "You will not feel well. But it will be okay." Her accent gives the word "okay" a quaint and charming lilt.

Aaron feels inexplicably comfortable with this person. He normally shrinks from contact, seldom permits anyone to get close. He knows something of Afghan customs. He speculates that Fatima is either a woman of great authority or a total non-conformist. Or both. She seems to be no man's property and follows no cultural dictates as to a 'woman's place' in society. That she sits beside him, imparting warmth, is as extraordinary as everything else that is occurring in this place so distant from what he considers to be home. But, he thinks, I 've had no home, anywhere, for such a long time.

"Im very scared," he confides. "Do you know anything about drug addiction?"

Fatima laughs gently. "People get addicted to drugs everywhere. With this war, many people with wounds use opium. Then they can't stop, because the wounds are deeper than the flesh."

Aaron shrugs the blanket off. He is sweating. His body is hot. His bones feel uncomfortable inside his skin. "I guess that describes me pretty well."

"You are a motherless child," Fatima states.

"Even worse than that; my mother is a demon. But how do you know?" Those five words, spoken by a woman of his mother's age, penetrates into some part of his being of which he has been unaware.

"I have seen that haunted look in the eyes of many orphans. Perhaps that's the pain you wish not to feel, the reason you take opium, the terrible loneliness of being unloved. And it is probably difficult for you to feel love, is it not? Have you ever loved someone more than life itself? Do you have a wife, children?"

Aaron is silent for some moments. He is examining himself ruthlessly. "I had a wife, and a child. When I was with her, I adored my daughter. At the same time, I held my love back. I was afraid of losing my freedom." He laughs softly in ironic self-contempt. How ridiculous that now sounds! "But after they left, after a few years passed......I just.....was so relieved to not have the responsibility that I forgot about her. And the only creature in the world that I love more than life itself is a dog. I fell in love with a dog. Isn't that pathetic?"

"Ah, but you have the dog. Love is never pathetic." Fatima's voice is almost a whisper, but thick like a tree trunk, resonant with the strength of her being. "It is not a child, a woman, a father or brother, but it is your angel. You will not be a whole person before Allah until you have brought that kind of love into the human community. What you are doing....I admire it. You are trying to change yourself. That is the greatest task any person can face."

"I have tried so many times before, and failed."

"No, you did not fail. Each time you try you are asking something of your spirit that your spirit can't deny. But it knows when you are ready. Your spirit has its own timing, its own logic that is difficult to understand. You will not fail. As long as you keep your hunger for truth, you will not fail, there can be no such thing as failure. You must never turn away from truth."

Aaron lowers his head into his chest. The air drains from his lungs, then comes rushing back in, cool and filled with starlight. Like Fatima, he holds the sound of his grief within him, but lets his body shake with sorrow.

"If you want, I will sit here with you," the woman offers.

"You need to sleep. I know I won't....it's impossible to sleep when this happens."

"I will sleep, here, sitting. But you will not be alone."

"Why are you doing this for me? I don't understand. I'm a foreigner, an interloper, a criminal, a smuggler."

"You are those things," Fatima agrees. "My son sees something in you, and he is a good judge of character. When I came out of the cellar, he said to me, 'This is a good man who is lost'. And besides, we Afghans are bound by ancient laws of hospitality. You are our guest."

They sit silently for many hours. Aaron hears Fatima's breath change as she falls asleep. He moves away so that his twitching will not awaken her. He waits for the dawn. It is always worst at night, the withdrawal. The darkness sucks him into pain that grows worse with each minute, and each minute lasts forever. When he wants to scream, he thinks of what Murid said to Fatima. "He is a good man who is lost."

Aaron combines that sentence with Fatima's statement, "You must never turn away from truth." He turns that into his night's mantra.

"I am a good man who is lost." he thinks. "I must never turn away from truth."

He re-lives the emotion he felt when the warrior invited him into the circle of prayer. He is a plant in a garden, being nourished by worship. He surrounds the sentences of his mantra with that feeling.

Again, god has provided him with what he most needs. This time he will not ignore god.

Far below, he can see glowing embers from the burned ruins of Kamchi.

At last, on the other side of the valley, light touches the mountain walls and comes drifting across the fields.

Hollow eyed, Aaron drinks a little water from his bottle and watches the others awake.

Bad tempered, reeking of sweat, the Afghans cast sidelong glances at Aaron as they disperse among the rocks to perform their morning ablutions. When they return, they wash their faces and hands in a bare teaspoonful of water.

The old man leads them in morning prayers. Fatima sits off to the side. Aaron brings his aching body to the the group and joins them.

The end of each phrase from the Koran is punctuated by a rumbling "Allaho Akbar". It gives Aaron a moment of peace, a moment of communion.

Someone says something and the group falls silent. Murid goes to the cave mouth and listens carefully. The throbbing of helicopter rotors slap at the air. It fades out, then became louder, then fades out as shifting winds rise with the sun's heat.

At an elevation almost even with their own, two Soviet MI-24 attack helicopters round the far curve of the valley and sway forward. Each has three round air intakes on top at the front, and rounded windows below, lending the craft its insect-like appearance. Two more choppers, MI-8 troop carriers, follow the lead of the first two.

A flare pops lazily out the side of each helicopter. One from the left, then one from the right, to deflect heat-seeking missiles. At intervals of six seconds, flares emerge from the sides of the crafts, arch with smoke trails and disappear as they burn themselves out.

Then, with a sound like that of ripping cloth, rotary guns cut loose across the remains of Kamchi. Missiles hiss from their harnesses beneath the stubby wing pods of the big helicopters. At first the explosions look like a line of grey and white blossoms pushing up from the earth. Then the sound and concussion reach the people in the cave.

Boom Boom Boom Boom! The sound is too loud to bear without placing hands to ears. Paralyzed with fascination, Aaron watches as the blossoms creep towards the place where the Land Cruiser is covered with tree braches.

It explodes, the gasoline sends an orange plume twenty feet into the air.

The impact rocks Aaron back so that he lands on his rear end. There suddenly seems to be no air to breathe. His mouth sucks like that of a fish. Heat burns his lips.

The troop carrier settles and disgorges a squadron of Soviet Special Forces, Spetznaz. The gunships hover protectively overhead.

"You're not getting back to Peshawar today," Murid tells Aaron, when the echoes have died down. He commands the other men with his eyes and his chin. They pick up their gear and set up a defensive perimeter around the cave.

"We'll have to wait here till tonight. Then we'll cross to the other side of the mountains and join up with Shah Massoud's people."

Murid has binoculars but does not like the angle of the sun. He knows it will cause a glint that might attract the attention of the Spetznaz. He lays on the floor of the cave with Fatima and Aaron. The other men vanish into the landscape.

One of the gunships peels off and begins passing along the flanks of the slopes, inspecting. Murid wriggles backwards into the darkness of the cave. Aaron and Fatima follow him, staying on their stomachs. The helicopter thwop- thwops closer, passing within twenty yards of the cave entrance. For the briefest moment, Aaron glimpses the crew with their helmets and microphones, and the black steel of a six-barreled gatling gun.

"Shit!" hisses Murid. "They're going to shoot into the cave."

He shouts something to his men. The helicopter has passed and is turning. Before it can come to firing position, there is a hollow sound from the right of the cave, Blang!, and a white vapor trail follows a rocket-propelled grenade out of its tube and connects with the MI-24. It is thirty yards out from the mountain face and the explosion breaks the machine in half just behind the crew compartment.

The world is speeded up and slowed down simultaneously. Pieces of metal whiz like flying razors, pocking the slope. The helicopter topples almost leisurely, spilling bodies, hot with

burning fuel. Mujahiddin are screaming. Aaron is screaming.

Murid grabs a piece of Aaron's shirt and throws him out the cave entrance.

"Run!"

Fatima races ahead, stops for a moment to see that Aaron is keeping up. The slope is alive with scattering Mujahiddin.

Across the valley, the second gunship is standing off, turning. Sparks come from its weapons pods and two dozen white streaks race across the valley.

Aaron follows Fatima. It is all happening too fast to think. From the corner of his eye, he sees the rockets coming. He almost flies up the face of a house-sized boulder, tumbles into its shadow, landing atop Fatima. A microsecond later, Murid lands atop both of them.

The rockets hold cluster munitions. Each of the twenty four warheads bursts open and scatters explosive pellets that whick into the mountainside, cratering every inch of the bare slope.

Aaron screams, air and sound emerge from his lungs, but he can hear nothing. He is packed into a crevice with his companions and can see nothing.

Then Murid's weight lifts from him. Aaron looks up into the man's distorted face, sees the hand reach down, feels Fatima push him from below.

They are up and running again. Aaron struggles to maintain his footing on a narrow shelf. Fatima catches at him, and they both fall about five feet into a trough that juts from an angle of the mountain.

Murid, refusing to abandon his mother, comes down to them.

Aaron lays where he landed, stunned, breathless, totally exhausted. He can 't run any more. He can hear Murid and Fatima panting. The sound of helicopter rotors echoes from the three walls of mountain enclosing the valley. Each thwop of its blades sounds like someone hitting an open tube with the flat of the hand.

"Look!" Murid points across the valley. "Somebody's got a Stinger." Aaron lifts himself enough to see an object looping around. It comes from low on the opposite slope, maybe two miles away. It angles steeply upward, leaving a white puffy smoke trail. Its path is erratic, it seemes to hesitate, sniff, then make a decision. Wind pulls the smoke into tatters. The missile finds its trajectory, speeds up as it homes on the second gunship, then plows into its underside.

There is one huge explosion followed by dozens of smaller ones as the helicopter's munitions go off in a rain of fire, black smoke and lily white magnesium.

The Spetznaz begin running toward their troop carriers. They are like tiny mites converging upon some sheltering plant. They disappear into the hatches of their transports and the remaining two helicopters fly back down the open side of the valley, low, firing anti-missile flares from their sides.

"Al-LAH! Oh, Al-LAH!." Murid says, looking at his hands.

They are covered in blood. His face turns white, his eyes go blank and he topples into the arms of his mother.

Fatima makes a sound for which Aaron has no metaphor, no personal experience from which he can interpret its animal intensity. It is horrible: he wishes he can un-hear it, unremember it, block it out of his consciousness.

The back of Murid's vest is slashed through, and blood oozes into the material of his clothing, turning it black. Aaron looks at this wound, dazed by the speed at which events are moving.

"Help me!" Fatima barks. "Bring him up here. Very carefully; keep his torso flat." She points upward from their precarious perch, toward the more secure area of the ledge. Heaving at the unconscious weight of her son, she moves him a few inches, turning him so that his upper body can be moved. Aaron jumps out of the indentation, then turns and leans back toward Fatima and Murid. He lays down on the rock and puts his hands out, taking Murid by each wrist.

With crazed irrelevance, he thinks, "I'm in a war movie from my childhood. Guadalcanal Diary. Battle Cry. Bataan. This isn't real. I'll put my wounded buddy on my back and run through the jungle, saving his life. I'll get a medal."

With Fatima pushing and Aaron pulling, Murid is put face down onto the pockmarked trail. In the sky, several vultures gather. There is still smoke in the air, and a stink of explosions, burned flesh, incinerated metal and electronic parts. Aaron helps Fatima scramble up, where she kneels by her son and begins tearing long strips from the bottom of her garment.

She examines her son's wound, pulling apart the shirt and vest to expose a deep laceration that runs from his shoulder halfway down his back. Without hesitation she takes two fingers and explores the wound. She brings out some bloody object, unidentifiable, shrapnel or rock, and tosses it aside. She returns to the wound, exploring for more shrapnel, soil, pebbles. She looks at Aaron with stunning ferocity.

"Give me your water!"

Aaron hands over his bottle and observes Fatima doing her best to clean the wound.

"Is there plasma in the supplies you brought?"

"Y...yes, I think so."

Fatima lifts her son and passes long strips of cloth beneath his torso, and begins applying a pressure bandage, wrapping it over and over, tearing new strips from her dress. She pulls at the ends of the strips to ensure maximum pressure, to slow the blood loss.

"Go down there and get it. And get clean bandage and betadine and antibiotics if you have them. But get plasma. Fast."

Aaron looks down at the valley floor. He can see the place where the wreckage of the Land Rover burns. He can see the place where he knows the supplies are stashed in the dry well.

He begins running. From the side of his eye he sees four or five of the Mujahiddin crawling from their places of shelter. He points back towards Fatima and Murid.

"Help!" he cries. "Somebody help!"

The old man comes pounding down from the slope and calls something in Pakhtun. Someone is screaming. There is a severed foot in Aaron's path. He jumps over it, runs past the cave entrance, looking desperately for anything identifiable as a trail. He finds the way and slides almost helplessly downward, tearing his clothes, cutting himself, barely in control of the speed of his descent.

He is aware of unusual processes in his own body. He feels none of the opium withdrawal. He would, under normal circumstances, be lying in a bed somewhere, twisting around, unable to rest, helplessly weak, every cell burning with a terrible thirst for relief. It is very strange to be so suddenly important, needed. It changes things. It gives him purpose.

He gets to the valley floor with amazing and reckless speed. First, he encounters the fragments of one of the downed helicopters. He doesn't want to look, but a trace of morbid fascination compels him to glimpse the corpses of the Russian crewmen. He regrets it. He runs across the wheat fields, past the destroyed vehicle, jumping irrigation canals. From this angle, it is more difficult to locate the well. He stops for a moment and re-lives the drive across the fields in the dark. He leaps into the eye of the vultures and looks down upon the landscape. He sees the valley, he sees Murid and Fatima, the old mullah, the survivng mujahiddin, the dead and mangled. He sees himself and knows that he must angle off to the right and follow the raised donkey path along the flank of the mountain.

In a few minutes he thinks he is atop the well. He walks around, kicking away branches and chaff. At last he hears his footsteps booming down into the hollowed depth. Getting to his knees, he throws off the the remainder of concealing wheat chaff and stones. The cover is heavy. Aaron finds a piece of tree branch and sets it beside the cover. He thrusts all ten fingers under the piece of wood and pulls with all his strength. It lifts, and he kicks the branch into the opening. Then he wrestles, pushes, pulls, kicks until the wooden circle shows him the interior of the well. There is a rope ladder fixed to two spikes, going into the darkness. He descends it and almost steps onto the crates that have come from Peshawar. It is too dark to see.

He feels among the boxes. It is easy to separate the ammo from the medical supplies, they are packed differently. His eyes begin to adjust to the dimness and he can see labels, written in Arabic. He doesn't remember enough to decipher them. He tears at a box with his hands, but it is sealed with clear packing tape. He is wearing a little silver amulet around his neck, a piece of Zuni jewelry studded with turquoise. It is blade thin, and he takes it from around his neck and uses it to slit the box open.

The plasma will be in rectangular flexible plastic containers with intravenous leads. He finds them in the second box. He tries to carry the box up the ladder but it is too heavy and clumsy. He begins tossing the packets up toward the daylight. When he has thrown half the box out of the well, he upends it, emptying it, then begins looking around for the other supplies. He finds the betadine and the gauze and surgical tape. Johnson and Johnson. He almost laughs. There is a box with scissors and surgical knives, each instrument wrapped in sterile plastic. He puts a few of the packages down his shirt.

Pieces of dirt fall on his head. He looks up. A face is looking down at him.

"Shit!" he screams. He has been so absorbed in his task, this apparition startles him even more than all the terror of combat. Before he can recover, a man is climbing down the primitive ladder. Gun barrels cover him from the lip of the opening. Aaron backs up against the rounded flank of the well, feeling its coolness seep into his flesh. He puts his hands in front of him, making them into claws. He is nothing but instinct. No one is going to fuck with him and these medical supplies.

"Za yu Afghan nem Mujahid," The man says. Pakhtun for, "I am an Afghan Mujahid." A flashlight clicks on and blinds Aaron. Then it turns up into the face of its owner and Aaron sees a beard, a white turban. "Khudai da mal sha. Sta nom sha Murid?"

"Murid is fucking bleeding to death, man! Help me with this shit."

It conveys what is necessary. The man scurries up the ladder and calls out to an unseeen companion. Hanging halfway up the rope rungs, he passes the supplies up and out.

"That should be enough," Aaron says after a few minutes. "Let's go, let's go!"

He gets out of the well. There are a bunch of Mujahiddin and two dozen donkeys, loaded with stuff. Disassembled machine guns are slung from the animals' sides in crudely made nets. There is an entire fifty seven millimeter DSHK, its barrel neatly fixed with duct tape so that it will not swing or interfere with the donkey's spindly legs. Mortars and RPG's bristle from the column. There are olive green tubes on the backs of two of the warriors, each of them topped with an awkward rectangular extension. Stinger anti-aircraft missile launchers.

Aaron brings an empty box with him and quickly dumps the supplies into it. He is making mental calculations. These men are faster and better conditioned than he is, they know the terrain.

"Up to the cave. The cave," he gestures up the mountain face.

The man who has come with him out of the well is evidently the group's commander. "I know where the cursed cave is," he says in English. He speaks to a man and thrusts the box toward this person, who takes it and begins sprinting like a goat up the mountainside.

Aaron sinks to his haunches, hands brushing the ground. He looks up at the commander.

"Stanford?" He asks weakly.

"No. Fresno State," the man replies. "Go Bulldogs!"

Chapter Forty Three

Beneath The Bottom

Konar Province

The altitude is getting to him. Everything is getting to him. He has seen things that are impossible to absorb. He was in San Francisco eight days ago. He had been hanging around with slimy disgusting people whose only goal in life was to find cocaine and heroin, get enough to sell, skim enough off of the top to get high, then find some more. He has been one of those people.

When the guerilla column on the valley floor passes the wreckage of the downed helicopter, the mujahiddin stop to mutilate the bodies of the Soviet crew. Three have been thrown clear of the burn zone and are relatively unmarked. The other three are charred. Aaron can find no place of moral outrage in himself. He squints when it happens. He doesn't look away, nor does he look. Only one detail maintains itself in his memory. One of the crewmen is Central Asian, an Uzbek or a Tajik. The Mujahiddin leave the body of this man alone. They touch the bloody forehead of the corpse, mutter "Allaho Akbar," then stoop to cut the genitals of the other crewmen. He suspects this is an act of policy rather than perversity. It is a message to the Soviets who will come later, looking for their lost soldiers.

Within the context of these experiences the irrelevance of his personal pain is a profound blessing. He hurts. His whole body is screaming, his lungs can not fill with air, his head is a searing thud, his guts are exploding. There are other men here with dysentery, wounds, blown off fingers, murdered loved ones. They keep moving.

If he wants to live, he will keep up with the column. Before starting up the flank of the mountain, a man shoves him an empty frame-type backpack. It is blue. It has a label, North Face, sewn into its flap. Made in California. Aaron fills it with medical supplies, hefts it, puts it on his back, follows the men.

Murid's lieutenant, Iskandar, looks back at him once, then begins to climb.

After about four hours, the column disappears into the mountains ahead of him. Aaron is looking at his feet, willing himself to step forward and upward. There is so little sound. Just a pad pad of donkey hooves, loosening stones tumbling backwards, men breathing hard. Forty or forty five people, armed with heavy equipment, all but inaudible, invisible. Earlier in the day a roar of jets filled the air and three Sukhoi Twenty Fives came in formation from between two peaks. Aaron looked ahead and there was no one to be seen. The whole guerilla band vaporized into the landscape. He stood there like an idiot until a stone struck him on the hand and he saw a man pop out of the rocks, throw his blanket over his head, then vanish back into the rocks. He had become a rock. Even the donkeys became rocks. Aaron got it. He became a rock. The jets zoomed deafeningly overhead but kept going.

Then the column is gone, really gone. He has been too slow, too tired, and he hadn't even noticed the mujahiddin pulling ahead until some silence even deeper than the preceding stealth impinged on his awareness. He looks up. He is alone.

He sighs with agony and keeps walking. The pain is so immense that he thinks it might be better to find some high perch and throw himself off it. He looks around for such a place. They are plentiful. But he is challenged. This isn't his death, to be giving up. If he is going to die, he will prefer that it be pushing ahead, pushing himself, his limits, his imagination and his comprehension. So he takes another step, and another.

He reaches the top of the range and sees in the distance really big mountains, plumed with snow: the Karakorums or the Hindu Kush. He doesn't know. Between himself and these colossi is a washboard of smaller ranges and valleys. He is, apparently, utterly alone in this majestic topography. He sees nothing below him on the descending slope.

"If I sit down," he thinks, "I'll never get back up."

So, instead of resting and obeying the massive depletions of his body, he takes one long sip from his almost-empty bottle. He still has the backpack. He has forgotten about it, until he is thirsty and wants the bottle. Then he realizes that he is still carrying fifty or sixty pounds of supplies.

"I am one stubborn motherfucker," he says aloud, and giggles. "I've been dead already a hundred times in my life. And I'm still walking. This ain't shit."

He begins carefully picking his way downward. It is all tumbled rocks, loose shale, wind and dust. His mind isn't really working. Dimly, he is aware that he might fall and that the fall can go on forever. "This is about it, " he decides. "I've tried and I've kept going and I still got the supplies, and this is okay. This is better than overdosing in an alley in San Francisco."

A hand comes from nowhere and pulls at his shoulder, righting his balance. It is Fatima. She turns him sideways, pulling on his shirtsleeve. "We are over here, " she says. She leads him through a crack in the mountain. There is an entire field hospital set up under a brow of stone that arches outward, leaving a deep indentation, not quite a cave, but protected from the elements. There are other women, dressed in burkhas, working amid wounded men. People with radios speak quietly. A mix of generators provides power to surgical lights and heaters. Some mujahiddin are laboriously cranking away on ancient generators, while a handful of Honda gas-powered portables hum in the far back of the shelter.

Murid waves weakly at him from a stretcher. The sun is sinking over the great range of peaks to the west. Aaron's legs turn to water and he falls backward. The pack is so full that its rectangular bulk arrests his tumble. He comes to a sitting position, propped by the aluminum harness made in California.

Chapter Forty Four

The Darker Fire
1982: San Francisco

Aaron steps out of the Greyhound bus station at Fourth and Brannan. Diesel fumes saturate the air. It is a nostalgic odor, it reminds Aaron of his innocent and excited days in New York City, or traveling in Zoot's Continental with the windows down, behind a truck hauling pigs from Kentucky to the meat packing plants in St. Louis.

It is three fifteen in the morning and he has been traveling for twenty two hours. His face feels pockmarked by airport grit and dust spewing from catalytic converters in poorly tuned cars. His western clothes feel alien on his body. The shock of arrival back in the United States is an icicle down his spine. He looks at the pale haunted faces of the denizens of downtown San Francisco, full of alcohol and dope, hopeless and disconnected from families, disconnected from culture, and he feels as if this is the true war zone, that the violence in Afghanistan is less than the psychic violence America inflicts upon its own citizens, the invisible virus of raised expectations ultimately dashed against the hard concrete and steel manhole covers of its streets.

He shudders, feels for his wallet in his pants pocket, and walks forward into his future.

He passes one hotel. All of these hotels are unwelcoming, but he hopes to find a building that doesn't look like it will spit him out again as a piece of human wreckage. On Sixth and Mission, he comes to the Arlen Hotel. It is a red brick structure that is four windows wide on Sixth, but runs all the way back to the alley between Sixth and Seventh. It isn't in any measurable way different from the other hotels he has passed. A red neon sign hanging in its glass door says "...ACANCY". He steps up three concrete steps and puts his hand through the steel loop handle and presses with his thumb on the release mechanism. The door is locked. He looks around and finds a rectangular buzzer to the right of the door. He buzzes. After about ninety seconds he hears a clang, followed by steps. A little dark man with a pencil moustache and a carefully wound turban comes down the steps. Bengali, Aaron guesses, too dark to be a Sikh or Rajastani, but too light to be from Kerala or Madras.

Cautiously, the man opens the door. "Yes?" he asks , and Aaron wonders how, with even a

single syllable, an accent can be manifested, how classically Indian the man sounds.

"Can I help you?"

I just know he pronounces his "V's" as "W"s, Aaron speculates. He will say, "please hand me the wacuum cleaner."

"I need a room. The sign says, well.....it says you have an 'acancy'.

"Yes yes, wery good, we have a room, sixty dollars for the week, only for the week or more, no renting to one nights, no renting to prostitutes." The syllables are as discreet and round as perfect green peas on a plate. The man looks for Aaron's luggage, sees none, makes a question with his eyebrows.

"I just got off the plane from Bombay, my luggage got lost."

"Bombay, Bombay, I too am from Bombay." He does not smile, but he opens the door and allows Aaron into the hotel.

At the top of the steps is a wrought iron gate, its narrow bars supporting an extra barrier of wire screen so that nothing can be passed from one side to the other. The night clerk puts a key in a big lock and pulls the door towards himself. He lets Aaron step through. Then he opens a wooden flap, steps behind the pitted and oft-carved reception counter, closing the flap behind him. He goes to the keyboard and takes one of three keys down from a hook and inspects it. He turns to Aaron.

"If you pay month it is two twenty five. Cash only. No welfare check, no food stamp."

"I have one question: do you allow pets? A dog?"

The clerk wrinkles his nose, looking at Aaron's money. "Big dog, little dog?"

"Little dog."

"Barking dog, not barking dog?"

"Not barking dog."

"Dog make crap?"

"Not in here," Aaron states firmly.

"Okay, you have dog."

Aaron counts out a hundred and twenty dollars. The bus cost two dollars and change. He has spent almost nine dollars on food. He has sixty odd dollars between himself and oblivion.

"I can do this," he inwardly asserts. "I can do this. I'll make it."

The Indian man counts the money, then hands him the key. "Room three oh three," he instructs. "Up the next flight of stairs. Where is dog?"

"I'll get him tomorrow. Thanks."

As he walks up the stairs and begins counting the numbers on the third floor, he hears a kind of muttering sound, as if all the hotel's inhabitants are talking in their sleep. Discreet bits of sound can be heard as he passes door after door. From one he hears a determined chanting of "Hare Krishna Hare Krishna," from another comes the laughter of a TV game show, and he distinctly hears the word "motherfucker" as he passes room three twelve.

The light is dim, there is a caged twenty five watt electric bulb every twenty feet. The carpet beneath Aaron's torn tennis shoes is a deep purple, worn through to the floor in spots, and not quite reaching the molding on either side of the hallway. The walls are painted a sickening phosphorescent green, somewhere between teal and lavender. The paint has been carelessly applied so that the cracks between the four-inch panels of wood veneer strips show the color of a previous paint job, a nauseating peach.

There is a smell of disinfectant in the air, emanating primarily from the two bathrooms, one of which is merely a toilet in a closet, the other a larger room with two shower stalls and four urinals. The lights in these rooms are controlled by dangling strings, each of which ends in a metallic bell shaped knob.

Aaron hears a racking cough as he passes the shower room, and a man's voice says to no apparent listener, "aaaawwwwh".

Rooms three oh two to three oh six occupy a cul-de-sac, a little five-room segment that turns off the main hallway. Aaron lets himself into three oh three, gropes for a light switch, finds none, then gropes toward the middle of the room until his hand brushes the string. He pulls and gets his first glimpse of his new home.

The bed is a narrow lumpy device set on a high steel-tubed frame whose paint is chipped and weathered. It is placed against the wall next to a window that looks out on apparently nothing. Just inside the door, to his right, is a porcelain sink. He knows, from other lifetimes in hotels like this, that the sink doubles as a urinal. There is a chest of drawers topped by a mirror whose silvering has long since vanished, an opaque piece of useless glass. Next to the bed is a night table with one small drawer and a cabinet with an embossed mace-shaped handle. The walls and carpet are identical to those in the hall.

Aaron lights the lamp atop the night table, and then pulls the overhead light off. He lays on the bed and groans, feeling the daggers of worn out springs poking into his back. He feels his courage beginning to slide away from him like a segment of ice on a polar glacier, cracking and beginning to fissure from the main body before sliding into the sea.

If it slides away, he will succumb to despair and merge with the drug culture of the streets and that will be the end of his story. He can not do that. He grabs the remnant of his strength and holds onto it. He remembers Murid and Fatima and the Mujahiddin and repeats to himself his new mantra: "I am not that person anymore".

He is not a drug addict. He is a man.

Aaron becomes aware of a strange presence in the room. He feels as if he is not alone, and it gives his body a chill, the hair on his neck begins to tingle and his eyes suddenly water.

He sits up, looking around, listening. There is no one. He peers into the murk outside the window. Apparently he is looking at a blank brick facade that only faintly reflects the orange sky glow from the city's lights.

He rises to his feet and looks into the doorless closet with its bent and twisted hangers. He stands on his tiptoes to check the shelf, runs his fingers across it and comes back with dust and mouse turds that sprinkle to the floor.

Then he smells a familiar smell, the smell of tobacco. Cheroot, he determines. Definitely Cheroot. Dutch Masters. Zoot's brand.

Aaron turns back to his bed and sees the outline of his long-dead mentor, standing elegantly in a tuxedo. He is seeing with an interior sense, not actual eyeball-vision, yet the ghostly presence is here, before him, in the room.

"Zoot," he says, "I've been on airplanes for more than twenty hours, I've been in a war, I've kicked dope, I'm in a crisis and I don't need to think of myself at this moment as being prone to psychotic hallucinations."

488

Zoot's ghost sprinkles ash from its cheroot into the ethers.

"Tough shit, man. I had to do some intricate maneuvering to get here in this form, Zoot's been dead a long time and it ain't easy to put on a personality like a suit of clothes."

"Ohhh," Aaron says, and has to cry, can do nothing but cry. He sits on the bed and the Zoot-spirit sits next to him. Aaron feels so immensely lonely, wants so desperately to be in contact with the spirit of Zoot Prestige, with someone who loves him and has known him a long time and sees his essence.

"It's okay, Aaron, I'm really here," Zoot says. "I know you can smell the cheroot, babe. That's the best I can do, I can't reach out and touch you, but I think the cheroot trick is groovy."

Then Aaron begins to laugh at the same time he is crying. Big swathes of tears run down his face and his ribcage twitches with sad ironic mirth.

"You gonna tell me," he giggles, "what happens after you die? You gonna reveal to me the mysteries of the universe?"

Zoot puffs and blows the smoke in a neat stream toward the ceiling. "The question is more like 'what happens after you're born?' To us folks here in the Big World, the world you're in, the world where you have discrete personalities fitted tightly into sometimes bad-tempered and capricious bodies, is the Little World. A place where you're born and die, where all this shit keeps whirling around. But, you know, I'm not here for metaphysical instruction and spiritual revelation, that's all ultimately bullshit, it can't begin to contain what's real."

Aaron inhales soberly and gets control of himself. "Then why are you here?"

"I'm here," Zoot says simply, "to let you know you're not alone. And to give you some courage, 'cause I can tell you need some."

Again, Aaron's emotions overwhelm him, and he sobs into his hands with gratitude, rocking back and forth, making the bedsprings creak. When he takes his face from his hands, Zoot is gone. The cheroot smell lingers, subtly, a faint waft upon the air.

Chapter Forty Five

Hauntings
1982: St. Louis

There is an old photograph in Marilee's closet, filched long ago from the family collection and held as an horrific icon, an object of secret obsession. It is Esther's high school graduation picture. To the best of Marilee's knowledge, it is the only picture from Esther's youth. It is contained in a grey patterned cardboard foldout. Inside, smiling from an oval frame, is Esther at eighteen.

Marilee can see that her mother had once been very beautiful. The photograph shows a smiling young woman with flawless skin, perfect teeth. Her hair is thick and barely confined to the stylish bun of the era. She is an archetypal Jewess, a radiation of a thousand years of Polish Jewish culture. She has a nose that is arched at the bridge, framed by high cheekbones, large eyes and a perfectly dimpled chin. There is an element of fragility to the expression, as if the smile is difficult to hold and has been held for too long so that her facial muscles are becoming fatigued. Other than that, Marilee can see no sign of the Esther-to-come.

Marilee's daughter, Rosie, will turn five on December Third. She is a stunning child, with wild curling black hair, peach-bite lips, a delicate nose, hazel eyes. Sometimes Marilee will hold the picture of her mother up to compare it to the appearance of her daughter. Rosie's eyes are a different color, but the resemblance is otherwise very striking.

It is snowing. Rosie is screaming with terror. It is her birthday. She holds back at the door to their house, her body becoming almost horizontal as she hangs in the grip of her mother's hand. Her feet are covered with red snow boots, and they are slipping out from under her as Marilee tugs relentlessly.

"We're going to the beauty parlor, for god's sake. It's your first time. What are you yelling about? You should be thrilled."

"I don't want to go, mommy, I don't want to go. Why do I have to go?"

Marilee is getting a rush of hot rage and can barely restrain herself from shaking the child.

"To make yourself beautiful, of course, just like mommy."

"No, no. I don't want to be beautiful like mommy."

Under her breath, Marilee hisses, "Fucking little bitch," thinking that Rosie can't hear it. But

Rosie always hears her mother's subvocalizations.

Marilee picks the child up. "Just get in the car!" She orders and whooshes the little girl into the back seat of the Cadillac.

Rosie becomes passive the rest of the way to the Beauty Salon.

The staff at Adele's Hair and Facial Stylings always cringe when they see the white Cadillac park in front.

"Here comes Perfect, " Adele says. After a moment, she adds, "Oh my god. Look at that. It's a tiny Perfect. She's bringing the baby."

Covertly, the other stylists look from their jobs to see, outside the salon's large display window, Rosie, being led sadly, as if to a sacrifice.

"Oh, she's adorable," says one of the ladies in a chair.

"She can't be, but she is," agrees Adele. "Poor baby."

Marilee enters imperiously, and gives her fur to the receptionist. She takes off Rosie's coat and thrusts her forward with a hand on the back of each shoulder.

"Here's my daughter Rosie" she announces. "She's ugly as a pig that's been rolling in a wallow. I know," she sighs dramatically, "it's not much to work with, but see what you can do to make her beautiful. Or at least presentable. Look, I'd be happy with just having her not be an embarassment. Think you can do that? We're going to a lavish affair tonight, and children are coming, too."

Marilee is impenetrable, totally unaware of the hostile stares from each of the beauticians and cosmetologists.

Adele kneels down and takes Rosie's hand. The little girl flinches but offers it. She sees kindness

in Adele's eyes, and it reminds her of grandpa. "I think you're very beautiful, Rosie. Very beautiful. We'll fix you up so your mom will be pleased. Will you stay here with us and let us curl your hair and manicure your nails? It will be fun, I promise."

Rosie nods her assent.

Marilee whirls, recovers her fur coat and opens the door. "I'll be back in two hours. I expect her to be immaculate, is that understood?"

"Yes maam," says Adele, trying to keep the contempt out of her voice.

Chapter Forty Six

1982: San Francisco

Aaron sleeps soundly for four hours. He is still so uncertain of his capacity for sleep that when he awakes and looks at his watch, he sighs deeply and pats his body with his palms, as if to affirm the existence of a miracle.

He remembers the colloquy with Zoot and smiles wryly. "That didn't happen, but it happened," he thinks, "and I'll just leave it at that."

There is one overwhelming priority on this day, something about which he has been obsessing since the moment he left San Francisco two weeks ago. He will get Diz out of the boarding place, make sure he's okay.

Putting the dog in a kennel had been wrenching, devastating. He remembers Diz's face as he placed the dog in a small wire cage. How can you do this to me? the dog's eyes plead. Don't leave me here with all these strangers.

I have to, Diz, he silently communicates to the dog, I have no choice. I have to go to Afghanistan and make some kind of deal and then I'll be back and we'll go rent an apartment in San Rafael where we can walk in the hills.

Aaron jumps from the bed and puts his clothes on. He'll be okay, he'll be okay, he repeats to himself. I left a deposit for two weeks and nothing's happened to him, he'll still be there.

The city bleats at him as he leaves the hotel. Fuck you, city, Aaron bleats back. I'll deal with you later.

He walks up to Geary and gets on the number thirty eight bus, going toward the park. Then he transfers to the Taraval streetcar and gets out to Nineteenth Avenue where he walks back towards Ocean and Wallach's Veterinary Clinic and Boarding Kennel.

The anteroom is exactly like that of a dentist's office. Aaron leans into a little window and sees the receptionist sitting in a steel-tube chair with a beige-upholstered back and seat.

"Hi,," he says, "I'm here for my dog."

"Oh yes, you have the cute little Spitz, don't you? He'll be so glad to see you. Let me find your bill." She rifles through a file cabinet. "It begins with a K, doesn't it? I remember."

"Kantro."

"Yes, here it is, let me see...." she pulls her glasses more tightly onto her face. Bringing a piece of paper up to the window, she passes it to Aaron.

"After the deposit, there will be a balance of sixty two fifty. I'll go get the dog."

"Wait, I paid you guys for two weeks. What's sixty two fifty? I'm on time."

"We gave him some antibiotics, see, here," she points with her pen at the invoice, "and a flea treatment, and weekly bath."

Aaron sighs. After paying this bill he will have less then five dollars. He counts out the money.

The woman stamps the bill PAID and goes to retrieve Diz.

Momentarily, the door to the reception room opens and the dog is led out on a disposable string leash. He has an idiotic little blue paper ribbon tied to his tail. He is sparkling clean, immaculately groomed.

The dog yelps once and almost climbs up the length of Aaron's body. His tail wags with ecstasy, his tongue slurps at Aaron's face, the little pulsating muscle of his canine soul leaps into its master's arms.

"Hey man, Dizzo, you clean little fucker, how you been?"

The receptionist smiles weakly and retreats back to the interior of the clinic.

Aaron swings the glass door wide and carries the dog onto the sidewalk. He snatches the blue bow from the dog's tail.

"You didn't fight or bite, did you? I hope you behaved yourself."

Aaron lifts the dog up and checks his underside. "Whew, they left your balls on. That's getting hard to do you know, I had to tell 'em you are a breeding dog. Ain't nobody gonna snip Diz."

The dog races in a circle around Aaron, winding the leash around his legs.

"We got a hell of a long walk, Diz. You remember that street corner, that day I almost wanted to kill myself, and I didn't because I would have had to kill you? Remember that?"

Diz barks and bounces on his legs as if they are springs.

"Know something, you got more brains than most people I know. Anyway, we're living about three blocks from that place, you'll hate it. And I have to find a job, I mean right now, today, I don't know how I'm going to eat. You'll eat, don't worry. We'll be okay. Got a long road to travel, a long way to climb, but we'll be okay."

The dog prances but keeps looking back over its shoulder, up into Aaron's face. Diz is smiling, his pink tongue lolls from the black mouth-skin, curled perfectly between sharp incisors.

He's so happy, Aaron muses. He has pure, genuine, uncluttered joy in being alive. Not mediated by self consciousness or thoughts, just Being itself. I should be half the creature he is, experience a fraction of the love he feels.

They cut over to Fifteenth Avenue and walk up the hill. To their left, the Pacific Ocean gleams like a silver coin in the sun.

Aaron needs to tire himself out. The residue of jumpiness from his drug withdrawal is still a t

ingling presence in his nerves. He takes the long way home, up Taraval to Dewey, up into Diamond Heights. At the very top of the hill, the city reveals itself in all its drama, like a beautiful woman who has taken a long leisurely time undressing.

"Look at that thing, Diz," Aaron insists. "Just look at it. Unbelievable."

The dog sits on Aaron's foot and wags its tail. All of downtown San Francisco lies at the bottom of the hill. To Aaron's senses it has an alien splendor, as if it has been whisked out of a future century. It is oddly silent, its distance drowned out by the passing of cars making the turn onto Clipper Street.

"It should be louder," Aaron says, "it should be like a great cymbal crash, or a Chinese gong." He squats, bending at the heels, and puts the dog on his thigh.

The dog slurps at his face. Aaron wrinkles his lips to one side. "Yeah, okay." He puts the dog back onto the sidewalk and they begin to descend from the affluent heights to the more commonplace grit of the city.

It takes almost forty five minutes to get to Church Street, where Aaron turns left, aiming for Mission and the employment agency down near Fifth. At the corner of Church and Twenty Fourth he passes a Texaco Station and notices the Help Wanted sign in the window.

He stops and watches the activity in the repair bays, watches cars enter from the street, ding the cable, stop at the pumps.

"I've only had two jobs, Diz. Professional musician and professional dope fiend. This is going to be a big change." He gathers the dog into his arms and walks into the station's office. It has two red vinyl upholstered chairs, its windows are pasted with scratched old Pennzoil decals. There is a cardboard life-sized Certifiied Amco Technician wearing a blue uniform and a blue officer's hat standing next to the glass door that leads into the garage section of the station. An old-style Coke machine, red with white letterings, rounded at the top, hums in one corner. There is a black Labrador retriever lolling indolently at the foot of the coke machine. It perks up as soon as Aaron and Diz enter the office, rises slowly from its sitting position and wags its tail.

Aaron's intuitive dog-menace censors register "safe". He puts Diz down and lets the two dogs sniff each other's butts.

A short man slides the door from the repair bay aside and enters the office. He is wiping oil from his hands with a red towel. He is compact, dark-skinned, with short curly hair.

"Oh what a nice dog!" He smiles without guile. "He and Jamshid get along."

The man finishes wiping his hands and throws the towel into a hamper just inside the door to a smaller, inner office. "What can I do for you?"

"Help Wanted." Aaron points to the sign. "I need a job."

"Oh, come on in here." The man points to the inner office. He ticks on a desk lamp and offers Aaron another red chair. Aaron sits at one side of a cluttered desk while the station's owner rolls back an office chair and slides himself into the desk's opening.

"I'm Bouzar Farzaddeh," he introduces himself, extending his hand.

Aaron takes it, noting its rough firmness, its strength. "I'm Aaron Kantro, and the dog is Diz."

"That's an unusual name for a dog. Is it from Dizzy? Does he play a trumpet?"

"Just a little," Aaron replies. "He dabbles with the piano."

"I usually call Jamshid 'Jahm'. He's an old dog, he's fourteen."

There is a bang from the repair bay and Bouzar rolls his chair out the door, looks through the glass, then rolls himself back into the office. He puts his fingers together, reverses his hands in a knuckle-popping stretch, then yawns.

"So, do you have any experience? Are you a mechanic?"

"None whatsoever," Aaron confesses.

"Eh...." Bouzar scratches the inside of his ear with his pinky finger, then folows its coils around, as if cleaning out debris. "I only need a pump jockey and tire-changer. Doesn't pay much, three seventy five an hour. We can teach you how to use the tire machines."

"You think I can bring the dog?"

Bouzar rolls his chair out once more into the main office. Aaron scooches himself backward to see what the dogs are doing. Diz is bouncing up and down in front of Jamshid, who regards him with an amused and tolerant eye and a friendly thumping of tail.

"What do you think, Jahm? Do you want company?"

The old dog licks its own grey muzzle and rolls over on its side. The tail continues happily thumping on the floor.

Bouzar shrugs. "It's okay with Jahm, it's okay with me. Can you start tomorrow morning?"

"I can start tomorrow morning."

"Good." Bouzar rises from the chair and slides the door to the repair bay aside. "Let me introduce you to Steve and Uncle Ali."

He leads Aaron into the repair bay, sliding the door shut behind him. A burly American in stained overalls and a purple t-shirt is bent over a Camaro.

"Steve, this is Aaron."

Steve emerges from under the hood. He is about six foot two, has wild long curly hair, a florid complexion and a Fu Manchu moustache. On his right bicep is a crude tattoo, a Gothic script rendering of the word "Decadence". On his left bicep is the word "Renaissance". On the right side of his neck and disappearing into his shirt is a much more finely wrought tattoo of a Chinese Dragon.

This is like wearing a sign or a placard, Aaron thinks, that says "I am an ex-con junkie". The tattoos hide track marks. The neck tattoos attest to such overuse of the other veins in the body that the man has resorted to injecting into his jugular. Aaron realizes at the same moment that he, too, is being "clocked," that Steve knows another dope-recovering scoundrel when he sees one.

They shake hands. Steve has a strange expression, one that Aaron can not decipher. "Groovy," he says, simply, then returns to his engine.

Bouzar leads Aaron out to an old man who is pumping gas into a black Mustang. He is tall, thin, and moves stiffly, grunting as he leans to take money from the customer.

"This is my Uncle Ali," Bouzar says fondly. "He doesn't speak much English."

He explains Aaron's new status in Farsi to the old man. Ali smiles to reveal gapped, yellowed teeth. He extends a hand to Aaron and speaks indistinctly. Then another car dinks over the cable and he turns to care for the customer.

"He's a dirty old man," Bouzar states. "He's an animal. I have to keep him from humping the lady customers." He shouts over his shoulder in Farsi to his uncle. The old man cackles wickedly and bends to his work.

"Okay, you come back tomorrow morning at eight. We'll get you started." Again, he shakes Aaron's hand. "Don't forget your dog."

"Not likely," Aaron says, following Bouzar back into the office. "Can he bring his trumpet?"

Without missing a beat, Bouzar responds. "I prefer piano, if that's possible."

Aaron has a good feeling about the place and its people.

He refastens Diz's leash and opens the door. "See you tomorrow." Bouzar nods absently and passes through into the repair bay.

Aaron leaves the station and heads down Church Street. I've got a job, he thinks, but I still don't know how I'm going to eat tonight.

He is about to go into a little corner grocery store to spend his last three dollars on dog food and a beef stick. Steve, the mechanic, comes from behind and taps him on the shoulder. Aaron turns and looks up into the big man's face.

"I remember you, now," Steve says. "You're the drummer. You were with Rob Weird. I saw you guys at the Cow Palace, in, what? Seventy two? Seventy Three? You were Aaron Kantro, right?"

Aaron nods. "I'm still Aaron Kantro."

Steve does a crazy little dance, jumping from one foot to the other. "All right!" He hoots, "that was a great band! That was some crazy smokin' music!" He pounds his open palm into Aaron's, a 'low five', then extends his hand upward, waiting for Aaron to take up the slack, and make the 'high five'. Aaron obliges.

"Hey, let me ask you something." Steve drapes a big arm over Aaron's shoulder and seems to create a little private space between them, in the middle of the teeming sidewalk.

"Sure," Aaron assents, "ask away."

"You got strung out, didn't you?" Steve backs away slightly and raises both hands. "Aint' none of my business, I know, but you are a famous rock and roll star and now you're looking for a job in a gas station, I mean, I ain't stupid, I been through some shit too."

"It's okay," Aaron says. The dog pulls once at the leash, then settles next to Aaron's leg. "Yeah, I got strung out. And I know you been through some shit, too. How long you been clean?"

Steve expands with pride. "Four years. Got my kids back, my wife back, got a job, stayed out of trouble. Life is good, life is groovy. How about you?"

Aaron sees no reason to deceive. "About two weeks."

"Holy Shit!" Steve takes another step back, as if Aaron's recently minted sobriety is a potential source of infection. An elderly Philipino couple walks between them and passes down the sidewalk. "Then you must be pretty raw. You all right?"

Aaron ponders the impossibility of explaining his experiences to anyone. "I'm all right," he says, cryptically, "I'm on the road to Damascus."

"Yeah, I can dig it," Steve responds, "and the sky opens wide, I remember that lyric, that is one of your songs, on the Weird World album. Well, hey, man, glad you're gonna work at the station, these Iranian guys are all right. Truth is, three years ago they were all sand- niggers to me, they were screaming ayatollahs, but after working with 'em they're just people, just normal people like us."

Aaron laughs so hugely that he surprises himself. He didn't think he was capable of such a laugh.

"Just normal people like us, huh, Steve?"

"Oh jesus, what am I saying?" Steve wipes his moustache with his oily fingers, then puts his arm back over Aaron's shoulder, recreating the little intimate space between them. It is a prison mannerism, a dope dealer mannerism, a way to not be overheard. "Listen, man, do you need a few bucks? I can loan you twenty, and after you've worked a few days Bouzar will cut you some slack, he'll advance you a little, he's a great guy with stuff like that."

"Hey, I don't want to..." Aaron begins to protest.

"No, no," Steve says firmly. "It ain't a problem." He takes a twenty from the pocket of his overalls. "You played so great with Rob Weird, this is just for being so great....know what I mean? Not everybody has a talent like that. People don't understand. Talent is a gift from God. I know how much work it is, I'm not sayin' it just happens, you must have worked your ass off for years, but still. Someone like you should never be hungry, never go without. You should be guarded and cared for like a precious treasure."

What a delicate and beautiful thought, Aaron reflects, coming from a man who looks like a junkie Hell's Angel. You never know, you really never know. He feels himself begin to relax. We'll survive, he says to Diz, inside his head. We'll survive. We're on the Miracle Train, now.

"Thanks," he tells the mechanic. He takes the twenty, puts it into his shirt pocket and shakes Steve's dirty hand. "Thanks a lot. This means a lot to me. See you tomorrow." He turns and enters the store.

Chapter Forty Seven

1982: Arlen Hotel, San Francisco

Aaron lets the desk clerk buzz him through the locked wrought iron door at the top of the stairs. Diz is tucked securely into his armpit. As he turns to make the next flight of stairs, a man races up to the desk.

"Strickland's trying to kill himself!" The man is tall, thin, sandy-haired, about forty five years old.

The desk clerk is a young American with a sallow triangular face and bad skin. "Is he doing it with a knife, a gun, a razor, dope or pills?"

"Pills." The man is panting. Aaron stands there. Footsteps from the third floor thump overhead.

The desk clerk shrugs. "So? Long as he doesn't make a mess, let 'im kill 'imself."

The anxious man turns to Aaron. "Do you believe this shit?" He jerks a thumb towards the desk clerk. "Serious desensitization."

"Can I help?"

"Sure," the man says, "Strickland likes dogs, bring the pooch."

Aaron follows down the hallway. Many room doors are open. There is a sense of bedlam in the air, sounds of radios, televisions, arguments, sneezes, coughs, hacking phlegm.

I dropped through a hole in the bottom of the world, Aaron thinks, and this is where I start climbing out.

The room is the last one in the main corridor. It has a bed; it is like every other room in this dormitory from hell. It is the same as Aaron's, it has a sink just inside the door, a chest, a mirror, a night table. There are psychedelic posters on the walls from the old Fillmore and Avalon days. There it is, the red and blue one, with the flowers and flames and endless Buddhist Gates. The Doors, it advertises, and beneath it, Zoot Prestige Trio. Aaron feels a pang.

Strickland is a chubby little man with hair like black wire spilling down his shoulders. He is blubbering and curled into a fetal position on his bed. "I took 'em! I took 'em all," he wails. The tall man opens the chest of drawers and removes a pill bottle. He shakes it, looks into it, opens the cap and spills the pills onto his palm, counting them.

"You didn't take any, George, not a one."

"Well give 'em here, then," George blubbers, reaching sloppily, ineffectively.

The tall man puts the pills back into the bottle and puts the bottle into his pocket. He sits on the other bed and offers Aaron a wooden slat-backed chair. "It'll be okay, George, I won't let them evict you, I promise." He takes a cigarette pack from the night table and lights one.

George turns his face to the wall. His rounded back looks like a dolphin's torso.

"You can't do nothin'," George mumbles. "The Hindus'll get you, they'll turn you into one of their slaves."

"Why don't you play with this cute dog, George, and stop worrying about everything."

"No!" George spits back, like a spoiled child. "It's okay for you, but I can't work, I can't count, I can't do nothing. The Hindus are gonna kick me out."

"Is he talking about the owners of the hotel?" Aaron asks .

"Yeah," the man says. "By the way, I'm Keith Wagers, but everybody calls me Wags." He points at the little man on the bed. "I kind of watch over George here, he ain't got nobody else, so I figure somebody's gotta do it."

They shake hands. Diz is sniffing around under the beds. "I'm Aaron. So what's going on here?"

"It's the system, the system in the hotel. If you fall behind on your rent you wind up working for

the Patels. And they find ways to jack you around so you never catch up. That guy at the desk? He's been working here four years. He's trapped. But if you're incompetent, crazy or just too fucked up, they put all your belongings in a plastic bag and throw you out on the street and keep your stuff. If you see two goons walking down the hall with plastic bags, that's what they're doing. It's the Patel goon squad. Can be you or me if we lose a disability check or food stamps. They'll have you manning the desk, cleaning out the toilets, fixing the furnace, it's their ready-made cheap labor force."

Diz jumps up on George's bed and begins sniffing at the man's ear. George giggles and turns to face the room. He scratches Diz on the head.

"What a pretty dog," he says in a gentle baby voice. "Pretty dog."

"I been taking care of George for eight months, since I got out on parole. His check didn't come this month. Patels are getting impatient."

"What'd you do time for?"

"Safecracking," Wags states blandly. "Sixteen months in Arizona Penitentiary."

"You clean?" Aaron asks .

"Not by choice." Wags responds, "but I'm workin' on it. How about you? Got any connections? "

"By choice," says Aaron. "I think I better go."

"Hey thanks for the help. Nobody gives a shit about George. Nobody but me."

Aaron gathers the dog into his arms. You've probably got George's check in your pocket, he thinks, and you'll get him out of the room but keep him in the neighborhood where you can milk him for his benefits. "Good luck, George."

By this time George has sat upright. "Wags'll fix it, won't you Wags?"

"Sure George, I'll fix it," Wags replies. He flicks his ash into an empty Dennison's Chili can.

Aaron goes to his room, puts Diz inside and then goes to the public telephone that is just inside the landing on the third floor. He puts some coins into the slot, dials a number.

"Hello?" Debra answers.

"Hi, it's me," Aaron says tentatively.

There is a long silence. Finally, Debra says, "Six years? Six years? You don't call, you don't write, you don't do anything, your child is growing up? Six years?"

"I know," Aaron murmurs guiltily. "I know. I'm calling now."

"What makes you think I even want to talk to you? Why should I say a single word to you?"

"I didn't call before because I had nothing to give but sickness. You were better off without me. I'm calling now because I'm changing."

"And where have I heard that before?" Debra derides.

"Don't say that," Aaron says firmly. "Don't say that. All I want is to know how you're doing, how Stefanie's doing? Are you still with Eric?"

"Yes, Eric is Stefanie's daddy, and we're doing fine."

"Good. What grade is she in?"

"She's in the third grade, she loves the piano, gymnastics, poetry and she gets straight A's."

There is another long silence. Debra's voice softens. "What about you? Are you okay? You sound different, somehow, I can't put my finger on it, but your voice is more calm, more peaceful."

"I'm okay. I've had some experiences.....I can't explain, but I'm not going back to that life. Being a dope fiend just isn't an option anymore. I'm not that person. I'm not sure which person I am, I'm just inventing myself as I go along. When I have more to give, I'll call you again."

"Okay," Debra says. "I'm glad you called. Stefanie knows Eric's not her biological dad. She doesn't remember you. It will be strange, but some day we'll figure out how you can see her. When you're ready."

"Right." Aaron's voice is a whisper. His nose wrinkles and he wipes his eyes. "I'll be in touch." He hangs up the phone.

When he returns to his room, he finds a small thin woman kneeling at his door. She is dressed in olive green sweat clothes and has a tightly wrapped tin foil helmet on her head. It is so carefully made that not a single hair shows from under its cover. It comes down the woman's neck and

ends above her shoulders in a sweep, like some ancient Amazon war bonnet.

"Excuse me, what are you doing?"

The woman looks up. She is about thirty years old. Her eyes are a watery blue and the skin of her cheeks is flushed. She has a pretty face but her expression is unintentionally comical. She looks like an actress playing an insane woman.

"I'm debugging you," she says confidentially. "I provide this service for free. No taps, no devices, no transmitters in the door. So far so good." She returns to her minute inspection of the woodwork.

There is a bark from inside the room.

"Hold on, Diz, I'm coming. Do you mind?" He puts his hand on the doorknob.

"Almost done here," the woman says, "I'll come in and finish the job."

"No, that's okay," Aaron demurs, trying to get into the room without allowing the woman access. She is pressing forward. Aaron keeps his arm on the door.

"You think I'm nuts, don't you?"

"Yes, I do," Aaron admits.

"Have you been depressed lately?"

"Of course I have."

"See? That's proof."

Okay, Aaron thinks, grist for the mill. I'm interested in craziness, I'm interested in everything human.

"Proof of what?"

"Look," the woman says patiently, "I can explain this and debug your room at the same time. It won't take me long, about fifteen minutes and I'll be out of your hair and I'll know there's one more room that ain't bugged. I gotta keep going over and over this hotel."

"All right, come on in. But I'm really tired and fifteen minutes is all you got."

S

he enters. Diz comes forward, wags his tail, sniffs at the woman and follows her around, observing her movements with his head cocked to one side. The woman begins passing a wand over the room's surfaces. It is made from tin foil, an ordinary kitchen fork and some copper wire.

"It's real simple," she says. "There's one satellite in geosynchronous orbit for each region of the world. They're put up by the CIA. They beam depression rays down into the minds of the entire earth population. The CIA wants to keep everyone in the world depressed. That way they buy more stuff, they consume to fill the horrid vacuums in their hearts, and the capitalist system keeps chugging along. That's why I wear the helmet. It covers my hair. The rays get in through your hair."

Aaron sits on the bed. "What about your eyebrows?" He asks . Then he notices they aren't there, she has no eyebrows.

She looks up from her work. "Plucked." She smiles impishly. The absence of eyebrows lends her face a crazed piquancy.

Aaron inpects the woman's wrists where they emerge from the sweat shirt. "Depilated," she says, in answer to his silent question. "All over. Takes a lot of work. Some depression gets in through the stubble, but I can handle that. I take ginseng and echinacea, the satellites don't like it. You should stock up. When the CIA finds out, they're gonna take all the herbs off the market, you won't be able to get any."

"You're as crazy as shit but you speak in complete sentences that I can understand," Aaron says. "What's your name?"

"Lori. But that isn 't my real name. I don't have a real name, not any more, too dangerous to have a real name." She passes her wand across the angles of the room, sweeps it across the ceiling, opens each drawer, then goes to the closet.

She pauses at the closet. "There's some strange energy in here but it reads as benevolent. Hmmm. Never seen that before." She gives her instrument one more cursory sweep.

"Done," she says. "What's your name?"

"Ruben Pondwater," Aaron replies. "Also not my real name."

"Glad to meet you Ruben. Your room is now safe from extraneous devices, but you should make yourself a helmet and take care of that body hair. And get some ginseng."

"Okay, Lori, will do. Time for me to take a nap." He gently eases her toward the door.

Chapter Forty Eight

The   Spook   Lady
1983: The Arlen Hotel, San Francisco

It's almost time for the Spook Lady to start her monologue. Aaron looks at the hands of the clock. The tired green radium is barely capable of showing that it's four thirty. He snaps on the light for a moment, to check. Yep, four thirty in the morning.

He turns off the light and listens to the sounds of the hotel and the city beyond. In this hour before dawn the world is like a rattle snake anticipating the sun. It's too cold to move. It can be poked and prodded without consequence. But in another hour, one will not want to prod. And in another two hours, one will not even come close.

Across the hall, in Room 303, the speed freaks are arguing about who got more dope. Upstairs, on the fourth floor, in the room directly overhead, someone is pacing evenly and steadily back and forth, like a soldier on guard duty. It's a kinetic tattoo, signature of god only knows what despairing thoughts.

Distant rock music. It never ends, he thinks, the sonic pollution. By ten it will be pounding on his walls, thumpety thump thumpety thump.

Now it's quiet enough to hear the voice of the Spook Lady. She lives next door in room 304. Since he checked into the hotel two weeks ago he can set his clock by the beginning of her four thirty harangue.

He has never seen anyone go to her room. During the day she takes her spot at the corner near the hotel door. She's dressed like a hooker from the thirties. She waits, stamped with loneliness. She's seventy, maybe seventy five years old.

She wears the same outfit every day: a vivid blue dress, elbow length mauve gloves, silk stockings full of runs, lace-up black heels. A fake carnation perches atop a decorative hair net. This shapes and restrains her brittle, dried hair.

She looks as if she's waiting for a trick, Aaron thinks. Maybe she gets tricks, who the hell knows? Nothing in this place could surprise me. Got a double amputee male hooker in room 301. A professional safe cracker in 297. Assorted psychotics. A woman who makes tin foil helmets to block CIA transmissions from satellites.

The Spook Lady must be waiting for the appearance of her vanished lover, thinks Aaron, the man she beats with her words, every night at four thirty a.m.

"You damn mothafucka!" There she goes, punctual as a Japanese train. "Who is that I seen you with....." The words fade in and out. Aaron turns to his other side, groaning, not wanting to hear it, needing sleep. He pulls the blanket up across his shoulder and looks out the window at absolutely nothing. There is a wall inches from his window. At night it sheds no light, it's just a piece of tar.

"Money?" the woman cries. "What fuckin' money? You don't fuckin'........" Bad tempered, jealous, she scours her spirit-lover. Does his ghost materialize in the hour before dawn? Does he wear clothes sixty years gone? Does he have spats, a cane, a diamond stickpin? Are there gold rings flashing, white teeth, a vivid red carnation stuck through the lapel of his double-breasted suit?

"A big man?," the crone derides hoarsely. "Ha ha, don't make me fuckin laugh. Hey, don't drop those.....oh you bastard!.......well, that's Jim so and so and he can eat my...."

This goes on night after night. It lasts about twenty minutes, then tapers off into silence. Names flow in and out of the ethers. Old debts, old crimes. Old revenge.

When I leave at eight this morning, she'll be there, Aaron knows, at her place by the door. She never returns my look, never meets my eyes, never acknowledges the essential fact of neighbor-ness. Her eyes are fixed on an invisible street, invisible buildings, invisible people.

She has observed the same routine every day that I've been here. Same place, same clothes, same fake flower, once crimson but going utterly white from the bleach of the sun. Buses wait at the light. Cars pile up, then surge forward honking and roaring. The city's life is flung like an acid onto the pavement. The Spook Lady sees big black Nash Sedans, high rounded Packards instead of Hondas and Camaros. When the sun sets, she goes to her room and waits for her lover in the mists of damaged memory.

Aaron wakes every night at four twenty five, exactly, taut with tortured anticipation. He can't help it. The Spook Lady has become one of the denizens of his insomnia.

She is suddenly loud. "Gimme that! Hey!" Something goes thump!

Aaron's ears are like huge radar disks, pulling away from his face, elastic, stretching.

It's quiet for a moment. Hotel sounds emerge from the background. Then he hears the woman weeping. "Ooooh!" She moans. "You black hearted son of a bitch!"

What did he do? Did he hit her? Is there a red hand print on her face, slowly fading? Can the shades of the past force blood through capillaries?

Sound of glass shattering, another thump, right against the wall behind Aaron's head. Then she laughs. "Ha. Ha. Ha. Ha." The indivdual "Ha"s toll like a cathedral bell. It is a sound so devoid of mirth that his skin crawls.

At eight, when he leaves the hotel in the morning, he can barely glance in her direction. He has been listening every night to a gaping red wound, one that pulsates and festers and never heals.

She doesn't know. She doesn't care.

In her mind, Aaron is the ghost.

Chapter Forty Nine

Spirits
1983: Arlen Hotel, San Francisco

Aaron wakes up. This is good, he wryly observes. If I wake up it means I've been to sleep. He reaches for his watch on the bed table. Six twenty. He went to bed at eleven reading a weighty book on psychology. He turned out the light at twelve thirty. At four twenty five he awoke to The Spook Lady's harangue but fell asleep before she finished. Almost six hours of sleep. His technique of using himself completely each day is working. Six hours of deep sleep is a victory, any night. He is beginning to sleep through the Spook Lady's corrosive monologues. The quality of his sleep is essential to his avoidance of relapse.

Diz stirs next to his ankle. The dog snores, lightly, a little wheeze escapes from his muzzle and his eyes open. He farts a human sized fart. Aaron laughs.

"We're still on Earth, Dizzo. Do you recognize me? I recognize you. I remember you from the incarnation on Capella Prime. It has a much brighter star than the sun, our planet orbited out where Jupiter will be, and the climate is sweet. You are a beautiful Strem, that's a kind of hermaphroditic courtesan, there are more genders on Capella Prime than here."

The dog yawns and extends its front paws.

"I can see you don't believe me. No reason why you should, I'm talking nonsense to hear myself talk."

As Aaron levers himself out from under the covers he hears the sounds of the hallway

floorboards being pounded by running feet.

"Goon Raid!" someone is shouting. "Goon Raid!"

Aaron belts on his pants and squeezes tennis shoes onto his feet.

"Stay here, Diz, I want to see what's going on." Of course the dog ignores his command and follows along, tail wagging, head tilted with curiosity.

He walks into the hall and follows the general sense of tumult, around the corner and into the main corridor. He sees someone charging down the steps toward the second floor. Other people are emerging from their rooms,. Lori appears fully dressed in helmet and sweat clothes.

"Someone's getting evicted," she says. "That's what happens when people ignore my advice about basic safety precautions."

Aaron descends to the first floor and passes the check-in desk, where a member of the extended Patel family is indifferently reading a newspaper.

At the end of the hall there is a little clot of people hanging outside the door of the room occupied by Wags and George.

Aaron pushes his way through. Two men are stuffing George's possessions into a plastic bag. Wags is standing at the back of the room with his arms folded, wearing an insincere expression of sympathy.

"Don't let them do this to me!" George is on his knees. "I'll die out on the streets, please please!" He turns to implore his companion. Seeing no comfort there, he turns to the two men who are confiscating his worldly belongings. "I'll pay, I promise I'll pay, I don't know what happened to my check, honest, I don't know, it's coming, I called Social Security, I called everybody, they say they'll look into it."

Aaron has an utterly visceral memory of himself standing outside the door to his house, pleading with his mother to let him back in, waiting for the Black Truck to take him to the orphanage. He squeezes his way to the back of the room and takes Wags by the arm.

"Come here, I want to talk to you, outside." The force of his anger seems to propel the tall man. He acquiesces, and follows Aaron out into the hallway, through the knot of people, around the corner , down into the cul-de-sac. Diz stays at his heels but walks with such dexterity that Aaron forgets he is there.

"Where's the check?" Aaron demands. "I know you have the check."

Wags shrugs his shoulders and grins. "I don't know what you're talking about man, I tried to help him but Social Security's full of shit, they don't do nothing."

The transparency of the lie is so obvious that Wags looks like a school boy trying to talk his way out of impending disaster at the hands of a righteous teacher.

Aaron takes a step forward. Wags is five inches taller, probably outweighs him by forty pounds. "You're a liar and thief, you motherfucker, where's the goddam check!"

Wags reaches into the waist band of his blue jeans. Aaron grabs the man's wrist and squeezes it, lifting it. At the same time he uses his chest to bang Wags into the wall. He is simultaneously enraged and exhilarated.

I'm not the agressive type, he muses detachedly. This isn't what I normally do.

The squeezing pressure on Wag's wrist is so intense that the man drops the sheathed knife for which he has been reaching. "Hey!" he protests, but Aaron bangs him again, then takes both Wag's forearms in his hands and pins him to the wall, squeezing.

"Ow, fuck!" Wags grunts. He struggles but can't bring his elbows forward. He tries a head-butt. Aaron dodges this maneuver simply be being shorter than his opponent. Wags' chin brushes the top of his head. Aaron stands on his toes and puts his face inches from Wag's face. The experience of his own physical strength is so sweet he can barely restrain gleeful laughter.

"You're not a dumb guy, Wags," Aaron snarls theatrically. "You've got a vocabulary, I know, you're a prison reader, you go to the library, you check out any book you can, you've read everything in three or four state penitentiaries. You know words like 'intimidate, harass, vindictive, pernicious, prejudicial, malignant, virulent, pestilential', you know all the words. Well I'm going to give you some new words, simple words. GIVE ME THE CHECK! If you don't give me the check I will teach you some other words, like 'crippled', like 'lesion, trauma, concussion, laceration, bruise, contuse.' Hey, how about 'WHEELCHAIR!' How about that one, Wags? You wanna find out how nasty I can be, how many times I can mess with your future?"

"It's in my back pocket, man, let me go, I'll give it to you!"

Aaron pulls Wags' shirt so that the man is forced to the floor, to his hands and knees. He kicks at each elbow so that Wags' arms collapse, leaving him with his butt in the air and his forearms driving into the gritty carpet. There is an envelope in the man's left back pocket. Aaron removes it. It is already opened. Aaron steps back and examines the check. Diz thinks this is a fine game and is bouncing back and forth in front of Wags' face, growling and waiting for a response.

Aaron examines the check. "Already endorsed and everything. Wags, you're a noble-hearted gentleman, and I'm sure an excellent forger." Aaron kicks the knife down the hall. He leaves it where it lays as he walks towards the room where the eviction is proceeding. He glances back at Wags, who is looking in all directions, more concerned with being seen getting beaten than with the getting beaten itself. The man crouches and waits for an opportunity to retrieve his knife.

Diz follows in Aaron's footsteps.

Aaron waves the check at the Goons. He makes sure they can read the name, George Strickland. "Found the missing check. Rent's paid."

The Goons look at each other, shrug, drop the plastic bag and leave the room. The onlookers sigh with relief. Aaron helps George get off the floor.

"Let's go to the desk, George, and straighten this business out."

George's mouth is open. "Where did you find that? How did you......?"

"Your buddy Wags had it. Watch your back, George, people you trust will steal from you. It's happened to you before, hasn't it?"

George walks his pigeon-toed gait. He is a helpless, mildly retarded fat litle hippie wearing a denim shirt and pajama bottoms. "I don't know. Has it? Wags is my friend, he wouldn't do that."

"Listen to me, George. I know Wags is company for you, I know you need to have him around. Just don't let him near your Disability check. Be careful." At this thin edge of survival it only takes a single slip, a slight malfunction of the "system" and a person can slide down into homeless oblivion. Most of the hotel's occupants have a buddy, someone to watch their back. However uneasy or corrosive, these relationships are better than loneliness. They are indispensable.

He escorts the sad little man to the front desk and waves the disability check at Shankar Patel. "Give us a a little while, we'll cash this check and pay George's rent."

Shankar Patel looks over his newspaper, rattles the pages a little, gives a bored nod of his head. He pats his turban with one hand, then picks up the telephone when it rings.

* * *

Aaron turns off the light at eleven forty five, closes his eyes, takes a deep breath and examines his state of fatigue. It should be sufficient. He will sleep, the drowsiness will come, his brain will produce adequate endorphins without chemical assistance. He has used himself up, another day. He feels sleep creeping up from his toes as if his body is a soda straw and he is sucking sleep into his cells.

Then he smells the familiar cheroot smell.

"Zoot," he says, "I can smell you. Where are you?"

"I'm in the closet," Zoot's muffled voice replies.

Aaron ticks on the light and gets out of bed.

Diz perks up and watches his companion walk to the closet.

"Up here," Zoot says.

On the bare shelf with its torn sticky paper there is the apparition of the bodiless head of Zoot Prestige. The cheroot dangles from Zoot's mouth.

"Damn," he says, "I gotta work on my pinpoint accuracy. The High Flyers are gonna laugh their asses off."

"High Flyers?" Aaron inquires.

"Never mind," says the musicians' head, "I ain't here to create no hip theology."

"Aw come on, Zoot, let's titillate the audience a little bit, you can't drop hints like that and just walk away."

"Take this cheroot out of my mouth, it's burning my eyes and I ain't got no hands."

This is really ridiculous, Aaron thinks, but he reaches up and puts his thumb and forefinger around the nothingness where Zoot's cheroot appears, and it comes away from the saxophonists' mouth.

"What am I supposed to do with it?" He squeezes the object but his fingers pass through it.

"Just wave your hands, it'll disappear."

Aaron complies. "Okay, Zoot, High Flyers, come on, let's hear it."

Zoot Prestige sighs. "I can't run down the whole hierarchy of the spirit world, it's too complex, man. But there are three basic kinds of archangels. There are High Flyers, Low Blowers and Deep Fryers."

Aaron smiles. "I can see that. Cool. And you're a High Flyer?"

"Apprentice High Flyer. I'm workin' on it. I still got some problems with the precision, as you can discern." The head turns a full circle, lifts from the shelf and floats out into the room. Zoot grimaces as if he is trying to force out a particularly reluctant fart. Part of his body begins to appear beneath the head, there is a faint flickering of tuxedo jacket, but it then rolls back up into the head. "Damn," he says, "if this was a gig they'd be throwin' shit at me. These freaking quarks are moving so fast I can't quite see the lattice."

"

Oh man," Aaron groans and sits down on the bed. He looks at Diz. The dog is staring amiably at Zoot's apparition, wagging his tail.

"The dog sees you, Zoot."

"Of course the dog sees me!" Zoot says testily. "He's a High Flyer, he's one of the greatest and oldest High Flyers. His name is

Dizoyonunykupti. He came here to help you through some rough times."

The dog scoots forward so that his paws dangle off the edge of the bed. His smile is as broad a dog-smile as can be imagined. His pink tongue laps at the air and his nostrils expand and contract.

"Dizoyonun.....what?" Aaron tries to form the syllables but gives up. "Okay, I can accept that Diz is a High Flyer. Do I want to run into a Low Blower or a Deep Fryer?"

"You done already run into them, boy, that's what I'm here about."

"Tell me more," Aaron prompts.

"You know, I don't provide functional information, I just provide encouragement, that's all I can

do."

"That's all I ever needed for you to do, Zoot."

"Well, I just wanted to point something out to you."

"Yeah, what's that?"

"

You know that shit that happened with George this morning?"

"Right, what about it?"

"That is a lot more satisfying than being a dope fiend, isn't it?"

"I enjoyed it at many levels. I'm not my dad, you know, I'm not gonna take care of everybody's crisis, but I saw something evil going down and it pissed me off."

Zoot grimaces again and the rest of his body appears.

"Hot damn, got it!" he exults. He sits down on the bed and puts a spectral hand on Diz's head.

"You dog, you," he laughs. "Why are you fucking with me this way?"

Diz pants and wags his tail and smiles and rolls over on his back, legs twitching in the air.

"Okay, okay, I'll tell him," Zoot speaks to the dog.

He returns his attention to Aaron. "There will always be a little bit of addiction in you, the rest of your life. It doesn't go away completely. But you won't live the life of an addict. You know another life awaits you. You come through the shadow, your addiction, you come through good. I'm proud of you, we're all proud of you."

"The High Flyers, the Low Blowers, The Deep Fryers, everybody?"

"Don't test me, boy. You made your walk and your deal and your shame with the Low Blowers and the Deep Fryers. You've come to a new relationship with pain. You know it's part of the structure of life."

Aaron runs the inside of his fingernail across his lower teeth, then looks at his fingers in the dim light. "Guess I do. Guess I have. I don't like it, necessarily, but I don't have to numb it away."

He looks up again, and Zoot is gone. Diz is still wagging his tail.

Chapter Fifty

Lights
1983: San Francisco

Aaron turns the key in his mailbox at San Francisco Main Branch and removes three months accumulation of grocery coupons, copies of Downbeat Magazine and assorted threats from collection agencies. He considers throwing the latter in the trash can, but girds himself to begin paying his old debts. It is impossible to repudiate his earlier life, impossible to banish the outraged screams from the victims of his irresponsibility, however institutional.

There is an envelope from ASCAP, the organization responsible for collecting royalties on music under his copyright. It is a joke. He gets checks for sixty two cents, or thirty eight cents, twice a year. He has a few albums to his credit. There is "I Left My Socks In Heaven," "Feral Tenderness," "Electric Needlenose Pliers" and his best-seller, "Barking Platypus At Midnight." All received critical raves and then vanished without a trace, and are now only available at collector's record shops. The title song from the album "Barking Platypus At Midnight" sold some thousands of copies and got airplay in unlikely places, like Sierra Leone and Lichtenstein.

He considers throwing that envelope away but holds it for a moment. He throws away the junk mail, sets the magazines and bills on the countertop, and tears open his piece of mail from ASCAP. There it is, the statement, the check. Idly, he looks at the amount. Eight thousand two hundred eighty six dollars and twenty three cents. He looks again and his heart nearly freezes. This isn't real, he decides. He examines the statement. "Barking Platypus at Midnight," is being played in Australia, New Zealand, Fiji Islands, Japan and Thailand. It has somehow resurfaced. The statement shows an acceleration of plays, month by month, over the last six months. It is growing. It is a hit.

Daily life, Aaron decides, is merely the interval between thunderbolts.

"Diz, look at this," he waves the check at the dog as he returns to the sidewalk. He can't help himself, he jumps up and down, laughter boils from inside him, then tears.

"We're out of the Arlen Hotel, Diz! We can leave the eighth circle of Hell!"

Diz needs no help being happy, but he is appropriately excited. Aaron takes a knotted-up sock from his jacket pocket and the dog immediately chomps upon it. Aaron lifts the creature into the air. Diz growls and hangs on, kicking his back legs. Aaron swings the ecstatic dog in circles. The animal's jaws hold fast to the sock. No amount of centrifugal force can dislodge him.

Goodbyes
1987: Muir Beach, California

Aaron buries Diz under the wind-bent Monterey pine tree in the front yard. An hour ago he had been prepared to take the dog to the vet, to take Diz on his last car ride. The dog has forestalled him by dying on his little bed, only seconds after Aaron makes the appointment.

"You knew what to do, didn't you, Diz?" Aaron carries the little white body out to the promontory. Zuleika watches from inside the house. Aaron's children, Rashid and Ehud crowd into her clasp, tears streaming from their faces.

Aaron wants to be alone with Diz. His grief had washed through him months ago, when he knew

the end was coming. He cried into his wife's breast when he saw the dog failing, ached with every new spasm and tremor, every moan of pain that came from the animal's mouth.

He has been spared the agony of euthanizing the dog. Diz has seen to that, has taken care of Aaron right to the last breath.

"Dizoyonunykupti". Aaron speaks the name Zoot's spirit told him belonged to the "High Flyer", his little white dog. He has no doubt of its truth. Sometimes only really crazy things are true. The dog saved his life. Diz kept love alive in him when nothing else could. That was a job for an angel.

He digs a deep hole at the foot of the tree. The wind is fierce but the sky is utterly cloudless. Aaron can see San Francisco, twenty miles south, can see Sutro Tower and the Sunset District. At the bottom of the cliff the Pacific Ocean collides with big rocks. It roars and hisses and booms. There is a brown swathe of water a hundred yards offshore, giving way to a deep blue. Near the rocks, underwater seaweed tints the surf green. Seals are calling, their jovial noise fades and amplifies as the wind shifts.

The pine tree is like a ferocious old man, bent from the wind but undeterred from staking its claim on existence. I will stand here above the ocean and take the storms, the tree seems to say. I will breathe the salt air and listen to the voices of the waves for three hundred years. I will slowly shape myself to the demands of the wind but I will continue to grow.

Aaron loves the tree. He buries his dog at the foot of Old Man. He slips Diz into a pillow case. It is so odd to see this beloved form, limp and lifeless, so odd to see the head lolling, the eyes closed.

He puts the pillow case in the hole and covers it with dirt. When he is finished, he stands looking at the ocean. He is aware of where he is, aware of his family, of his home, aware of his journey through life.

"You brought me full circle, Diz," he says. "You stayed with me on the downward slope, you were my friend in Hell, you were steadfast and undisturbed through the most harrowing initiations in the land of the Shadow. You were the difference between life and death for me, you kept me caring and connected to something. You brought me here, to this beautiful place, to be with these beautiful people. Zoot is right, you are indeed one of the highest of the High Flyers."

Aaron looks around, wondering if this will be a moment when Zoot's ghost will pay him a visit. There is nothing. There doesn't need to be anything more magnificent than the day, the view, the tree, the house, the family.

Aaron pats the dirt into place and returns to the house, to comfort his wife and children and to be comforted by them.

Chapter Fifty One

Psychotherapy On The Ground

"So....how much more psychotherapy do you think I'll need?"

Sarah is wearing a sleeveless V-neck sweater and an emerald skirt. There is a gold chain with the Hebrew letter "Hai" around her neck, representing the expression L'chaim, 'to your health'. Her hair is long and straight, flowing down her back. Her posture is relaxed; she inhabits the familiar old chair as if she is sitting in the lap of a maternal presence.

Serena looks at her watch. This is the ritual, always the same, at the beginning of each session. Sarah asks the question, then Serena looks at her watch, as if to say "another fifty five minutes."

"Have I ever told you my prostitution theory of psychotherapy?" Sarah wiggles her eyebrows teasingly.

Serena knows that Sarah loves to tease. "No, but you're going to....."

"In therapy, you buy a relationship," Sarah begins, "because you can 't sustain one under any other circumstance. The therapist gets paid to be supportive, tactfully critical, occasionally brutal, always empathic. The therapist is not a real friend, not part of your daily life, although you can call one on the phone in times of crisis. In short, a psycho-hooker."

Serena looks sideways at her client. "You are bad," she says. "You are really bad."

"I know, " Sarah agrees. "I am reconciled to my badness. I have no problem with the more abrasive parts of my personality. In fact, I enjoy them thoroughly. So why don't you and I cut through the crap, I'll pay you for this session, and I'll even buy you lunch. What do you say? Break the rules, be daring, my therapy is over, it's been many years and we're like sisters and I don't need for you to be a blank slate anymore."

"I appreciate the invitation but you never know, you might need me again someday, so we'd better keep this on a professional basis." Serena has neither gained nor lost weight in the years since she met Sarah. She is both irresistable force and immovable object. She is in her own permanent state of grace.

"You know," Sarah muses, "All I needed to do in therapy is be in the same room with you and

breathe the same air. I could never say a word, and the result probably would be the same."

"The results will have been the same even if you'd never come to therapy."

Serena opens the office door and allows Sarah to precede her. "Don't misunderstand me. That wouldn't have been true of just anyone. But you would have found a way, you would have figured it out."

"Then give me my forty thousand dollars back." Sarah demands.

"Too late. I already spent it."

Chapter Fifty Two

Near Kansas City

Mark is driving in circles around the Mid-West. He knows he should go to Mexico or get on a plane to Bangkok, but he can 't shake the need for familiarity, can 't let go of the American landscape, the American food, the American cars. Unconsciously, he is circling St. Louis, he is held centrifugally on a string by his birthplace, by his need for comfort, home, mother.

He dares not go to St. Louis. He has pulled off a heist in Las Vegas, stolen a suitcase full of cash from Russian gangsters. Now he knows that he stole from the wrong people. It was like the money jumped into his lap. Gavril asked him to take some money to buy a couple pounds of coke, and he just kept driving. If his enemies are still looking for him, they will be watching in St. Louis.

He gets off Highway Forty and slides over to the old Sixty Six, with its feeling of abandonment, with its drying-up souvenir shops and dying motels. There are still stoplights when the highway goes through towns, still wooden fireworks stands and places to buy cherry cider.

The suitcase with the money is on the floor of the pickup truck, on the passenger's side. It is driving him crazy. He wants to spend it on something big, something real, like a Cadillac, but he is probably on some kind of ten-most-wanted-list, after shooting the fucking Russian who came after him. He is sure his face is plastered in every newspaper, every post office, every grocery store. Actually he is just an afterthought, a squib on police briefings: if you see a man fitting this description driving a pickup, stop him for questioning. Armed and dangerous. Approach with caution.

Mark just keeps driving and staying in crappy motels and getting hookers. He stops for gas, for fast foods, for sleep. He drives in a thousand-mile circle around St. Louis. Indiana, Illinois, Arkansas, Kansas, Nebraska, Iowa, down to Kentucky, then back to Illinois, then back up to Iowa and down to Kansas.

He sees a stop light ahead, slows the Ford pickup. A shot-up green road sign announces the name

and population of the town. Belton. Pop. 1,308. It has a water tower with a grinning football team mascot painted on it, and the words "Go Wildcats". All over the happy Wildcat are sinuous spray-painted griffiti, "jerk 107," "Gloria's Pussy," and "fuckface".

Mark hopes he can find a hooker. He sees a blinking motel sign next to a truck stop. "Majestic Motel," it says, blinking green and white. "Vacancy".

He yawns and glances at his watch. It is ten thirty. The Kansas sky is obliterated by the little town's mercury vapor lights.. Spring has come. It is a warm night, moist after recent showers. A smell of earth and ammonia rise from the fields, a pervasive fertilizer fug that is drawn in on every breath. On the horizon a flash of sheet lightning glitters briefly in the west, crawls across the endless wheat-planted prairie.

After checking into the Majestic Motel, Mark walks across the parking lot to "EATS". It is a faded white stucco building. Inside, two fans rotate slowly on the ceiling, while a burnt-out flourescent tube flickers fitfully in one of the light fixtures. The smell of hamburger grease hangs in the restaurant, along with an air of hopelessness and boredom. Two truckers are sipping coffee at the counter, discussing basketball scores. The maroon vinyl stools squeak as the men shift their weight and turn to pour sugar and cream into their cups.

A woman sits drearily in one of the four booths, looking out the window, waiting for more trucks to come along. When Mark enters the restaurant she shifts her attention, patting her hair and adjusting her blouse so the cleavage is more evident. She is in her late thirties and has a large pimple on the right side of her chin. Her blonde hair is brittle and sits atop her head as if it is not organically attached to her body.

Mark, holding the suitcase with the money in his hand, approaches the woman.

"Are you working?" he asks simply. "Can I sit down?"

"If it makes a mess you can be my guest," the woman says cryptically. Mark takes this as assent, and puts the suitcase into the booth ahead of him, then slides onto the seat opposite the prostitute.

A waitress comes to the booth, squinting dubiously, chewing gum.

"You gonna eat something?" she says, holding her pad in front of herself as if it is a shield.

"Cheeseburger, fries, a coke, to go." Mark responds. "Anything for you?" he asks the prostitute. She nods her head negatively.

"I ate already. My name's Rita. Where you from?"

"I'm Mark. I'm from St. Louis, originally, but I'm just coming from Las Vegas."

"Really?" Rita perks up. "I'd love to go there, I've never been farther than Nebraska, when I went to cosmetology school in Lincoln." She raises her hands, to display elaborately painted teal-colored fingernails. "See these? I do these myself."

Mark pretends to be interested. "That's nice. Isn't it hard, painting your own fingernails?"

The waitress brings Mark's order in a paper bag. He gives her a ten dollar bill. "Keep it," he says, magnanimously.

"You want to go to my room?" he asks Rita.

She squeezes out of the booth. She is a big woman, bulges of fat dangle from the sides of her blue leotard top. Mark doesn't care. He takes the suitcase and his food and leads the way through two parked semi-trailers back to the motel room.

Inside, he puts the suitcase under the bed and devours his food, while conversing desultorily with Rita. God, he thinks, people are so boring. Don't they have anything to talk about besides sports, the weather, hair spray, fingernail polish? I can sit here and carry on a conversation for a thousand years, mouthing the same old shit over and over again, saying 'uhuh', 'yeah', and she will just keep rattling around in the same circles, repeating her two great philosphical ideas about life, the one about 'you never know what can happen' and the one about 'if you got your health, everything else is gravy.' She's probably got two kids in their early teens who are turning out bad, husband's been long gone, either in prison or killed in a car crash, she lives in a two bedroom brick house behind the gas station, does her friends' fingernails for free and comes out to the truckstop every night to give blow jobs to truckers for twenty bucks a pop.

After he finishes his burger and fries, Mark sits next to Rita on the bed.

"So, how much do you want for a blow job? No condom, nothing fancy, just let me come in your mouth and then you can go back to the truck stop. Don't take your clothes off, I don't want to see your body or anything."

"Forty bucks," Rita says, her voice rising on the word 'bucks', making it sound like a question rather than a statement, betraying her true price.

Mark likes to be generous. He isn't going to quibble with this poor old cunt about her price. He takes two twenties from his wallet and gives them to the prostitute. Then he unbuckles his belt and slides his pants off, lying back on the bed with his legs dangling over the end. Rita kneels at the foot of the bed, taking Mark's erect penis in her hand. It is on the smallish side, not abnormally so, just diminutive by conventional standards.

"Isn't that a cute little thing?" the prostitute says.

The next thing Mark is aware of is the fact that his hands are gripped tightly in Rita's hair and she is moaning weakly, and that somehow they have both traveled across the room and are hunched up in a corner near the steam radiator. Mark's heart is beating fast, his left hand hurts around the knuckles, and he knows he has hit the prostitute, has dragged her across the room in one of his fits of rage, the fits that he can never remember, of which he can only suffer the consequences later.

I'm going to become a serial killer of prostitutes, he tells himself, with a combination of dread and anticipation. If one more hooker insults the size of my dick she will be dead.

He lets go of Rita's hair. She is stunned and half-conscious. The right side of her face is turning crimson, as if she has a bad sunburn.

The door of the motel room flies open and two big men in sport jackets and hats come sweeping into the room, pistols cocked and pointed in loaf-sized fists. Mark falls backwards against the wall. His heart ratchets up a notch, beating with an intensity that he thinks must be unbearable. His mind goes into overdrive and words just spill through his brain nonsensically. This is it, he thinks, they've found me, it's over. Probably a good thing anyway because I'm a danger to humanity I should be dead I'm going to kill somebody going to kill my mother no she's already dead damn I should have killed her a long time ago before she killed herself I wonder if killing her would have made me feel any better probably not everybody's got mother problems only not quite so bad as me......

He grabs his chest, feeling as if someone has just stuck a dagger into it. He crawls forward on his face for a few inches, as if he's trying to reach the suitcase. He can't breathe, can't breathe, and pain is slicing through his middle as if his body is breaking in two.

One of the men takes Rita by the arm and says in a thick slavic accent, "Get the fuck out of here, don't say nahthing."

The prostitute stumbles from the room, mumbling incoherently.

The other man kicks at Mark's body, turning it over onto its back. "Mahtherfucker's dead," he announces, after feelilng for a pulse. "We don't even hef to keel him. He saved us the trahble."

The first man has found the suitcase under the bed, opens it, checks its contents. As he turns to go, he looks at Mark's disheveled form.

"Christ," he says, "hell of a way to die, weet your pents around your enkles. Like Elvis. Fect is," he says, contemplating Mark's body, "he kinda looks like Elvis, don't he?"

"Little bit," the second man says, indifferently. "The poor esshole haven't got much between legs for such a big guy. Bet Elvis had bigger dick than this."

Chapter Fifty Three

The   Lap   of   Luxury's   Barb
1995: Warson Hills, Missouri

Marilee rattles the doorknob to Rosie's room but it is locked.

"I'm your mother," she commands. "Let me in, this instant!"

There is a hollow laughter from the other side of the door.

"What will you do?" Rosie derides. "Ground me? Cut me out of your will?"

Marilee uses her fist and her toe simultaneously, but the door is made from solid oak and it jars her tennis elbow and her lower back injury.

"What I'll do is take a hammer to that precious car of yours, I'll rip it to pieces!"

This brings the desired result. Rosie opens the door and pushes her face through the crack, snarling. Her face is a mask of make-up, her eyes are bat-wings of dark rouge, her lips are black, her cheeks exaggerated in corpse-like paleness.

"What....do....you....want?" The nineteen-year-old daughter and the forty seven year old mother breathe into each other's faces with malevolent vigor. Rosie is taller than Marilee, thicker of body.

Marilee regards her offspring with a cool stare, a gesture stolen from daytime soap operas. She is the still-glamorous matriarch, the powerful pre-menopausal sexpot who "keeps herself up".

"I want to see what you have in there. I want to know that if you're living under my roof you're following the rules I've set down."

Rosie opens the door and bows, extending an arm, inviting her mother to inspect the premises. "You will find your worst nightmares, darling," she mocks. "Look in my drawers, look under my bed. Here, let me help you." She rushes to her night table and opens the top drawer. "Here's the heroin." She waves a small plastic baggie of white powder, then tucks it into her shirt pocket. She goes to her closet and reaches into the pocket of a raincoat. "Here's the grass." She waves a sandwich-sized baggie full of dried chartreuse buds.

Marilee lunges forward but Rosie evades her grasp, jumping onto the bed, holding the bag of marijuana high over her head. "I'm not done yet!" she screams. "I haven't shown you the crack pipe, the syringe, the videotape of me fucking Brian. I haven't told you that I have AIDS and if you touch me I'll bite you and infect you."

"That's enough!" Marilee backs away a step. "You're moving out tomorrow, you can go find your own place, take your dope and your boyfriend and make your own way in the world without my help."

"Bullshit." Rosie comes off the bed, stalks her mother around the room. "I'm not going anywhere. I've dedicated my life to staying by your side. I'm going to live here until you wither and disappear, I'm going to make sure you die miserable, that's what keeps me going, that's what fuels my will to survive!"

Rosie's arms are crossed in front of her face, as if she is attempting to make an anti-vampire crucifix to ward off the evil spell of her mother.

Marilee regards the large chunky form of her daugher. "You have fat wrists," she says icily.

Rosie holds her breath for a long time. I will kill her, she thinks; if I take one step more. If I say another word. If I exhale. If she insults me again. If I so much as move, or twitch, or blink.

There are clocks ticking throughout the house. There are appliances humming. There is at least one television set playing somewhere in the vast contemporary mansion on Warson Road, with its tilted and louvered windows, its assymetrical and derivative architecture.

Two people live in this opulent tombstone, a mother and daughter, locked together in a sulfur wind.

Marilee unkinks herself, moving in robotic jerks. I didn't get her to kill me this time, she muses. Won't she ever kill me?

She backs towards the door, eyes locked on her child's eyes.

I didn't kill her this time, Rosie sighs inwardly. I wonder how much longer we can keep this up? We're running out of ammunition. I've used dad's philandering, I've used my promiscuity, my addictions, I've used her aging and her feeble intellect, she's used my weight, my makeup, my skin, my height, my friends, my grades, I've threatened to flush her vicodin, she's tried to ace my stash, I've ripped her fur coats, she's going to smash my car. Somebody's going to die, sooner or later.

Retreating to her room with its futile double beds, Marilee flips the remote control on the TV until she finds Jay Leno. The banter is unintelligible, it is noise, laughter, voices, nothing more. She goes into the bathroom and opens the medicine cabinet. There are thirty-two bottles of prescription medication. Vicodin, Prozac, Ativan, Xanax, Serax, Darvon, Quinalone, Preludin, Allegra, Sorbitol, Lomatil, Welbutrin, Percodan, in one milligram, two milligram, four milligram, eight milligram, fifty milligram, hundred milligram doses, duplicate prescriptions from duplicate doctors, careless prescriptions from careless doctors, paid prescriptions from paid doctors who just did not want to know.

Marilee takes four Vicodin and two Ativan, then returns to the bedroom where she makes herself a vodka and orange juice. Sipping this beverage from a thick crystal juice glass, she divests herself of her clothes and dons light blue silk pajamas. She neatly folds back the silk sheets on her bed and inserts herself into the warm coccoon, where she lies stiffly, reaching her hand towards the night table occasionally to sip her vodka. She stares at the television screen and tries to decipher the words being spoken, but they seem to be in a foreign language. Jay Leno gestures with his hands, grins and quips, and some young female movie star in a newly released film leans forward and back, forward and back, giving the cameramen a glimpse of cleavage, or, from the side angle, an actual breast outline, never quite showing the nipple. The audience laughs, the sound is like an autumn gust, moving dry leaves across an empty field.

What are they talking about? Marilee thumbs the volume up but it doesn't help. From the opposite side of the house comes the thumping of Marilyn Manson or some such ghoul band. I hate that sound, I hate it, that mindless garbage, Marilee fumes. She increases the volume on the TV. A commercial for beer yells at her but the sound washes over her like sea spray across the prow of a freighter. She sips long at her drink, refills it from a conveniently placed flask and thermos. In about half an hour the pills will start to work and they 'll mix nicely with the booze

and I can forget about all this stress and go to sleep.

She wakes up two hours later. Conan O'brien is quipping emptily and haughtily to a rock star with a newly released CD. She still can not understand the words.

She unsheathes her body from within the clasp of the sheets and returns to the bathroom. She opens one of the drawers under the marble and gold-enameled sink and withdraws a package of razor blades. Taking two blades carefully from the little rectangular plastic container, she finds some adhesive tape and wraps layers of it over half of each blade.

Marilee is unaware of any thought processes. She is unaware of any emotion. She is as empty as a baseball stadium in winter. She pads through the immense house, holding her drink in one hand. Her muscles are so lax that she bumps into doorways, sloshing the drink over her wrist. She is oblivious. Sliding the glass door aside, she steps out onto the deck. Unbuttoning her pajamas, she slips her clothes off her body and steps into the hot tub, daintily. The water is very hot. The night is warm, crickets chirp, the sound of the fountain next to the swimming pool trickles lazily across the four acres of well-trimmed lawn.

Marilee swallows the rest of her vodka, and then draws crosses on each wrist, side to side, up and down, just to be sure. It is surprisingly easy; there is no real pain, only a stinging sensation that is swallowed in the water's heat. The tape on the blade enables her to press down hard, and gushes of red erupt under the water, spreading quickly in the current of the jacuzzi. Just to be sure she makes a tic-tac-toe pattern of cuts. She tries, with a weak spasm of humor, to place an "X" in one of the boxes but gives it up and drops the blades into the steaming tub. They float, she thinks, like little fishes. Isn't that cute?

Didn't her mother commit suicide? Or was that a heart attack? She can't remember. She has a sudden vivid memory of her mother stooping to tie her shoe. It is a school day. Everyone else is crying, screaming, oh what a mess!

Everyone complained about what an awful witch her mother was. She doesn't feel that way. Mama was okay; nothing great, nothing terrible. She can't imagine why her brothers and sister still carry such hostility, such complicated feelings about poor Esther.

Chapter Fifty Four

Flesh of **Flesh**
1995: Muir Beach, California

Telephones don't ring any more, Aaron muses. They beep, they burble, they chirp. Someone should make a telephone that still rings, a good old-fashioned clang-dinger that will really shake you out of your bed in the middle of the night.

The damn thing is somewhere in the bedding. Zuleika comes awake, startled. Aaron has already been awake. He is usually awake at four thirty. It is his "thinking hour". It is the hour of The Spook Lady.

The phone ringing at four thirty can not be good news. When he finds it, under the quilt at the foot of the bed, he presses the talk button with a chill of fear.

"Hello?"

"Aaron....." Sarah's voice is weirdly flat. "Are you awake?"

"What is it, Sarah, is it dad?"

"Yes, it's dad, but it's more than dad.....it's .....unbelievable....."

"Somebody's dead. Mark? Marilee? God, I hope Lisa's okay, tell me Lisa's okay."

"Lisa's okay. Mark and Marilee.....they're both dead. And dad is dying."

Zuleika sits up and leans over Aaron. Knots of her copious black hair fall onto his chest. "Both dead," Aaron says. "Mark....and Marilee....." A ringing begins in Aaron's ears. He feels as if someone has just slapped him in the side of the head. "Mark and Marilee are dead, " he repeats, for his wife's benefit. She puts the fingers of both hands on her cheekbones. Her mouth opens in silent alarm.

Suddenly Aaron can hear his own heartbeat. It goes thump thump in both eardrums. He is waiting for it to falter, or stop. He knows he is going to die. A family curse has finally boiled up out of his genes, it has taken his brother, his sister, and is taking his father, all simultaneously. This is how it is going to happen. A cellular alarm clock has ticked out its final seconds for the Kantro family; they are all going to be felled by their pre-programmed flaws.

Aaron looks at his beautiful wife. I don't want to leave her, he thinks. I fought so hard to get here, to have this love in my life.

Then he gathers himself, pulls his courage and his fatalism into one old Jewish lump and draws another breath, and another.

"What's going on? Just tell me piece by piece. Start with dad. He's an old man, he's sick." he says at last, to a weeping Sarah.

"He has cancer of the liver," Sarah explains. "The doctors think he's got a couple weeks at best, it's very advanced. You know dad....he just quietly endures his pain, he won't say anything, but I can tell, I made him go to the hospital."

"Yes," Aaron agrees. "He has too much courage, it becomes a vice instead of a virtue, it becomes sheer masochism."

"That's dad." Sarah's voice fades as she turns away from the phone.

"And Mark? Marilee?"

There is a long silence. Sarah is breathing hard.

"Wait a minute...." Aaron expostulates with sudden grisly humor. "Let me guess. Mark killed Marilee.....or Marilee killed Mark. They killed each other. Or somebody killed them. Or they killed themselves. Oh god, Rosie! What about Rosie? Is she okay?"

Sarah weaps and laughs. "You bastard," she says. "Rosie's as okay as Rosie can be. Mark had a heart attack in a motel in Kansas. And

Marilee cut her wrists in her hot tub. Rosie found her. That's…you know…complicated."

Aaron feels a chest pain beginning. He puts his hand over his left nipple. Through his t-shirt he can feel his heart pounding and pounding. His whole body is in a state of absolute terror. Alarm sizzles at the endings of each nerve. He jumps out of the bed to escape his fear, but it follows him.

"Our whole fucking family's being mowed down!" he wails. Zuleika looks on helplessly, her eyes are sweet tragic pools. "Do you feel like you're going to die, too?"

"Yes! Exactly!" Sarah exclaims. "I don't have any great love for either of our siblings, but they are flesh of our flesh, and I feel as if this flesh, this Kantro flesh, is predestined for doom, for early doom."

"No!" Aaron says defiantly. "That's our morbid imagination, that's you and me, artists and hypochondriacs, I know that part of me, I know that. Every case of acid indigestion is a heart attack, every goddam case of tendonitis is the beginning of Multiple Sclerosis. Fuck it, we keep surviving, Sarah, we survive!"

He wants to shake his sister. He wants to shake himself.

"Hang on Sarah, we're not finished, not you and me.....I'll be on a plane to St. Louis as soon as I can book one. Tell dad not to die until I see him."

"Okay," Sarah sniffs. "You're right. I'm not going to die, I'm not going to die, not going to die." She hangs up the phone. Aaron knows that she is still repeating the phrase, that it is her mantra, will be her mantra until some sense of normalcy and continuity returns to their lives.

* * *

"Does he know about Mark and Marilee?"

Aaron and Sarah are walking up the stairs to the oncology ward at Jewish Veteran's Hospital. Their steps echo up and down the empty wells.

"I haven't told him," Sarah says. "How can I tell him? He's so sick, he's dying, he doesn't need this grief."

"He'll find out. He'll wonder why Marilee isn 't at his bedside, wailing and screaming and carrying on. Or one of our big-mouthed relatives will tell him, nobody can maintain a secret in this family. They don't know. Nobody knows, except Rosie. Mark's body will be here tomorrow, it's coming as cargo on TWA. I have to pick it up at the airport. Will you come with me? It's really kind of creepy."

"I'm here for whatever needs to be done."

"The funeral is Wednesday, for both of them, they're going next to mom."

"Fitting place for them." Aaron pulls himself upward on the steel handrail. Sarah stops, just outside the door to the sixth floor. "Dad looks bad, I have to warn you."

"I've already imagined how he looks. What are his spirits like?"

Sarah hesitates, as if she does not quite know how to describe her father's mental and emotional state.

"He's.....he's peaceful. He's in great pain and won't take anything for it, not even an aspirin."

"Stubborn bastard," Aaron says. "I'd take dope in a second if I was in that kind of pain and knew I was going to die."

"Me too." Sarah looks through the glass at the hospital corridor. "Of course we come from a long line of expert drug consumers and pain avoiders."

Aaron responds with an ironic snort.

The stairwell is like an alternate universe, bare and poorly painted. Beyond the door is one of America's finest hospitals, efficient, clean, carpeted. "When I go," Sarah adds, " I want to be cremated, I'll donate my organs but the rest of me should go up in smoke."

"I'll be cremated, but nobody wants my organs. They've been too saturated with drugs. I have Hep C antibody but my liver works fine. Don't know how I did that; maybe Yoga saved my liver, I don't know." Aaron pats his abdomen gratefully.

After a mutual intake of breath, brother and sister push the door and enter the sixth floor. Sarah leads Aaron to the room. Its door is slightly ajar. Aaron knocks politely, then enters without waiting for a reply.

Max is lying on the bed, with a book resting on his chest. There are no fancy machines attached to him, only a glucose drip. His wife, Renate, is in a chair at the bedside, also reading a book.

"Look at you two." Aaron says. "Reading." He takes in his father's appearance quickly. It is not as bad as he feared. Max is thin, wasted, pale, but he seems in utter possession of himself.

Renate gives Aaron a wordless look of grief and exasperation, and kisses him on the cheek. "It's so good you can be here," she says. Her Czech accent is still thick, in spite of forty years in America. On her wrist, underneath a gold bracelet, is the sloppy Auschwitz tattoo, blue numbers across her tendons.

Aaron leans over and kisses his father. Max grunts. His eyes fog over with pain. Then, with some kind of superhuman effort, Max forces himself past his pain, and his face clears.

"Why don't you take something?" Aaron remonstrates. "What's the point of suffering like this?"

"I want to keep my mind clear," Max insists. "I'm only going to last another couple of days. I can handle it."

"That's a great big myth, that morphine 'clouds the mind', although I have to admit my take on the subject is less than objective." Aaron holds Max's hand. There has always been self-consciousness about touching between father and son, their embraces have been awkward and infrequent. Max squeezes Aaron's hand as if acknowledging this truth, hoping, now, to change it.

"Dad, pain can cloud your mind more than drugs."

"It's your suffering you want to alleviate, not mine," Max observes. "I'm used to pain. It's an old friend."

"Okay, okay," Aaron holds up his hands in surrender. "I know better than to argue with you."

Sarah pulls up an extra chair and takes her place beside the bed. Max eyes his children. He squints skeptically and wrinkles his nose.

"Something's up," he says, "I can smell it. You two are holding a secret. I know you too well. What's happened?"

Aaron and Sarah look at each other and shrug. Taking a big breath, Sarah delivers the news.

"Mark was found dead in a motel in Kansas."

Max pulls his lips tight with his fingers, kneading them.

"Oh my god," he says. "Did someone kill him?"

"No. Apparently it was a heart attack. We don't know what he was doing there. Maybe he was coming home."

Max's breathing lurches and then settles. "I always think someone will kill him, or he will kill someone. What else is there? Something else has happened. I'm psychic, you know, I've always told you I'm psychic. It's not Lisa because you would be out of control. So that leaves Marilee. She killed herself, I know it. She became her mother, she has always been her mother, the poor girl."

Sarah nods. There is a long silence in the room. Lunch carts roll past outside with dishes chinkling. Two nurses giggle naughtily as their voices fade down the hall.

Then Max begins to laugh. It starts slowly, a few 'huh's. It builds, becoming faster and deeper, until Max is laughing so hard his entire body shakes the bed.

Aaron has never heard a laugh such as this one, coming from his father. It is a laugh earned over a long life of suffering and struggle. Max laughs so hard that Aaron, Sarah and Renate can not help but laugh along with him. They hold themselves, doubled at the waist, twitch and roll and wipe their faces with the backs of their hands.

"I shouldn't laugh over such things," Max says, finally. His breath comes in fits but his face is pink and happy. "But I visualized the funeral. They'll all be there, the whole rotten clan, crying crocodile tears. The idea of Esther, Marilee and Mark being buried side by side, it's just......so fitting, so ironic, so perfect." He points a finger admonishingly at his children. "Don't you dare bury me there! Cremate me. Put my ashes in a dixie cup. Make an ash sno-cone, I don't care about that. Just don't bury my body near them."

"We wouldn't think of it," Aaron insists.

"It hurts, don't get me wrong." Max squeezes his own breast with bony pale fingers. "But I just can't take on any more pain than I've already got. Those poor bastards. They are my children, MY children. They are monsters, but still they are MY children. I don't want to imagine where their souls are right now. Is Rosie okay?"

"Rosie is both devastated and relieved. It will be tough for her. You know.... the more you hate a parent, the more difficult this kind of thing is," Sarah points out.

"Imagine such a fate. Having people relieved at your death. I won't have any of that. I did my best in this world, I know where I stand with God." Max holds out his hand for his wife. Renate takes it. They share a deep, loving glance and Aaron's heart twists with empathic terror. How would he feel if he lost his wife, today, tomorrow or thirty years hence? He feels as vulnerable as a nestling fallen from a tree. The price of love, he knows, is such vulnerability. How hard he has worked to protect himself from loving! How determined he was, when he was running from commitment. At the time, he deceived himself. He wanted his freedom, he wanted sex and fun! In truth, he couldn't tolerate the terrors of love. First, he had to learn to tolerate the terrors of himself.

Another secret lives in the room, held between Max and Renate. She is ill with cervical cancer. She will follow Max, in a few weeks or months. She is well content with this state of affairs. Their marriage of twenty four years has been a miracle, and she has no desire to live with her children into doddering and helpless old age.

"What's today?" Max asks . "Monday? Their funeral must be Wednesday." Wincing, he sits up and plucks the catheter from his arm. "Check me out of this place. I'm going to the funeral. Then you can take me home. I plan to die on Friday. I was born on a Friday, I can die on a Friday." He looks at what remains of his family. "You're not going to dissuade me, so don't even try." He swings his feet to the floor, and beckons Aaron to his side. "Just give me your arm, be my strength for a few more days."

"We'll take you home, dad," Aaron says. He doesn't try to squeeze his tears down, as he might once have, in the presence of his father. It is good, to let your dad see you weep for him. It is good.

"We'll take you home," Aaron repeats.

"It's better this way," Max says, his voice weakening as a wave of pain sweeps through his body. Then he pulls energy from some unfathomable source, and levers himself to his feet. "I don't want to die in a hospital. I've given the bastards enough money as it is."

He puts one arm around Aaron, and his other arm around his wife. He gives Renate a secret squeeze. It says a thousand things in a thousand languages, all of which translate the same: I love you. How grateful I am to have found you.

Chapter Fifty Five

Hounds **Of** **The** **Taliban**
1996: Kabul, Afghanistan

Taliban's rockets hiss overhead as they fall on Kabul, landing in the neighborhood of Kabul University. Aaron sees a cloud of brick-dust where a rocket has exploded, feels the concussion as it passes up through the car's wheels and suspension. Kabul is in chaos, there are people running in every direction, pulling wagons, driving cars, whipping donkeys, carrying mattresses on their heads. The city is in a state of collapse. There is no running water, no electricity, no police, no telephone. There is no government, just armed gangs contending for each block, each quarter, each neighborhood. Taliban is poised on the outskirts of the city, with tanks, jets, helicopters, artillery.

Aaron bounces into this cauldron as a passenger in an olive green Land Rover. He occupies the middle car of a three-car convoy. In front and behind, in identical dust-covered Land Rovers, are six mercenaries: two South Africans, an Israeli, a Belgian, a Frenchman and two Americans. There are white letters painted on the hoods and doors of each Land Rover. In English, Arabic, Farsi and Pakhtun they says, simply "Official". This is the idea of the Australian who occupies the driver's seat in Aaron 's vehicle, a man who calls himself Colonel Strathers. In the back seat are two retired sergeants-major from the British Special Air Services. The nine men are independent contractors from an international firm called Special Solutions.

Aaron has a special problem. Four days ago he had been celebrating Zuleika's birthday at Muir Beach. The house was full of people. Aaron loves odd conjuctions of people, he likes to mix friends from different areas of his life: Afghans, Hell's Angels, psychotherapists, Buddhists and musicians.

The phone rang. Aaron excused himself and ran down the stairs to take the call in the recording studio.

The voice on the phone is female, with an upper crust British accent. "Hello, I'm calling for

Aaron Kantro".

"That's me," says Aaron.

"You don't know me but my name is Catherine Sloan, I'm a correspondent for the London Times."

"I know who you are, Ms. Sloan.....I really admire the work you do. I've been avidly reading your Afghanistan dispatches." Aaron pulls his drum stool out from behind his kit and sits on it. He twiddles a drumstick through his fingers. "Why do I get the feeling this call is not good news?"

"I don't know what kind of news it is, let me tell you the story and then you can decide."

"Okay." Aaron's body is taut. He knows the call is about Murid and Fatima. They have returned, yet again, to Afghanistan.

"I was in a little town called Darrahe Zargal, about forty miles northwest of Kabul. It's a bad place to be, Taliban had taken it from Shah Masoud just as we arrived and we got caught in a no-man's land. Frankly, that's what we wanted to happen but we got a little too close to the edge, if you know what I mean. It was way beyond dangerous. Taliban stopped our cars. They dragged me out and threw a sheet over me like the sight of my exposed wrists was an affront to their eyes. They started beating my cameraman, and they took our guide away somewhere and were about to shoot him when a man jumped out of nowhere and started arguing with the Taliban soldiers. It was an incredibly brave thing to do, or a stupid thing to do, I don't know which."

"And that was Murid," Aaron states.

"That was Murid Syed Shah," Catherine Sloan confirms. "He bought us enough time to get our people back and get in our cars and drive to Kabul. He cited some Koranic text about the angels who visited Lot's house, how they were protected from the citizens of Sodom. That got the Taliban maniacs to arguing and consulting their Mullah. Murid knew they would come back to arrest him but he can't leave without his mother. So he told me to call you."

"And the last place you saw him was Darrahe Zargal?"

"That's the last place I saw him. I know what you have to do next if I'm reading this situation correctly."

"I'm sure you are. Any suggestions?"

"Do you have plenty of money?"

Aaron laughs. "Ever heard a song called 'Barking Platypus at Midnight'?"

Catherine Sloan makes a sound with her tongue, attempting to replicate the non-existent bark that has made the recording so comical. "You mean that crazy song they play on Japanese TV quiz shows? And the Australian Biscuit commercial?"

"That's the one. That's mine. Nobody in the states believes it. Anyway, money's no problem. Who should I call?"

"Try Colonel Strathers. He's in Tel Aviv right now but I know he's available and he's got men and equipment in Pakistan. I've got his number right here."

Another Taliban rocket hisses overhead, landing somewhere near Kabul Polytechnic. The Land Rovers lurch over brick and timbers in the street, turn right towards the ruins of what had been Kabul's architectural landmark, the Great Mosque of Puli Kishti. The bare flanks of the mountains loom behind the city, ominous and brown. Huge columns of smoke rise from Bagram Air Base, to the west, where Shah Masoud's army has occupied it after the Soviets evacuated. The Mujahiddin of the older generation are being bombarded by their own sons and nephews, the Taliban fanatics who grew up in Pakistan's refugee camps.

The streets grow more crowded. Colonel Strathers flicks on the siren and the rotating orange light mounted on the car's roof. He speaks into his hand-held radio. "Let's give 'em a bit of the howler, mates."

The other drivers put on their sirens and lights, and the convoy speeds through suddenly scurrying people.

"Amazing how that works," the Colonel laughs. He is a tall man with a face that looks as if a blacksmith has been hammering on it. In his late forties, he is dressed in local clothes, sporting a full beard. He has specialized in Central Asian trouble shooting since the late seventies. For twenty thousand dollars a day plus materials he and his men can solve problems anywhere in the region. Utlizing high technology, forgery, audacity and, when all else fails, sheer force of arms, he can find his way into and out of hostile situations.

The convoy has gotten into Kabul with the help of a global positioning sattelite device, driving through dry riverbeds and across a wasteland of bony pebbles. The roads are impassable. The border is choked with trucks and buses and Pakistani authorities are not allowing anyone to cross into Afghanistan.

Nonetheless Colonel Strathers has gotten them to Jalalabad, has pushed them upstream against a river of fleeing refugees and finally into Kabul. Anyone else would have said, "too dangerous, impossible, the roads are mined, there's a war on , can't do it." Strathers made his living doing the impossible. Aaron is impressed, in awe. He is also exhausted, and wonders how the Colonel and his men exist on such a steady diet of adrenaline.

"Turn left," Strathers barks into his radio. He has seen a knot of armed men a hundred yards ahead. There really isn't any "left" to turn into, just a crevice between buildings that closes around the vehicles until it is nudging the external mirrors on both sides. It debouches, finally, into a wider street, where only moments before it had seemed like a cul-de-sac, a trap. Strathers betrays no tension. He knows Kabul intimately. He watches Aaron exhale, and gives him the faintest hint of a mischievous wink.

Coughing brief commands, Strathers takes his three Land Rovers out the other side of Kabul without encountering a single roadblock. The convoy turns onto a rutted road leading to Darrahe Zargal.

Aaron has surrounded himself with this phalanx of centurions for one simple reason: to protect the money he is carrying, to enable him to spend an estimated fifty thousand dollars in cash, gold and diamonds. This isn't a Ken Follett novel, there isn't going to be a daring jailbreak with helicopters dangling rope ladders into impregnable fortresses. If Murid and Fatima are still alive, fifty thousand dollars can get them out of Afghanistan. It might cost Aaron half a million to spend his fifty thousand, but that's okay, that's Barking Platypus money.

The road runs alongside the Kabul River for about five miles, then turns to follow a little tributary. The terrain becomes steeper, the Land Rovers begin tipping back and forth as their wheels grind over eroded ruts. The Colonel chews intently on half a Tiger's Milk candy bar and works the gears, judging the road surface. Aaron digs on the floor of the vehicle through ammunition boxes and old candy bar wrappers until he finds a water bottle. He passes it to the Colonel and turns to look at the two Englishmen in the back seat. They are playing cards calmly, swaying with the motion of the vehicle, slapping their winning hands down on the armrest and holding them in place with their palms.

"Were you guys in the Falklands?" Aaron asks .

Jeremy, the taller of the two, looks up from his cards. "I was a corporal at the time, I was eighteen. Royal Lancers. We did the night assault. It wasn't any joke, let me tell you. Some of my mates got killed."

The other man, Scott, rolls down the window and spits onto the road. "It was nawsty," he drawls. "Jeremy crapped his pants, 'e was so scared."

Jeremy sails a card at his colleague. "Bugger, you were ten years old, you needed your diapers changed, your mummy was still giving you warm cocoa."

"I've seen me share of action," Scott bristles. "We can't all be grizzled veterans like Jeremy, boring all his pub-mates with stories of the 'orrible Falklands Campaign'. Eh?"

Aaron recognizes a routine when he sees one. The Colonel pours water over his head, then passes the bottle backwards. "These two," he explains, "have spent most of their careers pretending to be competent military advisors to various African dictators. They're an unsavory, disreputable lot, hardcore killers, willing to sell their services to the highest bidder. Not to be trusted."

The car lurches and its wheels spin fruitlessly for a moment, then regain their grip. Ahead of the convoy the road disappears into a defile between bare crags. Strathers speaks into the radio. "Let's pull over for a minute, mates, I want to consider the terrain. I don't like the look of that." He points towards the rocky notch, fingers gripped around the black plastic transmitter.

The three Land Rovers pull up in a cloud of dust. To their left, a hundred feet below the road, runs the small swift river.

Strathers gets out of the car, stretches, and opens up his laptop computer, putting it on the vehicle's hot roof. The other members of the convoy emerge from their respective Land Rovers. "Take the mine detector and make a sweep," he orders two men from the first car. "Let me know what else is up there." The rest fan out and make a loose perimeter around their position, assault rifles held loosely in their hands.

The Colonel consults a topographical map in his data base, but seems to derive no satisfaction. "It will take us a day to bypass this ravine. It's a beautiful spot for an ambush, but we've got no choice."

He speaks again into his radio. "You guys okay? What do you see?"

"No mines," the voice responds. "Little bits of metal, like there's been some fighting here, the MDR is picking up lots of little shards but nothing big enough to blow us up, unless it's plastic. There's been plenty of traffic through here recently."

The group waits by the cars. In the distance is a rumbling of artillery. It has become part of the sonic backdrop of Afghanistan. Occasionally a louder thump will emerge from the general muted thunder.

The Colonel drinks more water and paces away from the Land Rover to peer down at the river. Aaron walks alongside.

"I love Afghanistan," Strathers speaks sadly. "I love Afghans, from the Hazaris and Pushtuns to the Koochi nomads, there are no more lovely people on this earth." He sits down on his haunches and tosses a rock down into the gurgling stream. His bristly beard and loose clothing make him look thoroughly Afghan.

"This country is really fucked. It's going to be fucked for a long time. It's such a bloody shame. It's not really even a country. It's a bunch of tribes stacked atop one another. They should call it 'Af-Confuse-istan'."

Aaron lets a long breath out through his nose and wipes the dust from his face with a piece of rag. He is unable to comment. He has reduced the Afghan tragedy to a personal and private struggle to save his friends. All else is beyond his powers.

The colonel glances at him, squinting against the sun's glare as it bounces off the water in the river. "You married an Afghan woman, didn't you?"

Aaron nods assent.

"So did I," the colonel informs him. "Depends on the class and the tribe; some of them are not submissive like other Muslim women, they're ferocious and independent. But that depends on where they're from, what tribe, what area.....like Koochi women...my wife is Koochi, and she's a piece of work, she tells me where to get off when I need telling, believe me. I like that. I want a partner, not a slave."

"My wife is from an upper class Kabul family, educated, urban. No burqas, none of that stuff."

Thinking of Fatima, Aaron laughs. "Afghan woman won't like Taliban. They won't like being put back in the burqa and being taken out of their schools and jobs."

The radio coughs. "There's nothing up here that I can see," the voice says. "It's very tight and close, not much room to get out if something happens."

"All right, " Strathers decides. "Let me take the lead, bring your cars around behind us."

"Okay, boss."

When the two scouts emerge from the ravine, the group gets back into their cars and sort themselves out to enable Strathers to take the lead. The Colonel pulls at Aaron's sleeve as he is about to enter the vehicle.

"Why don't you go back to the middle car, no use in taking the point with me."

"No way," Aaron says firmly. "If something happens I want to be as close to you as possible."

"Have it your way then," Strathers allows. He then speaks to his soldiers. "I want everybody alert and ready. Scott, put a TOW on the roof." He is referring to a portable anti-tank weapon, a wire-guided missile launcher.

The men scramble to their positions on the Land Rover's running boards. Scott climbs onto the roof and lies atop the strapped-down Kevlar cargo containers, holding the TOW launcher across his shoulder and resting its weight on the luggage racks. To keep from bouncing off, he has worked his feet into the straps that crisscross the vehicle's roof.

The convoy inches forward, into the ravine. Shadows close in. Lizards scuttle into cracks in the rock as the three cars slowly grope around a curve. Each car maintains fifty yards distance from its nearest companion. Aaron can imagine the fissure in which they drive as being the result of some ancient collision of heat and ice, as if a giant had poured boiling water on a frozen mountain and it cracked open in sudden zigs and zags. It is impossible to see ahead for more than ten yards before the rock face hides the road from view.

The first corpse is just a smear with clothing. It has been covered in a seething black crawling mass of vultures that suddenly take flight when the Land Rover comes around an angle of the trail. A charred pickup truck is flattened against one side of the ravine.

"Watch the heights, watch the heights," the Colonel speaks into the radio, unnecessarily. All his men are aware of the dangers of moving through Afghan ravines.

There are more corpses, more vultures loft silently up onto the wind that is bottling through the canyon, carrying with it the smell of death. Trucks and jeeps and unidentifiable pieces of crushed steel cling to the ravine walls like bits of old wallpaper.

"They cleared this off with a tank," the colonel says. "Just rolled over the bodies, squashed the cars. Nice. Looks like it happened maybe two days ago." The Land Rover lurches sickeningly. Vultures land in their wake, flap up in the air for each car, then settle finally when the third car has passed. Aaron closes the window against the stench, then opens it rapidly to vomit. The other men are pressing their shirt tails to their faces.

"I smell diesel," Strathers says suddenly, putting on the brakes. The other cars stop and hold their fifty yard intervals. Everyone listens intently and sniffs the wind. There is a distinct smell of burning fuel. Then, before anyone can move, an olive painted behemoth burbles around an angle of the ravine face and appears on the road in front of them. It is a Soviet-made T-60 tank, its dome-shaped turret looking like a blister on a fist of tracked steel.

"Steady, mates," the colonel whispers. "If that gun lowers and aims, fire the TOW."

The tank and the convoy achieve a lethal equipoise, each standing before the other, blocking the way. The tank's cannon stays at a forty-five degree angle. A little hatch in front of the turret flips open and a face appears.

Its incongrous, thinks Aaron, to see a turban and a wild beard popping out of the driver's seat in a tank. The machine is sporting a crudely painted insignia, the crossed-swords logo of Taliban.

"What the hell is he doing?" The colonel wonders. Aaron picks up a pair of binoculars from the utility slot under the glove compartment and looks at the man. He is waving at Strathers' column, plainly gesturing for someone to approach. He looks like a toy figure, a pop-up creature in an arcade game of"bash-the-chipmunk".

Strathers opens the car door and gets out. "Anything happens, blow the fucker up and get out of here," he orders. When Aaron tries to get out his side of the car, the colonel holds his palm up, peremptorily. "Not this time. I don't need your help. You stay right where you are."

He walks ahead, his boots crunching on little rocks, and approaches the tank like a sacrificial Cretan virgin walking into the Minotaur's cave. For two mintues he speaks to the tank driver, then walks back, hands hanging loose at his sides, shoulders slightly hunched. He gets back into the car and puts both hands on the steering wheel and stares straight ahead.

"What?" Aaron finally asks . "What did he say?"

Colonel Strathers grins slyly and combs his beard with his fingers.

"He wants to know if we're here to buy the heroin."

Aaron laughs, then coughs and pats himself on the chest with his fist.

When he can talk, he says, "You didn't disabuse him of that notion, I trust?"

"

No, I did not. He wants us to follow him into Darrahe Zargal."

"Strip away the fundamentalism and the geopolitics and it all boils down to heroin," Aaron murmurs bitterly. "A hundred years from now historians will call this the Heroin War."

As he speaks, the tank's turret rotates one hundred eighty degrees and the huge vehicle throws its treads into reverse and begins crawling back the way it has come.

Darrahe Zargal had been a town of a couple thousand people. It has a mosque and a police station. Most of the buildings are smoking ruins, or stand with holes punched through their thick walls, revealing furniture and clothing like some pornographic display of private worlds made obscenely public.

Seventy or eighty Taliban soldiers squat in the main square or loll against trucks and jeeps. There are five corpses hung from hastily made gibbets, some dangling by their ankles from ropes. Aaron looks anxiously to see Murid's face among the executed. He does not.

"Don't meet any of their eyes," Strathers suggests, as if the Taliban are wild dogs liable to attack at any provocation. Aaron can feel the hostility in the air as their convoy follows the tank up to the front of the police station. The tank driver stops his vehicle and jumps out of the hatch to the ground. Jeremy drops his head into the driver's side window.

"Guess what?" he says to the Colonel. "They're out of ammo."

"How do you know?" asks Aaron.

"I know. There's a look, an 'out-of-ammo' look, that soldiers get when they've been winning and can't keep winning until they get more ammo. They've got that look."

"He's right," the colonel confirms. "Bet there aren't fifty rounds of seven six two in the whole town. They're waiting to be resupplied. They're hungry, too."

He lets out a huge sigh and his shoulders drop back into their natural position. "We still operate as if these dogs have sharp teeth," he admonishes his companions.

He speaks into the radio. "Looks like they're short of bullets, mates, but fan out and watch yourselves. We're going inside."

Aaron and Strathers get out of the car, while the two other cars park themselves at angles to the first car, circling the wagons, making a defensible perimeter. Strathers' men space themselves evenly behind the cars, watching in all directions.

Half dozen young men of the Taliban stand in front of the entrance to the police station. There is no door, it has been blown off. The men are filthy, dressed in the usual assortment of baggy pants, vests, long irregular turbans. One of them is pointing his AK-47 at Aaron and pulling the trigger. The gun goes click, click. The man then draws a finger across his throat, gesturing clearly. He smiles a sick, superior smile that makes Aaron's stomach churn with anger and frustration. Go fuck yourself, Aaron thinks inanely. Sometimes he hates human beings, hates the world they have made, that he too has made.

An older man comes rushing out of the police station and pushes at the younger men, shouting in Pakhtun, "Get out of here! Go away!"

Reluctantly, the fighters allow the foreigners into the police station. The older man shouts angrily at several more young men inside the police station. "Didn't I tell you to leave? Do you obey your mullah? Do you obey the writ of the Koran? Do you respect your elders?"

They depart, leaving Aaron, Strathers, the tank driver and the elder man alone in the blasted office. There is a desk, some file cabinets and a few wooden chairs. The officer takes a seat behind the desk and offers two chairs to his guests. The tank driver primes an assault rifle and stands guard at the open door.

"These young soldiers know nothing of the drug trade, they are innocents," the commander explains. "They think all these weapons and ammunition appear as if by miracle, at the command of Allah." He caresses his own forehead with the middle finger of his right hand, running it up from the bridge of his nose to his turban. The hand shakes slightly.

Aaron and Strathers seat themselves warily. A wind comes through the open window behind the desk and rattles some papers that are weighted down with a spent mortar casing.

"All right, let us proceed," the commander says. "My men don't want you here, they will kill you as enemies of Islam but I have persuaded Mullah Ibrahim that the Jihad is best served by this trade."

Aaron and Strathers understand that they have entered a transaction in mid-negotiation, that someone else has been communicating with this man, has arranged this deal. They look at one another briefly and Strathers nods imperceptibly, allowing Aaron to enter the breach.

"Let's get on with it," Aaron says, "Show us the drugs."

The Taliban officer stands up and takes a chain of keys from a drawer in the desk. "Follow me," he says, and walks towards the detention section of the jail. There is a door, which is unlocked by the commander. This leads to a small corridor, off which four cells are built, each covered by a stout wooden door into which a tiny grate has been set at eye level.

A voice comes from the first cell, speaking in plain English. It says, "I am here." It is Murid. The commander bangs with his fist on the cell door. "Shut up, pig! Be silent!"

Aaron says nothing. He follows the commander to the last cell. The Afghan opens the cell door, enters, and beckons Aaron to follow. Strathers remains vigilantly outside the cell.

Within the chamber is a small cache of arms and food. In one corner there is a wooden box with an eyebolt latch. The commander opens this box and tilts it so that Aaron can see inside. There are four bricks of heroin wrapped in transparent blue plastic, bound with white masking tape.

Playing the role, Aaron picks up one brick. A kilo of smack, he thinks. He uses his Zuni amulet to slice open one corner, and prizes a little dot of heroin from the package. He puts it in his mouth, pretending to test for quality. He knows quality, he doesn't have to pose as an expert heroin smuggler. It is heroin, it tastes like heroin, it smells like heroin. It is first rate heroin. Aaron's body memory surges upward and says "Give me some more, give me some more." For a moment, he wants to swallow the bitter powder in his mouth. It will ease his fatigue, relax his quivering nerves, soothe away the jet lag and the kernel of terror at the pit of his stomach as he sits among all these armed and completely crazy people.

Amazing, he thinks, how much of me still is drawn to this stuff, still wants to get high. In this bag are a thousand sighs of ectasy, a million groans of despair. "I'm still an addict," he realizes. "Zoot's spirit was right when he told me at the Arlen hotel, I'll be dealing with this desire for the rest of my life. I have to be very careful, very honest, and keep good people around me forever."

He puts the brick back into the box and spits onto the floor. He takes Strather's water bottle and gargles, spits again, ridding his mouth of the drug's trace. To be thorough, he checks the other bricks, opening each at a different place, drawing bits of rock-powder out of various parts of the object.

"

It's good," he says in Pakhtun. He now needs to guess how much the four kilos cost. He has put five thousand dollars into his vest pocket, fifty one hundred dollar bills. He takes out the envelope and counts forty of them, holds them in the air. The officer has silently counted out the money along with Aaron. With one glance Aaron understands that he is about to overpay. He puts ten more hundreds back into the envelope.

"Do you want the other two thousand?" he asks the man.

They assess one another's situations. Aaron is in a strange country with nine well-armed men, carrying money. The Taliban commander has a whole company, out of ammo, broke, hungry.

"What do you want?" The commander asks .

Aaron produces a photograph of Murid and Fatima. "Are these people here? Their relatives have authorized me to pay a ransom if I find them."

The man's eyes go to the first cell. He pretends to study the photograph but is thinking quickly.

"We are going to try them tomorrow morning, in Sharia court. Then we are going to hang them. I cannot let you have them without speaking to the Mullah."

"Let me see them," Aaron demands.

"See them, see them. Give me the money for the drugs, now."

Aaron hands over three thousand dollars. The wad of money disappears into the man's vest.

Aaron picks up the box of heroin and hefts it under his arm. On the streets of the United States the package is worth a million dollars. The profit margin for drugs is astronomical. The margin is determined by the drugs' illegality. A lot of people have a stake in keeping it illegal. Drugs aren't evil. The people determining policy, the people trafficking and supplying themselves with arms from the profits....that is evil.

The officer opens the first cell and extends his arm toward the two prisoners inside. Murid is lying on the floor, bloodied, barely recognizable. A female figure totally shrouded in a gray burqa sits at his head. Fatima.

Aaron shakes his head slightly. Be silent, he gestures.

The officer closes the cell door and leads the way back to the first room and orders the tank driver to find the Mullah. The sun's light is now slanting across the mountains, splitting into rays behind smoke and cloud.

"Would you like some tea?" The man offers. Aaron nods, takes a chair, kicking away bits of glass from around his feet. Strathers stands behind him, holding his assault rifle. A face appears at the door, and the commander barks, "Begone, fool!" The face disappears.

Strathers sidles to one of the blown-out windows and checks with his men in the square. They are waiting silently, while Taliban soldiers grumble all about them.

In ten minutes the tank driver reappears, leading a robed figure with a full beard, who wears a white turban wound around a red skullcap.

Aaron examines this figure. Weirdly, he has a memory of driving in the car with Zoot and Tyrone. It's Charlie Parker, he thinks. The mullah has round cheeks and greedy eyes, just like the picture of Bird on the album cover in the back of Zoot's Continental. The difference is that the Mullah has no intelligence, no humor, no mockery, not a trace of ironic self-contempt.

Aaron welcomed the sudden flash of insight. This man can be bought, he understands. I will get Murid and Fatima out of here, and it won't even cost me fifty thousand dollars of Barking Platypus money.

"Wa Salaam," he bows to the Mullah. The Mullah waves three fingers across his chest, like little sparrows.

"Wa Salaam, Aleikum Salaam," the Mullah responds, and takes a chair.

A glance is exchanged between the Mullah and the commander. Aaron sees the glance, knows its contents. We will be rich, it says, we can take our commission from this transaction and still continue the Jihad, just as Allah wills it.

A conversation ensues in Pakhtun that Aaron can not follow. Strathers listens intently. He answers a few questions.

"They want ten thousand dollars for Murid and Fatima," he says at length. "I told them we are in the ransom business and we know who their families are. Since we are going back to Kabul, we might make profit from them. I think he bought the story. We must wait till after dark to take them."

"Tell the Mullah that I will give him three thousand more dollars. Ask him to cool his men outside."

Strathers transmits this information. The Mullah counters the offer at eight thousand, the bargaining goes two more rounds and finally settled at sixty five hundred dollars for the prisoners. The Mullah rises ponderously from his chair and walks to the door of the police station. Young Taliban soldiers have been edging closer to the Land Rover convoy. If a single shot rings out, slaughter will ensue.

The Mullah raises his voice. His anger is as evident as his authority. He speaks for half a minute, and the soldiers begin to disperse. Returning to his chair, the Mullah makes a gesture with his hand, thumb and forefinger rubbing.

"I'll pay him tonight, before we leave." Aaron turns to the officer. "Open the cell and let us give food and medicine to your prisoners."

The man shrugs, rises and leads Aaron back to the cell. Strathers speaks to Jeremy through the window, and the mercenary brings in the medical kit.

Aaron enters the cell and kneels with Murid and Fatima. He turns back and gestures with his chin towards the commander, telling him to leave the cell. The commander complies, bored with the details now that money has been exchanged..

Murid groans. "You look horrible," he says, looking up at Aaron. His eyes are almost swollen

shut, his lips are twice their normal size.

"Maybe I look the way YOU feel," Aaron replies.

"I'm glad to see you, even if you do look horrible. Are we going to get out of here?"

"I think so." Aaron looks for a part of Murid's body that might not be in pain. He can only take his friends' index finger. "We'll be okay. What the hell are you doing here, anyway?"

Murid moves his eyes towards his mother. "She was here. Saving Afghan women. You know what she does. She agitates. She gets into trouble."

Fatima claws the mesh from her bourkha. "I despise these things, " she spits. "I loathe them!" Now her eyes can be seen, seething inside the hot gray garment. "Why do Muslim men exist in a constant state of sexual paranoia? Are they afraid the world will discover they're insensitive selfish lovers? The bastards!"

Aaron pats the woman's shoulder soothingly. "If we get out of here in one piece, you won't be able to come back to Afghanistan for a while."

"Don't you tell me what I will or will not be able to do in Afghanistan! Aghans hate being told what to do. We despise authority!"

"We can discuss this some other time," Aaron placates. Fatima sags. Her fury is spent. She leans back against the brick wall of the cell. Her chin droops onto her breastbone and her eyes close wearily.

Jeremy comes in with tea and medicine, while another of Strathers' men brings some blankets.

Eight hours later the convoy has cleared the "Defile of Death," as Strathers calls it, and are on the open road toward Kabul, driving along the river. Three Land Rovers are headed towards them in a cloud of dust. The sun is just rising. The sky is tinted pink at the horizon and is a startling cerulean overhead. The planet Venus is still clearly visible in the morning twilight.

Aaron looks through his binoculars and sees non-Afghan men driving the Land Rovers. "The heroin smugglers," he says. The two convoys close the distance after a brief hesitation, and are soon facing one another on the narrow road. They sit like that for a moment, then the smugglers back ponderously, one vehicle at a time, into a wide muddy place so that Strathers' convoy can draw up next to them.

A sweaty man with a two-day stubble of beard rolls down his window. He speaks in Dutch, but when Aaron shakes his head, he switches to English.

"What's up there?" he asks . "Is it safe to go ahead?"

"It's a death trap," Aaron says emphatically. "There's a Taliban massacre going on, bodies are everywhere. You can't go ahead, we barely got out with our lives."

"Shit!" the Dutchman curses. He speaks to the other men in his vehicle. They argue for a few moments. "We're going anyway!" he announces finally, pointing with his finger towards Darrahe Zargal. "They promised we will be safe." Then he punches his driver in the arm and the vehicle begins to move. Aaron thinks with desperate swiftness. He improvises.

"WAIT!" he shouts. The Land Rover stops a few yards forward. Aaron walks up and bends to the driver. "I think you should know there's a couple of Mullahs fighting a turf war over heroin. If you're involved in that, I don't care. I will just tell you to forget it because there isn't any dope there, not anymore. They burned the town, blew up the jail, nothing but a smoking ruin. Now they're headed this way. You go any farther down this road and I guarantee you won't be coming back."

"Fuck me fuck me fuck me!" says the Dutchman, beating the steering wheel with each "fuck me". Aaron looks into the man's eyes, recognizing every scumbag dope dealer he's ever known, including himself. He sees a dark hollow chamber of terror and quickly looks away.

A man sitting in the passenger seat speaks to his partner in Dutch. He is telling the driver to turn back. They argue for a bit, and Aaron simply removes himself and returns to his own people. The smugglers turn off their engines. The vehicles tick as their parts cool.

Aaron leaves them sitting there to sort out their own fates. He goes to the middle car of his own convoy and looks in on Murid. The seats have been laid flat so that Aaron's friend can lie on a stretcher. Fatima sits upright next to her son.

"Are you okay?" he asks . Fatima nods.

"Okay," she says, in that weirdly charming accent. "Let's go quickly!"

Aaron returns to the lead car and gets in. "Let's get out of here," he says to Strathers. The Colonel wastes no time putting extra miles between himself and the Taliban. At length, Aaron gestures to the side of the road, and Strathers brakes, slides a bit on the unstable surface, then comes to a halt. Aaron, taking the box of heroin, gets out of the car and goes to look out and down, to the river.

"This stuff should be legal," he says to no one in particular.

Strathers and Fatima come with him to the river's edge.

"If it was legal there would be millions more addicts," Strathers protests.

"First of all, that's simply not true. There will be exactly the same number of addicts as there are right now. And even if it was true, wouldn't it be better," Aaron postulates, "for there to be a billion legal heroin addicts in the world than to have all this war, violence, manipulation, deception and horror, all financed by heroin?"

Strathers considers this idea. "You're right," he says, "I never thought of it that way."

Fatima shakes her shaggy grey hair and washes her face in the river. "Men and their devices,"

she says contemptuously. "War is evil, all war is evil. War over drugs, war over political passions. It's all evil. You tell me....." she points accusingly at the weapons carried by the men in the cars. "You tell me how it makes sense to spend a trillion dollars to solve a billion dollar problem. You tell me how a country as poor as Afghanistan is flooded with expensive weaponry when there isn't enough food, enough schools, enough clean water.....it disgusts me!" She returns to the car and slams the door.

"I couldn't possibly agree with you more," Aaron says. He slits open one brick of heroin, peels back the masking tape until the packed powder hangs loose in its plastic bag.

There is still part of him that feels greed and excitement, even lust, about the object in his hand. God! Such great dope! Oh my! I can get so fucking high, and stay high for ten years!

The glamour and allure of addiction is so powerful, it captures him for a moment as he considers keeping the drugs, considers taking a little sniff right now. He struggles and it is brief. He considers the life he has made, the family back in Muir Beach, all the love with which he has surrounded himself.

Why on earth would he throw that away?

He beats the package with his fist a few times, to break up its caked consistency. Then he up-ends the bag and throws the powder into the river. He repeats this operation until the other bags of heroin have dispersed into the water, then tears the bags themselves into pieces, tosses them into the river and watches them flow downstream.

Chapter Fifty Six

2013: San Francisco

Aaron settles himself in the chair in front of the microphone. The studio is smaller than he expected, but it is modern, comfortable, sound-proofed with angular blue foam and partitioned by almost invisible glass.

Bob Plochette, the host of KQED's weekly radio show, Creativity Alive, watches the digital clock tick down the seconds. His engineeer counts down with his fingers on the other side of the glass, three two one, then a thumbs up. You're on. The radio host swings into his patter smoothly.

"Welcome to Creativity Alive, I'm Bob Plochette, and we ARE here, live, in the KQED studio, and we're privileged to have local music legend Aaron Kantro with us today, to help us explore and celebrate the music of another legend, the late, great Zoot Prestige. Welcome to the show."

"I'm glad to be here, Bob," Aaron says. He is aware that he is imitating the radio host's voice, his professional radio patter. Plochette's sentences always start on a C and rise to an A at the middle of the sentence, then dip to a D and end on a rather quizzical E.

"We've been playing some of Zoot's classic records for the last fifteen minutes," Plochette continues, "made in the late fifties through the late sixties. In fact, you are listed as drummer on Zoot's final four records, 'Hot Sax, 'Barbecue Bop', 'Honk If You Bop', and 'Bopped Out'. I have to ask you, what was it like to play with Zoot Prestige? What kind of person was he?"

Aaron understands that there isn't supposed to be any 'dead air', that he is on the radio and his gestures are invisible. So, without pausing to think, he begins to speak.

"Zoot was the most well-read man I ever met. His intellect was phenomenal, but he carried it with an absolute lack of pretension. He was a kind of Zen master, a funny guy with a deep comprehension of life. Zoot was warm. You know, there are a lot of good people in the world. There are a lot of dull people in the world. There are a lot of good, dull people in the world. When you meet a person who's not only good, but consistently interesting and entertaining, that's a treasure. I can only describe Zoot Prestige as a treasure."

Bob Plochette smiles. Good answer, good talk, he seems to indicate with a tiny nod. "Then he was as much fun in person as his recordings seem to indicate?"

"More fun. You have to understand that working the Circuit is sometimes dangerous and pretty hard. I only saw him lose his composure once." Aaron is about to describe the Jason's Lounge gig when Zoot's spirit materializes behind Bob Plochette's chair. He is wearing a white robe and a turban and looks like a Haji, a pilgrim to Mecca. Zoot winks and points at Aaron and says "Run with it, man, sing my praises like I ain't here."

Bob Plochette hears nothing, apparently sees nothing. The moment
of dead air is enough to prompt another comment from the radio
host. "Zoot's last recording was made in 1969 with you on drums
and the incredible Tyreeza Terry on organ. It was reissued as a CD
last year. My favorite cut is Zoot's original tune, 'Put on the Sauce,
Mama'. Let's have a listen to this." He cues the engineer and the
sounds of Zoot's last record emerge from the studio's monitors.
Tyrone/Tyreeza vamps on his/her Hammond B-three, the chords
starting the song with a classic mid-tempo blues feel. Aaron's
drums slide lazily behind the groove, and a rim shot clicks the
snare on two and four. Then Zoot's big tone oozes into the melody.
It takes Aaron a moment to repress his emotion, to push the tears
of love and gratitude back down inside himself.

"Doing pretty good, Aaron," Bob Plochette says. "I'm going to ask
you another couple questions about Zoot's career....."

He talks to Aaron but Aaron doesn't really hear what he is saying.
Next to Zoot, another spirit is manifesting, also wearing the robe of
a Haji. It is John Coltrane. The great saxophonist's features looked
as if they have been chiseled from some warm dark marble
quarried from a deposit deep in the ancient Nubian desert. His
expression is that of a prophet in rapturous conversation with God.

Aaron feels a chill of awe run down the back of his neck. Zoot's
spirit says, "Relax, babe, some High Flyers are coming through."

Another spirit appears, dressed in the garb of a medieval monk. It
is the poet Rilke. He has a homely horse-like face, and is speaking
words that Aaron can not hear. Then a nun appears and Aaron
knows without being told that it is Hildegarde Von Bingen, the

renaissance composer. Other spirits crowd into the studio, Frieda Kahlo, William Blake, Syvia Plath, Beethoven, spirits of painters, musicians, poets, visionaries, some famous, some vanished into the mists of time, anonymous but powerful.

Bob Plochette is saying ".......we can plug your new CD, of course, towards the end of the show....."

The radio announcer twitches, reaches a hand to the back of his neck, looks around, blows air through his lips.

"Jesus," he says, "I just had the weirdest sensation." He looks at his engineer. The song is coming to an end. They are back on the air.

"That is, of course, Zoot Prestige, being accompanied by our guest, Aaron Kantro, in the 1969 recording of 'Put On The Sauce, Mama'. Our show is called Creativity Alive on National Public Radio, and we have Aaron Kantro for the rest of the hour, to reminisce about Jazz legend Zoot Prestige, to play some cuts from the heyday of Zoot's long career, and maybe even to play cuts from Aaron's new CD, 'Suit for Zoot'.

He gestures for Aaron to come in and fill some air time.

"Sounds good to me, Bob," Aaron says, leaning back in his chair, folding his hands together. The spirits are all over the studio. No one else can see them. There is nothing Aaron can do but get through the rest of the hour in the invisible company of the world's artists. There are Egyptian sculptors and Cro-magnon cave painters, weavers of baskets, makers of pots, spinners of tales, singers of lullabyes, builders of monuments, tinkerers with machines, investigators of matters cosmic, microcosmic, common, uncommon, domestic and strategic.

The radio show is finally over, and Aaron escapes into the building's parking garage. The host of creative spirits follow him, surround him. He gets into his car and closes the door. Zoot sits next to him in the front seat. Coltrane is in the back, Charlie Parker is next to Trane, Lester Young squats on the hood, and Emily Dickinson hops onto the fender.

"Zoot," Aaron says at last. "What am I supposed to do with all this?"

"Get used to it," Zoot responds, puffing on an ethereal cheroot. "You're gonna see spirits the rest of your days and then some.....and you can't tell anybody."

"I wouldn't dream of telling anybody! They'd lock me up."

"

Naw they wouldn't. They'd flock to you in the thousands, they'd pay fifteen bucks for your books, buy your CD's, request personal readings, beg you to find their mom, dad, old friends. You'd be a big time guru."

"I don't want to be a big time guru! What can be more ridiculous!"

"Twenty years ago, you would have jumped at Big Time Guru."

"Twenty years ago I didn't have anything better to do."

"You're doin' fine, now, babe." Zoot spits a little piece of non-existent tobacco out the car's window. "Just get on with your life. With company, out- of- this- world type company. After a while you'll be able to hear them talk, just like you can hear me. And you'll work it out, how not to answer them except when you're alone." He flips the cheroot and it vanishes as if it has been sucked into an invisible time-warp.

"You're psychic, just like your dad, who sends his love by the way." Zoot pats the plastic dashboard of Aaron's Jeep Cherokee. "Ain't like the old Continental. Now, that car was elegant! That car was Spasmoferocious!"

Then Zoot is gone. All the spirits are gone. Aaron exhales with relief. He turns the key in the ignition, drives from the garage and heads north, toward Muir Beach, toward home.

Addendum: Zoot's Greatest Story

1968: On the road somewhere near Cairo, Illinois

The Mississippi river appears frequently to the left side of the road, as the Continental digests miles under its Goodyears. The river is like a giant python at the bottom of the bluff, twisting its silty way towards New Orleans. At Cairo it meets the Ohio River in a megalithic "Y". The different colors of the different rivers make discreet etchings in the basic silver brown in the serpentine body of The Mississippi.

Zoot is snoring lightly, slumped in the front passenger seat with his elbow on the armrest, his head bumping gently against the rolled-up window. The car's air conditioning is roaring like a distant storm, its wind coming from black plastic vents in the dashboard.

Aaron is in the back seat, trying to read a science fiction novel. The car's motion is making him sick, so he puts the book down and watches the River as it appears and disappears amongst rows of trees.

Zoot jerks awake suddenly, yawns, rubs his eyes. He inspects Tyrone's driving, looks at the speedometer. "You're going a hundred miles an hour, man, and you in the slow lane. There's a cop that cruises this road by name of Furley Robinson and he will love to jail my ass, so ease it on up."

Tyrone looks innocent. "I don 't know how that happened, Zoot, sorry." The speedometer drifts in fits and starts back down to seventy.

Zoot cranes his neck to see Aaron, slumped boredly in the back seat.

"I ever tell you the story of my true musical roots, of my Arkansas heritage?"

Aaron perks up and leans forward over the soft leather upholstery.

"Which one? The one about Preacher Scarby and the girls in the choir?"

"No, no, this one even earlier and more rooty than that one."

"Let's hear it, Zoot, we all ears," Tyrone says, lighting up a cigarette.

"This is back when I was five, six years old," says Zoot. "All the black farmers in Arkansas get together once a year for a musical festival, a Pig Squeezin'. They'd come from evahwhere, they'd come from Dawes County and Little Creek and Big Creek, from

Meaty Bottom and Cradle Cave. They'd bring their best musical pigs and their women and children would barbecue up some ribs and haunches and they would contend for the position of Master Pig Squeezer. "

Aaron smiles. Tyrone wrinkles his brow, hoping to concentrate on the road but sneaking glances at Zoot, trying to discern just how far in his cheek is his mentor's tongue.

"The greatest Pig Squeezer of all is a big fat gentleman by the name of Eufustus Rathbone. Y'll understand, Pig Squeezin is a subtle art, it combines animal genetics, musical training, weight lifting and other forms of athletics and requires a fine hand at dealing with the hogs. You gotta take em when they're tiny piglets and get em used to the feel of your armpit, your knees, you get piglets that like bein' squeezed and handled evah which way. Takes a calm and pliable pig to squeal and bellow on cue. Why, Eufustus Rathbone can get a note out of both ends of a pig just by flexing his bicep, he is that good. He has a pig named Joby that can fart an E flat and squeal a perfect third above it."

Aaron pats both his thighs hard, then pats them again, more softly.

Zoot pauses to light his three o'clock cheroot.

"You're putting us on, right?" Tyrone swings his head sideways, then back to the road, then sideways, then back to the road.

"Lord's Truth," Zoot swears, solemnly. He winks at Aaron.

"This must have been nineteen ten, nineteen eleven," Zoot continues. "It was my first Pig Squeezin and I thinks I is in heaven, they is so many people, so much food on big long tables, all kinds of little girls runnin' round in checkered dresses with pretty hats."

He exhales his stream of smoke languidly, cracks the window a bit to clear the air inside the car.

Tyrone lights yet another in a constant string of Camels.

"You're smoking too much," he admonishes Tyrone. "You know that stuff wilts your dick, don't you?"

Tyrone hastily stuffs out the butt in the ash tray. "Damn," he says, "one fun thing fucks up another fun thing. Doesn't seem fair."

Aaron puts his chin into the crevice between the front seats, as if to prompt Zoot to continue his story.

"Okay, after two solid days of Squeezin', there's only three Squeezers left who can get up and withstand the sheer virtuosity of Eufustus Rathbone. This man has been Squeezin' Master for six years runnin'. He has raised himself a breed of musical hogs that are light of weight but solid in volume and tone. He gets up on the stage that is built right there in the middle of Hanky Parkins' fresh-mowed soybean field. He's got Joby in one hand, he's got two piglets named Squeak and Tweak on rope leashes, and he's got an old sow named Hester draggin' her udders on the floor boards. Hester is like his old standby, a reliable bass pig. He can just give her a jiggle and she will go 'honk' on the downbeat and the upbeat."

Zoot's left hand waves in the air and pictures seem to flow from his fingers, apparitions in the drifting smoke that lazily spiral up from the cheroot held loosely in his right hand.

"Eufustus starts out with The Star Spangled Banner, just to keep things simple, not to raise expectations or nothin'. The pigs squeeze in perfect counterpoint. Eufustus is sitting on the low three-legged Squeezin' Stool, and he's got Joby between his legs where he can control the pitch by bringing his thighs together, he's got Hester under one foot and he's got Squeak and Tweak in each armpit. After the national anthem he looks around as if to say, 'can anybody top that? The crowd goes wild, everybody claps, looks like it's all over. But when the noise dies down, a youngster by the name of Chester Wankus comes up the steps leading just two little piglets. There's a gasp from the crowd, people saying 'he can't do shit with no two piglets, who he think he is?' But Chester just scoots that Squeezin' Stool over, sits down and starts squeezin' these piglets and he gets them fartin' and squealing and he plays "Battle Hymn of the Republic" real fast and he's tapping with his feet too. It is amazing. Old Eufustus puffs up his chest like nothin' happened, takes the stool back and plays the "Overture from The Marriage of Figaro". The crowd falls silent, they figure that's it, all over, nothin' can top that. Chester leaves his piglets on the stage, jumps off the back, picks up a two hundred pound sow like it's a twig and puts her on the stage, then jumps back up and gets her inside his legs. He takes a deep breath, everybody's waitin' for whatever's gonna come next."

Zoot leans forward and flicks the ash from his cheroot into the ashtray. He looks out the window. The sun is midway down the afternoon sky and its rays flash back from the river.

"Chester takes a minute to get himself braced, then he starts squeezin and out comes a perfect contrapuntal version of the opening of Beethoven's Fifth Symphony. The sow is a trifle flat out her behind but Chester compensates skillfully by increasing the pressure from his feet and the rhythm is powerful enough that Eufustus starts turning a darker shade of brown than he already is. Joby just lays down on her side and Chester's two piglets run over and start nursin' from her. You'd think that is the end of the story but just then up comes a teenage boy from Smith County, and he's got four piglets on leather leashes, he's got a three hundred pound sow and he's got a hairy wild boar in some kind of crazy harness. The judges take some time debating whether that is legal or not, but they allowed it, I mean a wild boar is a wild boar and they just have to give the kid points for difficulty."

"What's your name, kid?" the head judge asks.

"The kid replies, 'My name is Felix Twitty and I'm from Smith County near the town of Goose's Crack."

"Don't you think that's a little ostentatious, all them pigs?"

The crowd grumbles its agreement, I mean, if the kid can 't come through with something tremendous he'd be seen as a total poseur, a Nouveau Squeezer with a big ego. He just takes the stool nice and calm, positions that boar under his left arm, arranges them other pigs in various ways with one of 'em under his chin and he starts to play. At first nobody recognizes the music. It sounds good, it sounds mighty good, and finally the crowd realizes that the kid is playing Wagner's "Finale from Das Rheingold" and he is making the boar sing the part of Thor and making the piglets do the parts of the Rhinemaidens. It is spectacular! Everybody almost passes out from amazement and Felix Twitty sure as hell won the Master Pig Squeazer prize for that year and for the next five years. He's remembered as one of the greatest squeezers in history, and might have broken Tolly Scoobus' eight year run, 'cept he went off to France in World War One and got shot by a farmer who thought he was stealin' pigs. He was just playin' scales in the barn! All he wanted was a little practice. Mighty shame, that was. Mighty shame."

The occupants of the car drive in silence for a while.

"You're not pullin' my leg, are you?" Tyrone asks sincerely.

"Lord's Truth," Zoot swears.

Other Books By Arthr Rosch

The Road Has Eyes: A Relationship, An RV and a Wild Ride

http://bit.ly/2qpKoZG

The Gods of the Gift

http://bit.ly/1q6x230

www.ingramcontent.com/pod-product-compliance
Lightning Source LLC
Chambersburg PA
CBHW031019030726
47497CB00004B/921